Rita Bradshaw was born in Northamptonshire, where she still lives today. At the age of sixteen she met her husband – whom she considers her soulmate – and they have two daughters and a son, and a young grandson.

Much to her delight, Rita's first attempt at a novel was accepted for publication, and she went on to write many more successful novels under a pseudonym before writing for Headline using her own name.

As a committed Christian and passionate animal-lover – her two 'furry babies' can always be found snoring gently at her feet as she writes – Rita's life is a full and busy one, but her writing continues to be a consuming pleasure that she never tires of. In any spare moments she loves reading, walking her dogs, eating out and visiting the cinema and theatre, as well as being involved in her local church and animal welfare.

Rita's earlier sagas, ALONE BENEATH THE HEAVEN, REACH FOR TOMORROW, RAGA-MUFFIN ANGEL, THE STONY PATH and THE URCHIN'S SONG, are also available from Headline.

Candles in the Storm

Rita Bradshaw

headline

First published in 2003
by HEADLINE BOOK PUBLISHING

First published in paperback in 2003
by HEADLINE BOOK PUBLISHING

7

ISBN 0 7472 6709 X

Typeset in Times by Palimpsest Book Production Limited,
Polmont, Stirlingshire
Printed and bound in Great Britain by
Mackays of Chatham plc, Chatham, Kent

Papers and cover board used by Headline are natural,
recyclable products made from wood grown in sustainable
forests. The manufacturing processes conform to the
environmental regulations of the country of origin.

HEADLINE BOOK PUBLISHING
A division of Hodder Headline
338 Euston Road
LONDON NW1 3BH

www.headline.co.uk
www.hodderheadline.com

I dedicate this book to our friend Tony Haighway at Wolf Watch UK, with many thanks for the marvellous breaks Clive and I have enjoyed at the sanctuary, and the times we've gone to sleep listening to the wolves howling to the moon. Magic!

And dear Ayla, who totally disproved the 'Little Red Riding Hood and the Wolf' tale the first time I was introduced to her, when she rolled over for her tummy to be rubbed. She was an animal in a million, and I know Tony will miss her greatly.

Very special thanks go to Jake – Tony's magnificent black German Shepherd, who was twice as imposing as any wolf – for being such a wonderful companion when we visited the sanctuary and taking us so completely under his wing. He was a truly gentle giant and we'll remember the walks he took us on for ever. Long may his tail continue to wag in doggy heaven.

Acknowledgements

When the idea of a book built round the almost completely devastated small fishing communities of bygone days came to me, I didn't realise how hard the research was going to be.

I delved and dug in various ancient manuals, collecting a little gem of information here and there, but one book which was of enormous help and deserves special mention is *The Last of the Hunters, Life with the Fishermen of North Shields* by Peter Mortimer.

A Northern Fisherman's Lament

Come wives and canny bodies all,
Giv-ower thou chuntering and toil.
See yonder storm clouds bodeth ill,
'Tis time to wreak their fickle will
On us poor souls upon the sea,
Bonny owld laddies still we be.
So light the putting candles bright
To guide yon boats through tempest night.

ANON

Prologue

1884

'Mam, I don't think I can take much more. The others weren't like this.'

'Oh, aye, they were, lass, they were. It's just that you forget the pain in between times. If the Good Lord hadn't made it that way the human race would have died out afore it got started, that's for sure.'

'Oh, no, another one's comin'.'

'It won't be long, Mary, not now. It's always worse just afore you want to push, you know that. A little while an' it'll be born, lass.'

But would it? Nellie Shaw's back was breaking, bent as she was over the writhing form on the low platform bed, but she didn't straighten up. Her daughter had been experiencing birthing pains for the last eighteen hours but they were worsening now, causing Mary to start crying out.

As the contraction gathered strength and her daughter's nails bit into the flesh of Nellie's hand the older woman murmured words of encouragement even as she thought, The lass is nigh on spent, a blind man could see it, but what can be done?

It was twenty seconds or more before Mary's knees, raised involuntarily with the last pain, slid down again into the rumpled damp covers. 'Mam, this storm . . . it's not normal. Hark at it. An' there's George an' the lads out in it. I . . . I shouldn't have wished this bairn away at the beginnin'. This is God's judgement, His punishment for me wicked thoughts. He's goin' to take my man an' the lads.'

'Now don't you start talkin' like that, Mary Appleby.'

'It's true, I know it is. I wished the bairn away an' now—'

'I said, that's enough.' And then, as if realising her tone had been over-sharp, Nellie stretched out her hand, gently mopping the perspiring forehead of her daughter with a piece of cloth as she added, her voice softer, 'Speak it out an' it'll come to pass, lass. You know that as well as I do, now then. George an' the lads'll be all right. He's a canny man, your George, an' there's not a fisherman alive who knows the sea like him.'

The woman on the bed made no answer, and as the wind rattled the windows with renewed fury, lashing against the glass with enough force to make Nellie wince, she tried not to let the fear show on her face. Mary was right, this storm wasn't normal. Dear God, dear Lord Jesus, have mercy on us all . . .

The labour pains were coming with relentless regularity every couple of minutes but, nevertheless, Mary was so exhausted she was sleeping in the few seconds' grace before each onslaught.

Nellie continued to stare down at her daughter, pleading with the Almighty in her mind as her panic grew.

You know my Mary isn't a bad lass, Lord, and she didn't try to get rid of the bairn like some I could name. But falling like she did for this one when she thought her child-bearing days were over . . . it was a shock. That's what it was, a shock. Seven bairns she's borne in her time, and without complaint. Five of them surviving, and right bonny lads

2

too. She's been a good wife and mother and none knows it better than You. Dear God, have mercy on her. On us all, Lord.

A fusillade of hail pellets brought Nellie's head up again, and she looked towards the windowsill where a flickering tallow candle was burning. The storm was in full voice, howling and moaning, and Nellie shivered as she muttered, 'The candle'll bring 'em home sure enough, it's not failed yet. Aye, there's bin nights as bad as this afore.' Although not many, she had to admit, since she had first come to this cottage on the outskirts of Whitburn nigh on forty-five years ago. 'Course, in them days there'd only been a track on Sea Lane to Bent Cottages overlooking the seashore, and no way along the coast to Sunderland. She'd lived here twenty-five years before there was a road over the sand dunes to Fulwell. Then the pit'd been sunk, and along with the new miners' cottages had come a school and chapel and shop. Nellie frowned. She had no truck with the 'newcomers'.

What would her life have been like if Abe's boat hadn't been blown a few miles off course and sought temporary sanctuary in Marsden Bay all those years ago? Likely she'd have gone through with her betrothal to Frank Hammond, one of the Marsden fishermen from her home village who had also been her cousin.

Mary's knees came up and she let out another agonised groan. For the next minute or so Nellie's mind was focused on her daughter, and then Mary sank into the temporary opiate of slumber once more and Nellie found herself wandering back in time. It had been love at first sight, her and Abe. She shook her grey head at the fancifulness of the thought which she would never have dreamt of verbalising, but which she knew to be the truth nevertheless.

For him she had braved her parents' wrath for daring to plight her troth to a foreigner from four or five miles down the coast, knowing that was how Abe's family and friends would view her too. But they had never regretted it, not once. Abe had loved her like few men loved a woman, and even though she had only given him the one bairn, their Mary, he had continued to love her until the day he had died.

She still missed him. Nellie's deep grey eyes – which could be as bland as a newborn babe's on occasions when she deemed it prudent, especially when Mary and her husband were in disagreement over something or other – fixed themselves on the thin gold band on the third finger of her left hand. But at least Abe had lived long enough to see the first of his lusty grandsons before the sea had taken him, as it took so many.

Oh, she hated the sea; it was cruel, wicked. It might surrender its riches to the men it called but it demanded a high price in return, and wasn't chary about taking it neither. The miners had it hard all right, but there were more old miners to the pound than there were fishermen, and no mistake.

Nellie felt the sick unease within her rise up as bile into her mouth. She kept this fear buried most of the time – it was part and parcel of a fisherwoman's life, first learnt as a bairn at her mother's knee – but there were times when it wouldn't be contained, like now. A fresh torrent of rain hammered at the window and she glanced towards the candle again, whispering, 'Let it light their path home, Lord. Please.' And then her wrinkled brown face, the delicate features still holding a faint vestige of the beauty which had captivated the young Abe so many years before, was bent towards her daughter again as Mary stirred and groaned.

The child was born an hour later and it was a girl, a strong-limbed and lunged infant who squawked in protest as its grandmother cut the umbilical cord and wiped the tiny face before wrapping the baby in a clean piece of old blanket.

'It's a little lassie, hinny, an' bonny. Right bonny. Here, love.' Nellie settled the baby, who had stopped crying and was surveying the world through surprised wide-open eyes, into the crook of Mary's arm.

'A girl.' Mary's voice held a note of wonder. 'After seven lads I never thought I'd have a daughter, Mam.' And her tired face was shining.

'Aye, well, don't reckon on it bein' all plain sailin', lass, not with her bein' born amid tempest an' strife. It's a sign she'll be as headstrong an' self-willed as the elements that saw her given life. This one will never sail in calm waters.' And then Nellie's voice softened as she added, 'But she's bonny. Oh, aye, she's bonny all right.'

It was just after Nellie had cleaned her daughter up, washing her and changing the soiled covers on the low narrow bed in a corner of the living room – normally Nellie's own – that the women heard sounds outside the door and their heads turned as one. And then a deep rumbling voice and other, younger male voices filled the room, along with big bodies covered in filthy clothes and stinking of fish. But it was a smell sweeter than apple blossom and wild hyacinths to Nellie and the exhausted woman lying in the bed, because it meant their menfolk were home and they were safe.

George Appleby was a giant of a man, with a fine bass voice and springy tufts of grey hair which could never be tamed, but his big square face with its deep mahogany tan was tender as he looked down at his wife and new offspring.

'It's a wee lassie, George.' Nellie had moved aside as her son-in-law approached, the lads standing somewhat awkwardly behind their father. 'An' I was sayin' to Mary, born on a night like this she'll have a mind of her own.

Iron-willed an' as obstinate as a cuddy this 'un will be, you mark my words.'

George's callused hands were like great hams, the baby's minuscule as he reached down and touched the tiny white fingers for a moment after smiling at his wife. 'Aye, mebbe,' he said softly, his red-rimmed eyes scoured by salt spray and lack of sleep looking deep into his daughter's wide gaze as he searched the tiny face which was already distinctly feminine. 'Mebbe. But to my mind that's no bad thing. Yer don't get nowt handed to you on a plate in this world, an' them with the strength to fight for what they want are the ones who come through. What one might call iron-willed an' obstinate, another might name determined an' steadfast. Eh, lass?' The last two words were directed to the baby, and he touched the downy fuzz on the small head as he murmured, 'Determined an' steadfast, that'll be you.'

'Already got you wrapped round her little finger then, has she, Da?' one of the lads quipped, as another said, 'What you callin' her anyway?'

'Aye, that's a thought. We'd planned on David but that won't do now.'

'Daisy.' It was the first time Mary had spoken and her gaze was for her husband.

'Aw, lass.' He had only ever spoken of his twin sister – who had died of diphtheria when they were eight – to his wife, and now his voice was even softer as he said, 'Daisy. Aye, I reckon that'll do right enough, an' if this little 'un is half as bonny as the other one she'll turn a few heads when she's older. What say you, Miss Daisy Appleby? Yer granny says you're goin' to charter your own course an' I say you'll be a beauty. 'Tis a combination that'll leave its mark for good or ill, I'll be bound.'

Smoky blue eyes held his a moment longer before the

baby yawned delicately, settled herself further into the crook of her mother's arm and went to sleep.

Part 1
The Shipwreck
1900

Chapter One

She would feel buried alive, living in one of those stinking hovels in Cross Row or Wells Row.

Immediately the thought surfaced Daisy found herself apologising for it. It wasn't them poor folk's fault the way they had to live, but the smells seemed to stay up your nose for ages after leaving a bad street. Mind, some of the wives kept their houses cleaner than others and saw to it the privies stayed fresh, but that must make it all the more galling for them if they were stuck between two who couldn't care less.

Daisy took another great lungful of cold sparkling air, relishing its sharp bite after the stench in some areas of the town she had recently left behind. She hoisted her empty wicker baskets higher on her slender hips and continued to stride on.

Her da said the townsfolk thought fishermen stank, but the worst of the fish smells – even the guts and offal and such – was nothing compared to what some human beings were capable of. She hated the towns.

Daisy stopped for a moment, flexing her cold feet encased in heavy black boots with thick cobbled soles. It was a four-mile walk from home into Boldon and hard going in places but she didn't mind the journey back when the baskets were empty. She could always get a better price for the fish in Boldon, it being inland, than when she tried to sell the contents of her baskets door to door in Whitburn, and every farthing was precious.

She flicked back her two shining braids of raven-black hair before tilting her head and gazing up into the blue sky. It was a grand day. Not as nice as late spring when bluebells and cow parsley dappled the hedgerows and the heady perfume of wild lilac scented the lanes, but nice nevertheless.

And to see the sun shine again . . . Everything was better when the sun shone; people were nicer, kinder. There were castles in the clouds today, and even though the ground was still rock hard and frozen solid with the last of the winter snow, you could sense spring was on its way at last. It had been a hard winter, this one. Several times she'd had to clamber and lurch her way into Boldon on the crest of the snow-packed hedgerows, terrified she was going to find herself falling into one of the snow drifts which had been over seven feet or more deep. Her da would have gone mad if he'd known the risks she'd taken, but they'd needed the pennies selling the fish round the doors brought in, especially with one of the nets being lost recently. That'd been a blow. Her da had been like a bear with a sore head for days after that.

Daisy set her gaze forward again, jingling the coins in the pocket of her thick serge skirt before adjusting her calico cloak more securely on her shoulders. She loved this cloak. It had taken her hours to sew but when she'd finished her da had taken it to the tank and tanned it along with his nets, and it was the only garment she possessed which was a nice warm colour. Alf had said she looked bonny in it. But then Alf always said nice things to her, not like their Tom. Her small nose wrinkled at the thought of her youngest brother, the only one still living at home. Her granny said she and Tom were like cat and dog, and she was right.

Daisy started walking again, slipping and sliding on the icy ground as one part of her brain appreciated the stark white beauty all around her, and another began to list the multitude of jobs awaiting her on her return to the cottage.

She had collected a nice lot of driftwood along with nearly a bucketful of coal and coke first thing yesterday morning, and it would all be dried out enough by now. She'd banked the fire as best she could that morning with slack and damp tea leaves, but no doubt that would be her first task on walking through the door again. She had to make sure her granny was kept warm with the old woman's chest being so bad this winter. She would warm a few drops of the goose grease she'd bought from the farm the week before, and get her granny to rub it on to her chest, before heating a bowl of the broth she had made yesterday.

Good stuff, that broth was, as it should be considering she had boiled the big marrow bone the farmer's wife had let her have for hours. Her granny could always stomach a little broth when she couldn't manage anything else. The rest of them could have a mardy cake with the fat she had skimmed off the bone, and the flour and a few currants she had left in the larder, and she'd salt herrings to go with the cake. That'd do the night. And with what she'd earned today she could go to the mill and get a half-stone of flour tomorrow, and bake some bread. That would tempt her granny to eat, the smell of freshly baked bread. Daisy gave a little skip at the thought of it.

The lanes were winding, dipping and curving their way towards the coast, but Daisy's steps were light in spite of the conditions and the weight of her boots. She had sold all the fish, and none at a knockdown price either. It had been a good day. And summer lay in front of them. That meant calmer weather for the boats and all manner of extra food she could gather.

In the spring she could collect sorrel leaves from the lanes and hedgerows to flavour their food, and hunt out pheasant and partridge eggs and even the smaller guillemot eggs when she could manage to reach them.

The summer brought crab apples, haws, blackberries and sloes, and she knew just where to collect the best of them as the days shortened again. Farmer Gilbert, whose fields bordered the outskirts of Boldon, always let her have a supply of potatoes, swedes and turnips in return for a few bloaters and fresh cod, and he was always happy for her to go into the gleaning fields too. She liked that, the gleaning, with the scent of hay clinging to the warm breeze and the blue sky above. It might be back-breaking work, going along the stubble and picking up what was left to tie in bunches and sell to people who kept chickens, but she enjoyed it, especially when a bushel could be got together and she would take it to the mill and end up with a bag of fine wholemeal for cooking at home.

Farmer Gilbert never refused to take the sacks of acorns she collected for his pigs either, and always paid above the odds for them. She got a canny deal with Farmer Gilbert – he liked her, he did. 'Daisy Flower' he called her, and always with a twinkle in his eye.

Daisy smiled to herself at the thought of the stocky little man, her small white teeth gleaming against the honey-tinted skin of her face. Farmer Gilbert wasn't like Farmer Todd whose farm was much nearer the village. Her smile faded. She had had a run in with him the week before over the price of the goose grease. He had known she needed it quickly and had traded on that. Farmer Todd wouldn't give you the drips from his nose, and her da always said the milk his farmhand brought to the village every morning in backcans on panniers on the old donkey was watered down. Daisy nodded in agreement, thinking of it now.

Her mind full of the unfairness of miserly Farmer Todd, she continued to slip and slide her way along, keeping her gaze fixed on the black ice beneath her feet now. Consequently she nearly jumped out of her skin when her name was spoken very loudly just behind her.

She swung round, in danger of losing her footing on the treacherous ground. As she took in the chunkily built young man in front of her, Daisy's voice was unusually sharp when she said, 'Alf! You scared me half to death.'

'Me?' There was a grin on his tanned, good-looking face. 'Sorry, lass. I was leanin' against that tree over yonder waitin' for you, but you were far away.'

'All the more reason not to creep up on me like that,' she answered tartly.

'You sold all the fish?'

'No, I gave 'em away to anyone who asked.' And then, as if realising she wasn't being very nice, Daisy moderated her tone, adding, 'What's the matter anyway? I'm sure you must have better things to do than to wait for me to come back from Boldon.'

'Not really.'

Alf Hardy was a typical fisherman, barrel-chested with massive forearms and a body that looked as though it was built for endurance and would be capable of seemingly boundless energy, but now he appeared almost bashful.

Daisy stared at him. She had grown up treating Alf as one of her brothers – he was her youngest brother's best friend after all and eight years older than herself – but lately she had sensed a subtle shift in their easy relationship. It had been enough to cause her to become aware of him in a way she hadn't been before, and now, as she gazed into his mild hazel eyes, she noticed his perennially red ears were glowing even more brightly than usual. He was embarrassed. Alf was *embarrassed*. And suddenly she was too, and for the life of her couldn't think of anything to say.

'I . . . I wanted a word with you, without all the others

15

around.' Alf shifted uneasily, and his fingers – spatulate and with the evidence of tar and scar tissue from where they had split when pulling the nets up and down as a young lad – bunched together as he began to wring his hands before suddenly stuffing them into his deep pockets. 'I've bin tryin' to see you alone for weeks but it's like attemptin' to get an audience with the old Queen herself.'

Daisy forced a smile. He liked her, Alf liked her – in *that* way. Suddenly everything became crystal clear. But how did she feel about him? She wasn't sure. He was just . . . Alf. Dependable, kind, funny Alf. He and his old mother, who was a great friend of her grandmother, were almost part of Daisy's family. She could barely remember her own mam who had died of the fever when she was a little bairn of three, just the misty memory remaining of a warm pair of arms and a soft voice singing her to sleep at night, along with the vague recollection of her father holding her very tight as she had cried and cried on being told her mam had gone to talk to the angels in heaven. It had been Alf's mother who had stepped into the breach then and kept the household running for some years when it became obvious that the illness which had taken Daisy's mam had also badly weakened her granny's chest.

Daisy couldn't remember a time when Alf and Mrs Hardy hadn't been comfortably familiar figures by the fireside on those evenings when the fishing boats weren't out. The two old women would gossip over Mrs Hardy's homemade blackberry wine which she always brought with her, and Daisy's da and brothers and Alf would smoke their pipes and down a pint or two of the bitter beer her da made and served from the old Grey Hen, or stroll along to the public house for a tankard of ale.

Even now, when all her brothers except Tom were married and spent their evenings by their own firesides, nothing seemed to have changed. But it had, she just hadn't

16

seen it till now. Tom had his eye on a lass in Whitburn, she'd heard her brother mention something to her da about it only the other day. And Alf liked her . . .

'You must have guessed how I feel about you, lass? Everyone else has.' Alf rubbed his nose, his voice rueful. 'I didn't want to say anythin' afore but you'll be sixteen come summer an' plenty of lasses have bin courtin' for a year or two by then.'

Daisy shook her head, blushing as she said, 'I didn't know.'

He wasn't surprised she hadn't known despite what he'd said. Hadn't he argued as much when Tom had urged him to make his feelings plain? 'She don't think of me in that way, man. You know she don't. Looks on me the same as you, as a brother.'

'Then it's high time you changed the way she thinks.' Tom had been quite militant. 'Years you've waited to speak, an' that was right an' proper with her bein' so young an' all, but she's a grown lass now an' bin runnin' a household for years, don't forget. Me da always said she'd be a beauty an' he weren't wrong, there'll be plenty of lads sniffin' about our Daisy. I know me an' her always meet head on but you bring out the best in her, the softer side, an' marriage'll be good for her. An' you, eh?'

'Aye, but there's more to bein' wed an' such than runnin' a house. What if she don't like me? You know, as a lad.'

'Aw, man.' Tom had been irritable with what he saw as his friend's lack of gumption. 'You've got your own boat an' there's only you an' your mam in your cottage; I know any one of a number of lasses who'd jump at the chance to walk out with you. An' your face wouldn't crack no mirrors neither. Talk to her, for cryin' out loud, you know she thinks a bit of you.'

Alf looked at Daisy who now had her head lowered as she scuffed the snow with the toe of one boot. Aye, she

17

thought a bit of him, same as she did Tom and the rest of her brothers. But there were many different kinds of love, and never had this truth become so apparent to him as in the weeks and months since Daisy's fourteenth birthday. He had given her a little wooden box with a seahorse pared on the lid. Six months he'd been working on it in any spare moments he got, whittling away after he'd found a suitable piece of wood until it was all smooth and shiny and as bonny as you'd buy in one of the fancy shops in the towns. And all his work had been worth it for the delight she'd shown. Fair barmy she'd gone.

And then she'd kissed him on the cheek. Just a bairn's kiss, nothing more, but suddenly he'd known why he couldn't work up an interest for long in any of the lasses who made it clear they were willing. He'd sat and looked at her that evening, all the time pretending everything was the same as normal but it wasn't, not for him. And there was no going back.

Alf took a deep breath and then said evenly, 'Well, lass, now you do know, what's your answer? Can you see yerself learnin' to look at me as a' – he had been about to say 'man' but changed it to – 'lad?'

There was silence for a moment, and then Daisy glanced at him as she said quietly, 'I don't know, Alf. I'm sorry, but I don't know.'

He nodded. He'd hoped for more but at the bottom of him had been scared it would be less, that she would refuse him outright. 'Aye, well, that's all right. We've time.' He raised his eyebrows and smiled weakly at her. 'If me mam was here she'd add "God willing" to that, wouldn't she?'

Daisy smiled back as she nodded, glad he wasn't upset or angry.

By, but she was bonny. Alf's eyes moved over the face in front of him, its texture as smooth as satin and its colour like warm honey with a blush on it. She'd been daintily

appealing as a bairn, and as different in build from most of
the big-boned fishergirls as chalk from cheese, but now . . .
He gazed at her hair, her grey eyes, her small straight nose.
Apart from her granny he had never seen anyone with
truly grey eyes, but it wasn't just their colour or their thick
fringe of lashes which made them so bonny. They carried a
luminescence, as if they were lit from within somehow.

'I . . . I need to get back.'

'Aye, 'course you do.' Daisy's voice had been nervous
and made Alf belatedly aware he had been staring.

Had he frightened her? That was the last thing he wanted
to do. He turned, beginning to follow the path which led
to the village and talking as he did so. 'I looked in on your
granny afore I come up here. Made up the fire an' left her
suppin' a drop of hot barley me mam sent.'

Daisy hesitated for a moment before falling into step
beside him, acutely aware of the height and breadth of
him and the overall maleness of his hard compact body.
As Alf continued to talk she remained silent, but her head
was whirling.

He wanted her. Alf wanted her. It made her feel funny.
But he'd called in to make sure her granny was all right,
and that was nice of him. But he *was* nice, she'd always
known that. In fact, Alf hadn't got it in him to be anything
other than nice. Look how he had always listened to her.
He had understood when she was sad because she had
to miss so much schooling what with looking after her
granny and the house and everything. Her da and brothers
had said that learning was no use to a fishergirl, but if
Alf had thought that he hadn't said so. When she had
told him she wanted to know things, to understand more
about words and numbers and subjects like history and
geography, he hadn't guffawed and tweaked her chin and
called her doo-lally like Tom had.

'Don't worry, lass.' Alf was looking at her again but

now it was the old brotherly Alf, not the young man with hot, hungry eyes. 'I'm not goin' to keep on at you, you take all the time you need. But I felt it was right I made me feelin's plain, that's all. You understand?'

Daisy nodded. Yes, she understood, of course she did, and it was only to be expected that a good-looking presentable man like him with his kindness and sense of humour and all the other things which made him Alf, would want to find someone and marry and have a family one day. It was the order of things and right and proper, and if she'd had her head screwed on she would have wondered why he hadn't made his choice before this. And she wouldn't have liked it if he *had* said he was going to wed someone else.

This moment of self-knowledge came as a shock, so much so that as they turned a corner and Daisy looked across the white fields in front of her and beyond to where the sea – hypnotic, beguiling and lethal – shimmered silver-blue and calm, she didn't experience the usual rush of pleasure that told her she was nearly home. If she didn't want Alf to court any other lass – and she didn't – why hadn't she agreed to start walking out with him?

Daisy continued to wrestle with her thoughts as she and Alf followed the path towards the village. Depending on the season this could prove an arduous struggle through thick glutinous mud, or at the height of summer be baked hard and dusty with buttercups and wild thyme at its edges, or yet again – like today – a mass of frozen ridges of black ice and snow.

It was another five minutes before they reached the sloping sand dunes, an enchanted place in summer when fringed with delicate spiky grasses and tiny bright flowers. Now the cottages were in front of them, looking, Daisy always felt, to be somehow strung together like rows of herrings in the smoke house. They faced the wide expanse of the North Sea, with nothing between to cushion the worst of the elements.

The track widened to a rough road and as Daisy walked down it with Alf she was experiencing an emotion hitherto unknown to her, that of shyness. It suddenly seemed wrong – no, not wrong, that wasn't the right word, Daisy told herself silently, but she couldn't think of one that fitted how she was feeling. But walking together like this, where folk could see them, made her feel that everyone knew what Alf had asked her.

Apart from one or two boats the small fishing fleet was in, and most of the fishermen were either seeing to damage on their craft or repairing their nets with big wooden needles threaded with cotton treated with creosote. Daisy hated using this cotton when she helped her da with the nets. If it wasn't properly dried out her hands would be black in no time, and she would have to scrub them until they were raw to get the strong-smelling oil off her skin, and even then the smell would linger.

'Bad couple of days with that storm blowin' up out of nowhere.' Alf's eyes had swept down the higgledy-piggledy line of boats, some pulled close to the cottages and others at varying distances from the water's edge. 'The boats took a beatin' but we were lucky not to lose any.'

Daisy nodded. 'Me granny was worried. Not that she let on, mind, but when you all didn't come back the first night she had the candle burnin' from dusk the second.'

'Aye, well . . .' Alf raised his hand to one or two of the fishermen who had called to him. 'Likely it gives her a bit of comfort, same as me mam, but I've a mind it'd take more than a candle burnin' to stop old Neptune havin' his way if he decided your time was up.'

'Alf!' Daisy was shocked. She believed wholeheartedly in every one of the superstitions her mother had passed on to her with her milk, like her own mother with her.

Everyone knew you couldn't wash clothes on a day the menfolk went to sea in case you washed them away; same as a woman whistling was unlucky and watching the boats depart meant you'd be waiting for ever to see them come back. None of the old fishermen would allow a clergyman near their boat before it sailed – something Daisy had always secretly thought very strange, because weren't the clergy supposed to be God's ambassadors and go around doing only good? – and she had known from a small bairn never to mention the word 'pig' in front of her da or any of the other fishermen.

But the *candle*, that was the most important thing of all; it lit the way home for the boats, everyone knew that. Every fisherwoman in their village would make sure she had a candle in readiness for when her menfolk sailed, even if there was no food in the cupboard and she didn't know where the next penny was coming from.

Alf looked into the indignant young face frowning up at him, and his lips twitched. 'All right, all right, have it your way, lass.'

'Aye, I will an' all.'

This was so typical of Daisy that now Alf laughed out loud, partly from relief that she seemed to have reverted to being completely at ease with him again after their stilted conversation on the path.

They had been walking down the rough unmade road which passed in front of the cottages, dirt and sand blending with snow and ice to form a speckled, crunchy-surfaced toffee mallow underfoot, and now, as Daisy reached her door, waving to her father and brother who were working on the family boat at the water's edge, her voice was still reproving when she said, 'Thank you for seein' to Gran an' thank your mam for the barley drink.'

'My pleasure.' Alf grinned at her. He liked it when Daisy got on her high horse about something or other.

She might be a slip of a lass with a waist so slender he could span it with his two hands, but her sylphlike frame belied the spirit within. By, she could keep a man in line, could Daisy Appleby, and no mistake. But she was sweet-natured, as sweet as honey, and that's what made the difference between her and some of the other lasses he knew. Daisy hadn't got a spiteful bone in her body and he'd seen her in all her moods over the years, so he should know. *Oh, Daisy* . . . Alf forced his voice to betray nothing of the sudden surge of love that had swept over him when he said, 'There's a pot of me mam's crab-apple jelly on the table an' all. Mam thought it might tempt your gran to eat when she's feelin' a bit more herself again. She likes a bit of that on a drop scone, don't she?'

'Aye, she does. Ta, Alf.' Daisy smiled at him, her voice warm again. He was so *nice*, and Mrs Hardy too. And their cottage was bonny inside. Daisy didn't allow herself to think 'much nicer than ours', because that would have been disloyal to her da and granny, but there was no doubt that it was true. An old aunt of Mrs Hardy's had stepped out of the family's favour by going off to be in service somewhere or other years ago, gradually working herself up to lady's maid, whatever that meant. And when her mistress had died she had left one or two nice bits of furniture in her will to the aunt who, finding herself without a roof over her head, had been taken in by the newly married Mrs Hardy. Alf's mother had had her own mam living with her at that time too, according to Daisy's granny, and had thought it would be nice for the two sisters to end their days together.

So the aunt had come, along with her furniture, and after a period of time the sisters had died, leaving Mr and Mrs Hardy quite nicely set up for fisherfolk as the aunt had saved a bit too. But the icing on the cake, Daisy's granny always insisted, had been when Alf had come along after Mrs Hardy was getting on and had given up all hope of ever having a bairn. And with Mr Hardy being lost at sea when Alf was a young lad of seven or eight, the aunt's money had seen them through until Alf was able to go out with the fleet, and then later work his da's boat.

This story, which Daisy's grandmother had told her time and time again as a child when the little girl had crept into the old woman's arms for a cuddle, had always held a touch of magic for Daisy.

It was like a fairytale where everything came right at the end only it was *true*, and from Daisy's being a bairn it had added a touch of enchantment to Mrs Hardy's nicely furnished little home that would have made Alf's mother smile if she could have read Daisy's mind.

And she could live in Alf's cottage one day if she married him, Daisy thought as she watched Alf stride down the road. It would be her who would polish the fine pieces with lavender wax, and brush the two velvet-covered armchairs with bobbly beading round the bottom, when his mam was gone.

Eeh! She shook her head at the last thought, horrified it had come into her mind. How could she think about Mrs Hardy passing away? She was wicked, she was, though she hadn't meant it nasty like. She liked Alf's mam, loved her even. And such was her self-reproach that she opened the cottage door with enough force to make her grandmother start violently in her bed.

'Landsakes, hinny, whatever's wrong?'

Nellie was clutching her scrawny throat, eyes wide. Full of contrition, Daisy ran to the old woman lying on the platform bed pushed flat against the wall to one side of the range in which a good fire was blazing. 'I'm sorry, Gran. Did I give you a gliff?'

'Give me a gliff?' Nellie glared at the granddaughter who was the light of her life. 'If me teeth weren't me own I'd have swallowed 'em for sure.'

'Oh, Gran.'

'Aye, you might well laugh, miss, but me poor old heart can't take much of that. What's up anyway? You had words with someone? Someone upset you?'

'No.' Daisy hesitated. 'I've just been talkin' to Alf an' he was . . . nice,' she finished somewhat lamely.

'I'd hate to be in this bed when he puts your back up then, lass. That's all I can say.' Nellie looked into the fresh young face in front of her and what she read there caused her voice to become gentler. 'So, what's caused you to come in all of a lather then, hinny?'

Daisy stared at her grandmother for a moment before she said quietly, 'Alf's asked me to start walkin' out with him.'

'Oh, aye?' It was to Nellie's credit that she didn't fling her arms into the air and shout 'Hallelujah!' at this point, considering it was what she had prayed for ever since she had got wind of how Alf felt. Instead she made a play of fiddling with the worn grey blankets covering the lower half of her emaciated frame as she said, her voice steady, 'An' what did you say in reply?'

'I said I wasn't sure, that I didn't know whether I wanted to or not.'

'I thought you liked Alf?'

'I do, I do like him, but . . .'

'But?' Nellie's voice was still gentle.

'Shouldn't it be more than likin', Gran? Shouldn't you feel . . . oh, I don't know. Like you felt for Granda, I suppose.'

'An' what was that, hinny?'

'That you'd give up everythin', everythin' an' everyone, to be at his side?'

By, but this bairn of hers had a way of putting her finger right on the spot. Nellie stared at her. 'An' you're sayin' you don't feel like that about the lad?'

'No. Yes. Oh, I don't know, Gran. When I thought about Alf askin' someone else . . .'

'You didn't like it.' Nellie's tone was flat.

Daisy nodded miserably. 'But that's not the same necessarily, is it?'

No, it wasn't. 'How did Alf take it when you said no?'

'I didn't say no, not really. I said I wasn't sure an' he said he'd wait, that he would give me all the time I need.'

Thank you, God. Nellie relaxed a little. 'Then there's nothin' to get in a pother about, is there, hinny?' She reached out and took one of her granddaughter's hands in her own, squeezing it once before she said, her tone bright, 'Are them baskets empty? You sold the lot?'

'Aye, look.' Alf momentarily forgotten, Daisy reached into the pocket of her skirt and brought out the contents for her grandmother's inspection. 'Full price an' all. Tuppence each for them big bloaters, an' the cods' heads went straightaway down in the rougher end of town.'

Nellie nodded. 'They make a fillin' meal when they're boiled an' the flesh scraped off an' mixed with potatoes, as we know, eh, lass?' There was many a spell, especially in the hard northern winters, when they'd had to sell all the fish just to pay the rent and stay alive, and then the scraps of cod came into their own. But her bairn was a marvel and a natural housewife. Daisy had a way of making a penny stretch to two and she wasn't averse to hard work neither, although – and here Nellie sighed silently – it pained her when her lass's hands were raw and bleeding from helping George and Tom with the nets, or when she came in exhausted and sick to her stomach from gutting the fish and washing the offal.

'Da'll be pleased.' Daisy had left her grandmother's side and walked across to the range. Now she busied herself spooning two ladlefuls of broth from a big black saucepan standing on a battered wooden table to one side of the range into a smaller pan. She then placed this on the hob, pressing it towards the glowing coals before warming a few drops of goose grease and bringing the pannikin over to her grandmother. 'Rub this in, Gran, while I see to things.'

'Eeh, lass, you've enough to do without worryin' about me, now then.' Nellie slowly raised herself on to her elbows, and Daisy adjusted the straw bolster around the bony back before handing her grandmother the warm pannikin, whereupon she turned back to the range. And then she halted halfway across the room, glancing about her as she thought, This might not be as grand as Alf's mam's, but it's a palace compared to some in the streets I've been to today where the pervading smell's like sitting in the privy.

Some of the fishing cottages, of which Daisy's was one, had their own privies, square brick or wooden boxes with a wooden seat extending across the breadth of the lavatory and filling half its depth. These were situated outside the back door, and for those who were forced to share, the visit could be either foul-smelling or relatively odourless, depending on the fastidiousness of the last occupant. Daisy made sure a bucket of fresh ashes found its way to their privy every morning and evening, but the keen salty wind that was forever in evidence, even on the mildest of summer days, was the best purifier. She had been thankful she lived in the cottages situated on the shoreline ever since her first visit to the towns to sell fish. The strong odour of fish and seaweed and tar here, which clung to every cottage and infused clothes, bedding and furniture with its pungent smell, she did not even notice.

The cottage itself was very small, merely two rooms downstairs – the living room and a scullery – and one room above, although some of the fishermen's families had no upstairs at all. In the Applebys' case a third of the bedroom

27

at the end by the window had been partitioned off many years before by means of a ramshackle floor-to-ceiling screen, which George had made with odd scraps of timber he'd salvaged. This was Daisy's space, and there was just enough room in it for her narrow box bed – nothing but a foot-high wooden platform, again cobbled together by her father, and an ancient flock mattress – an orange box containing her meagre items of clothing, and two more boxes placed on top of each other to form a kind of table. These were draped with a piece of thick yellow linen which reached to the floor, and which had given Daisy great pleasure ever since she had found the cloth washed up on the shore years before.

This, together with the fact that she could sit up in bed and look out of the window – a mixed blessing in winter when the draught was enough to waft her hair about her face and ice coated the glass an inch thick – made her tiny bedroom a haven to Daisy.

The table held the sum total of her possessions: her hairbrush, a small, chipped but still quite exquisite vase – another beachcombing find – which Daisy filled with wild flowers from spring to autumn, and Alf's box holding some ribbons and hair grips which her da and brothers had bought for her birthday the year before, along with a small round hand mirror.

The upper floor of the cottage was reached by means of a steep staircase almost in the form of a ladder, which led directly out of the living room into the one above, but in spite of the range below being kept going day and night in winter the bedroom was always icy cold. Her father and brother, weathered by the hard life they led on the freezing, wind-swept expanse of the North Sea, seemed unaware of the cold, and once they were under their blankets in the two iron beds the larger space boasted – in one of which used to sleep Daisy's parents and the other her brothers, top and tailed – they were immediately asleep. Not so Daisy. Many was the night she shivered for half-an-hour or so in spite of her stone hot water bottle, finally drifting off to sleep curled round its warmth like a small animal.

A popping sound from the pot on the hob brought her out of the uncharacteristically pensive mood she had fallen into, and she quickly tipped the broth into a clean earthenware bowl and carried it across to her grandmother. 'Get this down you, Gran. An' all of it, mind. Remember what that apothecary in Monkwearmouth said when Da went to see him after your last bad turn. You need to eat little an' often. That'll be better than all the mustard poultices an' leeches an' sulphur baths, he said.'

'All right, me bairn. All right.'

Once her grandmother was settled and sipping the broth, Daisy walked through to the scullery. The floor here was stone-flagged like the living room, and on it stood a table on which were piled dirty dishes and pans from the family's evening meal the night before and breakfast that morning.

There was also a poss-tub and poss-stick, a large tin bath which was leaning on its side against the wall, an upturned bucket on which sat a tin bowl, and under the narrow window a smaller table on which lay a large marble slab used for keeping food cool during the warmer months. Next to this stood a barrel made of wooden staves with metal hoops round them. There was another just outside the back door of the cottage to catch the rain and this, together with the freshwater stream which ran on to the beach some fifty yards from the cottages, provided all their water. Daisy now scooped up half a bucketful, filtering it through muslin – ladle after ladle – to strain the dirt out, and carried it through to the living room. She tipped it into the black kale pot permanently suspended by a chain attached to a metal rod which could swing out over the fire when required, and which provided all their hot water for washing clothes and pans, and for bathing in the long tin bath.

'Lass, I know you've got things to see to' – her grandmother's voice was apologetic – 'but yer da wants you to work on the net.' Nellie gestured towards the big net on the far wall of the cottage, held in place by a double-pronged hook which was fastened to the tarred walls of the room and which held the nets secure when they were being repaired. 'Him an' Tom've done the heavy work down the sides, you'll only need the bone needles to mend what's left.'

'Aye, all right, Gran. I'll do the dishes an' get the mardy cake on for dinner first.'

Poor little lass. Nellie's sunken eyes watched sympathetically as Daisy's slim figure bustled about the cottage. The old woman would have been mortally offended if someone had reminded her that her own daughter had been brought up to do the same tasks, and then Nellie hadn't spared it a passing thought. The truth of the matter was that she had never loved her daughter like she did her granddaughter, her overriding disappointment at her own long-awaited child's being a girl instead of the boy she had wanted for her husband only abating to some degree when Mary had redeemed herself by producing one baby boy after another. And such is the inconsistency of human nature that Nellie had never thought it ironic that she should now love Daisy with what amounted to devotion, whereas her five surviving grandsons held little interest for her.

By the time George and Tom pushed open the door of the cottage the thaw which had been heralded by some of the old-timers – who considered themselves weather experts – was busy melting the ice and snow outside to thick slush and mud, something Daisy hated. Twilight had long since fallen, and inside the oil lamps had been lit.

Daisy was sitting working at the net on the stool they

kept for such a purpose, Nellie was dozing in her bed on the other side of the room, and the smell of the evening meal hung in the air. The mellow light from the lamps and the soft glow from the range showed the living room's meagre furniture to its best advantage. This consisted of a square wooden table covered with oilcloth around which six straight-backed chairs were placed, a wooden saddle devoid of cushions which stood flat against the wall opposite Nellie's low platform bed, and a smaller table to one side of the range upon which sat the pots and pans and big black kettle.

Daisy jumped up at the men's entrance; a sleety rain had been drumming at the windows impatiently for the last hour or more and she knew they must be wet through. 'You got her ready for tomorrow, Da?' Her father's boat, like so many, had been pummelled viciously throughout the winter, but the last fishing trip had been the worst yet. It added insult to injury that most of the fishermen had been forced to work repairing the damage to boats and nets throughout the next day which had been the calmest for some time.

'Aye, she'll do.' George was a man of few words but his smile was tender as he looked at his daughter. He was not a God-fearing man like some in the village who would no sooner have missed the Sunday meeting at Whitburn church than ceased breathing, but he believed his Daisy was a gift from the Almighty right enough, and made sure he thanked Him for her daily. And he knew his love was reciprocated. Daisy might be close to her granny – and that was good with Mary being taken when the lass was nowt but a wee bairn – but the feeling between him and his last child was something rare and precious.

In spite of his being away for days and nights on end, it had always been him Daisy had run to when she'd hurt herself as a bairn, even when Mary had been alive. Him

31

she'd told her secrets to, him who had received her baby kisses. He knew their Tom thought he was soft the way he was with the lass, but George didn't care. He hadn't cared from the day she was born and had gripped his finger with her tiny hand. He thought a bit of his lads, aye, and still mourned the two who had never reached their first birthday, but Daisy provided a light and joy in his soul that no one else ever had.

'There's your dry clothes in the scullery an' the meal'll be ready when you are.'

'Right you are, lass.'

George nodded at Nellie who was now sitting up in the bed as he walked across the room followed by his youngest son. As Tom passed his sister he tweaked one of her shining braids of hair, saying, 'I hope you've mended that net to my standards, little 'un,' which Daisy answered by sticking out her tongue at him.

Once the scullery door was shut she busied herself setting three places at the table and heating a little more broth for her granny. She didn't attempt to get the creosote off her hands, knowing from experience it would take a good while with the blue-veined soap and the scrubbing brush in the scullery before the stain would begin to shift, but as she began to serve up the meal she was humming to herself. If she married Alf, he wouldn't mind her still nipping along to see to her da and Tom and granny, she knew that. He understood that looking after her granny was like caring for a bairn, with the washing and feeding and making sure she was able to use the chamber pot when she needed it, and that her da and Tom would need a hot meal every night they weren't out on the water. Aye, he'd understand all that.

As Daisy began to sing 'Blaydon Races', more enthusiastically than tunefully, Nellie found herself relaxing back against her bolster again with a small smile touching her slightly blue lips. Her lass was singing and that was a good sign. It would all come right, Daisy and Alf, once the lass had had a chance to think about him as a lad and not as one of the family. Daisy was canny, she'd see what side her bread was buttered sure enough.

Nellie shut her eyes, the agitation and panic which had been making her heart race ever since Daisy had arrived home beginning to subside. She wanted to see her lass settled and happy before the Good Lord called her home, and there was none better for her than Alf. Not on this side of the ocean. Salt of the earth, Alf was, and he was right gone on the lass. Anyone could see that. Daisy would be safe married to him and she was too beautiful to be left to her own devices for long. They weren't all like Alf, not by a long chalk. But it would be all right; if she knew anything about Alf Hardy he wouldn't take no for an answer where Daisy was concerned.

A touch of excitement took hold as Nellie pictured Daisy on Alf's arm, and then as mistress of the bonny little cottage at the far end of the village. The next few months were going to be ones of change, she felt it in her water, and pray God it would all be good.

Chapter Two

Daisy was the first to rise early the next morning as was normally the case when her father and brother were taking the boat out. She always slept in her vest, flannel drawers and shift in the colder months, over which she wore a long calico nightgown, and after sliding her feet out of bed she made her way downstairs in the pitch blackness, feeling her way until she could light the oil lamp. Over the years she had perfected the exercise until now she moved without a sound.

Her granny's rasping snores told her the old woman was fast asleep. She made her way to the table, and once the lamp was lit padded into the icy-cold scullery where she stripped, hastily washing herself all over with water from the barrel and the blue-veined soap which never lathered.

By the time Daisy had donned her underclothes again her teeth were chattering, and after nipping through to the main room once more she quickly gathered her petticoat, thick serge dress, shawl and boots from a chair in front of the range where she had placed them the night before to catch any warmth from the fire.

After dressing she wasted no time in stoking up the range and putting fresh wood and coal on the fire, once she had raked out the ashes and tipped them into the bucket for the privy. Then the kettle was on the hob, and the big pan of porridge she had prepared the night before – so the oats were well soaked – was warming. She always made sure her father and Tom went out into the raw mornings with a full belly, and there was nothing like an outsize bowl of hot salty porridge made stiff enough to hold the spoon for warming a man through.

'You want a sup tea, Gran?'

Nellie had been awake for a few minutes but lying quietly. Now the old woman hitched herself up in the bed as she answered, 'When you're ready, me bairn, when you're ready.'

In the distance a ship's horn made a low, drawn-out sound, eerie and melancholy, and Daisy paused in mashing the tea, her gaze going to the window where a tired dawn was struggling to break through the greyness. The seagulls were already flying and calling in the thin early light, for all the world like hungry bairns crying for their mam's milk.

Daisy shivered. In spite of the fact that she had grown up with the plaintive sound she had never got used to it, and on mornings like this, when it was bitterly cold and windy and her father and Tom were going out on the water, the birds' cries always made goose-pimples prick her skin.

And then she made an impatient movement, shaking the foreboding away. She hadn't got time to woolgather, for goodness' sake. There was the breakfast to see to and the men's poke to get ready. After handing her grandmother a cup of black tea with a spoonful of sugar, Daisy sliced up the remainder of the mardy cake from the night before. She dropped this into the poke – a hessian bag which the men took on board with them – together with a couple of large potatoes which had been baked in their jackets in the ashes of the fire, the last of a piece of brisket cut into two hefty shives, and two apples from a supply stored on a rack suspended beneath the ceiling in the scullery.

That would keep her da and Tom going till they got home to a good meal. She already had the rent money put away, and with what she had got for the fish yesterday could do some baking today once she had been to the mill. The farmer's boy had promised to slip her a couple of rabbits when he brought the milk, so she could make a humpy-backed pie with one and a good pot of broth for tomorrow with the other. And she'd make a sly cake as well as some loaves of bread, and some drop scones for her granny to have with Mrs Hardy's crab apple jelly.

Daisy found herself smiling at the thought of the food and straightened her face quickly as she heard the menfolk descending the stairs. Eeh, they'd think she'd gone doolally if she greeted them grinning like a Cheshire cat, and Tom wouldn't miss such an opportunity to make some sly remark or other. And it was too early in the morning to chaff with her brother.

'Somethin' smells good, lass.'

It was her father's stock greeting in the morning but always said with genuine approval, and now, as George and Tom – fully dressed – seated themselves at the table, Daisy bustled about serving up the porridge and pouring cups of strong black tea.

Tom sat looking at the slender comely figure of his sister, but he was thinking about Alf. Had he asked her? Alf had been all fired up to take the plunge the last time they'd spoken, and about time too. And he wasn't just thinking about his friend here. He loved Daisy, 'course he did, she was his sister and a good lass at heart, but she was too headstrong, too wilful, for her own good. Fisherwomen were bred to be gutsy; in the harsh battle for survival they needed to be every bit as strong as their men, but they didn't all look like Daisy and therein lay the root of his concern. She was beautiful as well as bull-headed.

Tom ran his hand over his face as his conscience pricked him. By, he was a fine one to talk about bull-headedness, the mess he was in. He'd known he was sailing close to the wind when he'd taken up with Margery, her being a miner's daughter and all, but from the first time he had seen her one Sunday when he and Alf had gone for a walk into Whitburn, he had wanted her. He had broken the unspoken but nevertheless cast-iron rule that fishermen only went for fishergirls, a rule he himself was fully in agreement with – or had been until he had set eyes on Marge and lost all reason.

'Here, lad.' As Daisy placed a bowl of steaming porridge in front of him, Tom nodded his thanks, picking up his spoon and beginning to shovel the food into his mouth without really tasting it.

The fishing communities up and down the coast were close-knit and tight, they had to be to survive. Hadn't his granny told them tales of how hard she had found it to be accepted when she'd first come here, and her a fishergirl from just a few miles up the coast at that? But that was the way of things.

Tom took a long pull at the scalding hot tea, burning his tongue in the process. But a miner's lass . . . What did a landlubber know about gutting and sorting fish, mending the nets, smoking and wind-drying the fish, and a hundred other things besides? He didn't know a fisher lass who didn't have red swollen hands and skin as brown as a nut. They were born old. And there was Marge – white porcelain skin, hair as fair and fine as thistledown and blue eyes so light they seemed to reflect any colour she was looking at. But he loved her, and she loved him, enough to want to be with him as his wife and take on a new life that would be hell on earth at first. He'd warned her, aye, he had that to his credit at least. He hadn't dressed it up at all.

He would have to tell his da properly, this couldn't go on any longer. Six months he'd been seeing Marge on the sly, and the first time he had mentioned her to his da had been a week or so ago and then only in passing, while her parents didn't even know he existed. But after what had happened that time they'd been sheltering in a cave when a sudden squall had threatened to soak them through, he had discovered he couldn't trust himself alone with Marge. He had made sure they always stayed in the town after that afternoon, heaven though it had been. It was dangerous to be around other folk, there was always the chance someone might see them and go blabbing to her father, but once he had told his da he was going to marry Marge, he would go and see her parents. He'd had a bellyful of this skulking around.

'. . . eh, Tom?'

'What?' Tom came back to the present with a start, glancing at his father who had obviously been speaking to him.

'What's the matter with you, lad? You'd better wake up afore we get on the boat else you'll do neither of us no good. I was just sayin' to the lass here that we'll need a nice bit of coke an' wood for the smoke house when we're back, God willin'. The last couple of trips haven't given us much, we're due a good 'un.'

'I'll go up into the woods an' get some oak twigs an' such an' all, Da. They give such a nice taste, don't they?' Daisy, after one quick glance at her brother, filled in the awkward pause after her father had finished speaking. What was the matter with their Tom? He hadn't been himself lately. He had never been what you'd call a talker – not like Alf who was a born comedian – but he'd normally sit and chat with her da in the morning and last thing at night. Lately it had been all you could do to get a word out of him.

'Aye, you do that, lass. Makes all the difference, a bit of oak.' George's smoke house – a narrow wooden single-storey construction situated outside next to the privy – was his pride and joy. He had built it himself when he'd got married, using bricks for the floor from a derelict cottage he'd found one day on the way to Boldon. The tiled roof with its smokeholes had come from the same source, and with its rows of wooden rods on which fish were hung to cure it was a neat little enterprise, as was the wooden frame outside on which the fishing nets were hung to dry.

The men ate their food quickly; Daisy was only halfway through her bowl of porridge when they left the cottage. She knew better than to wish them well or look out of the window at the boats leaving, but by six o'clock the beach was devoid of any apart from one which had been too badly damaged in the recent storms to go out, and on which two fishermen of about Tom's age were already working. No fishing meant no money, and both men had young families to feed.

They paused in their work on the coble as Daisy walked past on her way to collect the milk and rabbits from the farmer's boy. Every morning he walked the donkey as far as the first cottage in the village and there he stood, whatever the weather, from half-past six until whenever the last of the milk had been sold.

'How's yer granny this mornin', lass? The wife heard she was middlin',' one of the men called over the rising wind.

'A bit better.' Daisy smiled back at their grinning faces. She liked these two and had danced at their weddings with the other bairns a few years before. Now she put her concern to them as she said, 'The wind's gettin' worse, isn't it? An' it's straight from the north, an' the sea's got choppier since the boats left. Do you think there's goin' to be another storm? I thought things would get better now it's a bit milder.'

'Aw, don't you fret, lass.' The man who had spoken before gestured at his boat. 'Old Neptune did enough damage last trip to keep him happy for a time. Fair ripped the guts out of her, he did.'

Daisy nodded. It was meant to be comforting, she knew that, but looking at their boat was just the opposite. The coble was the type of vessel all the villagers used – flat-bottomed for stability, shaped to be launched direct from the beach with the tarpaulin stretched like a tent across the bow and a long tiller handle the size of an elephant's trunk. The tillers were made of strong oak but this one had been snapped right off, and there was plenty of other damage too. And if she wasn't much mistaken it looked as though the storm clouds were gathering more thickly with every minute that ticked by after the relative calm of the day before.

Nellie said as much when Daisy entered the cottage with the tins of milk and two rabbits, the latter gained by bartering some fine red herrings which the boy's mother was partial to. 'Light the lamp again, hinny, it's grown as dark as night since you've bin gone. If you're goin' to get them oak twigs an' the flour, I reckon you'd better be quick about it.'

Daisy was quick, but by the time she got home again just before noon the weather had turned nasty. It took her almost five minutes of standing over the fire's glow to thaw out frozen, almost helpless hands and body, and then the tingling intensity of feeling was such that it brought tears to her eyes.

There were still the usual dirty coasters with salt-caked smoke stacks, schooners and square riggers on the horizon, but by late afternoon, when the smell of cooking was redolent in the cottage and elemental alchemy had turned slanting sheets of rain to sleet, the seething cauldron that was the ocean was deserted.

'Come away from that window, lass. You're givin' me the willies hoverin' about like a lost soul. The boats might well have put in up the coast till the storm's over. It wouldn't be the first time.'

No, and it wouldn't be the first time that the fishermen, desperate to land a catch, had hung on too long either. Times were changing for some folk what with the unions and all, but for her da and Tom and Alf there was nothing like that. Her da and a few more of the old fishermen could remember tales passed down to them by their great-grandas, which had come through *their* great-grandas and so on. Stories about the disease-ridden hovels built into the banksides of the Wear and Tyne, which were considered fit rat holes for fishermen. These labyrinths of stairs and dark passageways with a public house at every corner had also been frequented by the press gangs, and it was the fishermen who had suffered the most at the hands of those infamous ruffians. And who had cared enough to lift a finger? No one. Even now, according to her da, there still wasn't a band of people considered so expendable as ordinary fishermen. When they went to work they could simply disappear; as dangerous as life in the pits was, the death toll on the seas was twice as high.

Daisy said nothing, but as she turned to face the room again her face must have spoken for itself because Nellie's voice was dry when she said, 'Aye, well, mebbe I might talk out of me backside at times, hinny, but the only thing that's sustained me for the last seventy-six years is takin' it a day at a time. No use frettin' until you know you've got somethin' to fret about, now then. As me old mam used to say: Spit in the eye of the devil an' likely he'll be blind enough to leave you alone.'

Daisy nodded, walking across to the bed and taking her grandmother's wrinkled hand which was resting on top of the grey blankets, the veins tumescent. She wished she could be as calm as her granny, oh, she did, but she just couldn't. She wished her da and Tom, and Alf too, hadn't gone out today. And whatever her granny said, she had listened to the men talk well enough to know how many times they cheated death. At the end of a hard winter, like now, they took extra chances. There wasn't a fisherwoman alive who didn't know that.

'Shall I light the candle early, Gran?'

Nellie gazed into her granddaughter's enormous eyes with their thick smoky lashes, and what she saw there caused her to say softly, 'Aye, you do that, me bairn. You do that. An' we'll have a nice sup tea with one of them drop scones an' a bit of Enid's crab apple jelly, shall we? While we're waitin' for 'em to get back like?'

Daisy smiled and nodded, but once the tallow candle was lit and the ill-tempered wind lashed the sleet into vicious sabre-like squalls against the windows with its ever-increasing fury, she found she couldn't eat a thing.

George was tired, bone-gnawingly tired, and the icy chafing water which had been working on his flesh for hours had opened the crust on the salt water boil on his thigh which had been giving him gyp for days. A needle spray stung his face as it had been doing all night, but at least now, in the wild light of dawn, the silent angry wastes of the North Sea didn't hold the terrors they had in the pitch blackness.

He couldn't see any of the other boats, although when the storm had hit he knew none of them had begun to make their way home. It had been the inexplicable conviction that a big shoal was nearby that had done it, and he still maintained it had been there. But they'd stayed out too long, damn it. In this sort of sea even the big ships went down, and the cobles were matchsticks in comparison. Aye, they should have cut their losses long before they had.

George glanced across to where Tom was standing, his

son's face rigid and tight. It had been that way since their row the day before. Silly young so-an'-so. George ground his teeth irritably. What had the lad expected him to do when he had told him he was set on marrying a bit lass – a *miner's* lass – who didn't know one end of a gutting knife from the other? Fall on his neck and offer his blessing? Say it didn't matter? Well, it did matter, and he had never been one for beating about the bush as Tom well knew. By, to think a son of his could be so damn' stupid! No good could come out of such a union, it was doomed from the start. But it hadn't happened yet, had it, and if he had his way he'd make damn' sure this was one wedding which never took place. He'd rather be struck down this minute than have to watch his own flesh and blood being led by the nose by some bit miner's daughter.

Another wave, which seemed as high as a house, smashed into the bow, sweeping the small craft on to nowhere at a furious rate. Each time they crested a wave and slid down the far side, icy water swirled knee-deep into the bottom of the boat but at least they could see what they were up against now, thank God, thought George, crossing himself with one hand as he steered with the other.

Tom caught the gesture, his mouth curling at what he saw as hypocrisy, the harshness of his judgement mainly the result of yesterday's quarrel. Normally his father's ability to shape the Almighty into a comfortable concept he felt easy with – one which didn't include church on a Sunday or unnecessary religious fervour, but which definitely included the Creator taking an interest in George's personal affairs – didn't bother Tom at all. Today, however, his feelings were still raw from the bitter exchange which had flared up once he had mentioned Marge. Well, one thing was for sure, he didn't intend to keep coming cap in hand to his da, Tom told himself aggressively. He'd tried the reasonable approach and if his da wouldn't meet him halfway that was his lookout.

The grey water washing aboard reduced his limbs to salty numbness, but inside Tom was still boiling. His fingers were raw and split from where they had dug into the net earlier but he couldn't feel them; for the time being the lacerating pain was deadened by the anaesthetising effects of the freezing water. Not so the hurt within.

He would see about renting his own place once he was back, aye, he would, Tom thought angrily. Old Ken Upton's cottage would be coming up soon now his widow was going to live with her sister in Fulwell, and if Alf would be willing to have him on his boat he'd join up with him.

Another welter of white lather from the towering waves sprayed the boat as it continued to smash heavily into the next foam-topped ridge and then the next. Tom heard his father's voice, reedy against the din of the storm, call to him to take the tiller. He lurched over to him, noticing as he did so that the older man's face was grey with exhaustion and he looked spent. His da wasn't as young as he used to be. As the thought hit home it had the effect of cauterising the bitter aftermath of their hot words, even to the extent that Tom thought, much as George had done earlier, What the hell did I expect him to say anyway? He was never going to understand; how could he when I don't understand it meself? But I'll be blowed if I'm goin' to lose me da over this. It'll work out. When he meets Marge he'll understand why I love her, aye, he will. She will win him over.

He squeezed his father's sodden arm in the moment before he took the tiller, a quick gesture and without undue sentiment, but as he saw something lift in the grey face he was glad he had made the first move. He was a stubborn old blighter, his da, but then it took one to recognise one.

45

They had shot the nets several times the day before but each haul had yielded next to nothing, although his da and some of the other old-timers had said they felt it in their bones that the fish were waiting. If one boat had turned for home the others might have followed, that was often the way of it, but they had all needed a good haul and so they had pushed the gods just a little too far.

Tom looked over to where his father was standing on the freedeck, and was just going to call to him to ask if he could see any other boats when the coble spun drunkenly under his hands. And then he saw it, the mother and father of a wave coming broadside on, and he knew his father had seen it too when the older man turned an incredulous, fear-filled face to him, shouting something he couldn't hear.

It took three or four seconds for the wave to hit but Tom, unlike his father, didn't move, his whole being caught up in the ghastly fascination of the mountain of water descending towards them. By the time George snatched the tiller out of his son's hands, trying to pull it hard over to get the boat into the wind, it was too late. The sea picked them up and tipped them over as easily as a bairn playing with bits of twig in a puddle.

Daisy hadn't slept all night. A fear had settled on her, a familiar fear, and it was no use her granny saying she always felt like this when the boats hadn't come back because she knew that was true but it was no comfort. This storm was worse than most; in fact, she couldn't remember one of such ferocity lasting so long. Her granny had remained silent when she'd said that.

'I'm goin' to have a look outside again.'

'Oh, hinny.' Her grandmother's hand came out towards her in protest. 'It's still barely light, an' you've already got soaked to the skin once the day. If you up an' take a chill an' I have to start lookin' after you, it'll be a case of the blind leadin' the blind all right.'

The last few words had been said in a jocular tone, but when Daisy's tense expression didn't change the old woman in the bed sighed deeply. She might as well have saved her breath, the lass would have her own way in this. It was no use saying that the boats were likely resting at Marsdon beyond Lizard Point or even Frenchman's Bay if they'd got blown South Shields way, the lass wasn't of a mind to hear it. Daisy wouldn't rest until George and the rest of them were safely home, that was always the pattern of events.

'I'll be back in a little while. You all right for a few minutes? Drink your broth, Gran.'

'Aye, I will, lass, but I wish you'd have a bite of somethin'.'

'I will later, I promise.'

It was actually a relief to step out into the bitter cold although the wind, stiffened with sleet, stung Daisy's eyes as she immediately scanned the horizon. She was glad her granny didn't openly fret when the boats were delayed, of course she was, but at times like today the old woman's stoicism was almost irritating. Alf's mam was more of a comfort on occasions like this; Enid Hardy was always at sixes and sevens until Alf was back, and moreover was vocal in her concern.

Daisy picked her way over the mudbath that was the road, and on to the wet spiky grass dotted with pebbles and stones which led to the edge of the high bank below which stretched a long expanse of sand. She stood gazing out to sea as she had done earlier, praying soundlessly all the while. Let them come home, God. Let them come home. Let them come home. And then she turned as Enid Hardy came up behind her.

'It's not let up all night, lass, has it? An' here was me thinkin' the worst was over when the thaw started.'

'Hallo, Mrs Hardy.' Daisy smiled at the older woman, and Alf's mother patted her shoulder for a moment before standing with her and following Daisy's gaze out to sea.

'I know fishin' is fishin' the country over an' none of it easy, but I reckon our lads have it worse than most,' Enid muttered, pulling her shawl more tightly about her face as the wind whipped the ends. 'Do you know, lass, the first thing I can remember is the sound of the sea. There's them that say it's similar to the sound of your mam's blood pulsin' in her body afore you're born, an' that's what makes it "comfortin'"! *Comfortin'*! Comfortin' my backside, that's what I say. I'd as soon take comfort from the devil himself. Right from a little bairn I've hated it, aye, I have, even in the summer when it's pretendin' to be pally.'

Daisy nodded; she could understand Mrs Hardy speaking like this. She knew from her granny that Alf's mam had first lost her father and two brothers and finally her husband to the capricious moods of the ocean.

'I look at them pit villagers when they come for a plodge in the summer, messin' about an' splashin' each other an' larkin' on, an' they've got no idea what's what. They buy the scones an' cakes some of the old wives sell from their cottage doors, have a nice day in the sunshine, an' go home thinkin' they're hard done by the rest of the year 'cos they don't live by the sea.'

'I wouldn't want to go down a mine though, Mrs Hardy.'

'Aye, aye, there is that, lass. It can't be much fun down a mine for sure.'

They stood together, the old woman and the young girl, without speaking now. It was a little while later when Daisy, taking a step forward, said urgently, 'There's a ship out there, Mrs Hardy. Can you see it? A big ship, there, through the mist. But there's somethin' wrong.'

'A ship you say, lass?' Enid bent slightly forward as though the extra inch or two would help her failing eyesight.

By the time a couple of their neighbours joined them Daisy knew the vessel out at sea was foundering, and so quickly did she turn and run towards the cottage of one of the men she had spoken to the day before that Enid wasn't aware of her departure for some moments.

'Our Jed, lass?' The big woman who had opened the door to Daisy was heavy with her fourth child in as many years, her overall bulk increased by her enormous stomach. 'He's not here. He's gone with Dan to get a sack of taties an' flour an' bits, been's as they couldn't take the boat out. What's the matter anyway, hinny? Is it your granny?'

Daisy's heart sank. Apart from a few elderly men who were too old or too sick to fish anymore, Jed and Dan were the only fishermen who hadn't sailed with the fleet the day before. And now there was a ship sinking in front of their very eyes and no one to help.

Daisy gave Jed's wife a quick explanation and left the other woman shouting to her children to remain indoors while pulling a shawl over her head and following Daisy outside. But what help would a pregnant woman be? What help would any of the women be? It was one of the oddities of fisherfolk life that very few of their menfolk, let alone the women, had ever learnt to swim, the general feeling being that if they were unlucky enough to find themselves at the mercy of the North Sea no amount of swimming would help them. And no fisherman in his right mind would swim for pleasure.

Daisy glanced at the women clustered together on the shore, some four or five of them now as more of the cottagers became aware of the drama out to sea, but didn't join them. Instead she ran down on to the sand itself, her heart pounding as she saw that the ship was now listing badly. The women followed her down to the water's edge, mostly silent, several clasping their hands together and one or two praying out loud.

'We have to do somethin'.' Daisy glanced about her wildly.

'You can't do nowt, lass.' Enid's voice was low, her eyes fixed on the ship which had moved nearer to shore in its death throes but was now sinking fast. 'Them rocks out there are meaner than shark's teeth. Once they're in the water the cold'll finish 'em in minutes. An' look at them waves, lass. You'd be knocked off your feet even if there was a boat to launch. Poor devils, whoever they are.'

'It's goin' down . . .'

One of the women spoke and there was a concentrated drawing in of breath as the ship stood almost vertically in the water for a moment. As it remained there for some seconds the women heard a noise, either an explosion or perhaps the engines and machinery coming loose from their bearings and falling the length of the ship, and then it stopped, the ship first sinking back a little at the stern and then sliding slowly forward through the waves in a slanting dive as the sea closed over her.

'Oh, dear God, have mercy on them in the hour of their distress . . .'

Daisy was aware of Enid murmuring at the side of her and of one or two of the women crying while others were busy ushering children back towards the cottages and away from the debris which could now be clearly seen in the water. The waves were huge and it was difficult to discern any human beings amidst the wreckage, but once or twice Daisy thought she saw an arm lifted or what looked like a body or two clinging to anything which floated, but within a short while these had disappeared.

Mrs Hardy was right, no one could survive for long when the sea was like this and the coldness of the water froze the will to fight and resist. But in spite of her thoughts Daisy continued to strain her eyes out to sea, hardly breathing in her distress. Those poor, poor people, whoever they were. Mothers and fathers, sisters and brothers, sweethearts – there would be loved ones at home waiting for them. Oh, Da, Da, please be safe, and Tom and Alf. Were they still out on the water? If a big ship like the one that had just gone down couldn't make it safely to port, what chance did the cobles have?

And then she saw it. A small lone lifeboat being tossed about at random as the huge waves rose and fell. And someone was inside it.

Daisy clutched hold of Enid with enough force to make that good lady cry out in pain, but Daisy's fingers tightened further as she said, 'Mrs Hardy, there's a lifeboat that hasn't sunk an' someone's in it. Look, there. You see? Oh, we've got to help somehow, it could be turned over any minute. What can we do?' And then she answered herself saying, 'Quick, we need a rope.'

'Rope, lass?' Enid shook her head. 'You'll never get near enough with a rope.'

Daisy didn't waste time contradicting her, turning and hurrying up the beach and on to the high bank where Jed and Dan's boat was standing. She had noticed a thick coil of heavy-duty rope there the previous day and was praying the fishermen hadn't moved it when they had finished working on the coble. They hadn't.

Several of the women had remained with Enid at the water's edge, but now Daisy called to one or two who had come back up to the cottages and were standing in a small group a few yards away. 'There's someone in a lifeboat! Jenny, Maggie, quick, help me carry this rope down. *Come on*. We haven't got much time.'

The women had stared in amazement at first, but now all of them came running, lifting the massive coil of rope which had a small loop at one end and seemed to weigh a ton.

'What're you goin' to do, lass?' one of them gasped as they reached the others who had been with Enid, but who had come as a group to meet them halfway up the beach. 'Try an' lasso the poor blighter?'

'Molly! This isn't funny.'

Daisy heard one of the women remonstrate with Molly but her eyes were busy scanning the sea, and then her heart seemed to jump into her mouth when she caught sight of the lifeboat again just as a mighty wave seized it, tipping it over before covering it with a mountain of water. Now it was Enid clutching the younger woman's arm as they both stood silent and frozen for some moments, only to draw breath simultaneously as the swell dipped to reveal a body clinging to a spar of wood.

Daisy was already slipping out of her thick dress, kicking off her boots as she said, 'Give me your shawl, Mrs Hardy.'

Enid was now in such a state of alarm as to what Daisy intended that she passed over the shawl without a word, watching with the others as the girl joined it to hers, knotting them tightly together before passing them through the loop at the end of the rope. She then tied the material hard round her waist until she could hardly breathe.

'Lass, I hope you're not intendin' what I think you're intendin'.' Enid was beside herself. 'You'll drown as well as the poor devil out there, an' what good'll that do? There's no hope for 'em now.'

'I have to try, Mrs Hardy, an' I'll be all right if you an' the others hold fast to the rope,' Daisy said, her teeth chattering as the wind cut through her like a knife. 'If you all form a chain, and perhaps Jenny, Maggie, Molly and Lorna' – Daisy singled out four of the younger women who were stout hardy fishergirls and built like trams – 'come right into the water as far as they dare, I might just be able to reach whoever it is. If there's a problem all you have to do is to haul me back in. All right?'

'Don't do it, lass. Think of yer granny. What'd she do if anythin' happened to you?'

Enid realised she was talking to the wind a moment later when everyone was in place and holding fast to the rope, and Daisy was wading waist-deep in the water. And now the older woman's heart was beating fit to burst as she thought, Our Alf will blame me if anything happens to that lass, they all will. Why couldn't Daisy be like any other girl anyway? None of the others would have dreamt of doing this, not for a minute, and she'd no hope of reaching the poor so-an'-so on that bit of wood.

Daisy was thinking much the same thing. She couldn't believe how cold the water was, she had never felt anything like it before. As a wave knocked her off her feet for the second time in as many seconds and she struggled desperately to right herself, keeping her head above the surge, the futility of trying to pit herself against an enemy who was a hundred times stronger than her overcame her for a moment. And then she glanced back to where Jenny, Maggie, Molly and Lorna had followed her as far as they dare, and to the other women behind the quartet, and took heart.

The tide was coming in. Already the man – because she could see now the figure lying across the spar was a man – was nearer, and she couldn't have just stood by and done nothing. She wouldn't have been able to sleep at night. What if her da or Tom or Alf had been in similar trouble, and a bunch of women had just watched them drown when there was a chance they were near enough to reach them?

She blinked the blinding salt water out of her eyes for the umpteenth time and raised her arms high as she tried to jump another pounding wave. She was so deep now she could only just touch bottom with her toes and keep her head out of the water – and then she watched in horror as the slumped figure seemed to slide off the plank when the last wave covered it.

As the swell with its crest of white lather hit Daisy she lost her footing again, and by the time she had struggled, gasping and panting, to right herself all that could be seen a few yards away was the wooden spar floating unencumbered now. The man hadn't come up. Oh, God, God, help me. He hasn't come up! Let me find him, let me reach him.

Daisy wasn't conscious of launching herself towards the spot she had seen him last, but as her feet searched for solid ground and found only water the sea closed over her head and she took a great mouthful of salty iciness, flailing wildly as she realised Alf's mam's prediction was in danger of coming true and she would lose her life in this vain rescue attempt. She opened her eyes as she rose upwards and there, just in front of her, eyes closed and looking as though he was dead, was the body of a man, her man.

Instinct made her reach out and grab, and as her frozen fingers found a hold in the man's thick hair Daisy hung on for dear life, feeling as though she was being torn in half as the rope jerked madly round her waist. It was drowning her, she thought desperately, taking another mouthful of the disgustingly briny water as she fought to rise up for precious air against the pull of the rope which was curving her in two and keeping her head below the surface.

Daisy was aware of being towed through the water and that she, in turn, was towing the body of the man. As she kicked desperately with her legs she knew she couldn't hang on to consciousness much longer.

And then she was being hauled up by strong arms and when her mouth opened again it pulled in air instead of choking salt liquid. She still retained her hold on the man, even when Molly and Lorna lifted him up and Daisy found herself being carried back to the shore by Jenny and Maggie. They all fell in a heap on the wet sand once they were clear of the waves, Daisy immediately rolling over and emptying the contents of her stomach while one of the women, a sturdy female with forearms like a circus strongman, worked on the inert figure a few feet away.

'By, lass, if the salt water hasn't done for him you certainly will,' Molly commented as they watched the pummelling. The older woman lifted her head to give what was obviously going to be a tart retort, but just then the man's body went into a quivering spasm and he vomited water again and again.

Enid had been busy rubbing life into Daisy's frozen limbs before wrapping her in a blanket one of the other women had had the presence of mind to fetch. Now Daisy crawled over to the man as the retching ceased and his limbs gradually went limp again.

He was young, much younger than she had expected, probably Tom's age or thereabouts, and his clothes weren't those of a working man. Daisy gazed down at the waxen face as two of the women carefully turned the young man on to his back. There was an egg-sized lump on his forehead, and the right sleeve of his fine cloth coat was ripped, revealing a jagged gash on his forearm which, however, was not bleeding and did not appear to be deep.

All this Daisy gave only a passing glance to, her gaze caught and held by the almost beautiful face in front of her. The straight nose, the high chiselled cheekbones and firm but not over-large mouth reminded her of someone or something. And then she remembered. Miss Wright, the old school-marm in the village school at Whitburn, had been quite an artistic soul, and had brought in a book of paintings one day for them to look at as a reward for being well behaved. There had been one picture which had captivated Daisy, and Miss Wright had told her it was a photograph of a famous sculpture by an Italian gentleman named Michelangelo. The sculpture was called David.

'He . . . he's not movin', Mrs McCabe.'

Daisy appealed to the buxom fisherwoman who had ministered so roughly to the young man, and Ethel McCabe pursed her lips before saying, 'He's taken a fair crack on the head, lass. Look at the size of that bump. What with that an' the salt water he's lucky to be breathin', but it remains to be seen how he'll do.'

Daisy pulled the enveloping blanket more closely round her, then forgot all about how cold she felt when the man's long eyelashes flickered and his heavy lids rose. Piercingly blue eyes, the bluest she had ever seen, looked into hers, and she made a little inarticulate sound at the back of her throat as something leapt within her. She inhaled jerkily, knowing she ought to say something to reassure the young man he was safe, but the words wouldn't come.

Daisy was never very sure afterwards how long they stared at each other – it could have been just for a second or two or much longer – then his eyes closed again and the stillness which had descended on her mind and body was broken.

She shivered, swaying slightly as her body reminded her of its recent ordeal, and when Enid said briskly, 'Come on, lass, come on. It's a hot mustard bath you're needin' an' somethin' inside you a mite stronger than my blackcurrant wine,' Daisy did not argue. In fact she suddenly felt too exhausted to say a word.

She allowed Alf's mother to help her to her feet and

56

support her as the whole group trudged up the beach towards the cottages. Molly and Lorna along with Jenny and Maggie were carrying the young man between them, he appeared to be unconscious once more, and it was only when Mrs McCabe suggested the patient be taken to her house that Daisy found her voice again. 'Thank you, Mrs McCabe, but me an' Mrs Hardy'll see to him in my house. You've got the bairns to see to, an' likely he'll do better if he's kept quiet,' she added tactfully when it looked as though the older woman was going to object.

'Is that all right?' she belatedly asked Enid in an undertone. 'Could you stay for a while?'

''Course, lass. There's nowt at home that won't wait an hour or two with Alf bein' away.'

Daisy nodded, her thoughts immediately flying to her da and the others as she prayed silently, Let them be all right. Please, please let them be all right. But as she opened the door to the cottage and braced herself to meet the barrage of questions she knew would come her way from her granny, her mind had returned to the young man again, and she was thinking how odd it was, disturbing even, the effect one look from a stranger had had on her.

Chapter Three

It was around ten o'clock that same night that Daisy felt a sense of deep aloneness come over her. It was a strange feeling, not like loneliness or being companionless – more a recognition that if her da and Tom had been lost at sea she didn't know what she would do or how she would bear it, and that this night there was only her to care for the sick man and her granny so she had to be strong. She couldn't cry or give in to the consuming fear that was turning her bowels to water. Not yet.

Her concern for her father and Tom, and for her second youngest brother, Peter, who worked a boat with his best friend, had mounted steadily throughout the afternoon and evening.

It had been just after midday when the first of several boats had been sighted. These, it appeared, had all managed to shelter in Marsdon Bay, albeit only after they had taken a severe battering on the seas. Two more boats had sailed in at twilight by which time the storm had all but blown itself out. These boats, of which Alf's was one, had found refuge a little further up the coast at South Shields. There were now only three boats missing: Daisy's father's, Peter's, and Molly's husband's.

Alf had come to visit Daisy as soon as he had seen his mother. He told the white-faced girl that the three boats in question had been some distance from the others when the storm had hit. Likely they would be weathering out the worst of it together somewhere, and she mustn't worry. Her da was the finest fisherman Alf knew by a long chalk.

He had brought a pot of hot crab soup and a plate of freshly cooked fishcakes with him – Enid had sent a message saying Daisy had enough to do looking after her granny and 'the other one' to worry about cooking an evening meal. Once Alf had taken a look at 'the other one' he had been reluctant to leave, but Daisy had finally managed to shoo him away after half-an-hour or so by which time he had brought in a sack of driftwood and a bucket of coal and coke from the store under the dilapidated lean-to situated between George's curing house and the privy, and also filled up the water barrel in the scullery.

Daisy was grateful for his help, and overwhelmingly relieved he was safe, so she didn't understand why it was she hadn't wanted Alf to stay when he had offered. But she hadn't.

The stranger was still in the state of semi-consciousness he had slipped into down at the shoreline. Although Daisy had perodically fed him tiny spoonfuls of Mrs Hardy's renowned ginger beer – made with enough root ginger to make it hotter than the devil's pitchfork, according to those who tried it – along with small sips of rabbit broth, she knew he wasn't really awake. And this became increasingly unnerving as the hours ticked by.

When the women had carried him into the cottage earlier Daisy had hurried upstairs and dragged down her flock mattress, placing it close to the range. She had piled it high with the blankets from her father's and brother's beds as well as her own. While she had boiled hot water for the two stone water bottles, Enid had stripped every stitch of clothing from the young man until he was as naked as the day he was born, and then proceeded to rub his frozen limbs as hard as she could in an attempt to get the blood flowing through his veins. Once the older woman had dressed the inert form in Tom's spare trousers and a thick jumper she had called to Daisy, who was averting her eyes in the scullery, and the two of them had tucked him under the heaped blankets in front of the roaring fire with the hot water bottles at his feet.

Nellie, who had patently relished every moment of the unexpected drama, had sent forth a spate of endless advice from her platform bed which Daisy and Enid had borne with fortitude at first until Enid had finally snapped, barking at her old friend to *be quiet*. Daisy had actually felt sorry for her grandmother who had only been trying to help in her own way, but she had to admit the silence which had followed had been golden.

Now it was pitch dark outside and she was tired, so tired, but with a weariness that was in her mind as well as her body. Her da and the others . . . the thought of them was there like a constant drumming in her head and the worry had caused a physical ache in the middle of her chest which she actually rubbed a few times to try to alleviate it. She knew her granny was fearing the worst too now, since the other boats had returned. Not that she had said anything, but with her granny it was more what she didn't say. Peter's wife, Tilly, had come along to see them once she'd put her bairns to bed, and she was worried out of her mind. Five bairns, Peter and Tilly had, and the youngest only six months . . .

A mumbling from the figure on the mattress brought Daisy jumping to her feet again, causing her grandmother to say from the shadows, 'Easy, lass, easy. Looks to me as if it's goin' to be a long night so pace yerself.'

Daisy had thought her granny was asleep. Now she said, 'Do you want anythin', Gran? A drop of Mrs Hardy's ginger beer? There's plenty.'

'No fear, lass. Thanks all the same. The last time I had

a glass or two of Enid's ginger I turned inside out if you remember, had the skitters for days. Me backside wasn't me own for sure. No, the odd sip or two'll do the lad down there the world of good, but no one in their right mind would drink it for pleasure.'

Oh, dear, her granny still hadn't forgiven Enid for being a bit short with her, thought Daisy, as she knelt down by the mattress after taking the small pot of warm ginger from the side of the range. She raised the man's head slightly, supporting it with her arm as she trickled a tiny amount of liquid between the half-open lips.

Oh, but he was beautiful. The same thought that occurred every time she looked at him brought a pink tinge to her cheeks which had nothing to do with the heat from the range. She had never seen anyone so handsome. Her eyes moved to his hair, fair and silky and longer than the fishermen wore theirs, and then over his face to his throat and the wide broad expanse of his shoulders. She wished he would open his eyes and say something so she'd know he was going to be all right.

She dribbled a few more drops of liquid into his mouth, watching him swallow with a feeling of thankfulness. He couldn't be that bad if he was still swallowing, could he?

She shut her eyes, squeezing them tight for a moment as the enormity of it all – her da, Tom and Peter missing, and the sudden appearance of this disturbing stranger who was so utterly helpless – swept over her anew. Life was suddenly all topsy-turvy and fragile, and it frightened her.

When she opened her eyes again the sky-coloured gaze was waiting for her, its blue light even more concentrated in the soft glow from the fire in the range. Daisy stared back mesmerised for a second or two, and then she pulled herself together enough to say gently, 'Everythin' is all right, you're quite safe,' as her heart thudded hard against her ribcage.

'My . . . my head. The pain . . .'

'You've had a nasty bang on the head but don't worry about it, just rest now.' His had been a cultured voice, accentless, which went with the fine clothes. He was from the gentry, no doubt about it, and people would be looking for him. 'What's your name?' she asked very softly. And when he just continued to look at her, she repeated, 'Your name? What is it?'

'I . . . don't know.' And then the light in his eyes was extinguished when they closed again and he sank back into the deep sleep which Daisy found so alarming.

'I've seen this afore,' Nellie piped up from her bed where she had been watching proceedings with great interest. 'Your granda knocked himself out once; actin' the cuddy he was, though, not like this poor devil. Anyways, it was two full days afore he knew his arse from his elbow an' he had a bad head for a week or more. This 'un'll be all right, lass, now he's talkin' again.'

Daisy nodded. Maybe. 'Granda hadn't all but drowned though, had he?'

'No, no, there is that, hinny, but you can't do more than you're doin'. Look, you've got to get some rest or you'll be the next one flakin' out. Have one of them blankets, he don't need 'em all, an' settle yerself on the saddle for a kip. I'll give you a call if he wants anythin'.'

Daisy shook her head. If she gave in to the exhaustion which was dragging at her limbs she wouldn't come to again till morning, besides which her grandmother always slept the hours away, snoring loudly and with gusto, while proclaiming the next morning she hadn't slept a wink all night. She couldn't risk it. 'I'll stay awake a bit longer, Gran. You go to sleep.'

'All right, me bairn. I know it's no use arguin' if you've

63

made up your mind, but it'll be a long night, you mark my words.'

It *was* a long night, but by the time the inky darkness was finally stretched and broken on the rack of sunrise Daisy felt her patient's slumber was a more natural one. She had dozed once or twice, sitting sentry duty on the hard wooden saddle, awaking every so often with a start and immediately checking that the man was still breathing.

With the coming of the cold, mother-of-pearl dawn she roused herself fully, beginning the normal mundane chores like stoking the range and setting the kettle to boil. Chores that spoke of normality. When her da and Tom came home they would expect everything to be ticking along as usual, and ticking along it would be.

Once she had seen to breakfast and made her granny and the young man comfortable, she would slip along to Mrs Hardy's and ask Alf to make enquiries in Monkwearmouth regarding the ship which had sunk. It had been a big ship, important. Someone would know something. And likely her da and Tom would be walking through the door soon, and wouldn't they get a gliff when they saw the visitor? Aye, they would. Pray God, *pray God* they would . . .

Alf did not have to make the visit to Monkwearmouth. Before Daisy had even finished mashing the tea the first cottages in the village were astir, buzzing with the news that a search party was making enquiries regarding the ship which had sunk the day before. Of course they had been directed to George Appleby's place; it was his bit lass who had been foolhardy enough to risk life and limb rescuing a lad from the water, a toff by his clothes according to Ethel McCabe. As if any of the gentry would lift a finger to help a fisherman in similar circumstances! Less than the muck under their boots to the gentry, fishermen were.

She'd get no thanks for her trouble would Daisy, sure as eggs were eggs.

Daisy wasn't thinking of thanks as she faced the four men standing outside her cottage door. She had answered the impatient knocking as quickly as she could, considering she had taken the opportunity to nip into the scullery to wash her hands and face there while the tea was brewing, but it clearly had not been quick enough for the sour-faced individual who seemed to be in charge. He snapped at her the minute the door swung open, asking her name and then demanding entrance into the cottage in a manner which was offensive but brooked no argument.

Daisy's face was resolute and her voice low as she said, 'I'm sorry, but I shall need to know your business first.'

'Know my business?' Josiah Kirby had been valet to the master of Greyfriar Hall, situated south of Felling, the largest and best-run country estate in Durham – according to the army of servants who worked there – for thirty-five years, and considered this position superior to any other, even that of Middleton the butler. He had his master's ear in a way none of the other servants did and was the recipient of his confidences. All the staff were aware of this and treated him accordingly. He demanded and received the utmost respect, and now this little chit of a fishergirl dared speak to him in this fashion? His thin mouth became even thinner as he said icily, 'I am here as envoy for Sir Augustus Fraser. Let me pass, girl.'

'When I know your name an' your business.'

He would have slapped any of the Hall's maids had they dared to look at him as this baggage was doing, and seen to it they were sent packing without a reference. Daisy watched him straighten his slight shoulders and adjust the collar of the thick greatcoat he was wearing before he said, slowly and very deliberately, 'My name is Mr Josiah Kirby and I am making enquiries into the whereabouts of Sir Augustus's son, Mr William Fraser. I understand you are keeping a young man here, one who was travelling on the *Aquitania* which left France for England the day before yesterday.'

He made it sound as though she was keeping the young man a prisoner against his will. Daisy's answer was prompt and once again without undue ceremony. 'A ship sank out yonder yesterday mornin'' – she pointed to the wide expanse of ocean which was now shimmering calm and placid under a brightening sky – 'an' a young man was saved from the water, but he's in a poor way.'

She stood aside to let the men pass as she spoke but only Josiah Kirby moved into the cottage. After waiting a moment Daisy closed the door on the other three and turned to find their visitor kneeling by the mattress, saying, 'Thank God! Oh, thank God, sir. You're safe,' to the young man who had his eyes open. And then the older man swung round to glare at Daisy as he barked, 'What is the meaning of keeping Mr Fraser here like this? Why did you not contact the authorities? Sir Augustus and the family have been out of their minds with worry.'

She stared at the nasty little man, and resentment and indignation made her voice sharp as she cut across the protests Nellie was making from her bed and said, 'I wasn't in a fit state to go anywhere yesterday an' he couldn't have been left anyway. I was goin' to get someone to go into Monkwearmouth today.'

'Really?' It was said in a tone of disbelief. 'And where are Mr William's belongings and his clothes? What have you done with those?'

Was he calling her a thief? Daisy couldn't remember

when she had been so angry. 'He didn't have no belongings an' his clothes are dryin'.'

'No belongings?'

'Are you barmy, man?' Nellie's voice was deceptively soft as she entered the fray. 'The lass has just told you, the lad was fished out of the water when the boat went down – an' you've her to thank for that an' all. Without Daisy here riskin' her own life to save his, your master's precious son would be with the rest of the passengers an' their belongings an' such, at the bottom of the sea keepin' company with Davey Jones' locker. Look at him.' She pointed a bony finger at the figure on the mattress. 'He's still in cloud cuckooland an' likely will be for days, but he's a darn' sight better than he was yesterday, an' that's due to me lass.'

Josiah Kirby glared at the old woman before looking down at his master's son again, and when he saw the young man's eyes were shut and he appeared to be asleep the truth of Nellie's statement was borne out. 'He's sick.' His hand reached out and touched William's brow. 'You should have got a doctor to him at once.'

'He's had a blow to the head an' he was chilled to the bone from the water,' Daisy stated grimly. 'The most important thing was to make him warm inside an' out, an' that's what I did. No doctor could have done more. Besides which there was no one to go for a doctor as I've already said. All the boats were out an' they didn't come home till last night. He's best where he is for the present.'

'Where he is?' Josiah curled his upper lip. The smell of fish was overpowering, and although he had to admit this hovel was clean it was no fit place for Mr William. The very idea! The old hag in the bed was clearly useless, and the girl had already admitted she was the only one taking care of his master's son. 'I think not.'

'You prepared to answer for movin' him, eh, me fine feller?' Nellie put in slyly. 'Won't go down well with your master if his son croaks afore you get him home, will it?'

These people! Common as clarts and as cunning as a cartload of monkeys. What were they up to? But the warning in Nellie's words had hit home. Mr William was bad, no doubt about it, and they only had the open carriage and the morning was bitter. Josiah stood up abruptly, his mind made up. 'You had better make sure you attend to Mr William properly,' he said curtly, 'or you will pay for it, make no mistake. I shall inform Sir Augustus of the situation at once.'

'Aye, you do that, lad.' Nellie was openly enjoying herself now but Daisy was so angry she didn't trust herself to speak. She stood in silence, her cheeks burning and eyes hot, watching as the valet got to his feet and straightened his coat before tapping his bowler hat more firmly on to his head with a disdainful glance round the room again.

How dare he speak to them like that? He might be dressed up to the nines but he hadn't corrected her granny when she had referred to Sir Augustus as being his master so he was obviously just a servant, albeit a powerful one. Her granny had told Daisy tales about life in the big houses, passed on to her from Alf's mam who had heard them first hand from her aunt. The servants far outnumbered the family in many cases, sometimes as many as forty being employed indoors for a large country estate, her granny had said, and the aunt had maintained the upper servants lorded it over the lower ones to a point where they were more uppity than their masters and mistresses. Daisy could believe that now.

'I shall return shortly with instructions from Sir Augustus.' The valet spoke without looking at Daisy or Nellie, making for the door as though Daisy was invisible.

'Aye, I don't doubt that, lad,' said Nellie conversationally from her corner of the room. 'Gives you instructions on how clean to wipe your backside too, I'll be bound.'

The stiff little figure paused for a fraction of a moment, back bristling, before flinging open the door. He turned on the threshold, his hard black eyes going first to Daisy and then to Nellie, and it wasn't until he was looking at Daisy again that he said, quietly but venomously, 'Fishing scum! There's more than fish sold down at the docks an' the back alleys by the likes of you. I dunno what you thought you'd gain by keepin' the master's son hidden away but you've bin rumbled, girl, so think on.'

The door was slammed with enough force to cause the man on the mattress to stir and mumble, and then there followed a moment of dead silence which was broken by Nellie saying, 'By, lass, it didn't take him long to lose his cut-glass accent, did it? Prick his balloon an' he's as common as the rest of us, even if his linings might be of the finest linen an' changed daily.'

Daisy looked at her grandmother, and as a pair of sunken old eyes twinkled back at her she found herself grinning weakly. Her granny was one on her own and no mistake.

Daisy's slender shoulders went back and her chin lifted. She was blowed if she was going to let a little upstart like the one who had just walked out of that door get her down, even if his spitefulness had left her reeling for a moment. She wasn't so naive she didn't know some of the fishergirls who worked the docks in Sunderland and Tyneside were loose women, and that their activities had got decent fishing women a bad name, or that others who had lost their breadwinner to the sea were forced to take to the streets else let their bairns starve . . . but to tar them all with the same brush! She had done nothing to be ashamed of and nor would she, even if it meant working her fingers to the bone every twenty hours out of twenty-four, and she would tell Sir Augustus himself that very thing – should he ever condescend to put one elegant toe in such humble surroundings, of course.

Chapter Four

At exactly twenty minutes past eleven that same morning a further deputation from Greyfriar Hall arrived at the village. This consisted of Jack Mallard, first footman, and Jeremy Hopkins, second footman, in a carriage and pair, with Bernard McArthur, head coachman, and Bruce Fallow, groom, driving the covered coach behind, within which sat Josiah Kirby with the Misses Felicity and Cecilia Fraser.

Within three minutes of the coach pulling up outside the cottages William Fraser, wrapped in copious thick fleecy blankets and cradled as tenderly as any newborn babe by the two footmen and the groom, was deposited into the waiting arms of his sisters. They were the two younger daughters of Sir Augustus and Lady Fraser, the two elder being married women with homes of their own.

Josiah oversaw proceedings, and from the moment he entered Daisy's home, without even the courtesy of knocking first, until the footmen and groom had left with the young master, uttered not a word to the young girl and old woman within. His body rigid and his face like stone, he issued monosyllabic orders to the other three men, following them closely and shutting the front door of the cottage firmly behind them.

'Well!' The exclamation from Nellie said it all, and she didn't really need to add, 'The ungrateful so-an'-sos. That lad wouldn't have stood a chance without you, hinny, an' to take him without as much as a by your leave . . . Still, that's the gentry for you. An' you lookin' after him like you did an' all. You'll know what to do the next time you see someone drownin' in front of your eyes leastways.'

'It wasn't his fault, Gran. Mr Fraser's, I mean.'

Nellie looked hard at her granddaughter and when Daisy turned away to stare out of the window at the departing coach, her cheeks pink, the old woman said as though to herself, 'Aye, he was a bonny lad, but bonny is as bonny does. I can still remember when I was a lass a mite younger than you, an' a little lad from our village did a bit of night-time poachin' in the grounds of a big house Harton way. The fishin' had been bad, see, an' he thought a rabbit or two'd keep the family goin', but as it was he come across a pheasant that just sort of flew into his hands. But he got caught by the gamekeeper, didn't he, an' the young owner of the estate, a lad not much older than the one that was just carried out of that door if I remember rightly an' just as bonny, he had the boy done for seven years' transportation, an' all for the sake of a bird.'

The coach had gone but Daisy still continued looking out of the window as she said, 'Them times are gone, Gran. They don't transport someone for poachin' anymore.'

'Mebbe not, but the gentry'd still have the last drop of blood out of such as you an' me, an' not give us as much thought as the horses in their stables or their favourite dog. It's bred in 'em, lass, take my word for it, an' all this talk about unions in the mines an' the factories won't make a scrap of difference. Your da's right on that. It's power the gentry've got, the power of land an' money. This new party the unions got up a couple of months ago that your da an' Tom were on about, this Labour Party, it'll come to nowt. The mine owners an' the factory owners'll be havin' none of it.'

Daisy turned restlessly from the window. She didn't

care about the unions or the Labour Party or anything else except seeing her da and Tom. Everything else, even William Fraser and his family, paled into insignificance beside that. But she hadn't minded tending Mr Fraser. She pictured the handsome young face in her mind's eye, remembering the feel of his hair against her flesh when she had lifted his head for him to drink, and she shivered, her heart giving a funny little twist. Anyway, that was that, he had gone and she would never see him again.

She breathed in deeply, flung her two thick braids of hair over her shoulders and set about putting the room to rights.

The next two days were unpleasant ones. Daisy and Nellie and the other womenfolk had to face the fact that their men were not coming home, and their grief was over-whelming.

Peter's wife Tilly was inconsolable, and Daisy spent a number of hours each day helping her sister-in-law with the children and trying to keep things as normal as possible, while all the time each of them was waiting for confirmation of what they all dreaded. There had been some attempt by the authorities to salvage the big ship which had sunk off their coast, along with the grisly occurrence of several bodies being washed ashore amid other debris, but such was Daisy's state of mind that these events did not make a deep impression on her.

On the afternoon of the third day the body of a fisherman was hauled up in the nets of a boat working at Holy Rock, off Sunderland, but of the other five missing men there was no sign. Alf and the fisherman who worked his boat with him, Henry Ingram, volunteered to go and look at the body the next morning, and as soon as Alf walked into the Applebys' cottage on returning to the village Daisy knew the dead man was her da or Tom or Peter.

'Who?'

She hadn't needed to say anything more, and Alf had answered in like vein when he said, 'Tom.'

Later that night Daisy's three surviving brothers and their wives, along with Tilly, squeezed into the living room for a family assessment of what needed to be done. Daisy, her eyes still red and puffy from a bout of crying earlier, looked round at them all as George, the eldest and named after their father, began to talk.

He was thirty-eight years old, Ron thirty-four, and Art thirty-two, all three of them alive and well while Peter and Tom, the youngest two, were dead, she thought, the lump in her throat feeling as though it was going to choke her. It wasn't fair, life wasn't fair, they had still been so young. And yet could she have picked any one of the others to take Peter and Tom's place, or her da's come to that? Of course she couldn't. She sat up straighter in her chair and blew her nose. It was no use thinking about fairness or unfairness, she cautioned herself grimly, she'd go stark staring barmy if she went down that road. And she forced herself to take in what it was George was saying.

'So if we're all agreed the waitin' time is over there's only one thing for it as far as I can see.' George cleared his throat, glancing at his wife Martha before he continued. By, this was going to break them all, him and Ron and Art, but what else could they do? None of them would be able to sleep at night if Tilly and the bairns and Daisy and their gran weren't given a roof over their heads, although they'd be taking the food out of their own bairns' mouths to do it. 'We can't pay two extra lots of rent as well as our own' – George included Ron and Art in the sweep of his head – 'so we're thinkin' Tilly an' the two youngest can move in with me an' Martha, the other three'll bed down with Ron an' Rose, an' Daisy an' Gran'll go to Art an' Olive's. All right?'

'Don't talk daft, lad.' Nellie, never one for tact, spoke up from the platform bed. 'You're hand to mouth as it is, the lot of you. Where are you goin' to find the extra to keep us?'

'We'll manage.' This was from Martha, and said with a weary smile.

But they wouldn't. Daisy gazed round the assembled faces, her mind racing. She knew for a fact that all three households were well behind with their rent as it was, the winter having been such a bad one. Even if she left the village and sought work in the town somewhere, that still meant her granny and Tilly and the bairns would have to remain and it wasn't as if there was any spare room in her brothers' cottages.

George had six bairns, the two eldest big hulking lads, they were all squeezed into their place like sardines in a can as it was. Ron and Art's cottages were no better for space. And then there were all the extra mouths to feed and the bairns to clothe.

She rubbed her hand across her face, her stomach churning. If she married Alf he would take her granny too, there was no doubt about that. Her granny and Mrs Hardy would be tickled pink to live together most likely. Of course Tilly and the bairns would still have to be split up, which after everything that had happened was a blow to the family. The bairns would need to be close to their mam at a time like this and it wouldn't be the same for them living in separate cottages. If she could find work she could help out a bit with bringing some extra money into her brother's homes, she told herself, perhaps even enough to pay for Tilly and the bairns' food, and their clothes and things like that. She knew what sort of work a bit fishergirl would get, down at the docks gutting and packing fish, or maybe something in one of the roperies clustered along the banks of the river. Either way it would be filthy, back-breaking labour among the coarsest of companions for a pittance in pay, and whether it was up the coast at South Shields or down at Monkwearmouth or Sunderland's East End, she'd be treated as an interloper by her fellow workers without a doubt. But needs must. She couldn't say anything now, not until she had seen Alf, but if she did marry him it would relieve the burden a little, wouldn't it?

They all continued to talk for a while longer. By the time her brothers and their wives finally left Daisy knew there was no other option but for everyone to be divided up amongst the different houses. Their landlord, the owner of the brick and tile works situated west of Cleadon, would soon want them out once he found out their circumstances, and as George had said, there was no way her brothers could afford to pay two extra rents of two-and-six a week, or even one for Tilly's place. The rent man was fond of telling them how reasonable the villagers' rent was compared to some he had to collect for his employer, but two-and-six was two-and-six, and at the moment it could be ten shillings for all the chance they had of paying it.

Daisy looked round the cottage that had been the only home she had ever known, her heart heavy. They had enough food to tide them over for a week or so with her granny eating no more than a bird would, and with the wood and bits of coke and coal she'd collected from the beach the last couple of days they wouldn't be cold during that time, there was that at least. A storm always provided plenty of fuel once it had wrought its destruction, she thought bitterly.

'You all right, me bairn?'

Daisy was standing at the range warming some broth for her grandmother's supper. She turned quickly, stitching a smile on to her face. 'Aye, I'm fine, Gran. Don't worry about me.'

'We'll get by, lass.' Nellie's voice was subdued and she

wasn't her normal chirpy self. 'The Good Lord helps them as helps themselves, an' we've never bin ones for sittin' on our backsides in this family, have we?'

Daisy was prevented from replying to this piece of homespun wisdom by a knock at the door. It was opened the next moment and Alf stepped into the room. She stared at him and he stared back. She found she couldn't say a word and it was her grandmother who said, 'Hallo, lad.'

'Hallo, Mrs Shaw.' Alf turned to look at the old woman, his face grave as he said, 'It's heart sorry me an' Mam are for your loss. But you know that, don't you?'

'Aye, lad, I know that.'

Alf nodded and then his kindly eyes came back to Daisy. 'I . . . I wanted a word, lass. Perhaps you'd step outside a minute?'

She had known he'd come, but faced with the reality and the knowledge of what she was about to agree to Daisy wanted to run and hide.

'Take your shawl, lass, it's bitter out.' This was from her granny, and Daisy knew it was the old woman's way of telling her to hear what Alf wanted to say. For a second she felt a stab of resentment that she was being pushed into his arms and then she told herself not to be so silly, taking up her shawl and drawing it round her as she followed Alf into the night.

'It's a peasouper.' He had stopped just beyond the cottage and Daisy nodded a reply as she joined him. The air was salt-sticky and opaque, the muffled sound of a foghorn echoing across the water somewhere. Daisy had always hated the murky grey fogs which fell swiftly and with blinding intent, but tonight the feeling was such that it caused the fine hairs on the back of her neck to prickle.

When she was a child, her grandmother had told her that the poor lost souls of those drowned at sea who hadn't made their peace with God before they'd died were abroad on such nights. They were looking for folk who were silly enough to be wandering about, her granny had said, folk the spirits could lure to their deaths and thereby earn their own release from Hades. Daisy had been ten years old before she'd realised her granny's story was a ploy to keep her indoors out of harm's way when it was foggy, but the old woman had done her job well and the eerie sensation she always experienced made her uneasy.

'I know I said I'd give you time, lass, when we talked last, but things are different now.' Alf's voice was quiet as he stood close to her. 'You see that, don't you?'

Daisy nodded again, but then, as his arms went out to pull her towards him, she found herself stepping back a pace. *He hadn't got blue eyes*. What a ridiculous thing to come into her mind at such a time but it had, and with it the confirmation that the feeling she had for Alf was not the marrying kind. He was her friend, and she loved him in the same way she did her brothers, but that was all. He would never be able to make her head spin or her heart race. The thought of kissing him, of lying with him, seemed wrong, even distasteful. He deserved better than that in a wife and she couldn't marry him just to put a roof over her head. But then, this wasn't just about her, was it? There was her granny and the others to think of too. But she had to be honest with him, she owed him that at least. She couldn't pretend, make on she felt something she didn't.

The look in his eyes made her want to reach out and stroke his face, but knowing he'd interpret the gesture of comfort and concern as something else, Daisy said, 'I'm sorry, Alf. I don't want to upset you but I don't feel the same as you, and it's only fair you know that.'

'You don't love me,' he said flatly.

'I do love you but not in . . . that way. You're the same as a brother to me, don't you see?'

'I don't want to be your brother, Daisy.' The look on his face was paining her. 'Whatever else, not that.'

'I know.'

'You just need time, that's all. All this with your da an' Tom an' Peter has knocked the stuffin' out of you.'

'Alf, what if I can never love you like you want me to?'

'No.' His voice was harsh. 'Don't say that. Don't, lass, because I can't bear it.'

Oh, Alf, Alf. Daisy was out of her depth. She was hurting him and he was the one person in all the world she didn't want to hurt. But she couldn't lie to him, not over something like this. If he took her as his wife, he had to take her knowing the truth. She had her hand to her face, pressing against her mouth, but couldn't stop the tears from running down her cheeks.

'Look, you go in now.' His hand came out as though to touch her then fell back by his side. 'It'll all work out, trust me.'

Daisy brushed her hand across her face before she said, her voice small, 'Do you want to come in for a minute?'

'No.' He began to back away, his eyes still holding hers as though he was loth to break the contact. 'You're upset, lass, an' I can understand that, anyone would be with what you've gone through the last few days, but it'll get better, aye, it will. Things'll get back to normal by an' by.'

Normal? She watched him go until the mist swallowed him and still she stood there in the curling darkness, all thoughts of ghosts and goblins forgotten as the pain of the present made everything else unimportant. What was normal? Her da and Tom, the hard but happy life the four of them had led, that was normality and that was gone for ever, the sea had seen to that. Should she marry

Alf? Should she? It was the easy option, and everyone – her granny included – would tell her it was the right thing to do.

So why didn't she feel it inside, in her heart, where it mattered? She stumbled over to the wall of the cottage, shutting her eyes, but couldn't shut out the image that was burnt into her mind. It was a face, a strange face but a beautiful one. Yes, beautiful.

How long she remained outside Daisy wasn't sure, but when she realised she was shivering and the moisture was dripping off her face and hair she walked slowly to the cottage door, opening it quietly.

Her granny had propped herself on her elbows in an attitude of expectancy, and made it clear what she had supposed when she said, 'Where's Alf? Hasn't he asked you?'

Daisy walked across to the table, pulling out one of the hardbacked chairs and sitting down before she said, 'Yes, Gran, he asked me.'

After a moment's pause and a successful attempt to sound matter-of-fact, Nellie said, 'An' you said no.' Daisy raised her head, staring into her grandmother's eyes. 'Not exactly,' she said quietly. 'How could I with things as they are? But I had to let him know the truth. I couldn't pretend. Alf is too good a man to be treated like that.'

'An' the truth bein' . . . ?'

'That I love him as a brother but that's all.'

Nellie leant back against her cushions. 'I bet that fair made his night,' she said wryly. 'But if I know Alf he'll come to terms with it an' ask again, an' what'll your answer be then? Like you said, hinny, he's a good man. You could do a lot worse.'

'I know, Gran. Alf's grand.' It was an answer in itself and their eyes held for a moment longer before Nellie gave a satisfied sigh just before another knock sounded at the door.

'Not someone else on a night like this?' The old woman's expression of surprise was comical. 'By, lass, if we was one of them houses with the red light in the window an' no better than we should be, we couldn't do more trade the night.'

'Gran!' Daisy was truly shocked and it showed. Nellie gave a little chuckle that produced an answering smile in Daisy as she walked across to the door. Her gran! You never knew what she was going to come out with next, but she wouldn't be without the old lady for all the tea in China.

It had run through her mind that it might be one of her brothers or their wives returning to chat some more, or Alf to fulfil her grandmother's prophecy and say he would take her on any terms, so when she opened the door and saw a small slight girl with the fairest of colouring and without a hat or coat, she was too taken aback to do more than simply stare.

'Is . . . is this where Tom Appleby lives, please?'

'Tom?'

'Aye, they said' – the girl turned slightly, pointing back towards the first of the cottages – 'they said he lives here.'

It was only when the slight figure gave a convulsive shiver that Daisy's tongue was loosened, and she said, 'Oh, come in, come in. You must be frozen.'

The girl stepped into the living room past Daisy who shut the door behind her. Daisy saw her glance towards the platform bed but she didn't speak, merely rubbing her hand across her mouth, drops of water from her sodden dress falling on to the flagstones.

'You're soaked through.' Daisy had noticed that her granny was too surprised to say a word, which was a first. 'Come near the fire an' I'll get you a sup of somethin' warm. Here, have my shawl round you.'

Whether it was the kind words or the action of the shawl being drawn tenderly round her shoulders wasn't clear, but suddenly the girl was weeping, great shuddering sobs that seemed to be pulling her apart, and had slid down on to the cold flagstones at Daisy's feet.

After one stunned moment Daisy drew the slender – too slender – figure into her arms, cradling her as she would one of Tilly's bairns and making the same sort of murmurings as she said, 'There, there, it'll be all right. Whatever it is, it'll be all right. Don't take on so.'

The tears continued to rain down the girl's face for some minutes and by the time they had eased to hiccuping gasps the front of Daisy's dress was damp from the sodden clothes pressed against it.

'Look, lass, you sit by the fire a minute an' I'll get you a sup tea, all right? An' then we'll see about gettin' you into somethin' dry, you'll catch your death like this.' Daisy had reached out with one arm and drawn one of the straightbacked chairs from the table. Now she pushed the girl down on to it.

This had to be the lass she had heard Tom mention to her da once, the lass from Whitburn. And now the girl herself confirmed this when she said, 'I . . . I'm Margery Travis. Has Tom told you about me? I . . . I live in East Street,' in between the gulps and sniffles.

She couldn't say no, not with the lass in this state. Daisy compromised by saying, 'He mentioned he'd got a lass in Whitburn but that was all.' She had to find the words to tell Margery what had happened but it was going to be a terrible shock, and she looked none too good already. What on earth was wrong with her?

Nellie, decades older and wiser in the ways of the world, was already fearing the worst, her mind racing as she thought, Oh, no, not that. Not that now with the lad gone. Tom wouldn't have been so daft, would he? Fear prompted her to say, and so abruptly that Daisy glanced across at her grandmother in surprise as she placed the kettle on the hob, 'What's brought you out on a night like this, an' without a coat or hat?'

'I need to see Tom. He was going to come last night but I waited and waited . . .'

Margery's voice tailed off. Both Nellie and Daisy had noticed that this girl spoke a little differently from them. The northern inflexion was less noticeable and she pronounced her Gs, but not in a manner that seemed forced in any way.

'I have to tell you something.' Daisy left the teapot and cups and knelt down in front of the wan figure on the chair. 'Tom . . . him an' me da an' some others' – the big pale-blue eyes were enormous now and fixed on Daisy's face – 'they were caught in the storm a few days ago. They didn't come home, lass.'

'I . . . don't understand.'

The stricken expression on the girl's face told Daisy that Tom's lass understood only too well, but she gentled her voice still further as she said, 'They're gone, all of them. Me da, Tom, me other brother Peter—'

'*No! No!*' The words were desperate and then the girl bent forward, folding her arms round her waist as she began to moan softly.

'How far gone are you, lass?' Nellie's voice, in contrast to how she had spoken before, was quiet and sad-sounding.

The words hung in the air. Daisy blinked, looking first at her grandmother and then at Margery who had frozen and was now sitting in silence with her head hanging down.

A bairn? Tom had given this lass a bairn? He couldn't have, not Tom. And then a separate part of her brain which seemed to be working outside the situation said, Why not Tom? He was a man, wasn't he, and this thing she had glimpsed staring out of Alf's eyes once or twice, this hungry urgent thing, could easily take over if two people loved each other. She could understand that now, since the day of the shipwreck.

'Lass?' Nellie's voice was still quiet but there was a note to it which brought Margery's head up with a little jerk, although it was still slightly bent as she answered, 'Two . . . two months. I wasn't sure before but now I am.'

'Did he know? Tom?'

'No. Like I said, I wasn't sure until the last week when . . . when it didn't happen again. And I've been feeling bad the last few days, and I was sick yesterday and then again this morning.'

'I'm so sorry.' Daisy reached out and grasped one of the girl's fine thin hands in her own, and although Tom's lass didn't reply her other hand covered Daisy's, gripping it hard as the tears slowly dripped down her cheeks. 'We . . . it only happened the once, I promise. We didn't mean to.'

'Once is more than enough, as you've found,' Nellie said tartly, moderating her voice when Daisy raised a reproachful face and shook her head to add, 'But it's done now, lass, an' what will be, will be. What about yer mam an' da? Have you told them?'

The slight shoulders hunched. 'I wanted to tell Tom first but he didn't come last night, and then, when I was sick again this morning, my mam must have guessed something. She was waiting for me when I got home from work – I work for Mr Mallard, you know?' Daisy and her grandmother nodded their heads. They knew Mallard's corner shop in Whitburn which doubled as a grocer's and draper's. 'She went on and on at me until I told her, and when my da got in . . .' Margery's voice dropped to a whisper. 'He went mad and . . . and he threw me out.'

'Threw you out?' Daisy was horrified.

And now Margery raised her head to look into Daisy's face as she nodded slowly, saying, 'They . . . they said not to come back.'

'Your mam an' all?'

'She . . . she pushed me out into the street again when I tried to get back in.' Margery was sobbing loudly once more, and when she wailed, 'Oh, Tom, Tom. I want Tom,' Daisy and Nellie looked at each other helplessly.

What on earth were they going to do? Daisy was still holding Margery's hands in her own. Now her practical side came to the fore as she said, 'Come on, come on, lass, you'll be makin' yourself ill. Look, you can stay here tonight an' I'll go an' see your mam an' da tomorrow, all right? I'll explain about Tom an' say he loved you an' wanted to marry you—'

'They know that, I said that, but when they found out he was a fisherman . . .' Fresh sobs choked further words.

Daisy straightened her back. So that was the way of it? Tom wasn't good enough for their daughter. It wasn't only that Margery was in the family way, it was who had put her there they objected to. Her voice cool, she said, 'What does your da do, Margery?'

'He's a miner.' And then the other girl's head shot up as the frostiness of Daisy's tone registered, and she said, her eyes still spurting tears, 'Don't take offence, please. My mam and da have no cause to be like that. I . . . I loved Tom, I did. I would have been proud to be his wife.'

'Oh, lass.' Daisy felt awful, and it was by way of apology that she said, 'You sit still an' I'll make a nice sup tea an' somethin' for you to eat. You look done in. An' we'd better see about gettin' you into some dry clothes before you catch your death.'

*   *   *

85

It was eleven o'clock at night. Daisy had all but fed Margery the cold pease pudding and shive of bread and dripping she had persuaded her to eat, and now the other girl was tucked up in what had been Tom's bed with a hot stone bottle at her feet, fast asleep. Daisy had hesitated about putting her in Tom's bed before she'd told herself not to be so daft. It was more comfortable than her da's and the niceties didn't apply in the current situation, not with the girl carrying Tom's bairn.

It was with this thought in the front of her mind that Daisy plonked herself down on one of the chairs after coming downstairs again, looking across at her grandmother as she said quietly, 'I can't believe our Tom could have been so stupid.'

'Well, it weren't another immaculate conception, hinny, that's for sure.'

Daisy couldn't raise a smile. She sighed heavily. 'I feel responsible for her somehow, with Tom bein' the father.'

'Don't talk wet, lass.' Nellie's voice was sharp now. 'You've enough on your plate without takin' on more. They were old enough to do what they did, they're old enough to take the consequences.'

'But it's not they, is it, Gran? It's her, by herself. She told me a bit about her mam an' da when I was settlin' her in bed. Seems she's the only one, somethin' to do with her mam havin' a bad time when Margery was born, an' they've sent her to piano lessons an' all sorts. They even paid for her to have lessons out of school with the teacher in Whitburn to learn how to speak proper.'

'You're jokin'?' Nellie stared at her granddaughter, wagging her head in disbelief at the folly of some folk. 'Bloomin' hell, lass, our Tom could pick 'em, I'll say that. All the nice ordinary lasses that've bin after him in his time an' he has to go an' dally with her. An' not only dally but fill her belly an' all.'

'I think Margery is a nice lass, Gran.'

Nellie brought her chin into her scraggy neck. 'Mebbe. But all them fancy piano lessons an' such didn't teach her how to keep her knees together, did they? An' all right, all right, you might purse your lips at me, Daisy Appleby, but can you truthfully tell me a lass like that is cut out to be a fisherman's wife? Them upstart parents of hers had their sights fixed high, that much is for sure, an' you go an' see 'em tomorrow an' you're as likely to leave with a boot in your backside as a thank you for comin'. You think on, lass, I know what I'm talkin' about.'

Daisy stared at her grandmother. If she had spoken the truth she would have said she felt dazed by it all. Nothing was as it had been, nothing. She grieved for her da and Tom, and for Peter of course, and Tilly's misery was pitiful to see. Peter's widow was dreading the thought of being a burden – as she kept putting it – on George and Martha, and of her three older bairns going to Ron and Rose, but the alternative of the workhouse was an ever-present spectre at Tilly's shoulder. And there was Alf, poor Alf, who in a funny sort of way was presenting more of a threat than anything else. Daisy could see that if she married him it would help everything enormously – or perhaps that should be everyone. Everyone except her. She couldn't help it but that was the way she felt about it deep inside. And now this, Tom's lass.

The thought of the girl upstairs brought a strange feeling into her mind. Her granny, everyone, even Margery herself, would say she was ready for the asylum if she admitted to the fact that she was envious of Tom's lass. Not of the bairn side of things, oh, no, not that, but of the love that had brought them together. Margery had said enough for her to realise the two of them had been aware of the difficulties they were going to face in the future, but had been prepared to weather whatever came just to be together. She had never thought of Tom as being like that. And now he was gone and all that remained of him was the bairn Margery was carrying. How could she not help the lass?

'I'm goin' to see Margery's mam an' da, Gran.' And as she said it Daisy thought her granny of all people should understand how Tom and Margery had felt about each other. Hadn't she braved her own parents' wrath by marrying an outsider from another village? Hadn't she left everything to follow her own love here all those years ago? Daisy thought it odd that she had this insight while her granny seemed oblivious to any similarity.

Chapter Five

By the time Daisy reached the small terraced house in Whitburn the next afternoon, her heart was in her mouth. She had timed her visit to catch Margery's father when he had finished his shift at the colliery, mainly because Margery had insisted her mother wouldn't wipe her nose without her husband's permission. That being the case, nothing would be served by seeing Mrs Travis without her husband present.

There was a high wind blowing but thankfully it was dry as Daisy stood for a moment outside the house. It was identical to its neighbours to either side but for the fact that not only the front doorstep but also the pavement in front of the house had been freshly scrubbed and whitened. There was the usual motley collection of tangle-haired, snotty-nosed bairns playing in the roadway, one or two with the luxury of hobnailed boots – several sizes too large – on their small feet, but some of the children were barefoot despite the bitter cold. This surprised Daisy not one bit; in all the villages which had grown up a mile or so from the collieries where the men and boys worked, the bairns were the same. Although the coalfields spawned industry which made for the busy clangour, smoke and stench of prosperity, her da had always maintained the folk in the towns lived like rats in holes, and Daisy agreed with him in the main. And yet the miners and other townfolk looked down on fishermen, she thought, with the touch of resentment this line of thought always produced.

She pulled her calico cloak straight, clearing her mind of everything but the confrontation which was almost certainly in front of her, and stepping up to the neatly painted front door, grasped the shiny brass knocker in the shape of an elf on a toadstool and knocked twice. She had to repeat this three times before the door opened, although once she had seen the stiffly starched lace curtains twitch Daisy was determined she wouldn't budge.

'Aye?' The woman who had opened the door had a vestige of Margery's startling fairness but that was all, and none of her daughter's attractiveness. She stared at Daisy, her pale-blue eyes narrowing to slits before she said again, 'Aye? What do you want?'

'Mrs Travis?' Daisy kept her back straight and her voice low but firm. 'I need to speak to you an' your husband.'

'Do you indeed?' Hilda Travis continued to stare at the bonny young girl with the beautiful face and unusual eyes. 'An' would that be about me daughter by any chance?'

There was no point in prevarication. Daisy was aware her very clothes proclaimed she was a fishergirl. She nodded. 'Aye, it is. Margery came to us last night and—'

'We've got nowt to say to you an' your kind so I'd thank you to make yourself scarce.'

As the woman went to shut the door Daisy said quickly, 'I shall only knock again, Mrs Travis, an' again, an' again. Do you really want all your neighbours to hear what I have to say?'

She saw Margery's mother hesitate and then the woman was pushed roughly aside and a small man stood in the doorway, and such was the look on his face that in spite of herself Daisy took a step backwards. 'You threatenin' us, eh?' His voice was soft and deadly, and for a moment all Daisy could do was blink. Margery's father was a small

90

man but his body was a pack of tight hard muscle, and his face as dark and stony as the black gold he brought out of the ground.

'No, I am not, Mr Travis, but I do need to speak to you.'

In spite of her fear Daisy's voice had not been deferential, and she watched the muscles of his face tighten and the blue-marked cheeks darken to a red hue before he ground out, 'An' who might you be?'

'My name is Daisy Appleby. It's my brother Tom who . . .' Daisy found she didn't know quite how to continue at this point.

'Oh, aye? An' your brother's the type of scum who sends a lass to do his dirty work for him, is he? Well, I've nowt to say to you, but just send your brother to see us an' me fists'll do me talkin' sure enough.'

Daisy couldn't believe this aggressive individual with the inky-black eyes and mop of coarse grey hair was Margery's father. He was the very antithesis of the delicate and gentle girl she'd left behind with Nellie at the cottage.

'That won't be possible, Mr Travis. If Tom had been able to come he would be here now, but he died a few days ago.'

Jacob Travis stared at the bit lass who was glaring at him, and hadn't the smallest doubt in his mind that she was speaking the truth. He had always been an unerring judge of character with a reputation for being able to winkle out the weakness in a man as soon as look at him. Wasn't that one of the reasons he had got on like he had? He was canny, and although he was always careful to stay on the right side of the owners, as pit deputy he made doubly sure the men always remembered he'd been brought up as one of them, amid rags, poverty, disease and death.

'So she's been left high an' dry then? Sent you to pave

the way for her comin' back home, has she?' He raised his eyebrows at Daisy. 'Aye, well, mebbe this is where she belongs at that.'

It was too easy a victory, too quick a turnabout. Daisy stood looking into those bullet eyes and bit her lip. 'What are you goin' to do to her?' she asked suspiciously.

'Do to her? Nowt. Everythin' that could be done has already happened, hasn't it?'

'Not really.' She didn't trust this man. Margery had told her only that morning how fanatical her da was about being respectable. She had expected to have to argue and plead with him and his wife, and now Mr Travis was saying Margery could come home without so much as a curse or a threat. 'She'll need lookin' after. She's not very strong an'—'

'Don't you tell me what she is or isn't,' he answered sharply, temper making the veins on his forehead bulge. 'The little slut! An' she'll go where all the loose pieces go—' He stopped abruptly.

'You're going to put her in the workhouse?' Daisy was horrified.

'It's up to me how I deal with me own flesh an' blood.' His voice was deceptively low as the hard black eyes met hers again. 'An' I don't give a monkey's cuss what you think.'

'Her baby is Tom's bairn an' that makes it my flesh an' blood.'

She heard his teeth grind and the woman behind him say, '*Jacob!* Please, Jacob, don't lose your temper, not on the doorstep. You know the cuddy lugs next door's got on her.'

'You tell that little—' He stopped abruptly, his teeth clamping together. 'You tell her to get her backside home if she knows what's good for her.'

Daisy looked into the furious red face, her gaze taking

92

in the woman standing behind her husband too, before she said dully, 'She's not comin' home.' And she was fully aware of the irony of the situation as she spoke. She had come here intending to plead and beg for Margery to be allowed home, and now the girl's da was all for it and Daisy herself was refusing. But it was the right thing to do. She had never been so sure of anything in her life. Margery's da was going to put her away, most likely have her committed into the workhouse where she would have to remain for fourteen years until the child was old enough to leave.

Daisy had never set foot in the workhouse but she had heard enough horror stories about it to know what it would mean to a young lass like Margery. It wasn't the rigid routines and discipline that were unbearable so much as the more subtle deprivations and degradations that made the workhouse inmates lose all their dignity, like the inmates of prisons and lunatic asylums. Margery's bairn would be taken away from her to live with the other children in a separate section of the workhouse. The unmarried mothers, or 'unchaste women' as they were labelled, were excluded from the small privileges sometimes extended to the other inmates, who mostly consisted of the old, the sick, the handicapped and inmates' children, prisoners of a harsh system which showed no mercy.

The thought of Tom's bairn being sent to school in the workhouse uniform when it was old enough, of its being taunted and jeered at by other bairns who were probably less well fed and well clothed but who had proper homes, wasn't to be borne. Daisy thought back to the fights at her old school between the workhouse children and the other bairns, and it was enough for her voice to take on a note of authority as she said, 'Margery will never be comin' home, that's what I came to tell you. She's stayin' with us. It's what me brother would have wanted.'

'Oh, aye?' Margery's father was visibly quivering with rage. 'An' your lot are goin' to clothe her an' her bastard for the rest of their days, are you? Well, more fool you!'

'Goodbye, Mr Travis. I wish I could say it's been a pleasure meetin' you but it hasn't.' Daisy steeled herself to turn and walk away with her back straight and her head up, but once round the corner and out of sight of Margery's parents she leant back against a house wall, her heart pounding. Horrible man! And the look in his eyes when she had turned and left. If looks could kill she'd be six foot under right now. The next moment she nearly jumped out of her skin as a hand caught her elbow and a man's voice spoke her name.

'George?' The relief she felt on seeing her eldest brother after the unpleasantness she'd just gone through and the fright she'd had almost made Daisy forget herself and fling her arms round his neck in the street. Instead she composed herself and said quietly, 'What on earth are you doing here?'

'*What am I doin' here?*' George Appleby was a placid, easygoing kind of man like his father had been, so it said much about his state of mind that he shook his sister hard as he repeated, 'What am *I* doin' here?'

'Stop it, George. Get off!' Daisy kicked out in true sisterly fashion, her boot connecting with George's shinbone. She glared at him as she said crossly, 'What's the matter with you anyway? I thought you were all out on the boats today?'

'We were. A good haul brought me home early. But never mind that. Did he hurt you?'

'Hurt me? Who?'

George shut his eyes for a moment, beseeching patience under his breath. 'Who do you think? Tom's lass's da.' He didn't add that he had felt his heart jump into his mouth when he had seen Daisy looking like death as she'd leant

94

against the wall. 'An' what the hell made you come here by yerself anyway? Are you daft? Is that it?'

'No, I am not daft.' She would kick him again in a minute if he carried on. 'But you all left too early for me to say about Margery comin' an' it needed sortin' out. Anyway, I only wanted to talk to her da. That's not a crime.'

'Talk to him!' George shook his head. 'By, lass, you're fair mental, you are straight. The man threw his own daughter out last night an' was probably spoilin' for a fight, then you turn up on his doorstep. I couldn't believe it when I called in an' Gran put us in the picture. He might've knocked you into next weekend.'

'Aye, well, I didn't get hurt.' Daisy didn't add here that it was because exactly the same thought had occurred to her that she had made sure she visited Margery's parents before any of her brothers found out about Tom's lass and went to see the Travises. It hadn't seemed likely that a bit lass would inflame Margery's da like the sight of a fisherman on his doorstep would, although as it happened she didn't think he could have been much madder. 'But I can tell you now there is no way he's havin' Margery back without doin' away with her in the workhouse or somethin'. He made that perfectly clear. An' she's carryin' Tom's bairn, George, for right or wrong.'

'Aye, aye, I know that, lass.' By, did he know it. Tilly and the bairns and his grandmother were hanging like a lead weight round his neck, and now there was this other lass Tom had been messing about with. Where was it going to end? He didn't know about Margery ending up in the workhouse – they'd all be knocking on its door at this rate. It hadn't taken long for word to reach old Jefferson that two of his cottages were minus their breadwinner, although George hadn't let on to Daisy and Tilly and the rest of them about the visit he'd had from one of Jefferson's lackeys. Out by the end of the week, and that was being very reasonable, the man had said. Some landlords who weren't as considerate as Mr Jefferson would have made sure folk were evicted the same day.

It had been an uphill trudge leaning against the wind to the Travises' house, but such was Daisy's despondency on the way home that the walk seemed even longer. What were they going to do? How would they all manage? It was all very well for her to say Margery wasn't going back to her mam and da, but the reality was that they were going to have to be out of the cottage soon. She knew that and she also knew poor George was worried sick. But Tom's bairn being brought up in the workhouse? It couldn't be, she wouldn't let that happen, and she just knew Margery's da had that in mind. There had to be a way out of this.

Later that night, curled up under the blankets as she tried to get warm, Daisy knew she had only been putting off the decision that had been made the night before. She had listened to the other girl cry herself to sleep earlier, and had known then she had to go and see Alf in the morning. She would tell him she still felt the same, she couldn't lie about it, but that she would marry him if he could see his way clear to Margery and her bairn living with them along with her granny. She would still follow through on her plan to get a job and bring in some money although now it would have to stretch further. They could scrape through, they would have to – that was if Alf agreed to her conditions. But he would.

Daisy twisted restlessly in the bed, drawing her icy cold feet into her hands to warm them as she bent her knees. She had given her stone water bottle to Margery, and she was missing it.

Could she do it? Could she let Alf touch her and lie with her and do the things married couples did? She wasn't very sure about what happened in that realm, but she had heard enough talk among the women when they were all gutting fish or collecting mussels and such to know that some of them liked what went on and some didn't. The only information her granny had proferred on the subject, when she had talked to Daisy the day she had started her monthlies, was that the love a woman felt for her husband made her want to please him.

Daisy shut her eyes tight, her stomach churning. She wished, oh, she did so wish that the shipwreck had never happened. She wished she had never seen William Fraser because things would have been so much easier then. Her da and brothers would still have been lost of course, and Margery would still have turned up on their doorstep, but she could have married Alf not knowing . . .

The thought brought her eyes wide open in the darkness. Not knowing what? And then she answered herself immediately with, How you could feel when someone just looked at you, or how touching someone's flesh – even when they didn't really know you were there – could create little shivers in your stomach, or how a stranger could suddenly become so important. *Stop it*. It was a command to herself, and if she had spoken it out loud her voice would have been harsh. William Fraser was gone, he had never been part of her life and never would be. He was as far removed from her as the man in the moon.

She turned over on her stomach, putting her hands over her ears as though she could block out her thoughts that way. This would pass. She had often listened to the other lasses oohing and ahhing over some lad or other, and the next week they would be on to someone else. And she had more important things to worry about.

Oh, she missed her da. She missed him so much, and their Tom. Even now she still expected the door to open and them to walk in. How they'd all get through Tom's funeral in two days time she didn't know, and then they would have to go through it all again and again when – or if – her da and Peter were found.

It was another two hours before Daisy fell into a troubled nightmarish sleep, and even then she was still fighting against the images her subconscious conjured up – dark images, beings that wanted to subjugate and control her, to hold her and enclose her inside themselves.

And they all had Alf's face.

Chapter Six

The next morning was one of early sea mist followed by bright sunshine, the sort of day that spoke of a good summer ahead to the old-timers.

April would soon be bowing out to May and the change in temperature proclaimed this. It was several degrees warmer outside, although it would take more than a morning's sunshine to persuade the solid stone walls of the cottages to relinquish their damp grip on the occupants. Arthritis, pneumonia, influenza and chest infections produced a natural cull each winter on the old and very young, and the sea wasn't chary about picking off prime specimens of manhood all the year round.

It was still far too early to start the day when Daisy awoke. She lay listening to the distant pounding of the waves as she mulled everything over for the hundredth time. They probably had a few days' grace left at the cottage but that was all, and then what? Tilly and her family would be separated and squeezed into her brothers' cottages, and if Alf agreed to take Margery and her granny she would be beholden to him and his mother for the rest of her life.

At six o'clock Daisy flung back the covers, and by half-past she had breakfast ready. At eight o'clock Hilda Travis knocked on the door.

Daisy stood back a pace and surveyed Margery's mother as Hilda said nervously, 'Jacob is on the early shift from today so this is the best time for me to come. He mustn't know. I . . . I had to see Margery. I've brought her things, her clothes an' bits an' pieces.'

'Come in.' Daisy couldn't bring herself to smile at the woman, but she kept her voice civil as she said politely, 'I've just made a pot of tea if you'd like a sup?'

'No – no, ta, I have to get back.' As Hilda stepped into the living room Daisy saw her quickly glance round, taking things in, but she didn't walk over to her daughter who was sitting on a chair by the range, and neither did Margery stand up and move towards her mother. The two stared at each other, and then Hilda bent down and deposited the two large cloth bags she had been carrying on the stone flags. 'Here's your things,' she said quietly. 'You'll be needin' 'em, won't you, lass?'

'Yes.'

'How . . . are you feelin'?'

'All right.'

Hilda nodded her head jerkily. And then she turned to face Daisy, her voice low as she said, 'He . . . he's got this thing, this mania, about bein' looked up to, see? But he's not a bad man. He was all for Margery goin' to piano lessons an' such, betterin' herself. All we ever wanted was for her to make us proud.'

There was silence for a moment, and then Nellie stirred on her platform bed as she spoke up with the privilege of age. 'Strikes me no one ever asked the lass what she wanted.'

Hilda looked at the scrawny old woman lying on the narrow bed. She stared at her blankly for a few moments, and just when Daisy was thinking it was going to turn nasty, Hilda turned to her daughter who had risen to her feet. 'I'm sorry, lass, but that's the way of it,' she said, looking straight into Margery's tense face. 'We are what we are.'

'Doesn't that apply to me too, Mam?' There was a note of deep bitterness in Margery's voice. 'All my life I've tried to be what you wanted me to be, tried and failed. Oh, you might not have said so in so many words but it's been there right enough, in your eyes. When I wasn't top of the class, when I wasn't May Queen, when I wasn't bright enough to go on and train as a teacher like you wanted, and *especially* when I didn't want to start courting the lads you and Da picked out for me as "good enough".'

'Aye, an' look where that's got you now,' Hilda shot back.

Margery felt her stomach pulling itself tight as if recoiling from any contact with the woman who had given her life, and her voice reflected her feelings when she said, 'If Tom were here I would be the happiest lass alive today, bairn or no bairn. I loved him, Mam. I'll always love him, and I'm glad I'm carrying his child if you want to know. At least I'll have something of him for always.'

'How can you talk like that when you've shamed us all? An' before you start I don't mean because he's a fisherman. I'd say the same if it was John Lindsay or the doctor's son.'

'Would you, Mam?' Margery brought her head forward, her pale eyes piercing as they held those of her mother. 'Would you really? I don't think so, not for a minute. You'd be falling on my neck with thanksgiving if I'd said I was expecting and one of them wanted to marry me.'

'That's wicked.' Hilda was trembling as if consumed with rage. 'Wicked!'

'I don't want to argue with you, Mam, and I'm pleased you brought my things, but we'll never see eye to eye on this, or anything else come to that.'

'You've never said a truer word, girl.' All thoughts of conciliation gone, Hilda was now every inch her husband's wife. She turned on her heel, and as Daisy opened the door

101

for her walked through without a nod or a goodbye. And then she paused, glancing over her shoulder at the white face of her daughter as she said, her voice harsh, 'You've got all your things so there's no need for you to come to the house again, not ever. As far as your da an' me are concerned, we never had a daughter.'

And then she was gone, marching off fairly bristling with self-righteous anger.

'Don't upset yerself, lass.' Nellie spoke up as Daisy shut the door again and walked over to Margery to hug her. 'She'll likely come round when the bairn is born.'

'I don't want her to, Mrs Shaw. And I'm not upset about my mam and da, it's not that. I knew when I first met Tom that I was making a choice between him and my parents and that wasn't hard. It's just that I can't believe he's gone and I didn't even have a chance to say goodbye.' Margery's face crumpled and tears began to stream from her eyes.

'Aye, I know, lass, I know. Life don't play fair. An' you'd better be after callin' me Gran like our Daisy does now you're part of the family, all right?'

It was a massive peace overture by Nellie who had been covertly hostile since the moment the girl had arrived. As Daisy drew back from Margery and made a little face at the other girl, expressing amazement, Margery smiled through her tears. 'Thank you . . . Gran, I'd like that,' she said shyly.

'An' when you're all finished blubbin' I'd like me sup tea?' Nellie added in her own indomitable style. 'Me tongue's bin hangin' out the last half hour. Not that anyone's noticed the poor old gal in the corner, of course.'

If Hilda Travis had delayed her departure by fifteen minutes she would have been very surprised to see a smart carriage drawn by two fine chestnuts approaching the village. As it was, she missed the spectacle which set heads turning and curtains twitching.

A tall neatly dressed woman was sitting at the front of the vehicle next to the driver which left the two long seats within the open carriage empty. As the driver said, 'I reckon this is the one, Ellen. Bernard said it was the tenth along,' the woman glanced about her with interest.

So this was where the lass who had caused so much trouble back at the house lived, was it? Ellen Mullen nudged the first coachman, who was also her intended, as she whispered, 'Pongs a bit of seaweed an' that, doesn't it?'

'Aye, well, that's mebbe because we're yards away from the big stretch of water they call the sea, lass.'

'Oh, you.' As top-floor maid Ellen was privy to most of the intimate goings-on of her employers. Although Sir Augustus's wife Gwendoline had her own personal maid, the two daughters remaining at home were assisted in their toilette by Ellen. She had learnt very early on to say nothing and to listen hard and both women chatted quite freely in front of her. Ellen knew, therefore, that once the young master had come to himself he had been furious that nothing had been done for the fishergirl who had rescued him from the water. Mr William hadn't been satisfied with the suggestion that a sum of money along with a cursory note of thanks be delivered to the village. And once he got the bit between his teeth he was a devil for having his own way, was Mr William. Just like his father.

And so here she was with a summons to bring the fishergirl to the house, but what made this whole episode really interesting was the fact that this lass had thumbed her nose at Mr Kirby by all accounts. By, but he'd been in a fit when he'd come back after visiting the village. They had all wondered what was what but no one had dared ask, though from what Bernard had heard when Mr Kirby was leaving the fishergirl's cottage and then the snippets which had filtered through via Harriet, Lady Fraser's personal maid, it appeared this Daisy Appleby was a right one. Aye, a little madam with a mouth on her like a cesspit, Mr Kirby had told Sir Augustus and his wife, according to Harriet.

Ellen adjusted the collar of her serge coat nervously. 'You coming to the door with me, Donald?'

'Don't be daft, lass. What'd I do that for?'

'Because I want you to.'

'Oh, get yourself down an' don't be so wet. I'm here, aren't I? I'm not going nowhere. Just say what you've got to say an' then get yourself back up here. I tell you one thing, if this lass has got half the sense she was born with she'll be out that door an' in this carriage like a dose of salts. An' when all's said an' done she deserves something for her trouble. I'd think twice about throwing meself into the sea for me own mam, let alone a bloke I'd never met, I tell you straight.'

Ellen sent her betrothed a look which would have quelled a lesser man and flounced down from the carriage. Donald heard the door open after she'd knocked but kept his eyes studiously to the front the way Bernard, the head coachman, had taught him. In less than a minute Ellen had climbed up beside him again. He waited but she said nothing, so after a moment he glanced at her.

'Well?'

'Well what?'

'*Ellen.*'

'Oh, all right, all right. She's coming in a minute or two.'

'I told you.'

'Aye, but . . .' Ellen's voice trailed away, and when Donald said, 'What's up?' it was a second or two before she answered and then her voice was puzzled. 'She's not what I expected, not from what Mr Kirby said anyway. She's . . . nice.'

'Nice?' Donald wanted to throw his head back and laugh at her naivety, but he was here in the capacity of Sir Augustus's coachman and propriety had to be maintained. He therefore contented himself with saying, his voice scathing, 'Look, Mr Kirby reckons she's as bold as brass and typical of some of the fishing girls down at the docks who'd go with anyone. 'Course she was nice, you'd brought her news the master wants to see her. Besides, that type know how to turn on the charm with men *and* women. There's some as cater for both, you know.'

'*Donald!*' Ellen's cheeks were scarlet, and the coachman, realising he had gone too far, was suitably chastened.

He was still apologising when Daisy exited the cottage, standing for a moment by the carriage until Ellen said, her voice clipped now, 'Climb up then, we haven't got all day.'

Daisy wanted to fiddle with her hair and clothes – she had noticed a black blob which was obviously tar on her skirt – and not least her nails on the way to Greyfriar Hall. She had scrubbed and scrubbed them in the few hectic minutes she had had before she'd left the cottage, but the minute or two with the big scrubbing brush and washing soda had only served to make her red hands even redder, and still her broken nails were black-rimmed.

She only had one change of clothes which fortunately had been clean, or as clean as the poss-stick and plenty of elbow grease could make them, and her calico cloak covered the worst of the darns in her thick linen blouse. She couldn't do anything about the tar stain though.

She restrained herself from fidgeting, painfully conscious of the two stiff backs in front of her. The others might not be looking at her but she felt as though they had eyes in the back of their heads. Consequently Daisy sat as still as the deep potholes in the road would let her.

It was the first time she had ever ridden in a vehicle – unless you counted Farmer Gilbert's great hay wagon which was pulled by his two huge shire-horses – and in spite of her nervousness at what lay ahead, the experience was thrilling. The fields on either side of the lane fairly sped by, and they passed East Boldon and West Boldon and then Laverick Hall before turning sharply south, and within a short time were passing through the massive iron gates of Greyfriar Hall and into the estate.

The wheels of the carriage scrunched on the gravel drive and then Daisy saw the big house which seemed to stretch away endlessly beyond the smooth lawn in front of it. The carriage skirted the lawn, driving round the side of the house and into a huge courtyard in which were two more carriages, a covered coach, and what was clearly the stable block by the number of horses peering out of their stalls.

The carriage stopped, and Daisy noticed the woman in front jumped down quickly without waiting for the assistance of the man next to her, ignoring his, '*Ellen*, please. I've said sorry, haven't I?'

When Daisy was standing on the cobbles the woman said, her voice still abrupt, 'You've got to come with me to the kitchen and then they'll ring when they want you upstairs. And wipe your feet well on the cork mat outside the door. Cook doesn't like her floor messed up.'

Daisy looked down at her heavy hobnailed boots which were very different from the maid's neat trim ones, and something in her expression caused a softening in Ellen's tone when she said, 'Don't worry, it'll be all right. They've got a lot to thank you for after all.'

'I only did what anyone'd do if they saw someone drownin' in front of their eyes.'

Did she really mean that or was she just saying it for

effect? Ellen stared hard into the unusually lovely young face before her. 'Lass, I can assure you few would do what you did,' she said, her tone very dry. And when no reply was forthcoming added, curiosity overcoming the need to keep herself at a distance, 'The authorities told the master that a number of fishermen were drowned in the same storm that sank the *Aquitania*. Did you know any of them?'

The smoky grey eyes with their thick lashes gave the maid her answer, even before Daisy said quietly, 'Me da an' two of me brothers, an' another three from our village.'

'Oh, how awful.'

Daisy's heart was beating painfully as she scraped the mud off her boots before following Ellen into the house. She found herself in what appeared to be a large scullery, part of which seemed to be used as a cloakroom by the number of rough coats and shawls hanging on wooden pegs along one wall, under which stood lines of boots, large and small. She watched as Ellen stopped at one peg, taking off her coat and hat and smoothing her hair before she changed her footwear for a pair of thin-soled shoes. Then they walked past the big boiler, poss-tubs and deep white sink set to one side of two large rough tables piled high with vegetables and a number of dead chickens, pheasants and other game.

'The cook's name is Mrs Preston but she's mostly just called Cook. Keep on the right side of her, she can be a tartar if you start off on the wrong foot.' Ellen whispered this in an aside just before she opened the kitchen door, leaving Daisy no chance to enquire why she should be expected to keep on the right side of anyone in the house. She was only here for a brief visit after all.

Once in the kitchen she stared round her in amazement, completely overawed. It was vast, enormous; the range alone seemed to be as large as the living room at home and it was beautifully black-leaded with shining brasswork. There were marble-topped units down one wall upon which sat pots and pans of every shape and size, cupboards galore, shelves everywhere, two big sinks and numerous small tables holding quantities of food and large wicker baskets and the like, and in the middle of it all, the biggest table in the world with long benches down either side of it. The room seemed full of people at first, but when Daisy was pushed down on a cracket by Ellen and told to 'keep still', she realised after a minute or two that in spite of the hustle and bustle there were just seven people present. They all seemed to be doing something, and although there had been a brief lull in the noise and conversation when she and Ellen had first appeared, activity had quickly resumed.

Daisy was conscious of several veiled glances in her direction but only one girl, a young lass who couldn't have been more than twelve or thirteen, smiled at her from where she sat peeling an enormous pile of potatoes, and then it was a quick nervous smile before she lowered her head to the task in hand. The personage who seemed to be in charge, a tall, eagle-eyed woman with sharp features whom Daisy took to be the cook, ignored her completely.

It was only a minute or two before Ellen reappeared but it seemed much longer to Daisy's tightly stretched nerves. Bending over her, Ellen said, 'Jack – he's the first footman – will come for you shortly.' And then as before her tone softened a little as she added, 'You all right, lass? You don't look too good.'

She didn't feel too good. Her heart was thumping against her ribs with enough force to crack them and she felt dizzy, whether from the heat in the kitchen which was excessive or dread of what was to come, Daisy wasn't sure.

'You want a cup of tea?' Ellen was still bending over her and when Daisy shook her head, the other girl said, 'Oh, go on, I'll have one an' all,' whereupon she walked across to a huge brown teapot sitting on two flat steel rods over the range. She lifted it, shaking it slightly, and then poured two cups of black liquid into a couple of mugs she took down from a long rack on the wall.

'And what do you think you're doing, Ellen Mullen?' The woman Daisy had taken to be the cook stopped her pummelling of a basin of dough.

'She's feeling bad, Cook,' Ellen said shortly, spooning sugar into each cup and adding a good dollop of milk. 'You want her passing out up there and the master saying we didn't look after her properly?'

The cook moved closer to Ellen, lowering her voice as she said, 'Mr Kirby won't be best pleased if he catches you fussing round her. You know what he thinks about all this.'

Daisy imagined the cook thought she couldn't hear what was being said but she had always had cuddy lugs – according to her granny – and when Ellen whispered back, 'Aye, well, I'm not so sure he's got her right. She seems a nice young lass to me,' she was glad her cheeks were already burning from the heat. So the valet had been nasty about her, had he? Perhaps she should have expected that.

'She's no better than she should be and an upstart with it, and you're too trusting by half, me girl.'

'The fact remains she saved Mr William from drowning, and perhaps Mr Kirby had better remember that when—'

'What do you mean, I'm no better than I should be?' Daisy had risen to her feet, and the hubbub in the kitchen turned to absolute silence in the space of a breath. 'Well?' She advanced on the cook as the assistant cook, the kitchen maids, the vegetable maid and the two scullery maids watched with bated breath, not daring to move. To speak to Cook like that!

'She didn't mean anything, lass.' Ellen was distraught.

She had been sent 'specially by Sir Augustus and Lady Fraser themselves to fetch this girl with the minimum of fuss – those had been the master's exact words – and now for this to happen! She would get the blame, sure as eggs were eggs. 'Did you, Cook? You didn't mean anything.'

The cook, her thin-lipped mouth set tight, stared at the fishersnipe who had dared to challenge her in her own kitchen, and what would have happened next if the first footman hadn't appeared on the scene, no one knew.

As it was, Jack Mallard – a protégé of the butler, Mr Middleton, who had been coached by that same gentleman in the art of detecting and averting awkward incidents which might embarrass or upset the family – acted swiftly.

'Come along, lass.' He had taken hold of Daisy's arm and whisked her out of the kitchen before she knew what was happening. Once the door was closed and they were in the long corridor which led to the hall door, he said, 'You having a run in with Cook? You don't want to take no notice of her, lass.'

'She – she said—' Daisy found she couldn't repeat to this stranger what the cook had implied, however kindly he seemed. 'Mr Kirby has told lies about me and she believed him.'

Jack Mallard wasn't surprised. From the first day he had come to work at Greyfriar Hall some fifteen years ago, he'd known that there was no love lost between Josiah Kirby and Stuart Middleton. The valet and butler vied for supremacy both with their master and the rest of the staff, and you were either for one and against the other or the other way round. He'd decided to throw in his lot with the butler and had never regretted it. Josiah Kirby was a nasty piece of work and vicious with it, but certain of the staff – of which Cook was one – thought the sun shone out of his backside.

Now Jack had no compunction about saying softly, 'Look, lass, I don't doubt what you say is true, but Mr Kirby has the master's ear and you won't do yourself any favours if you repeat what you just said to me, all right? You're here to see the master so forget about Mr Kirby, he don't matter.'

Daisy stared at the footman and nodded slowly. He was trying to help her, she could see that, but the thought of Mr Kirby's lies made her blood boil.

And then her escort opened the door and they stepped out into the hall, and all thoughts of Josiah Kirby fled.

She was standing at the entrance to another world, she had to be, and she had never imagined anything like it in her wildest dreams. Daisy stood quite still, her gaze struggling to take in the great expanse of polished mahogany panelling and seats and small tables, the enormous gold-framed pictures on the walls and the acres and acres of deep rich red carpet. The footman had to repeat himself twice before she heard him, and then the words themselves were lost on her until he said again, 'The master and mistress and Mr William and his sisters are in the morning room, all right? Don't speak except to answer anything they might say, and curtsey to Sir Augustus when you first go in. Have you got that?'

Had she? Daisy stared at him, her eyes wide, and for a second the urge to bolt was strong. She saw herself running back down the corridor and through the kitchen and scullery until she was outside again, and only the thought of how much Mr Kirby and the cook would love to see her at such a disadvantage kept her where she was.

The sensation of the thick carpet under her feet was strange as she followed the footman down the hall, and never had she felt so tiny and insignificant. A huge and winding polished staircase rose up out of the centre of the endless space, but they passed this before her escort stopped at the last door on their right before the grand entrance directly in front of them.

'I'll knock and then open the door and announce you. Got it?' Jack Mallard was feeling sorry for this young lass who was so clearly out of her depth and scared to death. He had been expecting someone quite different from all that Josiah Kirby had intimated. If this lass was on the game he'd eat his hat. 'And just remember, all you have to do is speak when you're spoken to.'

'Aye, I'll remember.' Daisy was grateful for the solicitude she sensed but it had the effect of putting iron in her backbone. She was just as good as these folk, any of them – including Mr Kirby. She glanced at the liveried clothing of the man next to her which was intimidating in itself, and swallowed silently.

The footman didn't wait for an answer to his knock on the morning-room door, something Daisy thought odd because why bother to knock at all if you were going to open the door immediately? His voice was flat but penetrating when he said, 'It's the fishergirl, Sir Augustus.'

'Thank you, Mallard.'

The footman stood to one side for Daisy to pass him, and as she did so hissed out of the side of his mouth, 'Don't eyeball the master, lass, what are you thinking of? Keep your eyes on the floor,' but for the life of her she couldn't obey the order.

Beneath her feet was another carpet, this time a blue one, again so thick she couldn't hear herself walk, but it was the room in front of her and not least the five people in it which held her spellbound. The wooden panelling was a lighter colour than that in the hall and more intricately worked, being almost entirely festooned with leaves and flowers carved into it. An enormous full-length window with blue curtains took up half of one wall with a bookcase to either side of it, and a large cabinet, an occasional table, a screen partly obscuring another door and several very grand high-backed upholstered chairs were dotted about.

A roaring fire was burning in the marble fireplace, and to the side of this in an alcove was a large writing desk at which sat a grey-haired man. Directly in front of the fire in a position to catch all the heat were two chairs. The young man she had rescued from the sea was in one, a thick blanket over his knees, and an impassive-faced woman in the other. Two equally impassive but considerably younger women were sitting on a chaise-longue placed at an angle in the other alcove to that which held the desk. All five persons were looking at Daisy and she, in turn, found her eyes darting from one to the other.

William, she noticed, was very pale and even more handsome than she remembered. But after this one thought Daisy kept her eyes from returning to his chiselled features and didn't allow herself to think of Sir Augustus's son by name.

She had expected the master of the house to speak first, and when the young man spoke up, saying, 'I owe you a great debt, Miss Appleby. Please, won't you be seated?' Daisy felt the shock of hearing that deep pleasant voice for the first time register in her body.

She looked full into his face then, the piercing blue of his eyes striking her anew, but before she could answer or make any move towards the chair he had indicated, Sir Augustus said coldly, 'William? We agreed I would deal with this,' and the tone of his voice brought all Daisy's attention to him.

Sir Augustus Fraser considered that life had dealt him a series of blows in his latter years. Born a baronet, he had been encouraged from birth to remember the immemorial antiquity of his line and to look down upon nobility of more recent vintage. When it had come to choosing a wife, he hadn't even considered taking a female from one of the wealthy families of Low Southwick, Monkwearmouth, Sunderland and surrounding districts, who had mostly made their riches and titles in the nineteenth-century development of the area and were therefore shipbuilders, glassmakers, coalmine owners and the like.

Sir Augustus was a landowner, a member of one of the oldest county families, and only a wife of equal breeding would do. So Gwendoline had been selected and they had duly married. She had found the procedure involved in producing an heir more than a little distasteful, but that had neither surprised nor worried him. He had his mistresses for entertainment, a wife wasn't supposed to enjoy that kind of thing.

What had surprised and worried him, however, and more so as time had gone on, was Gwendoline's inability to produce an heir. One female child after another had been born, and to add insult to injury his daughters, without exception, had inherited neither their mother's fair graceful comeliness nor his darker good looks, but had fallen somewhere between the two and were remarkably plain. And then, at last, he had heard the words, 'You have a fine healthy son, Sir Augustus.'

As soon as Gwendoline had risen from her bed after the four weeks of confinement following the birth, she had moved into her own quarters in the west wing, making it clear all intimacy was finished with, and he had been content to let her go. He had his son. His wife had persevered in her duty, and he wanted nothing more from her from that point on but to be a graceful hostess and a worthy recipient of his name.

But Sir Augustus had found as the boy had grown that his long-awaited heir irked him. Although tall, William had taken after his mother in colouring, having her fairness and blue eyes, and bore nothing of the strong dark looks characteristic of the Frasers. And it wasn't only the boy's outward appearance which irritated him. William was seemingly unable to grasp the implications of his position. Sir Augustus's daughters had no problem in accepting that they had been born to be looked up to and served as of right, but his son, his *heir* who bore in his loins the seed of future Frasers, seemed intent on consorting with common people.

And now there was the affair of the fishergirl. True, she deserved some recompense for assisting his son, although he doubted if her part in the proceedings had been quite as dramatic as William would have them believe. Sir Augustus had tried to tell his son that these half-remembered images and memories he had could just as likely have been caused by the bump on his head than be based on truth, but the boy would have it that he had been sinking to the depths of the ocean before this fishergirl had intervened. Certainly Kirby seemed to think the rescue tale had been grossly exaggerated in favour of the young girl standing before them now. But Sir Augustus would get to the bottom of what had really happened. He had spent too many years meting out justice as a local magistrate not to recognise fabrication when he heard it.

Sir Augustus looked at the person in question and saw to his annoyance that the chit was staring back at him. So Kirby had been right. This girl, young as she was, was clearly used to earning her living in a manner which made her bold.

'I understand from my son that you played a part in assisting him on the day the *Aquitania* was lost. Is this so?' His voice was quiet but every word distinct and clear.

Daisy blinked. She didn't understand where this was leading but it felt odd, strange. It was almost as though Sir Augustus thought she had done something wrong, but how could it be wrong to save his son from drowning? She found she had to moisten her lips before she could say, 'Yes, sir.' And although she didn't look at anyone but Sir Augustus she was conscious of four other pairs of eyes trained on her.

'I would like you to relay to me the series of events which took place from the first moment you saw the ship. Can you do that?'

He was talking to her as though she was half sharp, an imbecile like poor Amy Croft with her slobbering mouth and unintelligible ramblings. Daisy stared into the hard dark face before her and unconsciously brought her shoulders back and her chin up. 'Of course I can do that, sir,' she said evenly, and then she spoke a word she hadn't even realised was in her vocabulary, but which had been planted there on witnessing an altercation between Farmer Gilbert and a shop owner who had come to the farm complaining the farmer had short changed him on the number of potato sacks he had delivered. 'An' there are plenty of folk back at the village who can corroborate what I say an' all.'

Sir Augustus's expression didn't change by so much as the flicker of an eyelash, neither did he move, but Daisy was aware of an indignant rustling of taffeta from his womenfolk, and of William throwing the blanket to one side as he stood up, saying, 'I am sure that will not be necessary, Miss Appleby. Please, do come and sit down and make yourself comfortable, and then perhaps you would be kind enough to do as my father has asked.'

Silence fell, and continued while Daisy sat down on the exquisitely upholstered chair William had indicated. She knew she had turned rosy red, but it was less to do with her temerity in daring to speak as she had than with the look on William's face when he had smiled at her. He hadn't just smiled with his mouth but with his eyes, and they had applauded her firm stand.

'William, sit down, dear.' Gwendoline was a lady born

116

and bred, and everything about her proclaimed this from her softly spoken voice to her gracious manner. She came from an old and wealthy county family but her grandfather had had the foresight to reach his fingers into all sorts of pies, including boat building, thus reinforcing the family's assurance of their own superiority as natural leaders.

As far as William's mother was concerned the world was quite simply divided into those who led and those who were fit only to be led, or as Lady Warwick put it, rural society was 'a small select aristocracy born booted and spurred to ride, and a large dim mass born saddled and bridled to be ridden'.

Consequently she was furiously angry with her beloved son right at this minute for forgetting himself so far as to address this common fishergirl as an equal, but the only sign of this was in the rigidity of her back. Her voice, manner and face were as gracious and cool as ever, even when she had to repeat herself and say, 'William, dear? You know you should be resting. The doctor said no exertion.'

'I don't think he meant I had to be cocooned in cotton wool, Mother, and the heat from the fire is excessive.' So saying he took a chair a few feet to the left of Daisy, and as he sat down, said, 'When you're ready, Miss Appleby.'

He shouldn't be talking to her the way he was, his mam didn't like it. Daisy's senses, which had always been more finely tuned than most people's, were alert to the tension in the woman. And the rest of them were the same. Her gaze flickered over the two elongated plain young women with smooth hair and cold eyes who were sitting on the chaise-longue. But it was nice of him to try and put her at her ease, which was what he was doing. William was kind, she could see that, and different from the rest of his family. Daisy took a deep breath and began to speak.

117

She was careful not to embroider the facts at all but neither did she think this was a time for false modesty, and although she paused once or twice to collect her thoughts her voice was clear and concise as she related exactly what had happened that morning on the beach.

When she came to a halt at the point where Josiah Kirby had first knocked on the door, silence reigned again. Felicity and Cecilia Fraser looked at their mother and Gwendoline looked at her husband, then they all looked at William who hadn't taken his eyes off Daisy, and Augustus broke the silence by addressing his son. 'It seems you are a very fortunate young man, m'boy.'

It was Augustus's way of saying that he believed Daisy's account of what had happened and William recognised it as such, but at the same time as a feeling of relief made itself known he experienced a surge of anger. Why couldn't they simply thank this girl for saving his life? Why was it so hard? There was nothing difficult about it as far as he could see. What did they think she would want as a reward, for crying out loud, the family silver?

He brought his eyes reluctantly away from Daisy's pink face and looked straight at his father. 'I couldn't agree more. I think you would be hard pressed to find anyone – man, woman or child – in the whole of Sunderland and Newcastle or beyond who would attempt what Miss Appleby did, and for a stranger at that. Yes, Father, I am indeed a fortunate young man to have made the acquaintance of Miss Daisy Appleby.'

Sir Augustus kept a smile on his face with some effort. This was exactly the sort of response which so irritated him with regard to William. His son should express proper appreciation for what had certainly been a courageous act, of course, but the girl was a menial of the most base kind and a little restraint was in order here. This misplaced sympathy for the lower classes had caused William to

118

embarrass them all greatly not so long ago when over dinner one night his son had all but accused a guest, a wealthy and influential mine owner, of employing slave labour in criminally unsafe working conditions. That had resulted in the boy being sent on his latest trip across the Channel to stay with his French cousins, out of harm's way. It had been on his return from that trip that William nearly lost his life. And here he was now, acting almost as though there was no difference between himself and a common fishergirl.

'Quite.' Sir Augustus turned from his son and trained cold eyes on the person in question. He didn't like to admit it but this was one of the rare occasions when he had been surprised by someone. From what Kirby had intimated he had expected to see a coarse, brash young woman brought to the house, but although Daisy Appleby had spirit he saw now he had been mistaken in his initial assumption that this boldness went hand in hand with brazenness. He had sampled many of her class in the whorehouses of Newcastle and Sunderland when he had fancied a little diversion from his more cultured mistresses, but this girl was no prostitute. Not yet anyway. She had an air of untouched innocence about her which would make her a better actress than Lillie Langtry if it wasn't genuine. She had spoken concisely, and appeared very clean – her clothes, although threadbare and patched, were proper – but there was something more, and it annoyed him that he couldn't quite define it. If she had been other than she was, a fishergirl, he could have thought it a self-possession born of dignity.

He had been of the mind when William had first insisted that something must be done for the girl to summon the wench to the house and give her a generous purse, but now, having seen her and heard her story, he wasn't so sure. Surely it would be a more fitting reward for her service to his son if the girl was given the chance to escape her background.

She could train as a maid of some kind. He could leave the finer details to the redoubtable Mrs Finlay – he understood from Kirby that his housekeeper kept the indoor staff on their toes, which was all to the good. And perhaps, if the chit proved suitable and of a pleasing disposition, she could progress to attending his daughters? She was presentable enough. Sir Augustus inhaled deeply, feeling rather pleased with himself as he said, 'I understand you told Mullen that your father and two of your brothers were lost at sea in the same storm in which the *Aquitania* went down? Do you have other family?'

Daisy lifted her head. 'Yes, sir. Three brothers, all married with families of their own, an' there's me granny. She lives with us – with me,' she corrected quickly, flushing again.

Sir Augustus nodded abruptly. He wasn't interested in the girl's family but from what Mullen had discovered it would appear Appleby had lost her provider. 'So you are in a position to take up employment, should it be offered to you?'

Daisy stared at him, completely taken aback, and then she became aware that her mouth had fallen open in a little gape and brought it shut quickly. What was he saying? He couldn't be offering her work, could he? Not here, in this house?

Lady Fraser had obviously been wondering the same thing because she made a small movement in her chair and said, 'Augustus?'

He ignored his wife – a not uncommon occurrence – and spoke in the manner of one bestowing an enormous honour when he said, 'How would you like to go into service here, girl? Work and live in Greyfriar Hall?'

'No.' It was an instinctive response and spoken from

120

the heart without any consideration for where she was or to whom she was speaking. Daisy immediately tried to remedy any incivility, saying, 'Thank you most kindly, sir, but I can't work here.'

'You are refusing my offer?' Sir Augustus's voice displayed little emotion, but his Adam's apple moved rapidly up and down, betraying displeasure. 'You have other employment?'

She could lie. She could make out she had other work and then that would be the end of it. Daisy's head was in a whirl. But her granny always said that lies – proper lies, and not the little white ones you said not to hurt folk's feelings and such – had a way of tripping you up when you least expected it, and then before you knew where you were, you found yourself up to your eyes in muck and bullets.

Daisy's heart was thumping, but she forced herself to speak carefully although she couldn't help stuttering a little. 'I . . . I haven't got other work, sir.' If she had spoken the truth here she would have gone on to say that she had seen enough in the last few hours to know she would rather labour gutting fish on one of Sunderland's quays from dawn to dusk than try to fit into the set-up here. Apart from hating the thought of being trapped indoors from sunrise to sunset seven days a week, and being so far from her granny and everyone, it just wasn't in her to bow the knee constantly to this family, let alone stomach the hierarchy among that lot in the kitchen and the rest of the servants. And to *live* among them – she'd be fit for the asylum in a week. However, truth often needed to be measured out in drops and not bucketfuls – another of her granny's sayings – and so she added politely, 'It's just that bein' brought up out of doors so to speak, I couldn't be inside all day an' in such a great big house an' all. I . . . I'm sorry, sir.'

'Father—'

As William began to speak, Augustus brought up his hand in a sharp cutting movement which forbade his son to continue. He caught his wife's eye as he did so, and read from Gwendoline's stiff expression that she hadn't approved of the notion of this low creature living under their roof. It only served to spur on his ideas a step further. His wife irritated him nearly as much as their son did.

Sir Augustus glanced at Daisy again, sitting with her hands lying neatly on her calico cloak which she'd pulled round her to hide the tar stain as she had sat down. Her large grey eyes were fixed on him. He cleared his throat and said, 'There is another position which I know of in a smaller establishment where your duties would be that of nurse companion, involving morning and afternoon walks and things of that nature. There is a small staff of three or four. Is this of interest to you? Oh, and I understand your village is no more than a mile or two from Evenley House?'

'Evenley House? Aunt Wilhelmina?'

One of the two young ladies on the chaise-longue spoke up, and such was her tone of voice that Daisy's eyes opened wider.

'Yes, Aunt Wilhelmina.' Her father's reply was terse. 'It seems that once again your aunt is in need of a nurse companion.'

'I'm not surprised.' This from William who, in spite of his father's furious expression, continued speaking directly to Daisy as he said, 'My aunt averages two or three companions a year. I think the longest one has lasted is seven months. Aunt Wilhelmina is what you might call . . . idiosyncratic.'

Daisy hadn't heard the word before but she didn't need further prompting to understand what was being implied.

'Thank you, William.' Sir Augustus's tone was icy but it seemed to have no effect on his son who sat back in his chair, shaking his head as he muttered, 'Aunt Wilhelmina.'

Daisy was at a loss. She looked from William to the cold elegant woman sitting in the chair in front of the fire, but what she read in that lady's expression of disdain brought her eyes quickly back to the master of the house. Sir Augustus was glaring at his son but as he felt Daisy's eyes on him turned to her, and now he was every inch the master of the household as he said, 'The position is not one which would normally be offered to someone of your' – he had been going to say 'kind' but knowing how his son would react changed it to – 'age, but in view of your service to my son I felt it appropriate. Of course my sister herself would have to decide whether you are suitable or not. You would be paid monthly, and in view of the circumstances it would be more generous than normal. Shall we say . . .'

He thought swiftly. His servants were paid anything from a pound a month for the scullery and chambermaids to nine pounds each for Kirby and Middleton, and in the allowance he paid his sister he knew Wilhelmina put by a monthly provision of fourteen pounds for her staff. These comprised a cook-cum-housekeeper, the cook's husband who acted as chauffeur-cum-gardener-cum-handyman, and their daughter who was the maid, along with the resident nurse companion of the time.

He did not ask Wilhelmina for a breakdown of their respective wages in the accounts she had to provide each year, but if he suggested to his sister that he would be willing to pay for this particular nurse companion himself, she would most certainly jump at the financial saving she would make.

'Shall we say six pounds a month?' he said smoothly. 'And of course your uniform, along with any other incidentals will be taken care of.'

123

Daisy stared at the tall autocratic man in front of her. She could see no resemblance to William in his father. It was a strange thought, a ridiculous one for such a time as this, the moment when she had been offered the world in one huge bountiful package. Six pounds. *Six pounds*. With six pounds a month she could pay Tilly's rent for her and provide for her sister-in-law's family as well as her granny and Margery. No, no – it would be better for Tilly and her bairns to come to her da's cottage and keep that going. Her da had built his smoke house there and he had the lean-to for the wood and everything. Their cottage was much better than Tilly's. Her granny could sleep where she'd always slept, and Tilly and her bairns could have the two big beds and Margery Daisy's tiny bedroom. The two younger women could see to her granny, and Margery would have family round her when the bairn was born. It was the answer to everything. It was, it was.

But what if Sir Augustus's sister didn't like her? Or if William's aunt's house was similar to this one? Could she stand that? Could she? And when the answer came it was as though it was from someone else, someone years and years older. Of course she could stand it – what had to be endured *could* be endured. It was as simple as that.

Chapter Seven

The drive to Evenley House on the outskirts of Fulwell close to the old quarries was an uncomfortable one for Daisy, despite the luxurious carriage, although she was glad to be returning to the area she knew. Sir Augustus's sister's establishment was no more than a couple of miles from Daisy's home village. Nevertheless, the seven or so miles from Greyfriar seemed to stretch on for ever, despite the swiftness of the horse and carriage in which Daisy and the Misses Felicity and Cecilia were travelling.

William's sisters had said not a word – except to each other – since the carriage had left the grounds of their home, but their very silence towards Daisy was an eloquent and bitter statement of their resentment at having to accompany a common chit to their aunt's residence.

They had known better than to argue with their father, however, when he had given the order after sending Daisy to the kitchen for some refreshment. Only William ever dared to do that, and he always paid dearly for it. They had watched and listened as their mother, livid with a rage that made her look years older, icily enquired of their father whether he had gone quite mad. His answer had been such that their mother had done something they had never witnessed before, leaving the room in a swirl of silk and satin and taking no heed of her husband's command to remain.

They had then had to sit and listen to their father

explaining to their brother the philanthropic reasoning behind his decision to inflict a fishergirl on their aunt. Neither Cecilia nor Felicity had any fond feeling towards Wilhelmina Fraser, in fact they disliked their father's sister intensely, but that was beside the point. Impossible and difficult as Aunt Wilhelmina was, she was a Fraser, and that meant she was entitled to a servant who had been trained to a good standard and who knew their place. Whereas this baggage . . . She might look clean enough, but they wouldn't be at all surprised if the first job their aunt's other servants had to perform was delousing.

In all their murmurings, neither Cecilia nor Felicity had remarked upon the unusual beauty evident in the girl despite her shabby clothes, but it had rankled with them nonetheless.

The sisters were well aware of their own plainness; they would have been even if their father had not referred to it at least once a week in some way, along with mentioning that their two elder sisters had managed to snare a husband each despite being afflicted with the same ailment.

While Cecilia and Felicity assured each other that they would rather die than take on Bernice's ageing widower who had been three decades older than his young wife when they had married, or Susannah's middle-class attorney who wasn't *quite* a gentleman and whose family had links with – they always whispered this word – tradespeople, they didn't mean a word of it.

A London season – which some years earlier had acquired husbands for their sisters – had come and gone without so much as the sniff of a suitor for either of them, and it had been agonising. Now, at twenty-three and twenty-four years of age, Sir Augustus's younger daughters were facing the terrifying prospect of permanent spinsterhood.

*　　*　　*

It was just after midday when the horse and carriage stopped outside a pair of imposing iron gates set in a high stone wall. The coachman jumped down and opened the gates without being told to do so, and left them open after he had climbed back into his seat and the carriage had rumbled through. They had passed several farms on the journey, and far in the distance Daisy had caught a glimpse of the wind vanes of Fulwell Mill, but once inside the grounds of this house a border of mature trees enclosed them in a small but very private little world.

Daisy hadn't been sure what she'd been expecting, but as they clip-clopped along a pebbled drive of perhaps some two hundred yards, she saw green lawns and neat flowerbeds on either side with the odd wooden bench placed here and there. The flowerbeds were ablaze with colour and there was a distinctly pleasant scent in the air. Then the carriage came to a halt and the house was in front of her.

Oh, it was bonny! Daisy thought of the stark grey-stone mansion she had just left, and which she had been half expecting to see again – albeit in smaller form – and instead gazed in delight at the long, two-storey whitewashed house, covered in red and green creeper and with a massive thatched roof which hung down over mullioned windows. Grand undoubtedly but bonny with it.

The coachman appeared and opened the carriage door, and when Daisy hesitated, waiting for the ladies to go before her, one of the women flicked her hand, holding up a lace handkerchief under her long thin nose as though there was a nasty smell in the carriage. 'Go on, go on.' It sounded irritable and curt, and both women drew their voluminous skirts away from any contact with Daisy's cloak as she scrambled out, her cheeks burning.

She watched the coachman, the same one who had driven the carriage to Greyfriar Hall earlier, help the two ladies down from the carriage, and when they moved towards the heavy oak front door Daisy fell into step a few paces behind. Before they had had a chance to knock the door was opened from within, a small maid clad in a black alpaca dress and starched apron and cap dipping her knee as she said, 'Miss Cecilia, Miss Felicity.'

Neither woman acknowledged the greeting, brushing past the maid as though she didn't exist, and apparently the girl must have been expecting this because she said quickly, 'The mistress is in the drawing room, the parson's just leaving.'

'Oh, lord, not the parson again.' Cecilia didn't bother to keep her voice down as she tossed the remark over her shoulder to her sister.

Daisy was inside the hall now which was large and wide with a graceful curving staircase rising from the tiled floor some yards in front of them. The doors leading off the hall and the wooden staircase itself were stained a deep mahogany, but the walls were papered in a gold and cream geometrically patterned paper which generally lightened the interior, as did the gold curtains at the windows to either side of the front door. It was bonny, Daisy thought again, watching the plump little red-cheeked maid assist William's sisters to divest themselves of their fur capes and hats although both women kept their thick cloth coats buttoned.

As the maid turned towards Daisy, Cecilia Fraser snapped sharply, 'Leave her, and announce us.'

'Yes, miss.' After depositing the capes and hats on the iron hallstand, the maid hurried along to a door at the far end of the hall, the Misses Cecilia and Felicity following at a leisurely pace with Daisy making up the rear. Corridors branched off to either side at the end of the hall, but although large, the house did not carry the same impersonal feel as Greyfriar. A pair of tables holding bowls of brightly coloured flowers stood against the far wall, and the pictures on the walls were of pleasant country scenes rather than the succession of grim portraits Greyfriar Hall had boasted. Nevertheless, the size and splendour of it all was overwhelming, and as Daisy glanced down at herself, the shabbiness of her clothes and in particular the tar stain on her skirt hit her afresh.

She heard the little maid knock upon and then open the door, announcing the sisters to her mistress, and as the two women swept past the girl Daisy wondered for a moment if William's sisters expected her to follow them into the room or wait outside in the hall. It seemed presumptuous to do the former and so she stood where she was, and it must have been the right decision because the door closed, opening a few moments later as the maid exited wheeling a large wooden tea trolley on which reposed various dirty dishes and a coffee pot and cups. She shut the door carefully behind her before lifting her head and smiling at Daisy who smiled back.

'The mistress had a late breakfast with the parson.' It was said in explanation of the trolley and Daisy nodded. 'She wasn't expecting the family to call, you see.' Daisy nodded again, she didn't know quite what else to do, and was a little taken aback when the girl, after hesitating for a second, left the trolley where it was and nipped across to her side. 'I don't know why you're here, lass, but don't take no notice of them two in there, all right?' she said under her breath. 'You'd have to be a lord or a duchess to get a civil word from Miss Cecilia or Miss Felicity.'

Daisy stared into the pretty little round face, the girl's kindness warming her. 'I'm here about the position of nurse companion,' she whispered back. 'Sir Augustus sent me.'

'Did he?' Kitty Murray tried to hide her surprise, not wishing to offend this lovely but lost-looking lass who she didn't doubt had been treated like muck by the mistress's nieces. The airs and graces them two put on you'd think they never had to visit the privy like everyone else. But this lass *did* look church-mouse poor, and young with it. Anyone less like a nurse companion she'd never seen. Still, it was none of her business. And then contradicting her last thought – something Kitty did fairly frequently – she said, 'You done anything like that before then?'

'No . . . no, I haven't.'

So why had Sir Augustus sent her here with those two? And then, as voices rose in the drawing room, Kitty said quickly, 'Sounds like the parson's going, I'd better take the trolley along. 'Bye, lass.' And she scooted off with a nimbleness that belied her very nearly pear-shaped body, her roundness of girth tapering towards the top of her head where a precarious bun of thick curly brown hair wobbled.

She was nice. Daisy stared after the departing figure with the feeling her last friend in the world had just deserted her, and then turned her head back towards the drawing room as the door opened.

A man came out, obviously the parson from his dress, and said to someone within the room, 'Don't be silly, I am more than capable of seeing myself out. This is my home from home after all,' before he closed the door behind him. It was a precise action, and his footsteps were precise likewise as he crossed the hall, stopping in front of Daisy to say, 'So you are the valiant young person who rescued Miss Fraser's nephew from the sea? How do you do, young lady?'

This kindness was unexpected, and the courtesy more so. Daisy found herself struggling for words, which was unusual, but managed to say, 'How do you do, sir?' fairly coherently.

'Oh, how remiss of me. I am Parson Lyndon, a friend of Miss Fraser's. And you are . . . ?'

'Daisy. Daisy Appleby, sir.'

'Well, you have done the Frasers a great service, but of course you know that.' The parson smiled.

Daisy made no answer to this but smiled back into the pleasant young face in front of her.

She had always somehow imagined that parsons and such were getting on in years, but this one seemed nowhere near as old as her brother George, and he was tall and good-looking to boot. His hair was dark and so were his eyes, his features fine – it could all have appeared severe on someone else, but the kindly expression in his deep brown gaze didn't allow this.

'I must be going.' Hector Lyndon gazed down at the fishergirl who, it seemed, had turned the Fraser household on its head, and had to admit to a feeling of surprise. This fresh young face, obvious shyness and patent innocence were not at all what he'd expected after what had been said in the drawing room, but then he should have known better than to form an opinion from anything Wilhelmina's nieces said. He wasn't so naive as to believe the sun of social harmony set bright in an unclouded heaven over England, and although he'd only met Sir Augustus once had thought the gentleman very like his daughters in his chilly self-satisfaction and absolute conviction that he belonged at the top of the heap.

The clergyman became aware of the girl in front of him shifting her feet uncomfortably. 'I'm sorry, I was daydreaming.' He smiled again, but this time her answering smile was uncertain.

He had disturbed her. Oh, dear, dear. She must be finding this visit overwhelming to say the least and he hadn't exactly helped matters. What could he say to put her at her ease? This would never do.

But the opportunity was gone when, in the next instant, the door to the drawing room opened and Felicity's voice said coolly, 'Appleby? My aunt will see you now,' her cold gaze moving over the two of them in such a way that Hector found himself hastily taking his leave.

When Daisy stepped into the drawing room her overall impression was of its richness of colour, followed almost immediately by a renewed churning in her stomach when she found herself facing the mistress of Evenley House. Wilhelmina Fraser had the family colouring and strong features, her black hair – in which no grey was apparent – piled high on her head in intricate curls which would have done credit to a woman half her age. Her eyes had the dark lustre of polished ebony, but the sickly-pale quality to her lined skin and the blue tinge to her lips betrayed her ill health. The main impact of her appearance, however, was an impression of indomitable authority and steely determination. It was this determination which had kept Wilhelmina alive for the last ten years since the heart condition first diagnosed in her as a young child had worsened.

The grand lady stared at the fishergirl, and when one of William's sisters opened her mouth to speak Wilhelmina forestalled her niece with a pre-emptive, 'So you want to work for me, do you?' directly to Daisy.

'Yes, ma'am.' Daisy hadn't expected it to be put quite so bluntly.

'Why?' Those black eyes were fixed on her face and were full of animation, their brightness only serving to emphasise the dull, parchment-like quality to skin drawn tight over the bones beneath.

'Ma'am?'

'It's a simple enough question, child. I asked you why you wish to take up employment as a nurse companion to an old lady, work which will involve seeing to all my needs and dancing to my whims on occasion, because the elderly can be difficult. Were you aware of that?' The piercing eyes

132

flashed towards her nieces for an instant but Wilhelmina continued speaking with scarcely a pause. 'Is it because you feel you have a vocation or a leaning towards such a position, or is the inordinate amount of money my brother is offering the chief inducement?'

Daisy's eyes narrowed. In spite of her obvious ill health and age, this was not a woman in her dotage. Although they were poles apart in station, Sir Augustus's autocratic sister reminded her of her own granny, and her granny had never been one for blathering but preferred to call a spade a spade. And she didn't like being humoured either. Daisy continued looking straight into the obsidian gaze even though her heart was pounding so hard it was threatening to choke her as she said, 'It's the money, ma'am.'

She heard a quick intake of breath behind her, and one of the sisters murmuring, 'Well, really!' But Wilhelmina Fraser's face had not moved a muscle.

'And for the sum of six pounds a month you will endure working for a crabby old woman who is perverse, trying and vexatious, and enjoys being that way?' she asked.

'For six pounds a month, I'd endure much more than that, ma'am.'

'Really, this is too much! You can't let this . . . this *person* speak to you in such a way, Aunt.' Cecilia's long face was suffused with angry colour, her thin nose fairly quivering as she stepped round Daisy to stand in front of her aunt. 'Surely you can see now that this whole scheme is utterly preposterous?'

Wilhelmina considered the girl's shrewish face for a moment. Her nieces were as plain as pikestaffs, and with as little shape too. Their private tutors had taught them a smattering of French, and impressed on them that the ability to sketch and paint in watercolour was an essential part of their education, along with accomplishments like playing the piano and fine stitchery. But it wasn't their placid acceptance of the constrictions their father had placed on their minds and bodies since birth that made her dislike them so intensely, and not even their unshakeable belief in their own aristocratic supremacy. No, it was their meanness of mind, their spitefulness, and she was seeing these attributes in full measure today over the matter of this fishergirl.

Wilhelmina reached for the small brass bell on the polished table at the side of her chair without answering Cecilia, and it seemed to Daisy that no sooner had it been rung than the door opened to reveal the maid. 'My nieces are leaving.' Her voice was glacial.

'But, Aunt—'

'And when you have shown Miss Felicity and Miss Cecilia out, you may inform Cook we have a guest for luncheon, a guest to whom the Frasers are deeply indebted incidentally. This is the young person who pulled my nephew out of the sea when he was foolish enough almost to drown himself, Kitty.'

'Pleased to meet you, miss.' The maid bobbed her head at Daisy, lowering it again quickly but not before Daisy had noticed the twinkle in her eyes. Kitty had caught the message her mistress had sent her and was relishing the bristling outrage evident on the faces of the two younger Frasers. So was Wilhelmina, if the gleefully vituperative expression on her face was anything to go by.

'Have you a message for Father?' Cecilia had swept over to the door with Felicity at her heels.

'Only that I am delighted to avail myself of his kind offer.'

'Very well. Good afternoon, Aunt Wilhelmina.'

'Good afternoon, Cecilia. Felicity.'

Once the door had closed Daisy was conscious of a feeling of relief which made her want to sag, and it was with some effort she kept her back straight and her chin up.

'Don't stand there as though you're on parade, child.' It was irritably spoken. 'Sit down and tell me about yourself. And as you may have gathered there is no excess formality in this household, but that does not mean I am a soft touch. I might look old and decrepit, but it would be a brave man or woman who'd attempt to pull the wool over my eyes. Do we understand each other? You will doubtless rue the day you walked through that door. Everyone else seems to.'

Daisy sat down on the small upholstered chair her new mistress had indicated and looked full into the tired old face in front of her. Her voice was soft when she replied, 'Not everyone surely, ma'am. Your maid seems very happy.'

'Kitty? Oh, Kitty is a good girl,' Wilhelmina acknowledged drily, before adding, 'Bright as a button, aren't we, miss? I hope that continues when you're called in the middle of the night to attend me when this wretched heart of mine disturbs me. And I need help to bathe and walk on bad days, and insist on a tour of the garden every day which means, whatever the weather, you will be assisting me while I take the air. But enough of that. Tell me about yourself.'

'Yes, ma'am.' Daisy paused, not knowing where to start or how much Sir Augustus's sister expected her to say.

'Start at the beginning, child.'

Startled, Daisy raised her head to meet those bright black eyes again – eyes that seemed anomalous in the rest of the lined face and emaciated body. It was as though Miss Fraser had read her mind and that was a little unnerving.

Obediently she began to speak and continued for some time. When at last she was silent it was a few moments before Wilhelmina said, 'I can see now why the six pounds a month is so important. Will it be enough?'

'I'm sorry, ma'am?'

'Will six pounds provide for all the needs you have to meet?'

135

It was a simple enough question, but spoken as it was, in a deeply moved voice which was soft and kind and quite at variance to anything which had gone before, it nearly proved Daisy's undoing. She had to gulp several times before she could say, 'Aye . . . yes, ma'am. Yes, it will be enough.'

Which words heralded the beginning of her life at Evenley House.

Part 2
The Green Baize Door

Chapter Eight

It was five days after Tom's funeral, and the first day of the month of May, when Daisy presented herself early one morning on the doorstep of Evenley House.

The two-mile walk to her new abode had been a very pleasant one. She had passed dew-spangled gossamer spider webs in the hedgerows of the country lanes, and in the last few days spring had announced itself with a vengeance, as though to make up for lost time. Although it was still cold, bright sunshine had lit the morning, and the banks to either side of the lanes had been starred with daisies, buttercups and dandelions. It was a day for cuckoo song, for flowering laburnum, lilac and larch, and in spite of her sadness Daisy had felt her spirits lifting a little once she had left the fishing village behind her. For the moment the sight and sound of the sea was a constant reminder of the father and brothers she had lost, and she was not sorry to be removed from it.

The funeral had been harrowing, but the grief and heartache had been tempered slightly by the fact that Tilly and her bairns would not now be separated but could all live under one roof along with Nellie and Margery. Tilly in particular had been overcome with gratitude when Daisy had put forward her plan for the future to her family, and each one of Daisy's brothers had privately expressed their own thanks to her for the huge weight she had lifted off their shoulders.

Daisy's new mistress had advanced half her first month's wages at their initial meeting, which had meant the rent was taken care of and Daisy was starting work secure in the knowledge that she was leaving her granny and the other two women well able to afford food and other essentials such as oil and candles.

Her granny had hugged her tight in an unusual display of affection which had touched Daisy greatly. Although she knew Nellie loved her all the world the old woman was not physically demonstrative, and to have the gnarled old arms holding her close while her granny had whispered amid tears that she was a brave, bonny lass and her mam and da would have been proud of her, had caused the lump in Daisy's throat almost to choke her. Tilly and Margery had embraced her too, their faces as bereft as if she was travelling two hundred miles instead of two, causing Daisy to remind them all that she would be seeing them in six days' time, on her half-day off.

She had sniffed and gulped on the first half-mile of the walk to the house, but then the bright blue sky overhead and the singing of the birds as they busily went about the business of feeding their young had quietened her heart. She was doing the right thing, the only possible thing. Whatever the future held she had to face it head on now.

It was Kitty who answered her knock on the door, and the little maid's beaming smile along with the words, 'Oh, lass, it's right good to see you, I've been hoping and praying you wouldn't change your mind,' did Daisy the world of good.

'Come along to the kitchen, the mistress isn't awake yet,' Kitty continued as she stood aside for Daisy to enter the hall and then shut the door. 'She rarely rises before nine 'cos she don't sleep too well most nights and likes a lie in. You'll find it's normally a slow start to the day here.'

Daisy followed Kitty down the hall and then into the

right-hand corridor she had noticed on her first visit to the house. 'Back there' – Kitty paused and turned for a moment, gesturing to the left fork – 'is the mistress's bedroom, bathroom and private sitting room. It used to be a study and library but when the mistress got too bad to use the stairs, Sir Augustus had it all altered. Lovely it is, but you'll see that and the rest of the house later. The drawing room you've seen, and the morning room is on that side as you come in the front door. On the other side is the main sitting room and the dining room, all right?' Kitty continued walking again, saying as they passed another door, 'That's the breakfast room but it's not used much now as the mistress always has a tray in her own quarters, 'cept when the parson comes, and then they have the trolley in the drawing room. And here's the kitchen.'

So saying Kitty flung open the door in front of them to reveal a large, long stone-flagged room which, although smaller than the one at Greyfriar Hall, to Daisy's quick glance seemed just as well equipped and appeared beautifully clean.

There was a welcoming glow from the large range which was a closed type with what looked like two ovens for roasting and baking set to either side of the enclosed grate which had the most enormous clippy mat Daisy had ever seen spread in front of it, thick and brightly coloured.

This and the solid kitchen table at which Gladys and Harold Murray, Kitty's parents, were sitting over breakfast, were the two things which registered first in Daisy's whirling mind. She had met the couple briefly on the afternoon she had been engaged, Sir Augustus's sister having summoned the Murrays to the drawing room for the purpose of introducing her new nurse companion to the rest of the staff. In the presence of their mistress the cook and her husband had been all smiles and ingratiating charm, but now, as Daisy smiled politely and said, 'Good morning,' neither responded beyond a cursory nod.

'Sit down, lass.' Kitty pushed Daisy down into one of the straightbacked chairs around the table, and it was only then that Gladys raised her head and really looked at her, her voice flat as she said, 'You've arrived then.'

'Aye . . . yes.'

Their breakfast looked to be a very substantial one. The cook's plate was heaped with eggs, ham, fried potatoes, tomatoes, mushrooms and broiled haddock, and there was a large plate of toast and another of shives of white bread in the centre of the table, along with a platter of butter and various preserves.

Gladys barely paused in her task of shovelling the food from her plate into her mouth, and her husband, who was as thin as his wife and daughter were plump, continued doing likewise as Gladys said, 'Aye, well, that's all to the good 'cos we need to get a few things straight afore the mistress rings for her tray.'

Daisy stared into the woman's fat, rosy-cheeked face, aware her stomach was turning over the way it did when she knew some kind of confrontation was looming.

'Me and Harold have been with the mistress ever since Sir Augustus first set her up in her own place when he got wed,' Gladys said stolidly, food splattering out of her mouth and on to her plate as she spoke. 'The mistress had been in charge at Greyfriar afore then, of course. With Sir Augustus's parents having died when him and his brother, Mr Francis, were no more than youngsters, it was Miss Wilhelmina who took on the role of guardian to 'em both, her being a good few years older. She used to act as hostess for all the fancy balls an' such Sir Augustus was fond of once he reached marrying age, but then he met his wife and the two of them – his wife and the mistress – didn't hit it off by all accounts. Two women stirring the same pot with different spoons, you see. The mistress liked things done one way, and Sir Augustus's new bride had her own way of thinking on matters. Which brings us to you.'

'Me?' Daisy had been wondering where all this was leading but she still didn't see what Kitty's mother was getting at. The woman was clearly rattled about something but her heavy-jowled face was giving nothing away, although there was a distinctly shrewd gleam in her button eyes. As for her husband, ferrety would best describe his slight frame topped by a pointed face and teeth that were blackened and fang-like. But Harold must be a hard worker, she added silently, almost by way of apology for the previous thought. The garden was a picture.

'Aye, you. The fishergirl who's landed on her feet.'

'Here, lass, get this down you while it's nice and hot, an' help yourself to milk and sugar.' Kitty broke into the conversation, ignoring a dark look from her mother as she placed a large mug of black tea in front of Daisy, pushing a basin of sugar and a small white jug filled to the brim with creamy milk in front of her a moment later. 'You had your breakfast?' she continued cheerily. 'There's plenty if you're peckish?'

'I ate before I left home, but thank you.'

'*Excuse me, miss*.' Gladys was fairly bristling as she glared at her daughter. 'Whose kitchen is this?'

'The mistress's,' Kitty returned cheekily, purposely mis-understanding her mother's meaning, 'but as she isn't here, I thought I'd do the honours.'

The other girl winked at Daisy as she turned from the table and walked over to fetch her plate from the long slatted steel shelf above the enormous range where she had obviously placed it to keep warm before she answered the door.

'Any more of your lip, my girl, an' I'll give you a skelp o' the lug.'

Kitty said nothing to this, merely settling herself down at the table and beginning to eat her food. Daisy glanced from one to the other. It was clear Kitty and her mother did not get on, and the father seemed well under his round little wife's thumb.

Gladys gave her offspring one last vitriolic look before turning back to Daisy. 'Like I said, we've been with the mistress for donkey's years, and there's nowt that goes on at the big house we don't hear the ins and outs of. Am I right, Harold?'

He nodded without raising his eyes from his plate where he was mopping the last of the yolk from his eggs with a piece of crusty white bread.

'Aye, when Sir Augustus comes to visit the mistress, Mr Kirby's not above sitting and passing the time of day with us and sampling a shive of fruit loaf or gingerbread, which shows how well we're thought of at the big house. A real gent Mr Kirby is an' no mistake, isn't he, Harold?'

It was said with the clear intention of provoking her, and Daisy knew this. She would have known it by the expression on the woman's face, even if Gladys hadn't taken care to labour the point that she and Harold were fully aware of the state of play between Mr Kirby and the new nurse companion.

Daisy's mind was moving very swiftly now. She would have liked to have told Kitty's parents her real opinion of Sir Augustus's valet, and she sensed this was exactly what Gladys was expecting her to do. For some reason the cook had decided to dislike her, and her husband was obviously of like mind. But not Kitty. The maid was for her, and equally set against her parents. This was clearly a divided household. Oh, dear, and just when she had thought she might have sailed into calm waters for a while.

Daisy breathed in to steady herself and said lightly, 'You are, of course, entitled to your opinion of Mr Kirby.' She allowed the merest pause before she added in the same tone, 'As am I.'

There was silence for a moment before Gladys spoke again, and the sarcasm in her tone was evident when she said, 'And him of you. Oh, aye, him of you all right. No one can pull the wool over Mr Kirby's eyes, however much they may lick the boots of the gentry.'

Don't lose your temper. Start as you mean to go on. If you let her get under your skin now you'll be forever scratching. It was as though her granny was in the kitchen with her.

Daisy forced herself to take a sip of tea before she said coolly, 'Sir Augustus thought highly enough of my suitability as a nurse companion to recommend me to his sister, Mrs Murray, and he didn't strike me as the type of man who would appreciate having his opinion challenged. Of course, I could mention to the mistress that you and your husband are unhappy about my appointment in view of what you have apparently heard from . . . other quarters? I'm sure the matter would be investigated very thoroughly, and then we would all know where we stood with our respective employers. I, for one, would have no problem with that at all. Of course, I can't speak for Mr Kirby.'

She didn't know where the words were coming from or how she had restrained herself from going for the cook, but she blessed the strength of mind that enabled her to take another sip of tea, as though she wasn't in the least concerned about what this horrible woman had insinuated.

The cook's face was burning now, colour suffusing it until it was almost scarlet. Gladys glanced at her husband who had just started on a piece of toast and was keeping his head down, and then at her daughter who was not bothering to hide her wide smile. She ran her tongue over her lips, and then said tightly, 'No need for that, I'm sure. I was only saying, that's all.'

'Perhaps it would be better if you waited until you had all your facts straight in the future, Mrs Murray?'

She had done it now, Daisy thought. She had burnt her bridges with this particular woman and they would never be friends, however long she worked here, but it couldn't be helped. The cook's antagonism needed to be faced and dealt with or Gladys Murray would have thought she'd got the upper hand and made her life miserable.

Her da had always said that when you weren't the person who started the trouble, you had to make doubly sure you were the one who ended it. 'Turn your back on a fight an' likely you'll end up with a knife atween your shoulder blades.' She had heard him say it time and time again to the lads when they had been younger. 'Face 'em, an' ten to one you'll find you're bigger an' uglier than the other bloke, an' if you're not, you might fool him you are.' And then he would grin. *Da*. Oh, Da, Da, Da. Suddenly the longing to see her da's face if only for a moment or two, to see the love in his eyes, was so strong it was a physical pain in the middle of her chest. But she couldn't, she couldn't ever, see him again.

'By, it comes to something when I can't have a bit crack in me own kitchen.' The words were muttered through the cook's gritted teeth.

Daisy rose from the table. She needed to get out of here for a few minutes. Now the unexpected confrontation was over she felt sick and shaky inside but she couldn't let the cook see it. She glanced at Kitty, who had pushed her plate aside and also risen, and said quietly, 'Could you show me where my room is? I've left most of my things at home' – she hadn't, but she would rather have been hung, drawn and quartered than admit in front of the cook and her husband that her pathetic little bundle was all she possessed in the

146

world – 'and I might as well get packed away before the mistress wants me.'

'Aye, lass. Come on. The air's fresher once you leave here,' said Kitty stoutly. Once they were outside in the hall, however, the maid's brashness disappeared, and she said softly, 'Don't take no notice of me mam, lass. She's a sour old wife if ever there was one. I reckon that rhyme the bairns sing was made for her.'

'Rhyme?' The girl's kindness was more debilitating than Gladys's spite, and Daisy had to gulp hard before she could speak.

'Aye, you know, the one all the wee lasses skip to when they're bairns.'

And when Daisy shook her head, Kitty began to chant softly, pretending to skip with an imaginary rope:

> 'Sour is as sour does
> And sour suits the lemon.
> Not so though the bonny wife
> Who at the start of wedded life
> Did give her man the sort of strife
> That sent poor Jack fair barmy.
> That's why he joined the army.
> One, two, buckle her shoe . . .'

As Kitty continued with the rhyme, her eyes bright, Daisy began to laugh, and when the other girl paused, panting, Kitty said, 'You mean to say you've never skipped to that one as a bairn?'

There had never been any spare time for playing games or skipping when she was a bairn, and she'd been running her da's house at eight years old. Daisy didn't go into all that, merely shaking her head as she thought, She's as good as a tonic, this lass.

'Mind you' – Kitty now thrust her head closer, her voice

conspiratorial – 'me da never joined the army. Had it too cushy here for a start. Besides which, if ever there was a Jack for a Jill, it's me mam an' da.'

'You're not close to them then?'

'Close to me mam an' da? Blimey, lass, I'd as soon be close to a dose of the fever.' Kitty grinned at her and now Daisy laughed out loud.

There was something immensely likeable and funny about the little maid with her wobbling bun of curly brown hair and her smiling face. Daisy found it amazing she had come from the two in the kitchen.

'Look, you take no notice of me mam, like I said. She's got the jitters, see? All on edge you'll step on her toes and get on too well here. Me mam fancies she's like that' – she joined her two hands together in a handshake – 'with the mistress, but I reckon the mistress know's what's what. She's not daft, her, but me mam's a good cook an' me da's a hard worker and so they suit. Me mam's been used to having it her own way with the other nurse companions that have come and gone. They've all been scared to death of the mistress and too anxious to please everyone if you ask me, but from what me mam heard about you she clicked on you're not like them. They were all educated, you see, gentlewomen fallen on hard times and so on. No match for me mam. But you, you're a tough 'un and she hasn't got the edge with you.'

Daisy blinked. Kitty meant all she had said as a compliment, but it was odd to be told she was no lady, uneducated and hard-nosed to boot – as a commendation. She must remember to tell her granny all of this, word for word. She'd split her sides laughing, her granny would.

'Come on, I'll show you your room.' Kitty continued talking as they climbed the magnificent staircase, saying, 'There's five guest bedrooms now the mistress's old room is one too, but it's once in a blue moon anyone comes to stay overnight. People just visit in the day, and then they don't stay too long 'cos of tiring the mistress, you know?'

At the top of the staircase there was a thickly carpeted corridor branching to right and left, and as in the hallway below there were fine pictures hung on the grey-painted walls.

'The mistress's old quarters, the master bedroom you might say, is right at the end there and has its own bathroom.' Kitty pointed to the right. 'Next to it are three other bedrooms with another bathroom between them. Both the bathrooms have a dry closet attached to them. This way' – Kitty turned to the left – 'there's two connecting rooms which was the nursery when the old owners had it, and that has its own bathroom an' all.'

They passed the door to this suite and then stepped down on to what appeared to be another small landing which had one door leading off it. When Kitty opened this, Daisy noticed that the other side of the door was covered in green baize. Kitty followed her eyes and said briefly, 'You're in the servants' quarters now. Your room's the first one and it's the best of the lot. Me mam's always hankered after it but they – me mam an' me da, that is – are right at the far end. I'm next to them and then there's another small room the size of mine that's just used for storage and such these days, and that's between your room and mine.'

Daisy glanced about her. The walls were whitewashed and clean but there were no pictures and no carpet in this corridor, just plain unvarnished floorboards. The only light came from a small slit window situated at the top of the wall below the ceiling.

'There's a bell above your bed that clangs if the mistress needs you in the night, the pull's next to her bed. Sir Augustus had that done when the mistress had to move downstairs,' Kitty continued, adding, as she pointed to the door they had just passed through, 'An' mind the step out there, lass. I've lived here all me life and still I've tripped up more than once when I've been seeing to the slops. Nearly had a bucketful all over me and the carpet. I empty all the slops up here every morning and put fresh water in the jugs for washing once I've seen to the mistress's room. If you want extra water you'll have to see to that yourself. This is your room.' Kitty nodded towards the door nearest the green baized one. 'Oh, and if the mistress is really bad any time there's a couch for you to sleep on in the dressing room off her bedroom.'

After a moment's hesitation Daisy said, 'Why wasn't a room set aside for her nurse downstairs when the library and study were altered? Wouldn't that have been better?'

Kitty pulled a face. 'Aye, Sir Augustus thought that an' all,' she said ruefully, 'but the mistress wasn't having any of it. According to her she's not an invalid, see? Eeh, she can be right stubborn when she wants to be. Said she didn't want some nervous nitwit hovering over her every two minutes to see if she was still breathing. She likes her privacy, that's the thing, but then old people get like that, don't they?'

Not if they're stuck in a one up, two down fisherman's cottage. There was little dignity left for her granny. But it was no use saying so to Kitty so Daisy merely nodded, and then opened the door to her room as the other girl said, 'I'd better get back, there's the fire in the drawing room to see to before I take the mistress her breakfast tray.'

Alone now, Daisy looked round the room that was going to be her home from home in these strange surroundings. She stood just inside the door for a few moments as the sheer space that was all hers overwhelmed her after her tiny niche in the bedroom of the fishing cottage. It took her a second or two to realise that although the room was a good size, the fact that it was sparsely furnished made it appear even larger.

It held a single brass bed with a faded patchwork quilt, a chest of drawers and small wardrobe, and a stout marble-topped oak table with a jug and basin on it painted with bright red poppies. The floorboards were again bare, but a thick and new-looking clippy mat lay on the floor to one side of the bed and there was a rather enormous chamber pot, again decorated with poppies, under the bed.

Daisy walked over to the small square window through which sunlight was streaming, her heart lifting at the knowledge that this clean, bright room was hers. It had a friendly feel to it which was enhanced by the bright yellow curtains. The colour reminded her of the piece of cloth covering the makeshift table in her small nook at home, and when she looked out of the window on to the kitchen garden below her eyes were misty.

It was a minute or two before she left the window and walked across to the wardrobe. Once she opened it a musty smell tickled her nose. She pulled apart her small bundle of belongings which had been wrapped in Tilly's spare shawl. It didn't take long to hang her other set of clothes and cloak in the wardrobe, and place her two pairs of red flannel bloomers and vest in the chest of drawers. Lastly she placed her hairbrush and hand mirror, along with Alf's box, on top of the chest of drawers. Her unpacking completed, she walked across and sat down on the bed for a few moments, trying to clear her mind.

She was here, she had done it. She glanced across at the lovingly carved box and for a second or two remembered how upset Alf had been at her decision to work and live away from the village, and then she resolutely put the image of his face out of her mind. She couldn't think about Alf now or dwell on the feeling that she had let him down in some way, not when she needed to be strong.

And she certainly needed to be strong, not only to cope with Miss Fraser but with those two down in the kitchen.

And William? The name sneaked in as she sat in a shaft of sunlight on the bed, and she shut her eyes tightly for a moment. She probably wouldn't even see him again, she warned herself for the umpteenth time, and if he did visit his aunt he might not want to talk to a servant anyway. Although . . . she didn't think he was like that. And then she remonstrated with herself quickly. How on earth did she know what he was like? She had to stop thinking about him all the time, it was daft, stupid. Her feelings for him could come to nothing, she knew that, even if she didn't know exactly what those feelings were because she had never felt the same way about anyone else. A young lass's romantic fancy, her granny would say if she shared her confusion with her. Nellie had certainly dropped enough hints over the last few days to warn Daisy that any regard for Sir Augustus's son was born purely out of starry-eyed fascination, and although they hadn't discussed William at all he had been there between them both nevertheless. And perhaps her granny was right, Daisy thought reluctantly. She usually was.

She opened her eyes and glanced round the room again. This was a bonny room *but it was in the servants' quarters*. When – *if* she corrected herself sharply – William called, it would be to see her employer, and she would address him as befitted the young master of Greyfriar Hall. There was a chasm between them and it was unbridgeable. Those were the facts.

She stood up, smoothing down her skirt and adjusting the woollen shawl at her shoulders. In spite of herself her eyes were drawn to her heavy hobnailed boots. William, *Mr William*, was used to ladies whose dainty feet were shod in fine shoes with silver buckles and pretty little bows; ladies who had never done a day's work in their lives and would have a fit of the vapours at the mere idea of it. The upper class. Funny, but she had barely given the matter of the class system a thought until recent days, but then why would she? She had been too busy working and living.

Daisy shook herself – a physical action although it carried a mental admonition at the heart of it – and took a deep breath before walking over to the door. She must go and meet her mistress whereupon she would be instructed in her duties and learn what was expected of her. This was reality, working-class reality.

Daisy was halfway down the staircase when Kitty appeared at the bottom of it. As the maid saw her she said, 'I was on me way to get you, lass. I've just taken the mistress her tray and she wants you to go along. Come on, I'll take you.'

Daisy followed Kitty along the hall and into the left-hand corridor. There were two doors in this section of the house, one situated halfway along the corridor and the other at the far end facing them. This had a highly polished table with a fresh flower arrangement set in front of it, however, and was clearly not in use.

Daisy's first impression as Kitty opened the door was that she had stepped into another little house. She was standing in a beautifully decorated and furnished sitting room, and this, Kitty informed her, led on to Miss Wilhelmina's boudoir. 'That's to one side of the bedroom and bathroom,' the little maid continued as they walked across the room, 'with an office on the other. On the days she's not feeling too good she only needs to walk a few steps that way, you see. The bedroom and office overlook the orchard and it's grand in the summer and autumn.'

Daisy made no reply to this, feeling overwhelmed.

Kitty knocked at the door to the bedroom and as a voice from within said, 'Yes, yes, come in,' stood aside and waved for Daisy to go through as she whispered, 'I'm off to see to the drawing room.'

'There you are, child.' Wilhelmina spoke as though Daisy had just stepped into the other room for a while, and as she stared at the old lady she tried not to let her amazement show in her face at the sight of the strange apparition lying propped against numerous pillows in the huge bed in front of her. The room itself was a somewhat fierce assault on the senses, decorated as it was in various shades of pink with a salmon-coloured carpet and roseate curtains, but nevertheless it was the personage nestled amidst the rose silk covers Daisy's eyes focused on.

Her new mistress's nightwear was such that it wouldn't have been out of place in a house of ill repute, and topping the vivid pink nightdress and negligee adorned with black bows was a lace-bedecked bonnet affair which tied under her chin with great bows. An article which suggested the reason for the bonnet was residing on the glass-topped dressing table, and as Daisy's eyes flickered to the huge wig of black curls, Wilhelmina made a small movement with her head and said, 'I know, I know. You think I'm a strange old bird, and you're probably right.'

Daisy hesitated for a moment and then advanced further into the room as she said quietly, 'Not at all, ma'am. This is your home an' you should be able to live as you please in it.'

'Well said.' The bonnet bobbed in approval. 'My sentiments exactly. But we can't always do what we should be able to do, my dear, as I've no doubt you have discovered even at your tender age. In my late father's will he left me a portion of money – enough to buy this place – but the rest of my inheritance is in the form of an allowance which is controlled by Sir Augustus. Now, I am considerably older than my brothers and my father was well acquainted with the fact that I was not going to behave like a silly young thing, but still he decreed the allowance should come through my brother, his heir.'

Daisy didn't know what to say and so she said nothing. She really wasn't sure how to take her new mistress. Surely Sir Augustus's sister shouldn't be talking like this to a member of her staff? She didn't imagine so anyway.

'Because of this' – Wilhelmina patted her chest over her heart – 'it was made clear I should not entertain the idea of marriage. Indeed, if the doctors were to be believed I should not have reached my twenty-first birthday. But doctors are not always right. Remember that, child. Doctors are not always right. I believe I could have married and had a normal life. Certainly if I had known in my youth what I know now, my life would have been different.'

And then, with a sound of irritation deep in her throat, Wilhelmina said, 'Don't stand there like that. Come and sit down, here, in this chair next to the bed. And don't be timid. You didn't strike me as timid the last time we met. I can't abide timidity in man or woman, that's why so many of my previous companions have left in tears thinking me a wicked old woman. They allowed me to frighten and browbeat them, you see. No blood in their veins. Have you blood in your veins, Daisy?'

She hadn't expected Sir Augustus's sister to use her Christian name. These high-born folk seemed to favour their servants' surnames from what she'd seen and heard at Greyfriar Hall. Daisy stared into her mistress's lined face and hers was unsmiling as she said, 'Aye, ma'am, I've blood in my veins.'

'I thought so. Sit down then, child.'

Daisy sat, feeling somewhat bemused, and with scarcely a pause Wilhelmina continued, 'Where was I? Oh, yes, timidity. It is bred in the type of woman who becomes a companion, you see, that's the thing. When we spoke

155

last it seemed to me you cared deeply for your father, that you loved him. Did you?'

With some bewilderment, Daisy said, 'Very much, ma'am.'

The bonnet bobbed again. 'Then you are fortunate. I hated mine. He was a bully, cold, sanctimonious, rigidly controlling every aspect of my childhood and youth. Because I was a high-spirited and imaginative child I was punished frequently. I rebelled, I am still rebelling, that's why all this' – she waved her arms to encompass the room – 'is important to me. My father would have thought it disgraceful.'

The last words were said with a great deal of satisfaction and Wilhelmina stretched her scrawny neck as she peered at Daisy. 'So, child, do you think we are going to get along?'

She had been right to think Miss Wilhelmina was like her granny. In her own way she was a fighter and determined nothing would get her down. Daisy was finding she liked the old lady more and more with each passing minute. 'Yes, ma'am, I do,' she said with a wide smile.

'Good.' Wilhelmina smiled back. Then she said with one of the mercurial changes of mood Daisy was to learn was habitual with her, 'Kitty was concerned you would change your mind about taking up the position. She is starved of companionship, poor girl.'

'She . . . she seems very nice, ma'am.'

'Kitty? She has limited aspirations.' It was said dismissively. 'Now to practicalities. We cannot possibly have you walking around in those clothes. I have arranged for my dressmaker to call this morning at eleven oclock at which time she will measure you for the wardrobe required of my companion. You will need day dresses, afternoon attire and at least two or three evening dresses, along with coats, capes, stoles, gloves. And nightwear . . .

new nightwear and underwear. The shoemaker is calling tomorrow afternoon and the milliner an hour later. Be firm with him, very firm. He is Italian.' This was obviously felt to be adequate explanation.

'But, ma'am?'

'Yes?'

'The clothes . . . I can't . . .'

'My companion is a reflection of myself, Daisy. You must be properly attired at all times. Life is informal on the whole at Evenley House, but on the occasions I have guests for dinner you will be expected to join us and you will be suitably dressed. Do you understand me? Added to which . . .'

Now it was Daisy who enquired, 'Yes, ma'am?'

'My dear brother has graciously consented to pay all your expenses including your wardrobe. Let's enjoy ourselves, shall we?'

And for a moment Wilhelmina Fraser looked positively roguish.

Chapter Nine

It was now summer, a full-blown one in which hollyhocks, delphiniums, sweet-peas, ox-eye daisies, roses and a host of other flowers provided a glorious display of colour, and scented the garden of Evenley House with their heady fragrance. In the kitchen garden behind the house, runner beans, potatoes, carrots, and all manner of vegetables contentedly grew fat, while the small orchard beyond the kitchen garden looked set to produce a bumper crop of apples, pears and plums.

Daisy found it hard to believe she had only been living in these wonderful surroundings for three months. She looked forward to her half-day every Sunday at the fishing village, of course, and still missed her granny more than a little, but she had to admit that there barely seemed enough hours in the day in which to enjoy all the new experiences flooding into her life.

And there was William . . . Daisy paused just a moment before continuing to button the bodice of the afternoon dress she was changing into. This was one of the formalities her mistress insisted on; morning attire was strictly that. Once luncheon had been served and eaten a fresh outfit was the order of the day, and should they have a visitor or Miss Wilhelmina feel up to eating in the dining room in the evening then one of Daisy's three evening dresses must be worn.

The last button secured, Daisy inspected her reflection

159

in the mirror on the door of the wardrobe. A sparkling-eyed face stared back at her, cheeks flushed and lips slightly parted in happy anticipation. William had told her the night before that he would accompany his father on Sir Augustus's weekly visit to Evenley House, and she knew he usually arrived at two o'clock and left two hours later. It was now ten to two.

Daisy lifted her hands to her hair which was arranged on top of her head in a thick shining coil, patting it even though there wasn't a strand out of place. William said he had never seen hair with such a sheen to it, like raw silk he'd described it. But then he said so many nice things, and yesterday evening had been no exception. He had taken to calling several times a week lately, and at least one or two of these visits were in the late evening, often when Miss Wilhelmina had already retired for the night, or else when her mistress was having a bad day and had taken a rest in the afternoon. On those occasions it would be just the two of them in the drawing room, and once the weather had become so hot she had consented to take a walk with him in the garden a few times.

Daisy now pressed her hands to her cheeks which burnt at the memory. They were heavenly, those times, and yesterday had been the best of all. She was always very careful to make appropriate conversation, but at one point William had stopped in the middle of what he was saying and taken her hand, telling her she was the most beautiful thing he had ever seen. She quivered now, much the way she had done the previous evening. She had seemed to drown in the blue of his eyes before she had come to herself and had the presence of mind to remove her hand from his, but even as she had thanked him most properly for the compliment she had known her face was alight with joy. That was the trouble when she was with William, it was difficult to contain her feelings as any nice young woman should. But he more than made up for all the spite and hostility which came her way from Gladys and Harold Murray, and the slights Josiah Kirby always managed to inflict when he accompanied his master on his visits.

As though her thoughts had conjured up the occupants of Greyfriar Hall Daisy heard the carriage scrunching to a halt outside her open window, and with one final glance in the mirror she turned and left the room.

'You ought to be a fly on the wall here, Mr Kirby.' Gladys was talking, her chins wobbling with indignation as she passed a plate of freshly made bilberry tarts and another of hot girdle scones to the valet. 'Brass-faced she is. Aye, brass-faced the way she makes up to Mr William. An' the airs and graces she puts on! By, you'd think she was a lady born an' bred, you would straight, and butter don't melt in her mouth where the parson's concerned. She's pulled the wool over the mistress's eyes from the first day she walked in here.'

'That doesn't surprise me, Mrs Murray.' Josiah bit into a bilberry tart, smacking his lips before he said, 'Your pastry melts in the mouth as always.'

'Oh, Mr Kirby.' Gladys simpered her appreciation. He was such a gentleman.

'But as I was saying, it doesn't surprise me the girl has wheedled her way in, Mrs Murray. Didn't I warn you she would do just that very thing before she started? I told you to be on your guard because I'd got her measure all right. She's a strumpet. No decent man is safe around her, not the young master or the parson. She'd have them both and think nothing of it.'

'She's turned our Kitty's head an' all.' This was from Harold who had been quietly munching his way through a plateful of hot girdle scones dripping with butter.

'Aye, she has.' Gladys nodded her agreement vigorously. 'Kitty won't hear a word against the girl' – the three of them rarely referred to their common enemy by name – 'and my lass has taken to going to the fishing village of a Sunday afternoon alongside her. Thinks the sun shines out of her backside, my Kitty does, and no mistake.'

'You want to stop her going to that village.' Josiah's face was grim now. 'It's no place for a girl like your daughter, Mrs Murray, an innocent. There's some there who'd get her working the Sunderland waterfront for a bob a time as soon as look at her.'

'Oh! Oh, I told you, Harold, didn't I? I said to him we had to stop Kitty going, but the lass was determined and the mistress had given her blessing so . . .' Gladys shrugged beefy shoulders. 'The mistress has even ordered I get a basket of this an' that for the girl to take to her granny each week, *and*' – here the cook's red face grew redder still with indignation – 'she inspects it afore the girl goes.'

Gladys didn't add here that she had been chary about including all the items her mistress had listed for her to pack, a fact which had come to light when Wilhelmina had enquired of Daisy if her grandmother had enjoyed the roast chicken in cranberries – the same roast chicken in fact that Gladys and Harold had had for their supper.

Josiah shook his head sorrowfully as he finished the tart and reached for one of the warm scones which were filling the kitchen with their fragrance. He had his own opinion of his master's sister but wouldn't have dreamt of expressing it to Gladys and Harold. He deemed it in his own best interest to keep the relationship between the Murrays and himself cordial – they were a useful source of information as to the goings-on within this household, and the master liked to be kept informed about his sister's callers. Personally, however, Josiah had little time for Miss Wilhelmina's staff. As for the lady herself, there were occasions – as in the matter of the fishergirl, for instance – when Miss Wilhelmina behaved in a manner distinctly unbecoming to the Fraser name. When he thought of the licence his master's sister had given that chit!

Josiah had been privy to some of the old lady's outrageous views in the past while attending his master, views on matters no real lady should concern herself with, and to his mind his master's sister had gone a little funny in the head in her old age.

'. . . don't you think, Mr Kirby?'

He came back to his surroundings to realise the cook had been speaking and he hadn't heard a word. 'I'm sorry, Mrs Murray? I was enjoying your delicious cooking too much.'

Gladys wriggled with pleasure. 'I was just saying she needs taking down a peg or two, the fishergirl.'

'Indeed. Yes, indeed. But be patient and it will happen. All her fine clothes' – and Sir Augustus had been apoplectic when he had received the bills for those – 'won't make a scrap of difference in the long run, you mark my words.'

Josiah took another scone and basked in the almost reverent admiration of the others round the table. Yes, he would see his day with Daisy Appleby sure enough. However long it took, he would see his day with the little baggage. Sitting there in the drawing room right now as though butter wouldn't melt in her mouth, who did she think she was fooling? She was aiming high, no doubt about it, but that was all right. The higher she went, the harder the fall, and he would make sure she fell right back into the gutter where she belonged. Her days were numbered. No one cocked a snook at Josiah Kirby and got away with it, least of all a little chit from the bottom rung of the ladder.

*   *   *

163

He could sit and look at her all day long. She had been lovely before, her beauty his only clear remembrance in those first foggy, nightmarish days and nights after the shipwreck, but now, dressed and coiffured like a lady . . .

William settled himself further into the chair he had chosen on first entering the room an hour earlier with his father. He always made sure this was placed just behind Sir Augustus but at an angle where Daisy was clearly visible to him. It seemed almost impossible on such occasions that this slender, finely boned young woman had risked her own life to manhandle him out of the sea, but he had been sinking for the last time when he had registered that grip on his hair, his lungs bursting and the rancid taste of salt on his tongue.

Daisy had told him on one of his visits without his father that she would be sixteen years old in September, but looking at her now she appeared a woman full-grown. She carried her height well although she couldn't be more than five foot three or four, and the shining black of her hair had the effect of turning that wonderful skin to warm honey. He liked the fact that she wasn't concerned about letting the sun touch her; too many of the women he knew were like pale dolls with no warmth or life in them. Her eyes, though, were her main attraction. He couldn't ever remember seeing another human being with such distinctly grey eyes, and their thick lashes set under eyebrows which were fine and almost straight, and which did not follow the curve of the eye sockets, only served to make them more distinctive.

He watched now as Daisy served his father another cup of tea from the trolley at the side of her. When she turned to William she flushed slightly as she met his watchful gaze, but her voice was perfectly composed as she asked him if he would like another cup, and his was soft as he declined.

What was he going to do? It was a question William had asked himself more and more often over the last three months, especially after the times he had managed to see Daisy alone. They were enchanting, those visits, whether they had walked in the gardens or sat in the drawing room with Daisy presiding over refreshments he hadn't wanted but had accepted eagerly if it meant an extra few minutes with her.

He had found, much to his surprise, that he couldn't stay away from Evenley House for more than a day or two, especially after he had realised Parson Lyndon had his eye on Daisy. Useless to tell himself that the girl was too young for the parson or anyone else, that it would take years under his aunt's patronage for Daisy to grow into all the social graces and bloom as a woman. He was jealous, damn it, he admitted it, and the new emotion was not one William relished.

He knew his aunt had plans for Daisy – plans which his father seemed to be going along with, much to William's surprise. Already a tutor had been commissioned three mornings a week to further her limited education, and the man had reported that she was above average intelligence for her class.

For her class! William shifted in his seat, the irritation he had first felt when his father had repeated the comment coming to the fore again. That was the root of the problem that had him tossing and turning at night, this preoccupation of all and sundry with the matter of class. His Aunt Wilhelmina was taken with the girl and had already worked wonders in teaching Daisy the correct etiquette for various formal occasions, but her beginnings were such that she would never be accepted in good society in her own right. But then, who made up good society? Trace any of the better families back far enough and you eventually came up with murderers, cut-throats and rogues in the line, and half of them were mongrels with umpteen nationalities in their history.

William rose abruptly, annoyed with himself and the world in general, and then became aware of three pairs of eyes looking at him. 'It's too warm in here.' He smiled at his aunt as he spoke but it was forced.

There would be all hell let loose if he did what he really wanted to do at this minute and asked Daisy to take a turn with him round the garden. For months now his mother and father had all but thrust one woman after another into his arms in a manner he found positively blatant. Morning coffee, afternoon tea, dances, balls – there seemed to be no end to the occasions when friends of his parents would turn up with an unmarried daughter or daughters in tow, and archly suggest he might like to entertain the lady in question. And he used the term 'lady' lightly with regard to some of them.

'Maybe so, but I haven't got your red blood, m'boy. Mine is as thin as water,' Wilhelmina said briskly. 'Have a look at the garden if you like, Daisy will look after us in here.'

William kept the smile on his face with some effort as he declined the offer, something Wilhelmina noted. She liked her nephew as much as she disliked her nieces, and was glad she had consented to be his godmother and have the boy named after her when he was born, even though she had seen little of him until recent months. She was under no illusion as to what was bringing William to the house so frequently now, or should she say who? She glanced at Daisy as William walked over to the full-length windows, opening one and standing in the slight breeze it afforded. But although the boy came primarily to see Daisy, his visits at least meant the three of them sat and conversed together, and she was glad of the growing friendship between herself and her nephew who, up to this point in time, had taken

166

his cue from his father and mother and treated her as a somewhat troublesome old woman. And maybe she was. Yes, maybe she was at that, but she rather fancied the boy was finding out they had more in common than he had supposed. Of course there had been the odd strained moment when Parson Lyndon had been here when he'd arrived . . .

Wilhelmina pursed her mouth thoughtfully. William had an independent spirit and an enquiring mind, and these attributes had been strengthened over the last weeks, prompted in the main by the discussions the three of them so enjoyed. Daisy was not reticent about saying what she thought on most matters, and although it was true she was woefully unschooled, the child had a remarkably quick mind and instinctive insight. William found himself challenged by her on all sorts of concepts he had clearly accepted at face value before this.

Although perhaps that was a little unfair? Augustus was selective in what he told her about the boy, but she had gleaned enough to understand that William's last trip to Paris had been precipitated by his father's reaction to the young man's outspokenness regarding the ill treatment of some miners. Not a subject for the dinner table, Augustus had blustered when she'd told her brother that her sympathies were all with his son.

'We must be going. Gwendoline has arranged a rather elaborate dinner for tonight,' Augustus was saying now.

'Oh, yes?' Wilhelmina answered automatically. She wasn't in the least interested in another of her sister-in-law's endless dinner parties.

'The Chapmans and the Thornhills are coming, I think, and the Wynfords. Bringing their daughters. You remember Geraldine and Verity, Wilhelmina? Fine little fillies, the pair of them.'

167

A smothered groan came from the direction of the window.

So Gwendoline was still parading all the young local women of suitable age and pedigree in front of her son, was she? Wilhelmina could have groaned herself in sympathy for her nephew. She pictured in her mind's eye her sister-in-law's pretty face and delicate air which gave no indication of the fierce matchmaking urge beneath that insouciant demeanour. Augustus and his wife had decided it was time for William to make his choice and so start the business of producing more heirs for the Fraser name. Everyone knew what was going on: the other families, the girls themselves, even the servants no doubt. Wilhelmina had once likened similar spectacles to cattle markets and saw no reason to change her view. Now she said quietly but with an edge to her voice, 'Do they receive rosettes, Augustus? Blue for a winner, red for runner up, and so on?'

'Really, Wilhelmina, you go too far at times.' His countenance had darkened and his thin lips were drawn tight against his teeth, but Wilhelmina saw that her nephew was grinning and struggled not to smile herself when she said placatingly, 'I'm sure that's true, Augustus.' It was such a pity her brother had no sense of humour, it really did cover a multitude of sins.

'And have I mentioned that Francis will be with us in a week or two?' Augustus asked as he rose to his feet, his face cold.

'Oh, joy.'

'Quite.' For once Augustus didn't disagree with the sarcasm evident in his sister's tone. As difficult as they found each other at times, Augustus and Wilhelmina were united in disapproval of their younger brother who lived abroad for nine-tenths of the year where he spent his time in dissolute pursuit of all the vices known to man. A determined bachelor of promiscuous and inconstant taste in women, Francis Fraser was utterly selfish and incapable of either giving or receiving love. 'But at least he has had the grace to forewarn us of his arrival this time. Normally he appears on the doorstep without so much as a hail, well met, and the last time we were entertaining Lord Breedon.'

'How long does he plan to stay?'

'Who knows? No doubt his liver is playing up again and he imagines a few weeks away from his whisky- and wine-loving companions will set him to rights.'

'Or perhaps his gambling debts need to be paid?'

'Perhaps.' The two siblings studied each other for a moment before Augustus said, 'Whatever, he is a Fraser, Wilhelmina.'

There was another snort from the direction of the window, and Wilhelmina said quickly, 'Give Gwendoline my best wishes, Augustus.'

'Of course. Good day, Wilhelmina. I'm pleased to see you looking so well.'

Their leavetaking was as formal as usual, and it was evident Sir Augustus would not have acknowledged Daisy's presence but for his sister's replying, 'That is down to Daisy. I've never had such a stimulating nurse before, and I have you to thank for that, brother.'

'What? Oh, yes, yes.' Sir Augustus nodded abruptly at Daisy who had risen to her feet and now bobbed a curtsey in the way Wilhelmina had instructed her before she rang for Kitty.

Wilhelmina watched the graceful movements of the young girl she was growing increasingly fond of, and wondered if Daisy was aware that Augustus had only spoken so freely because he considered her a servant and therefore beneath his notice. Three times recently he had taken his sister to task on some small matter concerning protocol, but she knew full well what the real issue was. He objected to her informality with Daisy.

Augustus swept out of the room in his normal overbearing manner, Kitty scurrying down the hall to open the front door ahead of the visitors, but William lingered a moment or two longer. 'Goodbye, Aunt. Daisy.'

'Goodbye, m'boy. Don't keep him waiting, you know how it irritates him.' Wilhelmina's voice was brisk and matter-of-fact as though she wasn't aware how the two young people in front of her were looking at each other. Several times now she had noticed it and had to confess to an increasing anxiety where her nephew and nurse companion were involved. Of course it might be nothing at all but perhaps she would have a word with William when a suitable opportunity presented itself and they were alone. He was not an insensitive man but he was still a Fraser, and she wouldn't like to think he might treat the girl in a cavalier fashion. Not a girl like Daisy. No, she wouldn't like to think that at all.

It was one thing for young bloods like him to have intimate adventures among their own class, and goodness knew there were always enough young married women with boring elderly husbands not to mention middle-aged widows for that to be easy enough, but casual associations below one's station could only lead to pain and scandal for the woman concerned, whoever she was. She did so hope William took after his father, rather than his uncle, in matters of this nature.

Now Parson Lyndon, although obviously above Daisy in class, was a different kettle of fish entirely. It would be a wonderful match for someone of Daisy's origins if the parson should think enough of the girl to make her an offer. As a clergyman's wife she would be accepted far more easily into the lower-middle-class society the parson usually moved in. Yes, Wilhelmina could see that working very well.

170

She glanced at her young companion who was busying herself tidying the tea trolley, her cheeks flushed, and nodded mentally at the thought. But of course there were the girl's own inclinations to consider in all of this, and although Daisy was still very young she had a mind of her own.

Well, they would just have to see . . .

Chapter Ten

It was Sunday afternoon and the day was hot, the sky blue and high, but to the two young girls making their way along the shoreline towards the fishing village the weather was unimportant. Kitty had just survived a clash with her mother which had rocked the kitchen, and for the last half-an-hour had been trying to convince Daisy that the fight which had ended with Gladys cuffing her hard round the ear had nothing to do with her friend.

'I've always had barneys with me mam an' da, lass, you know that,' Kitty said, her plump face perspiring gently under her straw bonnet. 'If it weren't about me coming here it'd be something else. Before you came I'd often spend me half-day off inside, 'cos I'd got nowhere to go, and Mam always made sure she found me some job or other that couldn't wait. You know what she's like.'

Oh, yes, she knew what Gladys was like all right. Selfish and spiteful with a vicious streak that was quite at odds with her rosy-cheeked face and plump comforting appearance. Daisy glanced at her friend, who still bore the red imprint of her mother's hand on one cheek. She didn't like to think she had in any way provided an excuse for this latest physical assault. Kitty was already partially deaf in one ear as a result of her mother's frequent clips round the head which had been going on to a greater or lesser degree ever since she could toddle.

'Actually, lass, it was worth this' – Kitty touched the

side of her face where her ear was still ringing from the blow – 'to see the look on me mam's face when you came in the kitchen just as she clouted me and threatened to do the same to her if she touched me again. It'll make her think twice next time.'

Daisy smiled but said nothing. She doubted it. And she didn't understand why Kitty, who was so full of pluck and hardiness and spirit most of the time, didn't retaliate when Gladys got physical, if only to try to push her mother's hands away or something similar. It would be no exaggeration to say that Gladys often went out of her way to pick arguments and attempted to make Kitty's life miserable most of the time. And her father stood by and did nothing. If ever there was a hen-pecked man it was Kitty's da, all right.

'Eeh, surprise, surprise. Looks like Alf's decided to take a walk just about the time we come.' Kitty slanted a sly look at Daisy as she spoke. If she had expressed her true feelings she would have had to admit to a sense of bewilderment where Alf and Daisy were concerned. Here was a fine, good-looking man with his own cottage and boat who was clearly daft about Daisy, and yet she didn't want to look the side he was on. And he was so nice, Alf. Even Daisy said he was the kindest man she'd ever met. And kindness counted for something in this life, by, it did. Kitty touched her cheek again. Even without the cottage and boat she would have snapped Alf's hand off when he'd said he wanted to start courting, if she'd been Daisy.

'If it isn't me two favourite lasses come visitin' again.' Alf was smiling widely as he reached them, immediately taking the wicker basket with the hinged lid containing the food Wilhelmina had sent, and which the two girls had been carrying between them. 'An' bonny you both look, if I may say so.'

It was Kitty who answered pertly, 'Aye, you may, lad,

174

you may. The truth never hurt no one,' at which they all laughed, though for Daisy it was somewhat forced. Every Sunday he was waiting, even when it rained, and she wished he wouldn't. She had said so several times and tried to put him off, but still the next week he would be looking out for them – for her. And he was good to her granny and the others, regularly dropping in some fish when he'd had a haul and always making sure her granny had a couple of nice big crabs for the soup she loved so much.

Alf followed them into the cottage as he had taken to doing every Sunday, something else which disturbed Daisy. It was as though he was making a statement, one which said quite clearly he had a claim on her, and although he always divided his attention equally between them all, the hot look was in his eyes whenever she caught him glancing at her directly.

'Aw, lass, lass.' Nellie's face lit up at the sight of her granddaughter, and Margery, who had been sitting mending one of Tilly's bairn's torn smocks at the table, smiled too as she said, 'Hello, Daisy. Hello, Kitty.'

As Kitty seated herself at the table opposite Margery, Daisy walked across and hugged her grandmother before doing the same to Tom's lass, as she still thought of Margery. Then she said, 'By, it's quiet, Gran. Where's Tilly and the bairns?'

'The little 'un's had the skitters an' bin right middlin' the last few days although she seems to have turned the corner now. Her an' Tilly are upstairs havin' a nap, an' Rose took the others for the afternoon. I tell you, lass, that bairn might have had the belly ache but she's got a pair of lungs on her enough to wake the dead. There's none of us had a wink of sleep the last night or two.'

Daisy had been unpacking the basket Alf had placed on the table as her grandmother had spoken. Now she said,

'Miss Wilhelmina's sent you another cooked chicken, Gran, look. And there's some ham and eggs, and a full bag of sugar and eight ounces of tea. And she's sent some vinegar toffee and coconut ice for the bairns, and a drop of brandy for when you're feeling bad. She swears by a tot in her tea in the morning.'

'Does she? Well, I never.' Nellie stared in wonder, as she did every Sunday afternoon when the basket was emptied. 'You thank your Miss Wilhelmina for us, hinny.'

'Aye, I will.'

Alf had joined Kitty at the table and the two of them were chaffing each other over something or other, so while Margery brewed a pot of tea, Daisy busied herself putting the chicken, ham and eggs on the marble slab in the scullery. The tea and sugar she placed on one of the two shelves above the tin bath where other foodstuffs were kept, and then she came back into the living room and took the small bottle of brandy across to her grandmother. 'Keep this by you, Gran, for when you need it,' she said softly, smiling down into the wrinkled old face. 'And don't you give anyone else a sip, mind. Miss Wilhelmina was very insistent, it's all for you.'

'Oh, I'm all right, lass. Don't you fret about me. I've never had it so good an' that's the truth. This new mattress you got me makes me think I'm floatin' on air, I tell you. I've never slept so well in me life an' it's surprisin' the difference it makes to me poor old bones.'

'It'll be thick blankets for you next, and a feather bolster and new pillows.'

'Lass, I don't want you to spend your money on me, now then. It's yours, you earn it. Kitty let on to Tilly last week that sometimes you're up half the night with the old lady an' then dancin' attendance on her all day.'

'Gran, I like it. I like her, and that makes all the difference.' It did too, Daisy reflected, walking across to the table and picking up her tea and her granny's. When Miss Wilhelmina was feeling bad there was more physical work than she'd expected, what with lifting her and helping her wash and dress and things of that sort, but the old lady was skin and bone like her granny, and she'd been attending to her gran's needs for years.

Sometimes Miss Wilhelmina wanted her to read to her most of the night when she couldn't sleep, and Daisy still had to attend to her duties in the day, but that was all right. She knew just what medication to adminster now, and how to massage her mistress's back, limbs and feet to help her circulation, and she enjoyed pushing Miss Wilhelmina round the grounds for a couple of hours in the afternoons. That was always the best part of the day, even when the wheels of the chair got stuck and she had to heave and push until she felt her arms were going to snap.

And the money she was earning was the icing on the cake. It was grand that after she'd paid the rent due for the cottage and provided for all the household necessities, there were always some shillings left over – even when she had had to pay for the doctor from Whitburn to call and see her granny, like last month.

It was the first time they had been able to afford to have the doctor to the house; before this her da had always walked into Monkwearmouth and had a word with the apothecary. The doctor had come out with a list as long as your arm of things wrong with her granny, and now she was on all different sorts of pills and potions like Miss Wilhelmina. There was a noticeable difference in her health, however, so to Daisy it was money well spent each month.

She had saved the money left from her wages after the household was taken care of and recently had had enough to purchase a fine new feather mattress for Nellie. Once she had replaced her granny's blankets, bolster and pillows, she intended to put new mattresses and blankets on all the other beds and maybe buy a crib for Margery's baby. She had told Tilly to tell her when the bairns needed new boots and clothes, but they could shop at the second-hand market at Boldon or Monkwearmouth for those.

Daisy took the two cups of tea over to the pallet bed, perching on the edge of it and handing one to her grandmother. 'Here, Gran.'

'Ta, me bairn.' Nellie stared at her precious grand-daughter while slowly beginning to sip her tea. She looked at the fine clothes, which stated her lass had gone up in the world. By, but they'd had a crack or two the afternoon Daisy had first waltzed in dressed up to the nines, pretending to walk with a mincing air as though she was holding a parasol over her head. And then she had had them in stitches when she had listed all the items of clothing her mistress wore, acting as though she was climbing into them herself as she did so.

'Gran, you wouldn't believe it! I didn't know if I was on foot or horseback that first morning I saw everything,' Daisy had said. 'First there were thick woollen combinations, and over them white cotton ones with plenty of buttons. Then grey stays with suspenders and black woollen stockings, white cotton drawers with buttons and frills, and a petticoat-bodice with lovely embroidery and more buttons. There was a cotton petticoat and then a beautiful lace one with a flounce round the bottom. Honestly, Miss Wilhelmina was getting fatter in front of my eyes!

'On top of all that she wears one of her satin blouses, lovely they are, with a separate high starched lace collar fastened with gold studs. Oh, I hated them studs for the first couple of days, Gran, but I've got the hang of them now. Then a skirt which touches the ground, and a pocket watch – beautiful it is, all fancy gold and precious stones – fixed to the front of her blouse. Then, to finish off, round her shoulders she has a collection of silk and lace shawls, only the gentry call them stoles 'cos they're a bit like long scarfs. Then I lace her boots on to her feet. But they're not boots like we know, Gran.'

'They're not, hinny?'

'No. The leather is so soft it feels like a baby's bum and Miss Wilhelmina has more than ten pairs, all with different patterns on and beading and things. She doesn't like shoes, the mistress, but her boots are better than any shoes.'

And she had said to her lass, 'Her boots are better than the ones she's bought you?' as she had looked at the fine high button boots Daisy had been wearing, because she could hardly believe there was anything that'd surpass them.

'Twenty times better, Gran. Fifty! Oh, and she has scented hankies that are as fine as cobwebs, and so many hats, and a beautiful fur cape, and lots of other capes and coats.'

Aye, they'd had some fun that afternoon all right, Nellie reflected silently, but even then she'd had her concerns and they had mounted over the weeks and months Daisy had been at Evenley House. Look at her now, sitting as far away from Alf as she could get, and him like a dog with two tails come Sunday afternoon.

How many times did her lass mention Mr William on her visits? If it was once it was a dozen times during the hours she spent here. And her face would light up and her eyes would become starry . . . Dear God, dear God. Nellie continued sipping her tea, her thoughts racing. I've prayed to You to nip this thing in the bud and I'll continue praying till the breath leaves me body. Hadn't they had enough shame brought on their heads with Tom's lass? And Margery was a nice lass, a good girl, no doubt about it, but still the stigma of carrying a bastard would be with her to her dying day. And it'd be worse for her lass, her

Daisy. Tom would have married Margery and everyone in the village knew it, George and the others had made sure of that. But Daisy? If the worst happened she'd be packed off back here quicker than a dose of salts. That was the way of it with the gentry.

'Gran?'

When Nellie felt a warm hand close over hers she realised she had been staring at the lass without seeing her, and the look on her face must have been disturbing because Daisy was clearly agitated.

'You feeling bad, Gran? Do you want me to get your medicine?'

'No, lass, no.' How many times had she held her tongue lately? It was beginning to feel like too many. Her lass was blossoming, Daisy was more beautiful each time she came home, and she was frightened for her. Gut frightened. 'Lass, I want to say somethin' but 'tisn't easy. You . . . you might not thank me for voicin' it.'

Daisy smiled a small smile. 'Since when has that stopped you?'

Nellie couldn't return the smile and there was a tightness in her throat. It hurt her to say anything that might take the light out of her bairn's eyes, but she couldn't lie here another minute without speaking. She glanced across at the others who were chatting among themselves. They were used to her and her lass talking quietly for a while when Daisy first came home. 'It's the lad . . . Mr William.' The tone of her voice was different, she could hear it herself. Although still low and pitched so the others couldn't hear, it had a rough note to it.

Nellie swallowed and tried again. 'Lass, you know nothin' can happen there, don't you? Not between you and him?'

The girl's hand left hers and Daisy tossed her head but didn't answer. Nellie waited until the grey eyes met hers again and then she said softly, 'Hinny, he's a being from another world, an' whatever you're thinkin' he'll never leave it an' you can't enter it. You can't, lass. It don't happen.'

'Gran, you don't know that.'

'Oh, aye, I do, lass. I do. He couldn't survive a week workin' like Alf or your brothers, an' you wouldn't survive a day trying to live like the women he's used to. They wouldn't let you.' Nellie's face held sadness touched with pity. 'You might tell yourself it don't matter that he's never encountered hunger an' hardship, that he knows nothin' about workin' till he drops an' for a pittance that barely feeds a wife an' family, but it does, lass, it does. They think different, the gentry. Right from birth they do. He might be charmin' enough but he'll never marry you. He'd be content to take you down, oh, aye, he'd be quick enough to do that. But marry you? Never. Never, lass.'

'He . . . he's not like that.'

'Lass, they're all like that.'

Nellie watched Daisy bow her head, her voice a whisper as she said, 'Gran, you don't know him.'

'Neither do you, me bairn. Neither do you. Their world would never normally touch ours, that's the thing. Even in them big houses like Greyfriar Hall, the upstairs an' the downstairs still keep to their own worlds. But when you pulled him out of the sea it muddled things just enough to let you peep round the door sort of.'

'The green baize door,' murmured Daisy.

'What?'

Daisy raised her head and looked straight at her grandmother. Shaking her head slowly, she said, 'It doesn't matter.'

'You'll think on about what I've said? You know I'm right at heart, lass, don't you? An' it's only 'cos I care about you.'

Daisy bent over her and kissed the grey head, but she didn't say, 'Aye, I know you're right, Gran', or, 'Aye, I'll think about what you've said', as Nellie had hoped. Instead she reached for the empty cup in Nellie's hand and stood up, her voice quiet and flat when she said, 'I'll get you another sup, Gran.'

The air was soft and warm after the heat of the day on the walk back to Evenley House, and carried the scent of wild flowers and grass in its mild caress. Tiny gnats were dancing in dying shafts of sunlight and birds were singing. It was the sort of evening that normally filled Daisy with the inexpressible joy of being alive, but tonight, even as she responded with every appearance of normality to Kitty's chatter, her mind was going round in circles.

Her granny was worried about her, she knew that, and her granny was the last person in the world who would want to say anything which might hurt her, but Nellie didn't *understand*. William was different from his father and the rest of them. Her heart told her so. He didn't have a big opinion of himself, he was kind and gentle and – oh, just wonderful. She felt she really came alive when she was with him, even if Miss Wilhelmina was there too.

But when they were alone . . . The way he looked at her then . . . Her heart began to thud. Was she being stupid? He had taken her hand the last time they were alone; even before that he had always complimented her on her appearance and talked to her as though he valued her opinion and thoughts, but was that just his way? She couldn't take her eyes from his face when he was near her; did he think she was throwing herself at him? Worse, *demanding* the sort of attention he gave her? Her stomach turned over at the thought that William's regard might be prompted more by gratitude that she had saved his life than real interest in her as a person.

182

'Eeh, the carriage from the Hall is here, an' on a Sunday. That's unusual.'

Kitty's voice brought Daisy out of her reflections as they walked up the drive to Evenley House. Her head came up and she saw the waiting carriage. Was William here? Or perhaps it was just other members of the family? Lady Fraser and her daughters visited but rarely and never on horseback as Sir Augustus and William sometimes did. According to Miss Wilhelmina, Gwendoline Fraser was frightened of horses and had instilled this fear in her daughters.

Daisy compelled herself not to hurry but to continue walking at a sedate pace by Kitty's side, but once they entered the house by the kitchen door her heart sank as she saw Josiah Kirby sitting at the table. The valet's presence meant Sir Augustus was here, and even if William had accompanied his father she wouldn't have a chance to speak to him directly.

Josiah had been in conversation with Harold. Neither man acknowledged the two girls' entry into the kitchen, but the next moment Gladys appeared carrying a large silver teapot and looking more than a little flustered. Her small beady eyes flashed over her daughter and Daisy before she said to Kitty, 'You, get your uniform on. The mistress has company an' they want more tea.'

Kitty didn't remind her mother that her half-day fin-ished at midnight as Daisy had hoped her friend would do, especially after the scene which had occurred earlier. Instead she shrugged at Daisy and left the kitchen without speaking. As Daisy went to follow her, Gladys spoke again, her tone the same but the words phrased as less of an order. 'The mistress said if you got back afore Mr Francis left, she'd like you to go along to the drawing room.'

'Very well.' Daisy's face had no softness in it as she

183

looked at the cook. 'I shall go and tidy myself first
and be along directly.' She didn't allow her glance to
encompass the two men at the table who were now sitting
watching them, she never looked at Josiah Kirby if she
could help it. From her first week at Evenley House
it had been war, albeit a silent one, between the two
of them.

Once the kitchen door had shut behind her Daisy
moved swiftly along the corridor leading to the main
hall. Miss Wilhelmina hadn't spoken directly to her
about this brother, but Daisy had gleaned enough from
listening to her mistress's conversations with Sir Augustus
to know she needed to be perfectly composed and in
command of herself when she met him. She ran lightly
up the stairs and along the landing, but on coming to
the servants' quarters and opening the green baize door
she paused, fingering the coarse material for a moment
once she had stepped into the uncarpeted section of
the house.

Did William see her as being on one side of this
door and himself on the other? His eyes, his manner,
the way he looked at her sometimes could lead her to
think differently, but she was being foolish to hope for
anything more than what she now had, she knew that
at heart. Her granny was right. His class would never
accept her. Her chin came up in silent protest at the
thought. The more she learnt about the gentry and their
blue blood and this breeding business, the more . . .
nasty it seemed to her. Their morals were such that
often they didn't marry for love but for purely worldly
reasons regarding lineage or wealth, and it seemed almost
acceptable for them to have associations outside their
marriages. And yet they thought they had the blood-
bought right to look down on decent working men and
women who wouldn't dream of behaving in such a way.

It was wrong. And the more she learnt in her lessons with Mr Price, her tutor, and from her conversations with William and Miss Wilhelmina, the more she was beginning to understand that there were lots of things that were wrong at every level of society. Issues she had never questioned before.

The parson had said much the same thing the last time he had visited the mistress. He was a very intelligent and learned man, Parson Lyndon, and she had to confess she was in awe of him. He somehow seemed much older than his thirty-one years. Miss Wilhelmina had said this was because he was the only child of scholarly parents who had had him late in life and devoted themselves to his education. Daisy rarely said much when the parson was here but she enjoyed listening to the discussions he had with the mistress.

Kitty's door opening and her friend emerging clothed in her uniform brought Daisy out of her thoughts with a bump.

'Creeping Kirby would come today after the do with me mam,' Kitty said, adjusting her thick bun of curls behind her cap as she spoke. 'I bet he'd hardly got in the door before she was on about me.'

Daisy thought her friend's nickname for the valet was very apt, having seen him dancing attendance on Sir Augustus with an obsequiousness which was sickening. 'Kitty, your mam an' da might work hard but you work harder,' she said quietly. 'You're entitled to leave the house on your half-day and do as you please.'

'Aye, I think so an' all. I'll see you downstairs then.'

As Kitty's plump body waddled off, curls bobbing, Daisy opened the door to her room and stepped inside, flinging her straw bonnet on the bed. Five minutes later she was downstairs again after quickly changing her crumpled dress and washing her hands and face, reaching the drawing-room door just as Kitty emerged from the end corridor carrying the big silver teapot.

Daisy paused and waited for her friend to reach her.

'I've just had a right ear bashing from Creeping Kirby,' Kitty whispered indignantly, her cheeks scarlet. 'Going on about showing me mam respect and saying that me elders are always right, he was, as if he's in charge of us here as well as them at the Hall. He said your village was no fit place for a lass like me, and when I asked him what sort of lass that was – you know, sarcastic like – he nearly choked on his tea.'

'I wish he had done.' It was said with great feeling.

'Anyway, just as I walked out I told him the mistress was quite happy for me to go with you and if he didn't agree with that perhaps it'd be better for him to talk to her. To put his mind at rest like.'

Daisy was impressed. Kitty wasn't usually so outspoken. No doubt her friend's newfound courage with the valet would be laid at Daisy's door and seen as another nail in her coffin, but that worried her not a jot.

She knocked twice at the drawing-room door and opened it, allowing Kitty to precede her with the heavy teapot before following the maid into the room.

'Ah, Daisy. Come here, child.' Wilhelmina had inclined her head at Kitty and motioned with her hand for the teapot to be placed on the trolley. Now she focused all her attention on Daisy, patting the space on the sofa beside her.

She walked across to her mistress and sat down, silently chastising herself for the sharp pang of disappointment she'd felt when she had realised William was not present.

Sir Augustus was sitting at the far end of the room

near the french windows which were open to catch the warm evening breeze. After a cursory nod in Daisy's direction he returned to his languid contemplation of the gardens. His brother was seated in an ornate Queen Anne chair directly facing his sister and close to the sofa. It barely seemed adequate to contain his fleshy bulk.

'Francis, this is the new nurse companion who has been looking after me so well. Daisy – my brother, Mr Francis Fraser.'

Francis did not rise from his seat as he surveyed the young woman he had heard so much about, and from so many different sources. One did not show that courtesy to a servant. When Daisy rose and bobbed a curtsey before seating herself again, he said, 'So . . .' pausing for some moments before he continued, 'You obviously have hidden talents, m'dear.'

'I'm sorry, sir?' Daisy kept the polite smile on her face with some effort. She didn't think she had ever met anyone she found so instantly repulsive. Miss Wilhelmina's younger brother was making her flesh creep.

'A dainty little thing like you having the strength to rescue my nephew from the cruel sea,' Francis drawled mockingly by way of explanation.

He hadn't meant that at all. He'd been being nasty, suggestive, Daisy thought, dropping her gaze so she didn't have to look at the dark, somewhat rheumy eyes that were sliding over her face. The way he was staring was horrible.

Wilhelmina must have thought so too because her voice was abrupt when she said, 'Daisy, child, perhaps you would serve us all a fresh cup of tea?'

Francis Fraser was five years younger than his brother but now, at forty-five years of age, appeared twenty years older than Augustus, the penalties of a lifetime of debauchery evident in both face and body. Utterly self-centred and opinionated, he had been an unpleasant child and had grown into an even more unpleasant man, excelling only in his capacity for the wide variety of sexual perversions he so relished. Now, as he considered the slip of a girl who had caused so much trouble in various ways in his brother's household, and who had even got Kirby seething with resentment, he admitted to feeling a slight sense of disappointment.

From all that Augustus's womenfolk had intimated, and certainly from the little chat he had had with his brother's valet, he had expected to see a bold, brazen hussy who would be more than ready to meet him half-way in a lusty romp once his sister's back was turned. But that was obviously not the way this piece played it. Francis sighed inwardly. He had long since lost any inclination to cajole or inveigle, having found from experience that the type who demanded such treatment wasn't worth the trouble or the money, and rarely submitted easily to the more . . . unusual practices he forced upon them.

Still, this chit was comely enough, if a little thin for his taste these days. He allowed his eyes to wander over the slender waist and firm young breasts beneath the muslin dress. He liked his boys svelte and narrow; his females, whether young or old, he preferred with meat on their bones. Then again, the exceptions to the rule were what made life interesting . . .

'Do you like milk or lemon in your tea, sir?' Daisy had to force herself to look into the moist, high-coloured face which, although bearing the same unmistakable stamp as his siblings, seemed like a caricature of theirs. She didn't like Sir Augustus Fraser – Miss Wilhelmina's brother was cold and unfeeling and rarely acknowledged her presence – but there was no doubt he was a fine figure of a man and carried himself with authority, whereas Francis Fraser resembled nothing so much as a giant slug.

'Lemon.' He abhorred tea, in fact the last time he had drunk the obnoxious stuff must have been in this very room on his previous visit the year before, but Wilhelmina was always very chary of offering him anything stronger. As though a brief abstinence here would make any difference to the state of his liver! Augustus was the same; in fact they had had quite an altercation about his consumption of wine at dinner a year or two back, if he remembered rightly. Augustus had told him, in his usual icy manner, that if he wished to drink himself to death he was quite at liberty to do so but not at Greyfriar Hall. Damn it but he loathed the pair of them, and it was galling to have to tread so carefully. But he must, he must. Those gambling debts wouldn't wait and he needed Augustus's co-operation.

He watched Wilhelmina's protégée deftly using the lemon squeezer, his mouth twisting slightly. His sister was teaching her well, you'd think the baggage had been born to it instead of coming from the gutter.

Without a word of thanks he took the cup offered to him but in doing so managed surreptitiously to stroke Daisy's hand for a moment, feeling the recoil of the young flesh with a sense of amusement and resignation. She was going to insist he importune her, this one, solicit her attention before she consented to some sport. According to Kirby she had been at it from when she could walk, but now she had landed in clover with his sister maybe she thought she would assume the airs and graces of a lady? Well, he had nothing else to do in this dismal backwater, Francis decided, so he didn't mind playing along a little. But he could only be pushed so far.

It was almost half an hour before the two men took their leave of their sister, and Daisy wasn't the only one who found their visit trying. Wilhelmina had always seen Augustus as an inordinately proud and fastidious individual, and knew the only way the older brother could stomach the younger was to pay little attention to him, but it irritated her the way he had removed himself from the conversation that evening. She had no illusions about Francis either but had chosen not to probe into his life, sensing that besides his immoderate gambling and drinking there were other vices he indulged in that she would rather not know about. This evening, however, she had been forced to acknowledge that she really didn't want Francis within a hundred miles of Daisy, and had found this realisation disturbing. The girl was an innocent, Wilhelmina was absolutely sure of that, and the thought of her brother laying his hands on her . . .

As the sound of the men's departure faded, Wilhelmina cleared her throat. The more she had got to know Daisy, the more she had begun to think that if things had been different and she had been blessed with a husband and a daughter, the child she'd have wished for would have been very like the one sitting beside her now, in spirit and in nature. She had a duty to make things plain to the girl though of course it wouldn't do to refer to Francis directly, he was her brother after all.

She thought for a moment, reaching for her teacup and taking a sip of the tea which was now quite cold, before she said, 'It is a sad state of affairs but some gentlemen have come to think that the pursuit of respectability and moral purity in a girl is something to be overcome for their own gratification. Such individuals, of course, cannot be trusted.' She raised her head and stared into the grey eyes watching her.

Daisy's reply was without embellishment, probably

because the skin on her hand was still crawling from Francis's touch. 'Perhaps such men are to be pitied, ma'am, but whatever their position I really couldn't refer to them as gentlemen.'

Wilhelmina blinked. 'Quite.'

And after that there was nothing further to be said on the subject.

Chapter Eleven

His aunt had hit the nail on the head when she had likened these occasions to cattle shows. William glanced round the stately, shining dining table surrounded by glittering guests. The resplendent formality of the carefully displayed silver, crystal and fine china was only outdone by the brilliance of the jewels some of the women present were wearing.

William was very careful not to catch the eye of either of the Wynford sisters who had giggled their way through the ten courses presented to date, consisting of soup, fish, two hors d'oeuvres, two *rélèves* and four *entrées*. The girls were now partaking of the sorbets the footmen were serving to refresh the guests' appetite before they turned to the six roasts and accompaniments, which would be followed by a variety of puddings, ices and savouries, followed in due course by dessert, coffee and liqueurs.

The guests had been seated according both to the strict protocol their titles and wealth demanded, and – in the case of girls like the Wynfords sisters – their suitability to become the wife of the heir to Greyfriar Hall. The seating plan had accorded his mother sleepless nights William understood from his father, who had told him in no uncertain terms hours before that he was an ungrateful pup who didn't know how lucky he was.

This might be so, William acknowledged, his gaze drifting over Camilla Routledge who resembled the horses she loved so much but whose father was a lord, and Priscilla McKenzie who was as pretty as the Wynford sisters and just as empty-headed, but came with a higher pedigree. However, this was the third elaborate dinner party seating over thirty guests in as many months, and he was tired of them.

His eyes finally came to rest on Francis whom Gwendoline had seated opposite her son, much as she would have liked to banish her brother-in-law to the less important end of the table. But Francis *was* a Fraser.

His uncle was slobbering over a sorbet, his heavily embroidered waistcoat already stained with food. Not for the first time in the last few days William felt his stomach clench in protest that he was related to this pig of a man. It was unfortunate that Francis chose that precise moment to raise his head. The older man looked at the younger from under his heavy eyelids, reading the disgust etched on the handsome features before his gaze returned to his plate.

Insolent pup. Francis continued eating but he had ceased to taste the sorbet. William might not look like a Fraser but he was a chip off the old block all right, looking down his holier-than-thou nose at all and sundry just like Augustus, damn his eyes. Francis swore in his mind, the basest of oaths, but it afforded him no release. His nephew could justify playing the grand gentleman, couldn't he; William was going to be extremely wealthy one day, and through what? Purely an accident of birth.

Francis pushed his plate away, settling back in his chair as he drained his glass. He gestured to the footman standing behind him to refill his glass, and when the man hesitated for a moment before doing so, Francis ground his strong and surprisingly white teeth. So orders had been given to the servants to limit his intake? Damn it but he'd see his day with Augustus, with the lot of them.

He belched loudly, draining the glass again and indicating to the footman once more who this time obeyed instantly. So the man thought he might cause a scene, did he? Spoil his master's dinner party? Well, he might have at that. Although . . . Francis's eyes narrowed. If he went about this the right way he could teach them all a lesson they'd never forget without jeopardising his own position in the process. Kirby seemed to think that his master's son was taken with the fishergirl but that she was playing him for a fool, along with the parson fellow and plenty more greenhorns besides he didn't doubt. But exactly how far did William's interest in the chit go? Far enough to set her up in her own place so he had exclusive rights? He was still young enough to be idealistic, was William, and the fishergirl seemed wily enough to make the most of any opportunity, from what Francis had seen of her.

He sipped at the wine now, his mind – slightly befuddled by the numerous glasses he had consumed with his dinner to date, and not least the brandy from his hip flask which had been refilled twice during the day – struggling with half-formed thoughts. The first thing was to gauge how badly William was smitten, he'd find some opportunity to do that or contrive one. And he might get Kirby in on this, under the guise of being concerned for the young master's well-being of course. It wouldn't do to overplay his hand with the valet. If nothing else Augustus's man was devoted to his master and the family, although that was a weakness he might well be able to use to his advantage in this matter.

Francis smiled, feeling suddenly much more satisfied with life. He had an interest to keep him occupied in this wretched backwater, and one with the potential to provide him with some entertainment at that.

*　　*　　*

It had turned midnight. Daisy had just left her mistress's quarters after reading to the old lady until Wilhelmina had fallen asleep. The windows had been closed in both bedroom and sitting room and the suite had been stifling. Now, as Daisy crossed the hall, she suddenly rebelled against the thought of going straight upstairs.

On a night like this at home she'd often sat outside the cottage door and let the sea breeze tease her hair and skin once the chores were finished and her granny settled. Although the gardens of Evenley House were scented with the perfume of flowers and had no remnant of saltiness in the air, she needed to be out of doors again.

Her mind made up, without stopping to fetch a shawl from her bedroom, Daisy slipped quietly along the corridor towards the kitchen. She left the house by the back door, locking it after her and slipping the key into the pocket of her skirt.

It was cooler outside and Daisy breathed in the clean fresh air gratefully, staring up into the dark sky studded with stars for a moment before she began to walk. The events of the day crowded into her mind after a while – Alf, the talk with her granny, Francis Fraser – and she sighed deeply. For some reason life seemed complicated. And then she made a sound of annoyance low in her throat. For goodness' sake, what was the matter with her? She'd landed on her feet in a way that happened to few lasses, they were all in clover now. At home there was food in the cupboards and security in the knowledge that they could afford to buy more. What else could she ask for? Her granny, Tilly and the bairns, Tom's lass – she could make sure they wanted for nothing. Look at them poor devils in the workhouse . . . She shivered in spite of the warm air. Or even the folk stuck in the towns where blackened factories, slag heaps, running filth in the gutters and verminous dwellings were commonplace.

196

And then all other thoughts went out of her mind as, having skirted the main lawn, she stepped through the archway of willow which led to the rose garden. She had intended to sit awhile in the quiet of the night but in front of her, lit quite distinctly by the light of the full moon, was the figure of a man. She couldn't see clearly enough through the shadows to ascertain who it was, but from the height and breadth of him it was not Harold.

She hadn't thought she'd made a noise, but in the next moment she saw the figure turn towards her and experienced a second of real terror before William's voice said, '*Daisy?* Daisy, is that you? I don't believe it.'

He didn't believe it? Her fright made her respond just as she would have done to Alf or any of the other fishing lads as she said, her tone sharp, 'What on earth are you doing here at this time of night?' It was only after she had spoken that she realised fully William was actually here, right now, in this beautiful moonlit place, and her heart began to pound as he came towards her.

'I'm so sorry.' His tone was apologetic but amused too, and she couldn't help but smile back. And then he was at her side and she felt something similar to a punch in the stomach when she saw he was dressed only in a pair of dinner trousers, shoes, and a white shirt that was open down to his waist and showed the thick blond hair on his chest.

She said again, 'What are you doing here?' but even to herself her voice sounded breathless.

'Escaping from one of my mother's confounded dinner parties.' It was rueful. 'I stood it as long as I could, but when the ladies withdrew I took the opportunity to decamp.' He didn't add that he had been drawn to Evenley House like a moth to a flame, all the time telling himself he was acting like a lovesick adolescent. If anyone had told him a few months ago that he would find himself riding miles at midnight just to stand outside a house wherein slept

197

the object of his desire, he would have laughed in their face. Though Daisy wasn't asleep. She was here, in front of him, and he didn't know how to stop himself blurting out what he felt. But he must not. There were a thousand and one obstacles in the way of any liaison between them and he knew it.

'You rode here on Lightning?' In spite of the name Daisy had found William's pure-blooded black stallion a gentle creature, even going so far as to stroke the great velvet muzzle on occasion. 'Where is he?'

'Tethered outside the grounds. I came in by way of the far wall.' Again he didn't feel it prudent to add it wasn't the first time he had been attracted here at night since Daisy had taken up residence with his aunt, and that he'd now perfected the art of a silent entrance and exit.

'Won't you get into trouble? For leaving, I mean?'

Probably. Very probably.

'Of course not. My father and the others will continue to enjoy their port, brandy and cigars for some time, and the ladies will twitter over their tea or coffee and liqueurs for even longer. No one will know I'm missing.'

Daisy's expression suggested she was not fooled and William's blue eyes laughed at her. She stared at him, terribly conscious of the naked flesh below his throat. Why had he come here to Evenley House to escape the dinner party? Why not the grounds of Greyfriar Hall, or if the need to put more distance between himself and the house was paramount, why hadn't he simply taken Lightning for a midnight gallop in the surrounding countryside? It . . . it couldn't be anything to do with her, could it? And then she told herself not to be so silly. This was his aunt's house, perhaps he had always used it as a retreat from the stiff formality of his home?

'Everything looks different in the moonlight.' His voice was soft, throaty, and then, as her long, dark lashes swept down to hide the expression in her eyes, he made the effort to sound more matter-of-fact when he added, 'It's a real bonus, meeting you like this. I do enjoy our talks when no one else is around. Do you know what I mean?'

Daisy didn't say, 'Aye, I know exactly what you mean,' as she wanted to, but, 'I . . . I should go in.'

'Why?'

'Miss Wilhelmina would say this wasn't proper.'

'Nonsense.' William pointed to a bench a few yards away. 'Come and sit for a while, just a few minutes. Look at the sky, have you ever seen such a beautiful night?'

Daisy glanced up into the star-laden sky. It *was* beautiful, but it could have been pouring with rain and blowing a gale and still this would have been the most enchanting night ever.

She noticed William was rebuttoning his shirt as they walked across to the gnarled wooden bench which was a relief, although her cheeks continued to burn as she seated herself on wood which was still warm from the heat of the day. She felt almost light-headed with excitement, but afraid too, of what she wasn't quite sure.

'How is your grandmother?'

'She's all right.'

'And the rest of the family? You went to see them today, I presume, it being a Sunday?'

Daisy nodded, keeping her eyes fixed on a rose bush a few feet away which was covered with rich full blooms. 'They're all well.'

'Daisy,' said William, leaning towards her a little, 'don't be frightened of me. Don't you know I wouldn't do anything to hurt you? We're friends, aren't we?' His heart was pounding like a sledgehammer. He was close enough to catch the faint flower smell emanating from her skin and recognised it as the scented soap his aunt insisted on. But it didn't smell like that on Wilhelmina.

His throat felt tight and his stomach muscles had knotted. It took all of his self-control to lean back on the bench and say quietly, 'It's just that I was so sick of all the talk back at the Hall, an evening of conversation but without anything being said. Do you understand?'

She nodded again, turning to look at him.

'When you speak you *say* something, you always have.'

Daisy wrinkled her nose and it was all William could do not to pull her to him as she said, 'I say too much most of the time. My granny isn't one for beating about the bush and I take after her, I suppose.'

'Then she must be a wonderful woman.'

The pounding of Daisy's heart threatened to suffocate her and she told herself she must go back to the house *now*. But she couldn't move. She didn't want to move. In an effort to bring things back to normal, she said, 'She's wise, I think. She has never had the learning to read or write but her wisdom comes from deep inside.' She shook her head once. 'Does that sound silly?'

'Of course not.' Nothing she could ever say would sound silly. When he thought of the aimless prattle of Camilla Routledge or the Wynford sisters . . .

'I've just read H. G. Wells's *The Time Machine* and I was telling her about it, and do you know what she said?'

Daisy turned to him, her eyes bright, and William thought, She's adorable. Utterly adorable. He shook his head, 'What did she say?'

'"Life is a time machine, lass. You have to make sure the buttons are set for where you want to go, and once having set them you don't alter course".'

'She *is* a wise woman.' Had he set any buttons? Or had he accepted that they were all set for him?

'Mind, she said not everyone has the privilege of being able to pick and choose which buttons they press. If you're out on the boats at twelve years old, or down a mine, you don't have the time to think about where you want to go, do you?'

William shook his head, his eyes riveted on her face. 'Do you know where you want to go, Daisy?'

She turned from him, her lashes drooping, and then shrugged. 'Perhaps. I don't know.'

He gazed at her averted head, and found he was shaking slightly when he said, 'I think I am beginning to.'

She didn't answer and the moment stretched and lengthened before she rose quickly, saying, 'I ought to get back.'

This time he didn't detain her. 'Can I walk with you as far as the entrance to the house?'

'I . . . I don't think that's wise.'

Where did wisdom come into all this? 'Please?'

Her silence was acquiescence enough, and when he reached out for her hand as they began to walk he felt it quiver beneath his.

He walked her to the kitchen door and wasn't surprised when, on reaching the house, she deftly removed her hand from his as she drew the key out of her pocket. 'Goodnight, William.' It sounded almost prim and for a second the urge to crush her to him was almost overpowering.

'Goodnight, Daisy.' Dear, dear Daisy. And then she had opened the door and slipped inside, and he was alone.

To Francis's delight, the opportunity to probe William's feelings concerning the fishergirl came far sooner than he had anticipated, namely at breakfast the morning after the dinner party.

He had not slept well, an over-indulgence in food and drink causing acute indigestion which had kept him awake until a pink dawn began to lighten the sky. Consequently he slept later than he had intended.

A large number of the dinner guests of the night before

had stayed overnight at Greyfriar, a regular occurrence. The males in the party had enjoyed an early-morning ride over dew-drenched meadows. Consequently the atmosphere in the dining room was loud and jolly when Francis made his appearance just after nine o'clock.

Breakfast was always a substantial meal at Greyfriar Hall. A range of hot and cold dishes including cold game pie and devilled kidneys, ham, steaks, eggs, cheese, fried potatoes and onion, and a variety of bread and rolls, was always at hand, with a separate table of prepared fruits and another of beverages at either side of the main spread.

Francis joined one of the ladies of the party who was obviously another latecomer, making light conversation as they both helped themselves to a variety of dishes before taking a seat at the long dining table. Immediately one of the line of servants who stood hovering behind the chairs appeared to take orders for Indian or China tea, coffee, toast and preserves.

Cecilia was on his right, and after a cursory, 'I hope you slept well, Uncle?' his niece turned back to talk to Felicity seated on the other side of her before Francis had a chance to reply to the duty enquiry. He began to eat his breakfast without responding. The two girls were whispering, their voices inaudible to those around them, but Francis, who had always been exceptionally keen of ear, could hear every word in spite of the buzz of conversation and occasional laughter and high shrieks in the room.

'And Mother said Father told him he won't get anyone better than Priscilla. She's a beauty, she dances wonderfully and she's been fêted, feasted, courted and adored in one continual round of gaiety from the moment she came out. And William said' – here even Francis's acute hearing failed him as Cecilia bent closer to Felicity and murmured in her ear, but from the scandalised '*ohhh*' which resulted

202

William clearly hadn't minced his words – 'and they had the most dreadful row.'

'Cecilia, they are always having the most dreadful rows.'

'Not like this apparently. Mother said William was so unco-operative it has made her wonder if he has his eye on someone we know nothing about, perhaps one of the set in France. She asked me if he had mentioned a name to us, spoken of someone more often than anyone else, but I said not. I think she plans to write to Aunt Lydia and Uncle Claude and see if he has spoken to them or Pierre and Marcel.'

The two girls were interrupted in their tête-à-tête at that moment by the Wynford sisters, and as the four young women began to speak of other things Francis sat pulling at the ends of his moustache with his thumb and finger. So Gwendoline thought William was sufficiently serious about some unknown attachment to be disinclined to fall in with their plans, did she? Well, well, well. And of course his relations were far too stately and socially conscious to see what was under their noses – if, of course, he was right about this. But surely William wasn't seriously considering anything other than a romp with the girl, or at the most setting her up in a small dwelling in Sunderland or Newcastle?

Francis glanced over to where his nephew sat finishing his breakfast, somewhat apart at the far end of the table and with a closed expression which discouraged conversation. He rose to his feet and walked down the room, taking the seat at William's side as he said, 'Good morning, m'boy, I'm glad I've caught you. I've been wanting a quiet word, man to man as it were.'

'Yes?'

The tone was hardly encouraging but Francis continued, 'Now your father's a good man, none better, but

203

having been married for over three decades he's out of touch with certain . . . practicalities us bachelors need to entertain.'

'I'm sorry?'

'Of course the bawdy houses and such serve their purpose but when a little filly catches your eye . . .'

It was clear William didn't have the faintest notion where this was leading, and Francis took great satisfaction from the moment when he said, 'I'm referring to the fishergirl, m'boy, the wench who so kindly hoisted you out of the water. She's taken my eye and I rather fancy it's reciprocated. I just wanted to make sure I wouldn't be treading on any toes if I—'

'You keep your filthy hands off her.' His voice was low and deadly and such was the enmity in it that even Francis was taken aback. 'You hear me, Uncle? You come within fifty yards of Daisy and I'll kill you.'

'What did you say?' Francis's outrage wasn't entirely fabricated. 'Don't be a fool. The chit's ripe and ready for it.'

'You've got a cesspit for a mind, everyone knows it.' William was experiencing a rage such as he had never felt before. 'You leave her alone, I mean it.'

'I see.' Francis's voice sounded thin and cold and came through lips that scarcely moved as he struggled to contain himself.

'I doubt it but I'm warning you—'

'*You're* warning *me*? Why, you little popinjay you! I was seeing the world before you were even born. And what's all the fuss about anyway? There's enough to go round for the two of us—'

Francis's words ended in a gurgle as William's hands came out and grasped his collar to either side of his many chins, his knuckles forcing the older man's head back as he ground out, 'You're not fit to lick her boots and that's the truth. You're putrid – contaminating everything you touch. Do you hear me?'

Francis was trying to wrench his nephew's hands away from his throat, clawing vainly at the iron grip as his eyes began to bulge.

There had been sounds of consternation beyond the two of them, a concentrated drawing in of breath and one or two little cries from the ladies present, but William was oblivious to anything and anyone as he shook his uncle with each word as he repeated, 'Do you hear me?'

'I don't think he can answer you.' Augustus had reached his son's side and his voice was icy as he added, 'Remember where you are, William. I don't know what this is all about but conduct yourself as a gentleman.'

'A gentleman?' William threw Francis back into his seat with enough force to send the chair rocking. 'That is getting to be a dirty word in this house, Father.'

'*William.*' His son's voice had not been low and Augustus was white with rage.

William now took a deep breath, rumpling his table napkin with deliberate control and throwing it down on the table before he got to his feet, his face close to that of his father as he said, 'He's scum, Father. You know it and I know it.'

Augustus's eyes were like chips of black lead. Lord Routledge was in the room, along with Sir Irwin McKenzie and others. What on earth was the boy thinking of?

The boy was thinking of murder. It was in William's eyes when he bent down close to his uncle again, his voice quiet now but nonetheless ferocious as he said, 'You might well be relying on me for your allowance in your dotage, Uncle. Just remember that, will you? But for the moment I'm telling you – not warning you, *telling* you – to keep away from her.'

Francis said nothing but the hatred in William's eyes

was reflected in his as he fumbled with his collar and coat with shaking hands.

William straightened, and not a muscle in his face moved as he walked steadily from the room without looking to left or right. Within moments a well-mannered murmur of conversation rose again, with nothing more contentious under discussion than the morning's ride or the latest fashion, but even as Augustus schooled his face to show no emotion beyond urbane congeniality he knew this incident would be picked over and over with great relish until there was no more meat on the bone.

He would get to the bottom of this, damn it, if it was the last thing he did. The Frasers had always avoided even a whisper of scandal – wasn't that why he had packed Francis off to the continent early on when his brother's . . . peculiar tastes had become obvious? And he had been right to do so as this incident confirmed. Two minutes back and Francis was already causing trouble.

If Francis *were* at fault he would make sure his brother was promptly despatched whence he had come. And if it was William . . . Augustus's thin mouth became tighter. It was high time the boy started behaving like the heir of Greyfriar, and his father intended to make damn' sure he knuckled down and applied himself.

Chapter Twelve

It was the morning of Daisy's sixteenth birthday, and for a little while she had forgotten that nothing had seemed right for the last few weeks. Gladys had been her usual surly self in the kitchen but Kitty had more than made up for her mother's lack of warmth, shyly presenting Daisy with a fine new pair of gloves and a small box of chocolates and singing 'Happy Birthday' to her even though she herself looked a mite peaky.

Daisy offered to take Wilhelmina's breakfast tray through to her mistress's private quarters, and on entering the bedroom was presented with a thick woollen coat and cape by a smiling Wilhelmina.

'Oh, it's lovely, ma'am, beautiful.' Daisy raised shining eyes from the box on her lap where the coat and cape were displayed. 'Thank you.'

'A small reward for putting up with a demanding and tiresome old lady, Daisy. And I *am* tiresome, am I not?'

Demanding maybe, fussy and even hard to please on occasion, but never tiresome. Daisy's face was straight now and her voice soft when she said, 'I don't think so, ma'am.'

'Go on with you, child. I think you are employing a little flattery now, or what your grandmother would term . . . ?'

'Buttering up, ma'am,' said Daisy, grinning.

'Buttering up? Yes, that will do nicely. And your birthday having fallen most conveniently on a Sunday, I have asked Cook to provide a special birthday tea for you to take with you when you visit the village later. Harold can drive you there in the carriage if you so wish?'

'Oh, no, thank you, ma'am. Kitty and I will manage between us. We . . . we like the walk,' Daisy said hastily. Gladys would already be spitting bricks about the birthday tea, the idea of Harold being forced to escort herself and Kitty to the door of the cottage would send the little woman into a frenzy, and it would be poor Kitty who would bear the brunt of her mother's venom for the rest of the week.

'As you like.' Wilhelmina was aware there was little love lost between her nurse companion and the cook and her husband – between Kitty and her parents too, she didn't doubt – but such domestic complications irritated and annoyed her and so she ignored them.

Wilhelmina accepted she had never had an excess of equanimity or forbearance – it was a family trait – but she was also honest enough to admit that since her heart had begun to cause such problems her impatience and exasperation with those around her had reached new heights. Never one to suffer fools gladly, constant frustration now added to an already volatile temper. Therefore Daisy's stoicism in the face of what amounted to considerable provocation at times was genuinely appreciated, the more so because the old lady sensed it was her companion's kind heart – rather than the wage Daisy was paid – which enabled her to stay so unflappable.

Later that morning Daisy had just given her mistress her medicines and performed one of the daily massages Wilhelmina needed on her legs and feet as a consequence of her poor circulation when a tap at the door of the private sitting room preceded Gladys's entrance into the room.

'Sorry to bother you, ma'am, but Kitty's ailing and Harold's none too good neither so lunch will be a little late,' the cook said importantly.

'Ailing?' There was a note of alarm in Wilhelmina's voice. The bubonic plague outbreak in Glasgow was still spreading in that city, and people all over Scotland and the north east had been warned to look out for signs that the disease had escaped the city confines.

'Oh, it's all right, ma'am. They were both talking to the butcher's boy when he called, and he's gone down with influenza.'

'Influenza? Oh, dear, and I thought we had escaped that.' An influenza epidemic at the beginning of the year had taken old and young alike at its height, but over the last few months it had appeared to burn itself out. Nevertheless, influenza was preferable to the plague, and Wilhelmina's voice reflected this when she said, 'Hopefully a few days in bed will put them to rights, Cook.'

'Yes, ma'am.'

'Talking of which, I am a little tired today. I think I will have a lunch tray in bed later, after a nap. Shall we say two o'clock? And, Daisy, once you have tucked me up, why don't you get off to see your grandmother?' Wilhelmina added kindly.

'Thank you, ma'am.' Normally her half-day began at one and it was barely noon now.

'What'll I do with the hamper, ma'am?' Gladys had not budged from her position just inside the door, and although her face was deadpan the cook couldn't quite keep a trace of elation from coming through in her voice. 'It's too heavy for one to carry, and Harold is in no fit state to drive the carriage.'

'Yes, thank you, Cook.' Wilhelmina's voice was sharp and stated quite clearly she would not be played for a fool. 'I will let you know later.'

Once Daisy and her mistress were alone again, Daisy had just begun to say, 'It really doesn't matter about the hamper, ma'am, although it is very kind of you. I'll take what I can carry today, and the rest can be used up here,' when there was another knock at the door.

A subdued Gladys put her head round the door and said, 'It's the parson, ma'am. He's called in to see how you are on his way home from the morning service. I told him you were tired and going to take a nap shortly, and he asked if you could spare Daisy for a moment.'

Try as she might, Gladys could not keep her inner resentment from filtering through in her voice again. Asking for that fishergirl, indeed. What were things coming to in this household?

'Pop along and bring the parson in here, would you, Daisy?' Wilhelmina then turned to the cook, adding, 'And I am sure a tray of coffee and biscuits would be most welcome. Some of those shortcake ones the parson is partial to, I think, Cook.'

When Daisy entered the drawing room Parson Lyndon was standing at one of the large windows looking out into the bright September sunshine. He turned from it, his pleasant, good-looking face breaking into a smile as he said warmly, 'Good morning, Daisy, or is it afternoon now?'

'Afternoon, but only just, Parson.' Daisy smiled widely at this man she had come to like and respect as one of the most benevolent people she had ever known. His increasingly frequent visits to the house, and the way he had begun to include her in the discussions he shared with the mistress, had gone some way to making up for William's absence of late.

In the last month he had made only one appearance at Evenley House, and that had been with his father, but it wasn't just the fact he had kept away for the last few weeks so much as his manner when he had come that concerned her. He had seemed remote and withdrawn, as though he had something pressing on his mind. She was glad William's uncle had stayed only briefly in England, though. His one visit to see Miss Wilhelmina had been enough to set her teeth on edge for days.

'Your mistress is indisposed?' Hector Lyndon was aware he was detaining Daisy in order to continue gazing at her face. She was so beautiful and so unaware of it, her eyes like great saucers and such a dark soft grey, but it was more than mere outward loveliness that had drawn him to this young, untutored girl with such – his mind hesitated over the word 'passion' here and substituted a more acceptable 'eagerness'. Daisy's face reflected the true beauty which came from a charitable heart; an essential virtue in a parson's wife, he reassured himself righteously.

'Miss Wilhelmina's heart hasn't been too good lately but she seems merely tired today,' Daisy said quietly, although there was no chance Wilhelmina could hear them. 'She wants to see you though, Parson. I'm to take you through.'

'Capital, capital.' Hector hesitated. Should he give her the small parcel now or wait until Wilhelmina was present? He would like them to be alone when she unwrapped it, but convention demanded a chaperone should be in attendance when a gift was received by a young girl. Propriety won, as it always would do with Hector. He let Daisy lead the way to where Wilhelmina was waiting on the sofa in her private sitting room.

'Dear boy.' She patted the seat beside her. 'I've ordered coffee for the three of us if you're able to stay for a few minutes?'

'Of course, Wilhelmina. It would be a pleasure.'

Daisy reluctantly took a seat opposite the sofa. Her mistress seemed to have forgotten she had told her she could leave early.

'Now a little bird told me' – Hector smiled at Wilhelmina – 'that it is a certain young lady's birthday today? Happy birthday, Daisy.' He took the small, carefully wrapped parcel out of his pocket and passed it over to Daisy with a smile.

Her face expressed surprise and then pleasure when she unwrapped the package to find a copy of Charles Dickens's *A Christmas Carol*. After she had thanked the parson she passed the book to her mistress who had asked to see it.

Wilhelmina had to hold the volume right up to her nose in order to be able to study it properly, and after perusing it for a moment or two, she said, 'Are these wretched eyes of mine deceiving me or is this a signed first edition, Parson?'

'Your eyes are not deceiving you, Wilhelmina.'

She lowered the book and peered over the top of it. 'I see.'

Daisy wasn't sure what her mistress saw, but Gladys entering with the coffee took her attention and the moment passed.

It was five minutes after this when Wilhelmina said – rather suddenly and not within the context of the conversation they had been having about the recent Trades Union Congress resolving to champion old age pensions as a fundamental human right – 'It is such a pity, Parson. I had arranged for Daisy to take a birthday hamper home today to share with her grandmother, but now poor Kitty is not well, along with her father who could have driven the carriage. Still, I dare say you will be able to manage the cake, Daisy?'

'Yes, of course, ma'am, and a couple of other things besides,' she said quickly, hoping this meant she could be on her way.

'Perhaps . . .' The parson hesitated, and then as Wilhelmina prompted him, said quietly, 'Perhaps I might be permitted to take Daisy and the hamper to her grandmother's in my trap?'

Wilhelmina smiled faintly as she said, 'What a good idea, Parson. Why didn't I think of that?'

'Oh, I couldn't ask you to do that.' Daisy was horrified at the idea of the parson having to go out of his way for her and on a Sunday at that, his busiest day of the week. 'What about your lunch? And you must have lots to do.'

'My housekeeper always serves lunch at half-past one, not a minute before and not a minute after,' Hector said, smiling. 'That will leave me plenty of time to take you on the short journey to Whitburn and still be home with twenty minutes or so to spare if we leave now.'

'That's settled then,' Wilhelmina cut in, her tone brooking no argument as she added, 'go and put on your bonnet, child, and tell Gladys to put the hamper in the parson's trap. And do give your grandmother my best wishes, won't you?'

Daisy stared at her mistress, blinking in surprise. She opened her mouth to speak and then closed it again. The poor parson must have felt obliged to offer her a lift in his trap after what the mistress had said, she saw that now. She just hoped what he'd intimated about his lunch-time was true.

By the time Daisy came downstairs again, her shawl about her shoulders and her straw bonnet with blue ribbons tied under her chin, Hector was waiting at the front door for her. 'All ready?' he asked lightly, and as Daisy smiled and nodded he allowed himself to touch her as he took her arm and helped her into the waiting pony and trap.

He had to see her, he couldn't carry on like this and her birthday was the perfect excuse. William ran his hand over his face as he continued to pace up and down his bedroom, and then delved into his pocket and brought out the little silver trinket box he had purchased in Newcastle the week before. He opened it, staring at the small diamond and pearl pin it contained. It was dainty and exquisite, like her . . . He groaned, shutting the lid to the box with a snap. A brooch

213

wasn't the sort of gift one gave to a young woman unless she was a family member, and he knew it. A present like this was a statement of intent, he had known that when he had purchased it, so *why* had he done so?

He flung himself down on his bed, his hands behind his head as he gazed up at the intricately moulded ceiling where cherubim and seraphim flew in an orgy of holy, plump-cheeked joy, their angelic smiles mocking the life led below their plaster heaven.

He'd promised himself in the hours following the row with his uncle at breakfast that he would severely limit his visits to Evenley House. The dispute between his father, uncle and himself which had rocked all corners of the house, and which had caused his mother to become so ill a footman had had to be despatched at eleven o'clock at night for Doctor Woodrow, had had the result of forcing him to face some unpleasant truths.

He twisted restlessly on the satin eiderdown before springing up and marching across to the window, sitting down on the window-seat and gazing out across the rolling grounds in front of him without seeing them. A peacock strolled across the green lawns, emitting its mournful cry and drawing his attention to it before strutting off again. He watched until it had disappeared, his brows drawn together.

The scandal which would follow should he make Daisy his wife would render her life impossible. He would take her into no man's land – removed from her own people but not accepted by the circle he moved in, and he had seen at first hand how cruel they could be to those they considered beneath them. Respectability . . . how he hated that word. It exacted a heavy price in humiliation and censure when some poor soul didn't live up to the criteria it demanded.

William turned away from the window, his face grim. He had not admitted the extent of his regard for Daisy during the argument with his father and uncle, knowing instinctively it would result in his father dismissing Daisy, however much his aunt might object. At the moment Daisy was under Wilhelmina's protection with all the material benefits that involved, but just the idea that he might be in love with her would cause his father to have a seizure. His father hadn't even liked the explanation that he felt a responsibility towards Daisy, the girl having saved his life.

'I don't want you causing me problems with Wilhelmina, do you hear me?' Sir Augustus had growled. 'Gratitude is all very well but a girl like that might encourage you to sample the goods, if you know what I mean. They don't understand the finer emotions, the common people, and they're like leeches if they smell an easy ride. Before you knew it she'd be presenting us with a bastard and demanding we pay her off again, damn it. Are you listening to me, boy?'

William had been listening, and his answer had been such that battle had raged on even after Doctor Woodrow had been summoned. But at least his uncle's none-too-subtle enquiries about Daisy had meant his father had packed Francis off within hours. His uncle was a loose cannon in matters of a carnal nature and his father knew it.

William dropped into a deep leather chair placed at a convenient angle to the bookcase close to his dressing-room door. Resting his elbows on the padded arms he supported his head with his hands, gazing down at the worn Persian carpet which covered most of the floor. His father would certainly disinherit him if he made his intentions regarding the future and Daisy plain, there was no doubt about that. However, he still had the few hundred pounds bequeathed to him by his maternal grandparents. His father couldn't touch that.

He raised his head, gazing unseeingly across the room.

Of course, the rent on even a smallish house with a staff of three or four to run it in a respectable part of town would soon begin to eat into that, and there would be plenty of other expenses too. He would need to have an income of some kind, but what? His brow wrinkled. He would have to leave this district and everyone he knew for Daisy ever to have a chance of being accepted into good society, so a number of friends who might have been of help with some kind of career opening would be lost to him. Nevertheless, an education which had embraced the best schools followed by Eton had to be worth something, surely? He had enjoyed his time in the south east and had left university with a deep appreciation of all things literary. Perhaps he could try his hand at writing a book. Or something along those lines.

He had no idea of the income needed to support a wife and family, he realised suddenly. He had no idea about a lot of practical matters. But he could learn. A quiver of excitement caused his stomach to tighten. Yes, he could learn. With Daisy at his side he could do anything. They would come through together whatever happened.

He began to pace the room again, his excitement mounting. Snatching the box out of his pocket again, he opened it, staring down at the brooch inside. *It should have been a ring.* He should have bought a ring and then he could have done this properly, but he would hint at what he intended when he gave her the brooch, though without a formal declaration. And then this week sometime he could visit Newcastle and find just the right thing. Oh, Daisy. He put the box back in his pocket, glancing impatiently at his watch as he did so. She would stay at her grandmother's house until tea-time so he had another three or four hours to waste before she would be home, then he would be there at his aunt's waiting for her.

He had to do this. The last couple of months had been

miserable, he couldn't exist without her, he couldn't. And if it meant giving up Greyfriar, turning his back on his family and friends and everything he had ever known, so be it.

Chapter Thirteen

'An' he's comin' back for you at half-past five you say? Eeh, lass, whatever next?'

The cackle of laughter which followed Nellie's words grated on Alf unbearably. He glanced across at the old woman who was sitting propped up in bed, her mouth open wide in merriment showing her remaining teeth and gums, and had an urge to yell at her to shut up. There was nothing funny about this parson feller bringing Daisy home. He might be a man of the cloth but he was still a man, wasn't he? And giving her a book! By, the way she'd talked about that you'd have thought it had gold lettering at the very least. And she had barely looked at the little sewing basket *he* had bought for her birthday. (Alf refused to acknowledge the prick of conscience that said this last accusation wasn't quite true.)

He brought his eyes back to Daisy standing at the table cutting thick shives of birthday cake, the contents of the hamper spread out around it. It was a fine cake, different from any he'd seen before what with the fancy little curls of icing and this and that, and there was a ham, a cooked chicken, eggs, white soft-looking loaves of bread, butter, tea, sugar, tins of condensed milk, and plenty more besides.

'So you're gettin' on all right then?'

His voice was gruff, and Daisy looked up for a moment before she lowered her eyes to the cake again and said, 'Aye, I am.'

'The old lady thinks a bit of you, giving you all that an' a coat an' all. Still, she can afford it.'

Daisy raised her head again, staring at him for some moments before she said, her voice cool and face straight, 'Just because she can afford it doesn't mean she had to be so generous.'

'Aye, I'm with you there, lass.' Nellie wagged her head. 'In fact it's usually the case that them with plenty hang on to it like grim death. Tighter than a duck's arse, most of 'em are, unless it's somethin' for themselves, mind.'

Enid was sitting on the end of Nellie's bed, and now Alf's mother nudged her old friend as she said, 'You'd better watch your Ps an' Qs when the parson knocks on the door, lass. Likely he's never had an arse, only a backside.'

Both old women convulsed with laughter. It was Margery who asked quietly, 'How bad is Kitty, Daisy?'

Margery was sitting in one of two wicker chairs with flock cushions which had been purchased a few weeks before, and as Daisy handed her a piece of cake she thought how poorly Tom's lass looked. Apart from the mound of her stomach she seemed to have lost weight rather than put it on as her pregnancy had progressed.

'She'll be all right.' Daisy gave her grandmother and Enid a piece of cake each and then Alf, leaving her own on the table as she continued, 'Bugs just seem to bounce off Kitty, she's always better twice as quick as anyone else. Miss Wilhelmina says she's got the constitution of a horse.'

'Aye, well, mebbe that's the case but this influenza is a different thing, isn't it?'

Alf's tone was distinctly belligerent but before Daisy could voice the sharp reply she'd had in mind, Tilly and the children trooped in, fresh from visiting Tilly's sister in Seaburn, and the little ones' excited cries as they saw the birthday cake allowed the moment to pass.

The rest of the afternoon passed fairly harmoniously, but Daisy was forced to recognise she missed Kitty's presence in the house. She hadn't realised how much her friend talked to Alf and kept him amused, the two of them laughing and larking on like a pair of bairns most of the time. Today he sat quiet and morose, responding only in monosyllables to anything which was said to him. His demeanour cast a shadow over the precious hours she had at home, and by the time they heard the parson's trap outside the cottage Daisy was almost glad to leave.

She pulled her shawl round her shoulders as Margery climbed the ladder to the upper room as quickly as her increased girth would allow. The other girl had been horrified to learn the parson would call, her shame at being an unmarried mother seemed to swell with her stomach, and although Daisy had tried to persuade her to stay and meet Parson Lyndon Margery had become upset at the mere thought.

Once the introductions to the others had been made Daisy had expected they would leave immediately, but the parson seemed in no hurry, engaging first Tilly and then the oldest of her children in conversation and handing the bairns a slab of stickjaw for them to share.

Nellie watched the tall young man from her vantage point in the bed, and something in his gaze as he looked at Daisy made her heart beat faster. So that was the way of it. Did the lass know? She doubted it. Whenever she'd mentioned the parson Daisy had referred to him in almost reverential tones, and Nellie was sure her granddaughter saw him as a being apart from the normal throng, because of the man's vocation and also because he was a highly intelligent and learned individual according to the lass. But however Daisy saw him, he obviously liked her.

Nellie felt warm pride stir within her. There had been a change in her granddaughter over the months since she'd started having lessons with this tutor feller. A little learning had served to stimulate her lass's naturally inquisitive and searching mind. Daisy was brighter than most, Nellie would swear to it. She had always asked the most baffling questions right from a bairn, and had only been knee-high to a grasshopper when she'd wanted to know why the sky was blue, what made the tides come in and go out, and why coal burnt and stones didn't. Nellie had always passed her granddaughter's queries over to George, but – bless him – her son-in-law hadn't been up to all the answers as the lass had grown. But the parson now, he was different altogether.

Her Daisy had always been a peculiar lass – not in a strange way but in an extraordinary way – and some men couldn't cope with that. Nellie's gaze fell on Alf. The last months had shown her that the girl had been right to refuse him, much as she and Enid would have liked the pair of them to get wed, Nellie thought. Alf was a good lad, but he was a fisherman born and at heart wanted a lass who knew her place as his wife and the mother of his bairns, and that was all. Daisy was different from most of the fishergirls and this had become more and more apparent of late. Not that her wonderful Mr William would ever have been any good to the lass – just heartache and maybe ruin there – but the parson . . . It meant something if you were a parson's wife, by, it did, and she would be safe with him. And with all his book learning and such, she'd look up to him which was important in a marriage.

'It's right good of you to give Daisy a ride back to the house, Parson.' Nellie ignored Alf's stiff expression and spoke warmly. 'I hope it's not put you about too much?'

'Not at all, Mrs Shaw.'

'An' the lovely hamper Daisy's mistress sent! She's so kind to the lass is Miss Fraser.'

222

Hector smiled. 'A meek and willing spirit will always reap its own reward, Mrs Shaw.'

Nellie nodded but didn't reply to this. The Daisy she knew was willing enough, but much as Nellie loved her granddaughter she could never have described her as meek.

Daisy had been standing in the middle of the room, her shawl still round her shoulders. Now, as she reached for the empty basket, Hector said quickly, 'Allow me.'

'Oh, thank you.' Daisy was flustered and it showed. She kissed her grandmother and said goodbye to the others, and she and the parson were actually at the door when Alf said, with no lead up whatsoever, 'So you're not married then? You live in the Vicarage on your own?'

Hector turned to face the bronzed young fisherman. 'I have a very able housekeeper who comes each morning,' he said quietly.

'Still a big place to live in on your own, isn't it?'

Daisy stared at Alf's red face and now she was squirming inside. What was he doing, speaking to the parson in that tone of voice?

'Possibly.' Hector smiled, a soft deprecating smile. 'But hopefully it won't be for ever.'

Alf wanted to say, 'You've got your eye on a lass then?' but knew that would be going too far. Instead he said, his tone still distinctly confrontational, 'Nice, is it, the Vicarage?'

Hector seemed to consider his answer for a moment. 'Yes, it is very pleasant, but more importantly it is where God has called me to minister,' he said gently.

Put that in your pipe and smoke it, Alfred Hardy. Daisy glared at him and Alf glared back, but Hector merely nodded to the women once again and opened the cottage door. 'Shall we?' He gestured for Daisy to precede him out of the house and this she did, after one last furious glance at Alf.

223

'I'm . . . I'm sorry about Alf.' They had climbed up into the parson's trap which was a relatively new one with fine brass side lamps, although the pony was getting on a bit. Nevertheless, Primrose was as calm and placid as they come with great heavily lashed eyes and a gentle disposition, which was important in a parson's pony. It wouldn't do for her to be bad-tempered or untrustworthy, not with the amount of time she had to wait outside various dwelling places while the parson ministered to those within. But Primrose loved human beings and animals alike and always lowered her velvet muzzle to nuzzle at anyone who stopped to pet her. Daisy stared across the pony's broad furry back and didn't look at the parson as she added, 'I can't think what has got into him.'

'I think the young man is fond of you, and that being the case is a little over-protective,' Hector said quietly, adding, 'although that is no bad thing,' in case she thought he was criticising her friend.

Daisy's cheeks turned pinker. 'I have brothers who are more than able to provide any protection necessary. Alf . . . well, he knows where he stands on that score.'

So the fisherman had made his feelings plain to her at some point. Hector took a deep breath and said steadily, 'He may have taken exception to my bringing you to the village and then calling again.'

She didn't doubt it. Twilight was beginning to dampen down the vivid blue of the sky above and there was the scent of hay in the warm air. It had been a long hot summer and the farmers had made the most of it, harvesting the corn and getting it safely in the stack or in barns in plenty of time this year. No doubt lots of farm workers would have spent this Sunday afternoon walking round the parish admiring or criticising each other's efforts because a good corn rick was a work of art.

'See, over there? There are several goldfinches feeding on thistle seed.'

The parson's voice brought Daisy out of her thoughts and as she looked across to where the pretty little birds were busying themselves arguing over the choicest morsels, she thought, He's so nice, the parson. Most people wouldn't have given the birds a second glance, let alone stopped the pony and trap and commented about them.

She smiled back at him and for the first time, as their eyes met, Daisy realised the parson was really very good-looking and not all that old, or not for a parson anyway. It was disconcerting, seated next to him as she was, and suddenly Alf's rudeness took on a whole new slant. She had assumed his attitude was one of resentment because he saw the parson as part of the life which had taken her away from the village, but the way Parson Lyndon had looked at her just now put a different complexion on the afternoon.

Daisy dropped her eyes, her thoughts causing her cheeks to burn as she pretended to take an interest in the view on her side of the trap.

Hector smiled to himself. He had seen the sudden awareness and the ensuing blush of confusion, and considered this just as it ought to be in an innocent, artless young girl. Daisy was woman enough to have registered his unspoken declaration of intent and that was quite enough to be going on with for now.

He adjusted his long legs, making some comment about the lovely evening as he did so to which Daisy replied shyly.

He was fully aware that she looked upon him first and foremost as a man of the cloth, and, he liked to think, as a friend too, or perhaps a counsellor and teacher on a par with her tutor would be a better definition. Now she had been awakened to the fact that along with those things

225

there were others – that he was an ordinary man made of flesh and blood for a start. There would be plenty of time once she had adjusted to this realisation to present himself as a suitor, but she was still very young and he knew he had to be patient.

Hector breathed in the warm scented air, smiled again to himself, and allowed Primrose to continue at a steady pace as he engaged Daisy in conversation about nothing more contentious than how she had enjoyed her afternoon with her family.

'You are not seeing this clearly, William, and if it was just your well-being at stake I would say go ahead and learn the hard way. You will always have money behind you and furthermore will always be accepted into good society whatever errors of judgement you make while you bear the Fraser name.'

'The Fraser name!'

It was said with utter contempt and now Wilhelmina's voice became even sharper as she said, 'Yes, the Fraser name. Mock it if you like, but the fact remains you will be forgiven much on the strength of it. If, heaven forbid, this madness of which you speak did come to pass it would not last, you must be aware of that? And when the marriage finished you would recover and go on to make a good life for yourself among your own kind in this male-dominated society in which we live. Oh, yes, you would, and you needn't shake your head at me in that way. But Daisy . . . she would be cast adrift most cruelly. Tennyson, Ruskin and other writers habitually liken maidens to flowers, but believe me, William, girls of Daisy's class need to be as tough and enduring as oak trees.'

William almost fell so abruptly did he turn and march over to the drawing-room windows, and it was from there

226

he said, 'I thought you of all people would understand. I thought you had some regard for Daisy.'

'I have great regard for her which is why I am speaking to you like this.'

'What about all your talk of women's rights and how society is rotten from the inside out?' William's face was scarlet. 'Or does all that only apply when it doesn't affect your own family?'

Wilhelmina took a steadying breath. Dear, dear, the boy was in a state. Her heart was already palpitating violently from the force of the altercation which had begun some ten minutes earlier when William had arrived at Evenley House and showed her the brooch. She ignored its rapid throbbing as she said, 'I think you know me better than that, William. I am not speaking in this way because I agree with society, or because its strictures give me any pleasure. Nevertheless, it must be said that Daisy is still a very young woman who knows nothing, or almost nothing, of the world you and I were born into. Can you visualise the child giving orders to your servants? Or accompanying you to dinner parties and holding her own with the ladies who will be there? Women are never so cruel as when a beautiful member of their sex is at a disadvantage, as Daisy would be. In every way.'

'That's not true!'

'It is true, and even if you were foolish enough to give up Greyfriar Hall and turn your back on your family, scandal would follow you wherever you went. People would know who Daisy was and all about her beginnings, you can take my word on that.'

'We wouldn't be moving in circles where it would matter.'

'Of course you would. For goodness' sake, at least see this clearly, William, and don't talk such rubbish. You know as well as I do that there is a very strict code governing introductions, calling and dining, and there is a world of difference between calling and merely leaving cards which would make life unbearable for the child. None of the ladies would call upon Daisy even if they left their cards as a mark of respect to the Fraser name, you can be sure of that. Yes, it sounds so trivial but it signifies social endorsement or total exclusion – and Daisy would be cut wherever she went. The girl would be miserable – no, worse than miserable, destroyed.'

'But, Aunt, times are changing. You are basing all your arguments on how things were twenty or thirty years ago.' William strode back across the room, sitting down in the chair he had recently vacated and taking Wilhelmina's cold hands in his own as he repeated again, 'Times are changing.'

'There are some things that never change.' She stared into his earnest young face and kept her voice gentle. 'Don't do this, William, I beg of you. Daisy gave you the greatest gift one human being can give another when she saved you that day; don't repay her courage by ruining her life. There is another who will take care of her and love her as she should be loved, and with him she will not suffer the indignities and heartache which would be heaped upon her as your wife.'

'The parson.' William withdrew his hands, leaning back in the seat. His aunt had made sure he had seen Lyndon's gift when he had first arrived, and now William knew why. 'Daisy would never be happy with him, he's old. Oh, not in years, I grant you, but here, in his head, he is an old man.'

'That's not fair and you know it.' Wilhelmina's voice had resumed its habitual sharpness. 'Parson Lyndon is a young, good-looking man, and furthermore has some standing in the community. He can provide well for a wife and family, and as his spouse Daisy would have a full and rewarding life.'

She watched her nephew's face tighten and recognised the Fraser stubbornness when he said, 'Surely it is for her to make the choice between us?'

'Oh, don't be a hypocrite, boy! Any young thing from Daisy's background would be dazzled at the thought of making such a fine match as yourself, it is only natural. She would not see the disadvantages of such a union. But Daisy does like the parson, and would more than like him if you gave them a chance, I know it.'

It was some time before William spoke again. Wilhelmina sat quietly studying his bowed head, while all the time inside herself she was saying, 'Oh, William, William, don't do this.'

'I love her, Aunt.' When he eventually raised his head she saw his blue eyes were wet, and it took all of Wilhelmina's strength for her to say steadily, 'If that is really the case then allow her her chance of true happiness. Marriage with you would give her no peace or self-respect, society would make sure of that. The gap between you is too wide and love is not enough, William. In these circumstances it is not enough.'

He closed his eyes and put his hand tightly across them, muttering, 'I can't bear to lose her.'

'You will bear it. You are a Fraser, and however much you kick against the pricks there are some strong points in our heritage, boy. Courage, for one. It allowed me to face the fact that I would be alone and childless all my life, and that I will go out of this world without leaving anything of real worth behind.'

William's hand came away from his face and he stared at his aunt who was speaking in a low intense voice, one he had not heard her use before.

'I have never had the words "I love you" said to me,' Wilhelmina continued. 'Not by my parents who had no time to lavish on a girl child who was not the required heir; not by your father who was always a cold fish, and certainly not by Francis who was utterly self-absorbed from the cradle. I never had a suitor, or even an admirer.'

Wilhelmina lay back a little in her chair, her heart was beating so hard it was actually hurting her. 'But enough of self-pity, such a wretched emotion and one which I heartily despise.'

William bent forward and took her thin pale hands. Frail fingers curled round young strong ones and there was a long silence before he said, 'I should go. I would prefer not to be here when she returns.'

'I'll walk to the door with you.'

This was an unusual occurrence, and after William had helped the old lady to her feet and given her her polished ebony walking stick with the gold top, they moved very slowly out of the room and into the hall. It was not far from the drawing room to the front door, but nevertheless they had to stop twice for Wilhelmina to catch her breath.

William kissed his aunt on the forehead before opening the door. On the drive stood the parson's trap, and he was in the process of helping Daisy down from it. Neither Daisy nor Parson Lyndon was aware of them, William realised, and Daisy was smiling at something the parson must have said as she looked down into his upturned face. Her face was warm and glowing and her eyes bright and starry, and the sight was like a sword thrust straight through William's heart. He felt his aunt's hand tighten on his arm but for the life of him couldn't do anything but simply stare stupidly at the scene in front of him.

Wilhelmina hadn't been aware that the parson had offered to bring Daisy home and for a moment felt as stricken for William as the expression on her nephew's face revealed he was, but then she told herself it was all for the best. Whatever interpretation William put on this, he couldn't fail to recognise Daisy was not averse to the parson's company and it reinforced everything she had said earlier.

Daisy glanced their way the next moment as her feet touched the ground, and Wilhelmina saw William's face was wiped clean of all expression when he said politely, 'Parson Lyndon, Daisy, good afternoon. You are just in time to help your mistress back to the drawing room, Daisy, if you would be so kind. I didn't like to leave her without a hand at her elbow.'

'Of course.' Daisy stared at William and the light died from her face. The parson had been making her laugh on the way home by attempting to sing one or two of the songs from the operettas composed by Sir Arthur Sullivan and Sir William Gilbert even though he admitted to being tone deaf. She had been amazed in the first instance that Parson Lyndon knew anything other than the hymns they sang in church, and when she had admitted this he had gone on to express his taste in music which was wide and various. He had been attempting to teach her the words to one of the songs from *The Mikado* as they had arrived at the house, and, she suspected, deliberately trying to make her laugh, but it wasn't so much his efforts as the fact that she had spotted William's favourite stallion tethered outside which had suddenly lit up the evening with joy for her. But now here was William, standing in front of her, and his face was cold.

'How are you, William?' Hector's voice was pleasant. He could have been speaking to a man half his age by his demeanour, although in fact, there were only seven years separating the two.

'Very well.' William's throat was too dry for him to say anything more. He was battling with the insane desire to take this man of the cloth by the throat, much as he had done his uncle.

'Capital, capital.' Hector spoke as though he was quite

231

unaware of the atmosphere which had become as tense as piano wire, and as Daisy moved quietly to Wilhelmina's side in the doorway, he added, 'We have just returned from Daisy's village and the family were full of praises for the excellent birthday tea you provided, Wilhelmina. A veritable feast.'

He spoke as though he had been present all afternoon and this was deliberate. Hector did not dislike William Fraser – such an emotion would have been quite out of place in a parson and a grievous sin before the Almighty in one of His under-shepherds – but he considered Wilhelmina's nephew typical of the young bloods of the present age. The vast majority were intent only on having as riotous a time as possible, and he had dealt with more than one distressed family whose daughter had been ignominiously sent home from her place of service with a full belly. William was a handsome enough youth and furthermore seemed partial to Daisy's company which made him a hazard to her well-being. He needed to be discouraged from thinking he could toy with her.

The air was filled with unease after he had finished speaking and it was Wilhelmina who said quickly, 'I'm pleased to hear that,' her tone dismissive, before she turned to Daisy. 'Perhaps you would help me back to the drawing room, child? I confess I am a little tired and the night air strikes cool.'

He couldn't give her the brooch and she would assume he had not remembered her birthday. William's expression was as dark as his thoughts and he did not return the small smile Daisy gave him before she turned away. But then, what did it matter? She was clearly not ill-disposed to the parson's attentions and if she had invited the man to her family's home . . . He had always felt Daisy had an incandescence about her, something which could warm his heart or burn his fingers, and now he knew which it was.

William saw the parson hesitate a moment after the women had disappeared before he said, 'I mustn't delay you, William. Please give my kind regards to your father.'

He found he had to swallow deeply before he could say, 'Yes, I will. Good evening.'

'Good evening.'

The parson walked with measured steps into the house, shutting the door gently behind him, and then all was quiet except for the twittering of the birds in the surrounding trees. William stood for a moment more on the drive. He glanced across at the pony and trap which still had the wicker basket on its seat, and then he strode across to his horse and, once mounted, did not look back at the house.

Chapter Fourteen

'He's gone abroad?'

'To Paris, yes, child.' Wilhelmina busied herself with smoothing down her coverlet so she didn't have to look at Daisy's face because its expression pained her, and she prayed she might be forgiven when she added off-handedly, as though she wasn't aware what her words were doing to the white-faced girl, 'My brother seems to think there is a young lady William is rather partial to across the water. Of course he has spent a considerable amount of time with his cousins – Gwendoline's sister's boys – in the past, so that is quite feasible.'

Like someone mesmerised, Daisy continued to measure out the various pills and potions her mistress had to take every morning before she set foot out of bed, but all she could think was, He has gone. And he didn't even say goodbye.

It had been three long weeks since the day of her birthday and not once in all that time had William called at the house. But then, she had kept telling herself, there could be all sorts of reasons for that. Nevertheless, the longing to see him had grown with each passing day and for the past weeks Daisy had had a physical ache in her chest morning, noon and night.

She just didn't understand what had happened, she repeated silently for the umpteenth time. From calling almost every other day when she had first started at the house, he had suddenly curtailed his visits in the summer and for the last little while they had seen nothing of him at all. But she had her answer now, didn't she? In the shape of this nameless young French lady.

She bit hard on her lip. She couldn't cry, not now, not in front of Miss Wilhelmina, she told herself fiercely. Time enough for that when she was in the privacy of her room.

Wilhelmina was well aware of the struggle going on in the young girl she had come to love like a daughter over the past months, and for the first time in her long life she was suffering from the emotion of guilt. But, she reassured herself, this was all for Daisy's ultimate good. She would have a wonderful life with Parson Lyndon, and as his wife would be looked up to and respected in the small community in which they would live and work. There were times when you had to be cruel to be kind, and this was definitely one of them.

The parson had been calling even more frequently over the last weeks, and with William's continuing absence Daisy had obviously begun to look forward to his visits. Wilhelmina emphasised this to herself, sure it would all work out splendidly.

And William? She thought back to her brother's visit the day before while Daisy had been at the fishing village. Augustus had been more than a little annoyed at the boy's departure.

'Refused outright to consider Priscilla McKenzie or the Routledge girl, and wouldn't even attend Gwendoline's last dinner party,' he had grumbled darkly. 'Damn it, but the young cur needs a good horse whipping! I tell you, Wilhelmina, I was glad to see him leave for Paris. The boy is a disappointment, and his poor mother is beside herself at his refusal to take Priscilla after all our efforts to arrange the match.'

But William would be all right once he was with his cousins. He would be able to sow as many wild oats as he liked in their company without eyebrows being raised. Paris was like that, or so she'd heard. It was only in inferior novels a soul pined for unrequited love, and William was too handsome and too much of a catch to remain lonely for long.

Her nephew thus dealt with, Wilhelmina turned her mind to Daisy. She would suggest the child be driven into town to purchase a new hat – that was the very thing. The acquisition of a new bonnet was the cure for any indisposition in a young gel, and perhaps Daisy might wear it for church on Sunday if the weather remained clement?

It was a few days later, on a morning following a visit to Evenley House by Josiah and his master during which the valet had sat and conversed with Gladys and Harold at some length, that Hector Lyndon received a letter which disturbed him greatly.

The parson was already more than a little distracted – an uncommon occurrence – having been notified a day or two earlier that his only living relative, an elderly uncle who lived in Manchester, had succumbed to an outbreak of arsenic poisoning. This same outbreak had killed at least four people and left 2,000 more suffering from nervous illnesses in Liverpool and his uncle's home town. It hadn't helped Hector's state of mind that the cause of the outbreak had been traced to sulphuric acid supplied by a Liverpool company and used to treat brewing sugar. This had necessitated thousands of gallons of beer being poured into the sewers of both cities. His uncle, like Hector himself, had been a man of the cloth and regularly used his pulpit to preach against the demon drink and the need for abstinence by all good Christian souls, so the manner and cause of his death had left the parson unable to share word of his loss with anyone and feeling deeply ashamed of his own flesh and blood.

It was doubly unfortunate, therefore, that the letter should arrive on his doorstep at a time when Hector was feeling awkward and out of countenance with the world in general, and distinctly vulnerable regarding the integrity of his position.

Dear Parson Lyndon,

I feel it is my duty, as a good Christian, to acquaint you with some disturbing information I am sure you are not aware of. It is not right that a fine upstanding man of the cloth such as yourself should have the wool pulled over his eyes by a slip of a girl who is no better than she should be.

When Daisy Appleby was taken into Miss Fraser's employ some months ago she left a life which, sadly, was not respectable. It is even more sad that she now uses the wage of a good honest employer to run a house of ill repute in her home village. At the present time there are two women living in this property, overseen by the girl's own grandmother, and no man. Need I say more? One of the girls, unmarried of course, is due to give birth to a child in the near future.

I felt you would want to be advised of the above, and not least Miss Appleby's duplicity, in view of the fact that your reputation, up to the present time, has been one of high standing.

I am, sir, your obedient servant.

It was not signed.

Hector read the letter through twice and then a third time before sitting back in his seat at his desk and glancing round his study. Without even looking at them he was still seeing the lines of neat careful writing.

After a moment or two he rose, walking through to the kitchen where his housekeeper was busy preparing a meat roll for his dinner that evening. Mrs Finnigan looked up from wrapping the roll in a cloth preparatory to steaming it for three hours as the parson entered. It was not usual for him to visit the kitchen, normally he rang the bell and summoned her to whatever room he was in, and her apprehension was reflected in her soft Irish burr when she said, 'Is anything wrong, sir?'

'Wrong?' Hector forced a smile before he said, 'Not at all, Mrs Finnigan. I was just wondering if you saw who delivered the unstamped envelope this morning?'

Teresa Finnigan stared at the parson. She hadn't worked for him for the last few years without knowing when he had something on his mind. She glanced at the piece of paper he was holding against his leg, written side down, and then shook her head. 'No, I didn't, sir. It was on the mat when I opened the door before getting your breakfast, so whoever left it must have been up bright and early.'

Hector inclined his head without commenting and turned on his heel. Once back in his study he sat down at his desk with the letter in front of him, his head in his hands. How did he deal with this, and how much truth was there in the accusations? Wilhelmina had told him Daisy was supporting her grandmother and two sisters-in-law after the young women's husbands had been drowned, or he had thought that was what she had said. Of course he didn't believe Daisy was of easy virtue, not for a minute, but nevertheless . . . Dear, dear. He stood up, beginning to pace the floor. A parson and his wife had to be above reproach in every way.

At half-past one on the dot Mrs Finnigan served lunch in the Vicarage's small brown-painted dining room. She had informed Hector at the time he had taken over from the retiring Parson Tollett that she was quite happy to provide him with a tray in front of the fire in the sitting room any time he wished – 'Parson Tollett often liked to relax in his slippers come lunchtime, sir, so I'm used to it' – but Hector had looked askance at the very idea. Standards had to be maintained and propriety upheld, particularly in the home. Dignity bred respect, and in Hector's view this couldn't be earned by someone who was so slack in their personal habits as to eat from a tray in front of the fire.

Having said a solitary grace for the steaming bowl of mutton broth and three shives of stottie cake, Hector began to eat his meal. He would pay a visit to Wilhelmina next Sunday afternoon while Daisy was visiting the village and ascertain the truth about her relatives, but discreetly. He did not wish to give Wilhelmina the impression anything was amiss and had no intention of telling her about the letter. At the moment, however, he was grateful he had not spoken directly of his feelings for Daisy but had followed a prudent line. He had not compromised his own position and that was the most important thing. If there were members of Daisy's family – people who lived in her home at her expense – who were intent on a ruinous life, then he had to distance himself from her forthwith, however reluctantly.

The soup and bread gone, Hector carefully wiped his mouth on the linen napkin and left it, neatly folded, to one side of the empty soup bowl as he rose to his feet.

The person who had written the letter struck him as an educated individual which therefore rendered the contents worthy of consideration. This was not the missive of a fisherman or girl from Daisy's village who had a grievance against one of their own making good, he was sure of it. But for now he had a number of calls to make on the needy inhabitants of his parish, and his private affairs were of no account compared to his divine calling.

He brushed a few crumbs from his jacket, settled his clerical collar around his neck and walked swiftly from the room.

Margery's baby was coming and the delivery was not going well. Nellie had sent Alf to Evenley House to fetch Daisy when Margery's labour pains had gone on for a whole day and night, and once Daisy had reached the cottage she asked him to go into Whitburn for the doctor. Then she set about relieving Tilly who was looking exhausted herself, wiping Margery's forehead and trying to comfort the girl.

On the last day of November 1900 Margery gave birth to Tom's son. The baby took after its father and was healthy and vigorous but his arrival into the world cost his mother her life.

Although the doctor was very careful about the amount of chloroform he administered to his exhausted patient, Margery never regained consciousness from the operation he was forced to perform when it became plain the child would not be born naturally.

It was Daisy who first held the child after the umbilical cord had been cut. She gazed into the tiny face, at the miniature arms and hands clutching the air. This was Tom's bairn, the son her brother would never see, she thought, grief and wonder fusing together. And the baby was bonny, so bonny. Oh, Tom, he looks like you. I can actually see you in him.

The infant nestled further into the blanket wrapped snugly round him, yawning widely and showing small pink gums, and a rush of love so strong it was painful gripped Daisy's heart. This tiny scrap was so helpless and vulnerable and he wasn't going to have a father to protect and watch over him.

Tears were trickling down her cheeks as Daisy stood

cradling the child, and she was so wrapped up in the wonder of this new life that she was unaware of the doctor's increasingly desperate ministrations to its mother. The miracle of the perfectly formed little person in her arms left her speechless as she walked across the room and knelt down by the settle where Nellie was lying, the old woman having given up her bed to Margery when the labour had first begun. Tilly had been helping the doctor and Daisy but now stood up silently, her hands clasped together and held tightly against her waist and her eyes glued on Margery's still form.

'Eeh, look at that, he's Tom all over, lass.' Nellie was dry-eyed as she stared at her great-grandson but her lined face was softer than usual. Then she and Daisy heard Tilly give a little whimper deep in her throat from her vantage point at the doctor's side.

They both looked across at her, but it was the doctor who said, 'Miss Appleby? I'm sorry, there is nothing more I can do for your sister-in-law.'

'What?' Daisy rose slowly to her feet still holding the baby, ignoring Nellie's arms which had reached out for the child after the doctor had spoken.

'She . . . well, she's gone, I'm afraid. Her heart has simply given out. Did she have any problems in that way that you know of before she became pregnant?'

'Problems?' Daisy stared at the doctor blankly. She was unable to take in the fact that the fragile young girl lying on the soiled pallet bed wasn't breathing anymore. Margery would wake up in a minute, she had to. She had her baby to live for now, Tom's son.

It was Nellie who broke the silence, saying, 'I think her problems were more in the mind than the body, doctor. Folk, even the best of 'em, can be cruel when someone makes a mistake, an' the lass made a very visible mistake.'

Doctor Hogarth nodded his grey head slowly. He was a kind man which was why he had referred to his patient as being a married woman in spite of knowing the true circumstances within this family. Shame was a terrible millstone, he had known it break the necks of more than one patient in his time.

'The lass felt it more than she let on,' Nellie continued soberly, 'an' it got so she wouldn't budge from within these four walls. 'Course, the lad might have bin a comfort to her had she lived.'

Daisy's glance flashed between them before she lowered her eyes to Tom's son. Was she mad or were they? How could they calmly discuss the whys and wherefores when Margery . . .

'The parents will have to be informed,' the doctor said.

'Why?'

'Why?' He looked startled by the harsh tone of Daisy's voice.

'Why should they be informed? They were nothing to Margery, treated her like nothing. Right from the moment she was born she was supposed to live out her life in serving them. They made her feel she had to be the best at everything, and when that didn't happen they made her feel worthless, unloved. My brother saw that, I know he did, and loved her like she was supposed to be loved.'

Doctor Hogarth ran his hand under the stiffly starched collar of his shirt. He'd told his wife a hundred times to inform the maid not to put so much starch in the tub but still the collars came back so glassy his neck was constantly chafed red. 'They are nevertheless her parents, and the child's grandparents,' he said gently. 'They have the right to take the infant if they so wish.'

'They have no rights over my brother's son.'

Nellie shut her eyes for a moment. To answer back to Doctor Hogarth like that!

243

'Miss Appleby, it is clear you are upset—'

'Doctor Hogarth, those . . . people told Margery they never wanted to see her again,' Daisy said, her voice passionate in her desire to make him understand. 'If they said they wanted my brother's son it would only be so they could hide him away in the workhouse or something similar. My brother . . . well, he was an embarrassment to them. He wasn't good enough in their eyes and neither would his son be. Please, just leave things as they are. We'll look after the bairn and he *will* be loved. Surely that is more important than anything else? And it's what my brother and Margery would have wanted.'

'My dear child.' The doctor's voice was even more gentle now. 'Surely you understand they will get to know? With the best will in the world someone, at some time, will tell them the news.'

She had to make him *see*. Daisy schooled her voice to sound more matter-of-fact as she said quietly, 'I've met these people, Doctor, I know how their minds work. They want to pretend they never had a daughter because of what she has done, it's more comfortable that way. But should the bairn be presented to them they would take it and out of spite and . . . and shame they would get rid of it. I'm sure their intention was to put Margery in the workhouse when they discovered her condition. They wouldn't think twice about disposing of my brother's bairn in the same way. We have lost Tom and nothing can bring him back. Please don't make us lose his son too.'

Edmund Hogarth stared into the face he would later describe to his wife as memorable, but made no reply. Daisy watched him close his eyes after a moment or two, his head bowed and shaking slowly from side to side. The wait for him to speak seemed interminable but something told her not to rush him. And then he said, 'You are placing me in a very difficult position.'

White-faced and dry-eyed now, she said, 'You have advised us of the correct procedure regarding Margery's parents and if anyone asked I would make that perfectly clear, you have my word on that, Doctor. But I can assure you Margery's mam and da won't pursue their grandchild; as far as they're concerned they don't have one. Can . . . can we leave it at that? For all you know we are going to follow your instructions and inform them about the wee laddie.'

The doctor raised his head. 'Who would care for him? You provide for the family, I understand, and I'm sure your mistress would object to a baby being foisted upon her.'

'I can see to him, Doctor.' Tilly's voice was eager. 'With five of me own one more'll make no difference, an' with me youngest in the process of being weaned an' me always providing milk to feed twins we wouldn't even need to find a wet nurse.'

Doctor Hogarth stared into the rough, workworn face of the woman beside him who had lost her husband a few months ago and looked twenty years older than her twenty-eight years. Then his gaze moved to Nellie whose emaciated frame was positively skeletal but whose eyes had more life in them than he saw in many women half her age. Lastly his gaze fastened on Daisy. In the hurry and distress of the last hours her hair had come loose and a few shining silky strands were curling about her face. Those lovely eyes were beseeching him. He knew when he was beaten.

'I shall speak of this to no one,' he said gruffly, 'and of course it is no one else's business anyway.'

'Thank you.'

Doctor Hogarth said nothing. He was standing in a miserable fisherman's cottage that was without any of the niceties his wife would take for granted. It smelt, it was filled with the lowest of the working class, their enunciation poor and without refinement, and yet he knew this child was fortunate. He himself had been brought up in a rambling mansion overlooking its own private two miles of beach, the eldest of four boys who had all gone on to carve a niche for themselves in the medical world in some form or other, but there hadn't been an ounce of what he was feeling now in his childhood and youth. His wife too was very well bred, but – thank God, and he did, daily – Charlotte loved him and theirs was a marriage and home filled with the same closeness and support he sensed in this room, despite their disappointment about being unable to have children.

'It's a momentous task you are taking on, that of providing for someone else's child, and it will have far-reaching effects on your life. Do you understand this?' he asked softly after some moments. 'It needs thinking about, and very carefully.'

Silence fell on the room for a second, and then the young girl with the amazing eyes looked him full in the face. 'He's not someone else's child, he's mine now,' she said, even more softly, and such was the conviction in her voice that the good doctor knew there was no more to be said.

Part 3
Friends and Enemies

1903

Chapter Fifteen

It was Daisy's nineteenth birthday. The fierce gales which had been sweeping the country for over two weeks had blown themselves out, though not before wreaking havoc and destruction in the north. But now a September sun was shining warmly on the tall young woman making her way to the waiting carriage.

Daisy had changed considerably in the last three years. Not so much in her physical appearance, although her height had shot up some inches and she was now tall for a woman at five foot nine inches, the main transformation was in her manner and her speech. Thanks to the tutor Wilhelmina had employed for the first year of Daisy's stay at Evenley House her vocabulary and diction had improved enormously.

As well as encouraging her to delve into different areas of literature, Wilhelmina had made sure her young companion became acquainted with certain aspects of political and social reform, not least the case for women's suffrage. There was much which Daisy found disturbing as well as fascinating in her studies, but the more she learnt, the more determined she became that she would make a good life for herself and her lad – that was how she thought of Tom's little boy, as her son, her own – once her time at Evenley House came to a finish. Her goal was to have little Tommy with her all the time and she had thought long and hard about this, with the result that some time before she had purchased a book and was now teaching herself the rudiments of shorthand. However, Wilhelmina having become increasingly frail, Daisy was now in a position where she did almost everything for her mistress which left little free time, but the idea of a secretarial career in the future had been planted in her and Daisy was determined to hold on to it.

Her Sunday afternoons with Tommy were the most precious things in Daisy's life, and in spite of only seeing her once a week the child's feeling for her was something quite separate from the way he felt about anyone else, even Tilly. He loved Daisy every bit as much as she loved him.

The nature of Tommy's arrival and the bond which had been forged between them had played a large part in helping Daisy to come to terms with Parson Lyndon's defection. After he hadn't called for a week or more she had expressed concern that he was unwell to Wilhelmina, and it had been then her mistress had confessed about an altercation she'd had with him after he had called on her to ask a few pertinent questions. The good parson had clearly misjudged the intelligence of Sir Augustus's sister, and after she had forced him to explain himself further and the matter of the letter had been raised, he had received short shrift from the old lady who had terminated their friendship.

Daisy had been first angry and then terribly hurt, a feeling of humiliation taking hold of her which had been difficult to shake off for some time. She had thought Hector Lyndon was her friend, and after William's departure for foreign shores the parson's interest in her – which she had recognised as more than mere benevolence – had been a balm to her sore heart. Moreover, she had liked him very much. Whether anything more would have come from their friendship was another matter, but it had pained her that the parson could dismiss her from his life so cursorily and without even the courtesy of allowing her to defend herself against vile accusations. In such an atmosphere little Tommy's unconditional love had been all the sweeter, causing her often to count her blessings and eventually put the matter of the parson behind her.

This was not so easy where William was concerned. The way he had forsaken her, without so much as a goodbye, had cut deep, and as the months and years passed she'd made herself hate him. And she would go on hating him; it was vital protection for the day she would hear of his engagement to some fine lady or other from across the sea . . .

Once Daisy had seated herself in the carriage, Harold clicked his tongue and the pony ambled off. This had been accomplished without Daisy or he exchanging a word.

Daisy eyed the back of Harold's head upon which his flat cap sat like an aggrieved pancake. There was always the same cold silence from the cook's husband when they made a detour to this part of town after Daisy had taken care of any purchases Miss Wilhelmina wanted. Of course the network of streets stretching west from Monkwearmouth docks *was* grim, and the terraced dwelling Daisy had just visited was in a street close to Potato Garth, a well-known haunt of dockside dollies, but that was where Molly's sister lived so it couldn't be helped.

She had first heard of the desperate plight of this family, struggling to keep their heads above water and avoid the workhouse after the breadwinner had suffered an accident in the North Sands shipyard, a few months ago on her weekly visit home. Molly's brother-in-law had suffered serious injuries in the fall which had put him in the Sunderland Infirmary, and his wife and seven bairns – all under ten years old – had been in dire straits. It wasn't an uncommon story, but with the brother-in-law coming from the south and Molly and her bairns already having moved back in with her mam and da after Molly's husband was lost along with Daisy's father and brothers, there had been no help forthcoming from normal channels.

Daisy had gone to see Molly after Tilly had put her in the picture. She had always liked the big jolly fishergirl and felt an extra kinship with her somehow as a result of Molly's husband perishing in the same storm which had taken Daisy's father and brothers. The outcome of this visit had been a trip into Monkwearmouth on her next half-day off after she had spent some hours with Tommy, although she had persuaded Kitty to go straight home from the fishing village, knowing her friend would incur Gladys's wrath if she was late back.

Molly's sister's house had been steaming with the washing the woman was taking in in a desperate effort to make ends meet, and poverty was evident in her gaunt frame and the bairns' hungry faces. The gratitude the poor woman had displayed when Daisy had given her enough money to clear the backlog of rent and buy food and fuel for the week had been thanks enough for the depletion in Daisy's savings. Over the next few weeks she had made two more visits to Molly's sister's, and it had been the Monday after the last call when Wilhelmina had taken her to task.

Was it true she was in the habit of visiting a less than salubrious part of Monkwearmouth on her half-day off, her mistress had inquired, and in the late evening at that? Daisy had stared into Wilhelmina's cold face and for a moment it was as though the letter Parson Lyndon had received was right there between them. It took all her self-control to bite back the sharp retort which sprang to mind and to say, quietly and with dignity, 'Respectability is not confined to grand houses or clean streets, ma'am. The family I visit are good people who have fallen on hard times.'

'Explain.'

She had explained, and although it was clear Wilhelmina had believed her the old lady had still asked her not to visit them again but to send any gifts or moneys through Molly. It was only when Daisy said she couldn't hurt Molly's sister's feelings by cutting her in such a way that her mistress had said, and tersely, that if Daisy meant to persist in such a venture herself then she must do so in daylight hours during the week, and Harold would take her. Relations between Daisy and her mistress had been strained for a few days over what Wilhelmina saw as her companion's obstinacy, but when Daisy walked out to the carriage on the day the old lady had designated she'd discovered a hamper full of food along with a sack of potatoes and another of coal.

Wilhelmina had brushed her thanks aside with an abrupt, 'I'm sure you need the pennies you put by more than me, child,' but things were back on their old footing again and Daisy was glad. When Kitty had discovered it had been her parents who had caused the storm in a teacup after Gladys had sent Harold to spy on Daisy's visits, it had seemed poetic justice that Gladys had to prepare the food and Harold drive her to Monkwearmouth on future calls.

As the carriage left the oppressiveness of the town Daisy's thoughts moved to the coming afternoon. Miss Wilhelmina had said she could change her half-day off this week in order to see her family on her birthday, but she hadn't told her grandmother, aiming to surprise the old woman. Now she hugged the thought to her. Her granny would get a gliff and no mistake.

As it happened, it was Daisy herself who was surprised and not a little frightened as she approached the cottages by means of the road over the sand dunes from Fulwell. She suddenly felt herself lifted right off her feet by a brawny arm round her waist, and twisted frantically to see who had grabbed her from behind.

'Alf!' Her voice wasn't as strong as she would have liked.

'Who else?' He had been laughing but then, as he lowered Daisy to her feet and she turned to face him, his smile vanished as he took in her angry expression. 'Aw, don't go on, lass.' His voice was placating. 'It was just a bit of fun.'

'I don't like being manhandled.'

'Manhandled?' His voice expressed hurt now.

'Yes, manhandled.' His arm had pressed against her breasts, whether by accident or design Daisy wasn't sure, but she had not liked it. Every Sunday afternoon he met her and Kitty, come rain, hail or snow, and even today he had been waiting for her! Her voice reflected her irritation as she said, 'What on earth are you doing here at this time of the day? Why aren't you out on the water?'

Alf stared at her. If he told her the truth – that he'd suspected there was a chance her mistress would let her visit the village on her birthday – she would know he had planned his whole day around the possibility. He rubbed his face with the back of his hand. 'There's other jobs to see to on land. Anyway, maybe it's just as well I've seen you like this without the others around. I want to get a couple of things sorted once and for all. I might as well tell you straight, I can't carry on like this much longer.'

'Like what?'

He continued to stare at her, moving his head with a small jerk before he said, 'I'm tired of waitin', that's it in a nutshell. I want a wife an' family, lass. That's not too much for a bloke to ask, is it? Companionship, someone waitin' when I get off the boat of a night, an' don't say I've got me mam for that.'

She hadn't been about to say that. Daisy swallowed. 'I can understand that, Alf.'

'An' that's all you've got to say? Look, lass, to put it bluntly I want a wife afore I'm too old to enjoy being wed and I'd like it to be you, but you know that. Are you still sayin' no? An' before you say anythin' you ought to know this is the last time of askin'. The very last.'

Daisy's eyes widened slightly. He'd said that as though he meant it. Turning, she began to walk on, and as he fell into step beside her, said, 'Alf, you're my friend and dear brother and I can't think of you in any other way. I'll never be able to thank you for your kindness to Gran—'

A sharp movement of his hand stilled her voice. They had reached the first of the cottages, and his voice was rough when he said, 'It's no use hopin' he'll come back an' marry you, you know that, don't you? He's got bigger fish to fry.'

Her heart jerked in her chest and then began to thud hard against her ribcage. 'I don't know what you're talking about.'

'No?'

'No.'

'You're throwin' your life away, pinin' for him, and he's nowt. They're all nowt, in spite of their fancy clothes an' la-di-da way of talkin'.'

'I'm not pining for anyone, Alf Hardy.' She was angry now. 'Just because I don't want to marry you doesn't mean I want to marry someone else.'

'So that's me final answer then? You're determined to go on lookin' after that old crone an' actin' Lady Bountiful to every Tom, Dick an' Harry?'

Daisy took a step away from him, terribly hurt.

'An' don't look at me like that neither,' Alf said thickly. 'I'm not one of your fancy pals who mince about an' never say what they really think.' He swore, the first time he had

255

ever used a profanity in front of her, and then he grabbed at her, pulling her against the bulk of him. One big hand was in the small of her back and the other under her armpit, and he arched her rigid body into his as he took her mouth in a kiss which had no gentleness in it.

Daisy didn't fight him. They were in full view of the village and so she was quite safe, besides which she instinctively knew the only way to bring him quickly to his senses was to remain perfectly still. She stood stiff and unyielding in his desperate embrace for as long as the kiss lasted which wasn't more than a few seconds. And then he thrust her aside so violently she almost fell but for his hand reaching out again to steady her. 'If you don't want me there's one as does.'

His face was flushed, veins bulging in his forehead, but his voice was low and deep and held a note Daisy didn't recognise. She was trembling with the shock of it all but she managed to speak steadily when she said, 'That doesn't surprise me. You're a good catch for anyone.'

She saw the rage drain from his face along with the high colour and for a terrible moment she thought he was going to cry. Then he said, the words strangled in his throat, 'I'm goin' to ask Kitty to start courtin', Daisy.'

'*Kitty?*'

'Aye, Kitty. We . . . we get on an' she thinks a bit of me.'

Daisy stared at him. Kitty? Kitty and Alf? But then a separate part of her mind said, Why not? Why not indeed? If she'd had half the sense she was born with she would have seen long ago that what Alf said was true. Kitty did like him, she always had, but knowing how Alf felt about her, the other girl had never talked of her own feelings. And Kitty was bonny and jolly and as strong as a horse. She would make a perfect fisherman's wife, and the hard life wouldn't worry her at all. In fact, she'd take to it like a duck to water. So why, Daisy asked herself now, in view of all that did she feel as if the bottom of her world had just fallen away?

'You know she won't say yes to me if she thinks you are against it. She thinks the world of you.' Alf's voice was low and he didn't look at her as he spoke.

'I'm not against it.'

She stared at him until he looked up again, saying, 'I've had a bellyful of bein' on me own, lass, an' I'm not gettin' no younger. Kitty's a good lass an' I know we'd suit each other. It won't be the same as if we'd . . .' His voice trailed away and he shrugged his shoulders.

'Kitty would make anyone a wonderful wife.' Daisy's voice was stronger now. 'And you would be kind to her?'

'You know I would.'

Aye, he would. Alf couldn't be anything other than kind, and she knew he must have worked himself up into a right state to speak as he had about her and William. This last thought gentled Daisy's voice as she said, 'I wish you both every happiness, Alf.'

'I haven't even asked the lass to walk out yet.'

But he was going to do so, and Kitty would say yes. A strong feeling of gladness rose up in Daisy now. Alf would be so good for Kitty, providing that solid foundation her friend had never experienced before, not with her mam and da being as they were. The marriage would work, she could see it working very well, and the pair of them were her dearest friends after all. It was just the surprise of it which had made her feel odd for a moment or two.

'I'll make sure she comes with me on Sunday, Alf.'

He looked down at the ground for a moment. 'Aye, all right.' And then he jerked his head in the direction of the road leading out of the village and his voice was flat when he said, 'I've a few bits to see to in town. 'Bye, lass.'

She nodded. ''Bye, Alf.'

He moved away first and strode off rapidly. It was the first time he had ever chosen not to spend time with her when she visited her granny, and as she watched him go Daisy knew a moment of deep regret. Not regarding her decision; she could never have married Alf, and would have made both of them utterly miserable if she'd weakened in that respect. No, her regret was for how things would change from this point of time. In a way she would lose both Alf and Kitty, and it wasn't until this moment that she fully realised how much coming first with both of them had meant to her after William had discarded her as easily as he would a pair of old boots. But that was horribly selfish of her, she knew.

She stood without moving until Alf had disappeared from view and then began walking slowly, her head drooping. Somehow this didn't feel like a birthday at all. And then she pictured Tommy's little face with its wide infectious grin and her spirits lightened. She had her boy, her precious little boy. All right, so her financial responsibilities might be too great for her to leave Miss Wilhelmina's employ, besides which she felt a loyalty to the old lady which kept her at Evenley House, but one day circumstances would change and a door of opportunity would open and she'd jump through it, taking Tommy with her. It was all down to the time machine again and the buttons she chose to press.

She was going to make something of herself, and when she did Tommy would have all the advantages of a solid home and a good education or her name wasn't Daisy Appleby.

Daisy opened the door to the cottage, her face breaking into a wide smile at the childish shriek of joy which greeted her entrance. She bent and opened her arms to receive the scampering body, and as she did so, thought, This is what

258

it's all about. As the child wrapped his plump little arms and legs about her, for all the world like a baby monkey clinging to its mother, Daisy cuddled him close, glancing across at the smiling face of her granny and then Tilly who came bustling out of the scullery, her hands covered in flour. As their combined welcome flowed over her in a warm tide, she relaxed. She was home.

Chapter Sixteen

William took one of the newspapers a servant had recently ironed – it wouldn't do for the ink to rub off on a family member's hands – and pretended to read to escape the conversation around the breakfast table. In spite of having lived in Paris with his uncle's family for the last three years, he still found the discussions which invariably raged at breakfast a little too early in the day to be enjoyable. He knew Pierre and Marcel liked to bedevil their father, who was of the old school, with their radical ideas, and sometimes felt he would like to point out to his uncle that the two young men were only baiting him – it would certainly make for quieter mealtimes – but as this would spoil his cousins' fun he kept silent.

He raised a hand and immediately a liveried servant poured more coffee into his cup. There were thirty servants in all looking after the family of four and any guests his uncle had to stay in his town house, some of whom travelled with the family when they visited their château in the French countryside. On those occasions, though, William and his cousins often stayed in Paris where the night life excelled any other city's and hedonism was the order of the day.

His first lover there had been the young wife of an ageing count, and perhaps because Jeanette had been the first he remembered her more clearly than all the others who had followed although her face was now a blur in his mind.

Strange, when you thought about it, that it was the one girl he hadn't had, the one who had only allowed him to hold her hand, whose face was crystal clear whenever he shut his eyes at night. He forgot the others as soon as he left their presence and yet every detail of his time with Daisy was imprinted on his memory. He felt the familiar twisting in his guts and changed the direction of his thoughts ruthlessly.

His aunt and uncle were thinking of visiting their château for a few weeks and he might go with them this time. It would give Hildegarde time to cool down and accept that their affair was over.

As though his thoughts had conjured it up William became conscious of a footman at his elbow, holding out a silver plate on which reposed a pink-flushed envelope. He recognised both the paper and the bold black script of the writer and, sighing inwardly, took the envelope with a nod of thanks. Another of Hildegarde's faintly hysterical demands that he visit her, no doubt. She had caused quite a fuss at the Rothwells' musical soirée last night, even going so far as to hold on to his arm when he had tried to walk away after she'd cornered him in a recess of the drawing room. The woman was shameless, but then hadn't that been what had attracted him to her in the first place? She had wanted him and she'd made no bones about it, but that hadn't mattered so much when her husband had been abroad. Now Rudolf von Spee was back, and as German Ambassador to the French government he was not a man to mess with, being both important and influential. He was also a nasty piece of work.

William slit open the envelope, his eyes scanning the lines of writing. He read the letter twice before leaning back in his seat. The woman was deranged, she had to be to threaten she would tell her husband everything if he didn't resume their affair. What had he got himself into here? This could turn into the mother and father of a scandal.

He thought quickly. His uncle's château was not far enough away with Hildegarde in this frame of mind. Perhaps England would be better? It was the second week of September. That meant the King had spent a week or two at the Palace after his usual month's cure at Marienbad and would now be going up to Balmoral for the grouse and deer. Scotland would be the accepted place to be; no one would think it overly strange if he renewed his acquaintance with one or two university friends whose families had estates up there. It was time to show his face for a while anyway, it had been nine months since he had spent some time in England and eighteen since he had visited Greyfriar Hall, and that had only been a brief stay. Of course Daisy must be married by now, he could easily take up residence at Greyfriar again, but somehow the thought of seeing her on Hector Lyndon's arm was still as raw as the last time he had observed them together.

He rose from the table, and as he did so his eldest cousin, Marcel, glanced up and followed him out of the room, leaving Pierre and Claude still arguing. Marcel inclined his head at the envelope in William's hand. He, too, recognised the pink paper. 'Trouble?' he asked softly.

William handed his cousin the letter in reply, and after Marcel had read the contents he pursed his lips, his fair brows drawing together. 'Tread carefully with this one, Will. Hildegarde is just a silly woman but her husband is a powerful man with many friends, some respectable and some not so respectable. You know?'

Yes, he knew. William nodded. 'I've been thinking it's about time I paid a visit to the land of my fathers,' he said with a touch of self-mockery.

Marcel smiled. 'I think that would be a good idea.' He

hesitated before saying, 'Particularly so if the news I heard is true. It appears Francis is in Paris again.'

'He wouldn't dare show his face here, not after the last time.'

It had been two years ago, twelve months after he had left England, that Francis had turned up on the doorstep of Claude's town house asking to see William. He had given his uncle a chilly reception which had turned to frost when Francis had had the audacity to suggest his nephew act as intermediary in a reconcilation between Augustus and himself. He had been short of cash and heavily in debt – again. William had all but thrown him out of the house.

'Do not be so sure, cousin,' Marcel said drily. 'When the devil is pulling the strings . . .' He raised his eyebrows before adding, 'Hildegarde? Were you indiscreet at all?'

'Indiscreet?' William thought for a moment. 'No, I don't think so. There were no letters or anything of that nature.'

'Good.' Marcel then slapped him on the back, saying, 'I am late for my fencing lesson. I will see you later, Will.'

William watched his cousin stride away but did not move for some moments. Then, slowly, he began to make his way to his bedroom on the second floor of the house. At some point this morning it had dawned on him that his present life had soured on him. He was tired of playing the man about town, he had been tired of it for some months but it had been easier not to face the fact that at times he was sickened by the sight of his own face in the shaving mirror. He decided he had made a cuckold of a man for the last time. The next woman he took to his bed would be free to bestow her affection where she would.

He paused on the second landing, leaning with his hands outstretched on the polished gallery rail as he stared into the richly decorated hall far below. His aunt always insisted on the best and employed the finest designers to furnish the homes of her French husband. They had been good to him, his aunt and uncle, and more like parents than his own had ever been. It was hard to believe at times that his aunt was his mother's sister.

Once in his bedroom he flung himself down into one of the two leather armchairs placed in the bay of the window, leaning forward and clasping his hands.

He was twenty-six years old, and what had he to show for his life? Was his present existence what Daisy had risked her own life for?

His posture altered as William raised his head, flexing his shoulders and straightening his back. He had come here originally because he had not been man enough to stay in England and watch her marry someone else. That was it in a nutshell. But enough was enough. He was going to take control of his life again and begin afresh. The army maybe? The Fraser clan had long-established military connections, half his forebears had been Colonels or Brigadiers. Whatever, he was done with Paris. It had been good to taste what real family life was like with his aunt and uncle and cousins, and he'd always be grateful to them, but it was time to leave. To carve out his own future.

A dart of excitement, the first he had felt in a long, long time, brought him out of the chair and over to the walnut writing desk in a recess of the room. He needed to start making plans.

Later that same morning William found himself alone in the house. His aunt had persuaded her husband to drive to the Bois de Boulogne, one of the two grand parks Baron Haussmann had built four decades ago when the French Prefect embarked on his rebuilding of Paris. It was still the place to see and be seen, and Lydia had wanted to show off the new carriage and pair her husband had bought her for an anniversary gift the week before. Pierre, who had his eye on a certain young lady who might also be taking the air, had gone with his parents, and William was in the middle of writing a letter to the friend he hoped to stay with in Scotland when a maid knocked on his door to say, Francis had called.

As William entered the drawing room he saw his uncle standing by the open french windows, looking out over the rows of neat flowerbeds. He turned immediately to say, 'M'boy, m'boy,' arms outstretched as though William was the dearest soul on earth to him.

William walked fully into the room before he replied, and then indicated a chair to one side of the magnificent fireplace. 'Please be seated, Uncle.' It was coldly said. 'You wish to speak to me?'

The smile remained fixed on Francis's puffy face as he sat down, shuffling his fleshy buttocks deep into the seat. 'Indeed I do, m'boy. Indeed I do. And just between ourselves, if you get my meaning? No need to air the family's dirty laundry in public after all, or let word get back to the old pater, eh?'

William stared into the flabby, perspiring face. 'I'm sorry, I don't follow you.'

So that was the way the arrogant young pup was going to play it? Well, he didn't mind spelling it out. In fact, he'd get pleasure from it. Francis placed his hands on his knees, leaning forward slightly as he said in a low voice, 'I'm referring to your little . . . indiscretion with the German fellow's wife, m'boy. I hear von Spee is hopping mad.'

If Francis called him 'm'boy' once more he'd wipe the smile off his uncle's face with the back of his hand. William walked over to the door, opening it and standing straight and stiff as he said, 'Good day, Uncle.'

'What?' This wasn't what Francis had expected at all.

266

'Now look, laddie, I've come here to try and help, that's all. Family is family, what?'

'I don't need your help.'

Francis found himself momentarily at a loss and fought back with a short bark of laughter before he said, 'Don't be so sure about that. I just came to advise you to get out of Paris for a while. I know a few people—'

'I'm sure you do.' William cut across his uncle's voice. 'As it happens I am leaving for Scotland in the next day or two so you need concern yourself no further. Now, if there's nothing else?'

Francis's jaw tightened, and his next words came from between his teeth as he got up to leave. 'You'll regret crossing me one day, boy.'

'I doubt that.'

As his uncle passed him they exchanged one last glance of mutual enmity and then Francis stalked off down the hall, pushing the servant who had opened the door for him roughly aside and disappearing into the busy Paris street beyond.

By the time Francis reached the end of the road he was sweating profusely but he didn't stop walking until he was out of sight of the house, and then he leant against the iron railings which bordered a small front garden, his hand to his chest as he tried to catch his breath. If ever anyone deserved what was coming to them that little pipsqueak did. He fished his silk handkerchief out of his top pocket and mopped his damp face. But he had got the information von Spee had paid him for and that was the main thing. If all went according to plan, at the end of this little lot he'd be sitting pretty. With William disposed of he was the next in line to inherit after all.

He stood for a moment longer, straightening his hat and adjusting the lapels of his coat after he'd returned the handkerchief to his pocket. And then he began to stroll along the pavement, one hand sliding into the inner pocket of his coat and his fingers caressing the thick bundle of notes resting against his heart.

Two days later William's trunk and portmanteau had already been placed in the coach which was to take him to the port at Calais, a journey of one hundred and fifty miles, and now he was making his goodbyes to the family. He was touched to see both his aunt and uncle had moist eyes, and his cousins were trying to extract a promise he would return in the near future.

'You will be breaking a hundred ladies' hearts if you stay away, cousin. You know it, don't you?' This from Pierre and said with a twinkle in his eye.

'Come back for the New Year. You know how you enjoy the celebrations in gay Paree,' said Marcel.

'The New Year can be gay anywhere.' William smiled, but he hadn't realised just how much of a wrench it would be to leave them all. However, his mind was made up. First Scotland, and then he would inform his family he was joining the army.

The farewells over at last, he took his seat in the coach and nodded at the other occupants, hearing Marcel promise, 'I will join you in Scotland for a spot of shooting in a couple of weeks,' over the sound of the horses' hooves as they got underway.

'*Au revoir*.' He hung out of the window, waving, before settling back in his seat again, the middle-aged gentleman and young couple who comprised the rest of the passengers smiling briefly, before the gentleman made himself comfortable and shut his eyes, and the young couple began conversing quietly.

William followed the gentleman's example. He hadn't slept too well the last few nights with all he'd had to think about and he was tired. He dozed for most of the journey, and by the time the coach lurched into the courtyard of an inn at Abbeville its lamps had been lit for some time.

The gentleman was only travelling as far as Abbeville, and when the young couple asked William to join them at the evening meal the inn provided, he accepted gratefully. He had never felt so alone in all his life as during the last hours.

The young couple turned out to be a Monsieur and Madame De Quéré, a French couple who spoke excellent English and who were travelling to Calais to see Madame De Quéré's sister who lived close to the port. After a somewhat mediocre meal, only made enjoyable by the company and several glasses of very good wine, William went up to his room. He was asleep as soon as his head touched the pillow despite the hardness of the flock mattress.

A grey dawn was only just beginning to break through the darkness when he joined Monsieur and Madame De Quéré in the coach after a hearty breakfast, and for the rest of the journey it was just the three of them which made for pleasant conversation.

Calais looked and smelt like any big port as the wheels of the coach bumped over the cobbled quay, the universal smells of the waterfront vying with the odd whiff of eau de Cologne now and again from the fine lace handkerchiefs elegant ladies held pressed to their delicate noses.

A steady rain had been drumming against the windows of the coach for the last hour or two, and as William waited for Monsieur De Quéré to help his wife out of the vehicle before alighting himself, a clap of thunder rolled across the sky. It was a thoroughly miserable day.

William's uncle had tipped the driver of the coach handsomely to see his nephew's trunk and bags safely deposited aboard the *Mauretania* and, his goodbyes to his new friends having been said some moments before, William climbed down from the coach intending to make his way to the ship which he could see some distance along the quay. It was then he noticed that Madame De Quéré seemed to be in some distress. He caught her husband's eye as the man glanced about him in agitation, and William felt he could do no other than step forward and say quietly, 'May I be of some assistance, Monsieur?'

'My wife . . . I'm sorry. It seems she is not well.' As he spoke the woman leaning against his chest moaned softly and then appeared to swoon right away, her head lolling alarmingly as her husband struggled to take her full weight.

William had reached out to support her too when it had seemed Monsieur De Quéré couldn't hold her, and now he said to the slightly built man, 'I have her, Monsieur, don't worry. Perhaps if you could lead the way to the nearest physician's establishment?'

'No need for that. She . . . well, she is in a delicate condition, you know? And it is early days. Apparently it is not unusual for this to occur at such a time.'

'I see.' William glanced about him. 'Well, let's get her out of the rain at least, shall we?'

'I cannot impose on you, Monsieur Fraser.'

'Of course you can.' William smiled encouragingly at the poor man and tried to ignore the fact he could feel water beginning to drip down his neck. 'The driver is seeing to my bags and it is at least another two hours before I need go aboard. Let me help you get her to shelter and then perhaps a glass of water will revive her?'

'You are very kind.' There was the slightest of hesitations. 'If you are really sure you have the time my sister-in-law's house is only just round the corner. A minute's walk, that is all. It would be less distressing for my wife if we took her there, I think.'

William nodded. The woman was coming to but still clearly feeling unwell. Obviously she would welcome being with her sister. Monsieur De Quéré seemed quite happy to relinquish his burden to William and walked ahead, carefully picking his way over the wet cobbles towards a narrow path which ran directly in front of warehouses and other buildings and then into an alleyway. The end of this opened up into a street which seemed to incorporate more warehouses intermingled with houses. Compared to the dock itself which had been a hive of activity this area was quieter, and now that the alleged minute's walk had lengthened into several William became aware of a prickle of disquiet. He was just about to ask how much further the house was when Monsieur De Quéré said, 'Just down here, Monsieur Fraser, and we are there. I cannot tell you how much we appreciate your help.'

The side street had a pungent smell to it; William didn't like to think what was in the gutters and old broken boxes and crates and other rubbish piled high to either side of the road, but right now all he wanted to do was to get back to the waterfront. He watched as De Quéré knocked on the front door of a house halfway along the street, its flaking door and windows identical to the ones on either side. He hadn't imagined that the lady's sister would live in such a rundown, seedy area, but then ports the whole world over seemed to spawn such habitation.

He wished he could adjust his hat so the water would stop dripping down his neck; at this rate he was going to be soaked through to his underclothes by the time he boarded the *Mauretania*.

As the door opened he saw a youngish man peer at them in the dull grey daylight and heard Monsieur De Quéré speak rapidly in his native tongue, too rapidly for William – whose French was pretty good normally – to understand. And then Monsieur De Quéré turned to him, saying, 'If you could just help me in with her, Monsieur, my brother-in-law will guide you back to the waterfront. We do not want you getting lost.'

'Please, don't trouble him. I can find it all right.'

As William stepped into the dank, dark hall he had no time for more than a quick cursory glance about him as once again Monsieur De Quéré was leading the way, leaving him to guide Madame through into the sitting room. The woman had been leaning heavily on his arm, but as they came to the threshold of the room her posture changed and she straightened up, glancing at him in the fluttering light from a naked gas jet attached to a bracket on the wall.

The room was poorly furnished, holding nothing more than a large shabby sofa, a battered wooden table and three straight-backed chairs which had seen better days. At the back of these stood a number of wooden boxes and crates, which seemed to suggest the room doubled as a storage place. The only window was boarded up which made the light from the large oil lamp in the middle of the table inadequate. However, there was an element of cheeriness from the black-leaded fireplace which was stacked high with blazing coals, a scuttle at the side of the fire brim full.

All this William noticed in one swift glance, his attention being primarily on the two men facing him who had been standing with their backs to the fire, legs slightly apart, as they toasted themselves in its warmth. He smiled at them but the stolid faces didn't respond, neither did the men speak. It was Monsieur De Quéré who spoke first, saying, in quite a different tone from any he had used before, 'You can let go of her now, Monsieur Fraser. But of course, I was forgetting, you like handling what is not yours, do you not?'

William stared into the man's eyes and wondered why

he had not noticed their hard blackness before. At a sound behind him he looked round; the young man who had answered the front door smiled at him, gesturing for him to enter the sitting room. He was holding a two-foot iron bar in his hands.

William swallowed, fear sweeping over him like a wave, but he stepped into the room. He could do little else. As he did so the woman he had known as Madame De Quéré smiled at him and then tilted her head, saying over her shoulder as she turned and left them, 'I can't see what the attraction was myself, but then my man knows better than to leave me for weeks on end. Eh, Jean-François?'

Sniggering from the two men in front of the fire brought William's attention back to them. They were thickly made men, heavy-shouldered, short but powerful-looking. In contrast Jean-François, or Monsieur De Quéré as he had been up to this point, was slim and wiry, as was the man holding the iron bar. Nevertheless, four against one was poor odds. William decided to try sweet reason coupled with bribery.

'I take it your presence in the coach was all leading up to this point, Monsieur De Quéré? And from what you have already said, am I also correct in assuming Rudolf von Spee is at the bottom of this?'

For answer the man said, 'There are some people one does not cross, Monsieur Fraser. Were you not aware of this?'

'Whatever he is paying you and the others, I'll double it.'

One of the bullet-headed men said something in German and Jean-François answered in the same language. He then turned back to William, speaking again in English when he said, 'You cannot buy these gentlemen, Monsieur Fraser, so do not waste your time attempting to do so. You have annoyed their master and he has told them what is required.

For myself I do not indulge in . . . physical exertion. My wife and I like to think of ourselves as artists involved in the delicate profession of persuading clients to part with their wealth, that is all.'

'You are confidence tricksters.'

Jean-François's eyes narrowed on the young Englishman. Then he said, 'I would like to say that you would be wise not to annoy me, but in truth it really does not matter one way or the other. I was asked to deliver you to von Spee's friends. This I have done. My wife and I will now take our leave.'

This couldn't be happening to him. William could feel his stomach turning over. Were they going to kill him? He glanced beyond Jean-François and read the answer in the dull-eyed faces staring at him.

'Goodbye, Monsieur Fraser.' Jean François walked quickly past him, pausing in the doorway for just a second before shutting the door behind him.

William had moved sideways as the other man exited, and now had all three men in his sight. As their eyes fixed on him he concentrated on the slim man holding the iron bar, who was striking it rhythmically against the palm of his other hand.

With a lightning movement William reached out and grabbed one of the chairs, holding it in front of him like a lion tamer as the two gorillas approached, their eyes unblinking. It was a poor weapon when matched against the iron bar and the other two fellows' great ham fists but it was all he had.

When one of the men brought a mighty forearm sweeping against the chair it was all William could do to hold on to it; consequently he missed the crouching action of the man with the iron bar but he certainly felt the impact as the solid rod snapped his left shinbone like a dried leaf.

He was on the floor now, the agony in his leg obliterating

everything else. When von Spee's thugs began to use their boots on him he tried to roll or crawl away but to no avail. He could hear himself screaming and one of the men chuckling before he lost consciousness, then he was going into the red mist and although he knew it was all up with him if he didn't try and avoid the murderous intent of the steel-capped boots, he went willingly.

Not even William's mother would have recognised her son by the time the three had finished their fun. He didn't feel them strip him down to his blood-soaked underclothes after they had gone through his pockets, or hear the careful knock at the door which preceded Francis Fraser's entrance into the house with his nephew's trunk and portmanteau.

'You've seen to him then?' There was a note of disappointment in Francis's voice; he had wanted to watch when Augustus's son got his just deserts but von Spee had been specific in his orders. Once William was inside the house and it was apparent his uncle would not be needed in any way to lure William aside, should the other ploy fail, Francis was to intercept the trunk and portmanteau, paying the driver of the coach a handsome tip. The driver knew his passenger had been English; what could be more natural than the father coming to meet his son unexpectedly and changing their cabin to a double berth? And if the remuneration was generous enough the driver wouldn't quibble.

He hadn't quibbled, and after a brief word Francis left the house again for Paris, taking William's trunk and portmanteau with him to dispose of at his leisure.

The other three rolled the body in a piece of rough sacking, leaving it in a corner of the room until darkness fell and they could safely dump it in the accommodating waters of the murky dock. All identification was gone and one more floating corpse was neither here nor there in waters which saw plenty of them. But they hadn't reckoned on a door-to-door search by the dockside police working on a tip off about contraband from the Customs officers.

After a check from an upstairs window when a knock came at the front door at dusk, von Spee's men left by an attic door on to the roof, making their escape past smoking chimney stacks and brooding pigeons and seagulls. They took with them William's clothes and the contents of his pockets including his papers, but his body they left rolled up in a corner of the sitting room, secure in the belief that they had done their job well.

Chapter Seventeen

'Say "How do you do?" to Miss Wilhelmina, Tommy.'

'How do you do?' And then the child, overcome by his surroundings and more especially the grand old lady in front of him, buried his head in Daisy's skirts.

She bent down, lifting the small boy into her embrace, and when plump little arms wrapped themselves in a stranglehold round her neck and his face remained hidden, said apologetically, 'He's shy, ma'am.'

'Too shy to try a piece of coconut ice?'

One eye peeped at her. Coconut ice was one of Miss Wilhelmina's little indulgences and the old lady often sent a bag to Daisy's grandmother after the girl had told her Nellie had a sweet tooth. Several pieces always found their way into Tommy's willing mouth and the child had developed a passion for the sweets.

'Do you prefer pink, white or brown, Tommy?' Wilhelmina asked as the little boy twisted round in Daisy's arms to stare down at the large tin full of coconut ice the old lady was holding out. Gladys always coloured a third of the mixture with pink food colouring, and another third with coffee essence to give a Neapolitan effect.

Daisy crouched down with Tommy on her lap now, and as the little boy said, 'Brown,' murmured reprovingly, 'Brown, please, ma'am.'

'Brown please, ma'am,' the childish treble repeated.

Wilhelmina smiled. 'I think I like that best too.' And

then, as the child hesitated, she said, 'That's a nice big bit just there, Tommy. Try that one.'

A dimpled hand reached out and took the chunk Wilhelmina had pointed at, and when the little boy said, 'Thank you,' without any prompting, the old lady's face softened still more.

Daisy breathed a silent sigh of relief. When Miss Wilhelmina had expressed a wish to see the child she had to admit she'd had her doubts. The old lady was terribly frail now, unable to get from her bed to her private sitting room without help and then Daisy virtually carried her. For the last few months Daisy had been more of a nurse than a companion; she bathed her mistress in bed every morning, massaged her limbs constantly day and night, fed her when Miss Wilhelmina's hands were shaking too much to do the job, and slept almost every night on the couch in the dressing room.

They never spoke of Miss Wilhelmina's demise – the old lady was frightened of dying although she would never have admitted to it – but the fact that she had asked to see Tommy was indication to Daisy that her mistress knew her time was short. Daisy had wanted the old lady to meet him but in view of the child's boisterousness had wondered how Miss Wilhelmina would cope. Even the most sedate visitor tired her out these days. In the end it had been decided that Tilly would bring Tommy to the house on Daisy's next half-day off just an hour before Daisy was due to leave for the village, and it so happened that this was a Saturday rather than a Sunday because it was All Saints Eve which the village always celebrated.

That this fact was firmly on Tommy's mind was revealed when, having made short work of the enormous piece of coconut ice, he wriggled off Daisy's lap and put one hand on Wilhelmina's black-clad knees, saying, 'Are you comin' to the bonfire?'

'I'm afraid I can't, Tommy.'

'Why not?'

'I'm not very well. I can't run and play like you do.'

He traced his finger round the outline of a flower in the figured material. 'I'll look after you,' he offered solemnly.

Wilhelmina did not speak immediately, but when she did her voice was softer than Daisy had ever heard it. 'Thank you, Tommy. If it was at all possible that would have been lovely but I'm afraid I can't.'

'Tilly's cooked special cakes.' The child had clearly got over his shyness. Now he smiled up at the old lady, his huge brown eyes taking in the lined face and outrageous wig. 'An' she let us clean the bowl.'

'He means the children finished off the last of the mixture with their fingers, ma'am,' Daisy said in answer to her mistress's glance of enquiry.

'And did that taste good?' Wilhelmina asked, smiling.

Tommy nodded, his curls dancing.

'Perhaps you could see to it that Daisy brings me a piece of cake?'

'Aye, all right.' Tommy now turned right round, his little head tilted back on his shoulders, before coming back to face Wilhelmina again. 'I like your house,' he stated firmly.

'Thank you, Tommy.'

After that the hour passed quickly, although there was the odd moment of panic on Daisy's part when Tommy decided to jump off Miss Wilhelmina's footstool on to the sofa beside the old lady, and another when his small hand reached up to touch the carefully styled curls and waves perched on top of her head.

Tommy had milk and biscuits and more coconut ice, chattering away between mouthfuls just as he would do to Nellie as he looked at the pictures in one or two books

Wilhelmina had Daisy bring out, rolling about on the carpet like a puppy, fingers digging curiously into the unaccustomed luxury of the thick pile.

When it was time to go he walked across to the sofa where Wilhelmina was sitting, her face showing exhaustion now, and of his own volition offered his lips for a kiss just as he would do with Nellie. The look on her mistress's face brought a lump to Daisy's throat and Tommy, had he but known it, could have got away with anything for the rest of that day.

Daisy took the child up to her room with her while she washed her hands and face and collected her bonnet. He bounced on her bed while she got ready, talking nineteen to the dozen as always, and as she turned round after smoothing her hair into place and looked into his happy little face there were no words adequate to express the love that flooded her body for this small person.

Once downstairs again Daisy made her way to the kitchen with Tommy's hand in hers. Kitty was coming to the celebrations at Alf's specific request, and for him the little maid had braved her mother's wrath. Gladys didn't hold with such 'tomfoolery', something she made clear for the umpteenth time as Daisy walked into the room.

'It comes to somethin', aye, it does, when a bit lass can tell the mistress when she wants to work an' when she don't.'

Daisy prayed for patience for Tommy's sake, her voice even as she said, 'Miss Wilhelmina could have said yes or no to us changing our half-day, Gladys, but she chose to say yes. She is mistress here after all.'

'Huh!' Gladys glared at her before fixing her eyes on Tommy. So that was the little lad who was supposed to be Daisy's brother's boy? By the look of him he could be three but it was more likely he was four. Her brother's boy be damned! That child was Daisy's, she'd bet money on it. Had him just before fortune smiled on her and brought Mr William across her path, likely as not.

'All Saints Eve is special. All the celebrations would be over if we went tomorrow as usual,' Kitty piped up as she fixed her straw bonnet in place with a hat pin. Kitty's hair always acted like a spring with hats otherwise, causing them to fly off her head at the most inopportune moments.

'Ghosts, goblins and such! I don't hold with it, not any of it, and I'll thank you not to fill our Kitty's silly head with your foolishness, Daisy Appleby.'

Tommy was too young to understand all that was being said but he did know that the fat lady was being nasty to his Daisy. His little face bright red, he let go of Daisy's hand and took a step towards the cook, his voice shrill as he said, 'I'll tell Miss 'Mina of you! I will!'

'It's all right, Tommy.' Daisy whisked him up into her arms, inclining her head at Kitty who now followed her out of the kitchen, her hand over her mouth as she struggled to contain her laughter.

Once outside Daisy whirled Tommy round a few times until the child was screaming with delight, all thoughts of the nasty lady gone, and then she hoisted him on to her back, saying, 'A piggy home, all right?'

'Yes, yes.'

They had only gone half a mile before he was fast asleep, and it was a few minutes after this that Kitty said, her tone subdued now, 'Sooner or later I'm goin' to have to tell me mam I'm walkin' out with Alf, aren't I?'

It wasn't the first time they had had this conversation over the weeks Kitty and Alf had been courting, and now Daisy said, 'Kitty, she can't stop you. You're a grown woman. Stand up to her and she'll back down. All bullies do.'

'Aye, maybe, but it isn't just what me mam might say so much as . . .' Kitty stopped.

'What?'

'I don't know how serious he is, that's the thing, I suppose. If I tell me mam an' put up with all that'll follow for nowt . . .'

'For nowt?'

'Aye. He might not be thinkin' permanent, lass, might he?'

Daisy glanced at Kitty's face and her friend's expression caused her to say, 'Alf's not the sort to lead a lass on, Kitty. He likes you. More than likes you. Everyone can see that. And you're so good for him. You look up to him and he knows it. He's sort of grown in stature since you've been courting.'

'Aye, maybe.' Kitty's cheek were pink. When she changed the subject Daisy didn't press the matter but her friend's anxiety had disturbed her.

They reached the village to see the most enormous bonfire – as yet unlit – on the beach, with a number of children excitedly gathering more driftwood to add to it. Tommy woke up just as they reached the cottage door, and when Tilly's bairns called to him from the sands went running off to join them, his small face alight with the thrill of it all.

Every bairn knew that come nightfall they all blacked their faces with soot and called themselves guisers, marching round the cottages begging for money or sweetmeats while their mams and grannies prepared a feast to be consumed round the bonfire of roasted chestnuts, special cakes of sugar, cinnamon and sweet herbs, and soused herrings. It was a time when the whole village came together and afterwards many a small person was sick with excitement and too much cake. There would be a torchlight procession all round the village before the bonfire was lit, and then dancing to the accompaniment of a fiddle or two.

As always, Alf was hot on the heels of the two girls, but when he entered the cottage Kitty had to force herself to act naturally. She had loved Alf Hardy almost from the first moment she set eyes on him, even knowing how he felt about Daisy, but it was because she loved him so much that she couldn't lie to herself. He would always feel something for Daisy, she wasn't so daft as to think otherwise, but – and here her thoughts clarified – that didn't matter so long as what he felt for *her* was real enough. And she just wasn't sure about that. Oh, they had some right good cracks together but there was more to a man-and-woman relationship than larking about. More than love even. There had to be . . . what? Kitty struggled to find the words which would express the feeling she knew to be important. Tenderness, that was it. When a lad felt tender about a lass, and a lass about a lad, it sort of filled any little gaps. Aye, she'd settle for tenderness all right where Alf was concerned and count herself well blessed, even if that was all he ever felt.

He walked straight over to where she was sitting, tweaking an errant curl which was hanging down over her forehead as he said, 'Lookin' forward to the jollifications then, lass?'

She smiled back at him, nodding her reply. He always spoke to her first these days and his manner with Daisy was now that of a brother with a younger sister, but . . . Kitty glanced at her friend – slim and beautiful – and then looked down at her own bulkier shape. How did he really feel? She'd have to try and find out because she didn't think she could go on like this much longer.

'Aw, come with us. It won't be the same without you, lass.'

'Aye, you know how you've been looking forward to it.'

'Don't you stay on my account, lass, 'cos I'm big enough and ugly enough to look after meself.'

'You never said a truer word there, Gran!'

'An' less of your lip, Tilly Appleby.'

Daisy smiled as she gazed round the faces in front of her – Kitty's, Alf's, Tilly's, her granny's – but much as she appreciated their concern she had no intention of joining the others for the torchlight procession or the lighting of the bonfire and the dancing. She hadn't from the moment she and Kitty had talked earlier, and when she had managed to get Alf alone for a moment or two in the kitchen and whisper that Kitty was feeling a bit down, mainly because she wasn't sure where she stood with him, her decision had been made. Kitty and Alf might feel they had to stay with her if she went outside and it was important they had a chance to be by themselves, something that was hard to come by at the best of times.

She had made her grandmother her excuse, saying she wanted to sit with Nellie. Now she said, 'Me and Gran will sit and have a glass of your mam's blackcurrant wine, Alf, and put the world to rights. You're good at doing that, aren't you, Gran?' she added teasingly.

'Oh, you.' Nellie wagged her head at her granddaughter, but didn't add her voice to that of the others and remained quiet when they tried to persuade Daisy to change her mind again. There was something wrong with her lass. Did she regret refusing Alf now he was courting Kitty? But no, it wouldn't be that. Whatever was wrong, the lass had made her decision about Alf years ago.

'So?' The door had barely closed behind the last of them when Nellie spoke. 'What's wrong?'

Daisy poured two glasses of Enid's wine, which had the deserved reputation of having a kick like a mule, before she said, 'There *is* something I was going to tell you. Miss Wilhelmina had some news from Sir Augustus a few days ago.'

'Oh, aye?'

'About William.'

Nellie's sparse eyebrows rose but she said nothing. She was thinking plenty however. So the young master had finally got betrothed, had he? It had to be something like that.

'He's missing.'

'Missin'?'

Daisy nodded. 'It could be some sort of mix up, of course, but apparently he'd decided to leave Paris and spend some time in Scotland. When his cousin went to join him there he found William had never arrived. He went to see Sir Augustus to learn if William had contacted his father, and now the cousin and Sir Augustus have gone to Calais to see if anyone there knows anything. According to enquiries his father made before he left for France, William never boarded the ship he was supposed to travel to England on.'

'An' this cousin's got no idea where the lad could be?'

'He did say . . .' Daisy hesitated, and then continued, 'It could be that William changed his mind at the last minute and is staying with friends in France.'

'Got a lot of friends, has he?'

Daisy shrugged. Reading between the lines of what Sir Augustus had said when he had called to see Miss Wilhelmina just before leaving for France, it appeared quite a few of the 'friends' were of the female persuasion. Nevertheless, ridiculous though it was after all she'd told herself over the last three years, she was worried. She couldn't help it. The possibility that William was lying injured somewhere, or worse, had shown her that all her talk of hating him was nonsense.

285

'Aye, well, I'm sure he's all right, lass. Such as the young master buy themselves out of trouble. Likely he didn't want everyone to know his business and had something in mind he didn't want to let on about.'

'Perhaps.' Something involving a woman no doubt. Although she'd rather that than her worst fears come true. Which only proved she was as daft as a brush considering the cavalier way William had treated her. Daisy decided to change the subject. 'How has Tommy been behaving himself? Any more fighting with Tilly's youngest? Butter wouldn't have melted in his mouth at the house,' she added lovingly.

'Oh, aye, I can believe that. Charm itself when he wants to be.' But Nellie's voice was warm. The child was her favourite. 'He's a lad an' a half an' no mistake, but his da was the same. Come out of yer mam's belly with his fists raised, did Tom. But he's a bright little laddie, the bairn, an' comical with it. Did Tilly tell you what he said the other night when the bairns were all in bed? Mind, it weren't Tommy's fault really. The older bairns had been teachin' him an' the other little 'uns that rhyme about Christmas an' the workhouse, the one that goes:

> It was Christmas Day in the workhouse
> The happiest day of the year;
> Men's hearts were full of gladness
> Their bellies full of beer,
> When up spoke a bad, brave pauper
> His face as bold as brass
> We don't want your Christmas pudding!
> You can stick it up your arse!'

Daisy found herself grinning in spite of herself. 'The little monkeys!'

'Aye, still, that's bairns. Anyway, Tilly was hurryin'

'em along an' she'd promised each of 'em a piece of vinegar toffee if they were good. Cuthbert had said he'd call round, you see.'

Daisy nodded. Cuthbert Hartley had been a pal of Peter's and, his wife having died the year before after giving birth to their third child, had taken to calling in the evenings oft times lately, ostensibly to pass the time of day with Nellie. However, everyone knew he was sweet on Tilly and she on him.

'Anyway, Tilly was halfway down the stairs when they started playin' up some, so she tells 'em there'll be no toffee if they don't quieten down. An' young Tommy pipes up, "We don't want your vinegar toffee, you can stick it up your—"' Nellie lowered her chin.

'He never did?' Daisy was actually quite shocked although she had to bite on her lip to stop herself from laughing. But she didn't want Tommy speaking like that. Not her little man.

'Aye, wee monkey. 'Course, he didn't know what he was sayin', lass, not really. He was just funnin'.'

Daisy wondered about that. Tommy was indeed as bright as a button as her granny had said, and he had all of his father's cheekiness and then some, besides which Tilly was an easy-going and indulgent mother, indulgent to a fault. Her bairns all seemed to take after Peter who had always been the placid, gentle one in the family, whereas Tom had always been in hot water over something or other from the day he was born, according to her granny. Nevertheless, in spite of the fact that she and Tom had always fought like cat and dog, he had been the one Daisy had most in common with in a funny sort of way. But his son needed discipline as well as love and this was becoming increasingly apparent as Tommy left babyhood behind.

Of course the ideal solution would be for her to spend more time than just a half-day a week with the bairn, but Miss Wilhelmina couldn't spare her, ill as she was, and Daisy couldn't repay her mistress's many kindnesses by leaving the old lady's employ at a time when Miss Wilhelmina needed her the most. Besides which how could she provide for all those who were looking to her? The last three years she'd managed to pay the rent on the cottage, feed and clothe all its occupants and still supply little luxuries which made her granny's life more enjoyable. There was no worry about being able to call the doctor now; he came once a month bringing a bagful of pills and potions for her granny, and his visits and the medication alone cost more than most women double Daisy's age had a hope of earning.

She had seen the grey exhausted faces of some of those who worked fourteen to sixteen-hour days in the factories, mills and brickmaking works hereabouts when she drove into Sunderland with Harold for bits and pieces her mistress required. Ninety hours a week for three or four shillings in the shops too, and then some of them, especially those employed in dress shops, were expected to take work home to do in their 'spare time'. Bairns in those homes had no chance. At least Tommy was plump, healthy and happy.

Daisy now turned to Nellie and said quietly, 'I'll talk to him about it. He has to understand what's right and wrong, Gran, young as he is.'

'Aye, I dare say, hinny, but there's worse things than a bairn bein' a mite lippy, an' he's a lovin' little soul.'

Tommy definitely had his great-grandmother in the palm of his tiny hand!

The bonfire had long since been lit and was now a mass of glowing red embers, but the drinking and dancing were still in full swing when Tilly and Cuthbert walked through the door a couple of hours later.

'We've come to sit with Gran for a while, lass.' Tilly

cast a glance at Nellie who was snoring softly. 'You go and stretch your legs, Daisy, and join the others for the dancing. It's not fair, you missin' it all.'

She would have preferred to continue sitting at the table tackling some of Tilly's mending; she had been thinking about William for the last half-an-hour while her grandmother had been asleep and didn't feel like putting a merry face on. However, she'd rather fancied Cuthbert's face had lit up when he'd seen Nellie was dead to the world. It couldn't be often he had Tilly all to himself.

She put down one of the children's torn shirts and got to her feet, thanking them. Once outside she raised her face to the starlit sky. The scent of the sea and woodsmoke, and the distant crashing of the waves under a sky drenched with light from the full moon, made the night enchanting. It was rare to get such an evening at the end of October.

Where are you, William? She lowered her eyes to the folk on the beach as the fiddlers struck up a merry jig. Everywhere she looked there seemed to be couples although she was too far away to make out who they were. She found she couldn't face joining them. She turned and began to wander towards the sand dunes, intending to find a smooth rock on which to sit and look out over the moonlit sea.

She almost walked straight into them.

Afterwards Daisy blessed the fact that Alf and Kitty were so wrapped up in each other they were blind and deaf to anything around them. Of course in the first moment she didn't realise it was them, it could have been any young courting couple frolicking beneath the pearly sky. She blinked in surprise before quickly dropping to her knees above the deep dip where the two partially clothed figures were, hoping to edge silently away and avoid embarrassing them. The man had been lying half over the woman, his mouth to one of her breasts and her hands entwined in his hair, and the woman's legs had been naked.

Daisy was almost out of earshot when she heard Kitty's unmistakable gurgling laughter which caused her to freeze for a moment before hurrying on.

Kitty and Alf. When she reached the first of the cottages Daisy paused to catch her breath, the two names continuing to reverberate in her mind. Did this mean that everything was all right now? She did hope so. She could see her two friends being happy and raising bonny babies, and Alf would undo all the damage Gladys had done her daughter. Kitty was well overdue a taste of real happiness.

Daisy began to walk on slowly. She could also see her own situation changing very shortly with the state of Miss Wilhelmina's heart. She would not remain at Evenley House after her mistress's demise, not even if she got the chance to do so which was doubtful, but neither would she be content living in the fishing village again. Her shorthand had come on nicely but she hadn't had the chance to so much as put a finger on a typewriter, and if she was to earn enough to look after her granny and Tilly and her bairns . . . She had a small amount saved but it wasn't much; Molly's sister's situation had depleted it somewhat before Miss Wilhelmina had taken over the responsibility. Nevertheless, it was enough to give her a breathing space. She might have to take a post as a governess perhaps, while continuing with her shorthand and buying herself a secondhand typewriter when one cropped up in a pawn shop. She had been looking for one for ages but nothing had been forthcoming, and they were too expensive to buy new.

Daisy breathed deeply of the smoke- and salt-scented air. The one thing she wanted was to have her boy with her; if that could be accomplished she'd be the happiest woman on earth.

* * *

'Everything's all right now. Between me an' Alf, I mean.'

The two girls were walking home after the festivities and as Daisy said warmly, 'Oh I'm so glad, Kitty. I told you he was serious about you,' her friend turned a shining face to her.

'We didn't want to announce it tonight, what with everyone tied up with putting the bairns to bed and Alf's mam having already turned in, but he's asked me to marry him, Daisy.'

'Kitty!'

After the two girls had finished hugging and were walking on again, Kitty said quietly, 'He said some lovely things tonight, almost as though he knew I was feelin' funny, an' then one thing led to another an' he asked me. I . . . I love him so much, Daisy.'

'I know you do, lass.'

'An' I know he loves me now.' And she was sure. At last she was sure. Beautiful, he'd called her, through and through, and everything a man could wish for. She hadn't expected to be his first lass and it had made what had happened all the more special when he'd told her he'd only had the odd bit of slap and tickle with other lasses, that he'd been keeping himself for the one he married. But that was the sort of man Alf was. She was lucky, she was so, so lucky, and right at this minute she wouldn't swap places with any other lass in the world. Not even Daisy, beautiful as she was.

Chapter Eighteen

'Are you quite insane, woman?' Augustus raked back a lock of hair from his forehead, high colour darkening his cheekbones. 'I have told you over and over again, he did not board the ship which was to bring him to England. He and his luggage disappeared some time after the coach arrived at Calais. That being the case, how on earth could the girl have anything to do with it? Damn it, the chit barely leaves my sister's side.'

'I did not mean that she had spirited William away, and you know that.' Gwendoline Fraser's voice was clear and unswerving, her frothy hair and delicate appearance at odds with the burning hatred in eyes fixed squarely on her husband's angry face. 'You also know that the fishergirl was the real reason William left for France in the first place, and I do not believe you when you say you think he had a woman in Paris. Your *criminal* foolishness in placing that girl in a position which meant she had access to our son is unforgivable.'

'Give me strength!' Augustus glared at Gwendoline a moment longer before swinging away from his wife, demanding of his daughters sitting side by side on the chaise-longue, 'Is your mother being reasonable? Now is she?' He didn't wait for an answer before turning back to his wife. He wagged his finger in her face as he ground out, 'Plenty of young bucks take their pleasure with girls from the common people, it's a natural enough need and one which is easily met. It gets rid of excess . . . emotion when they are in decent society. If he did sport with her, which I doubt, that was all it was.'

At one time Gwendoline would have been intimidated by her husband's fury, but now neither his voice nor his manner had the slightest effect on her. She loathed him. She had always disliked him although she hadn't recognised this until the first night of their honeymoon. It had been only then she had discovered exactly what being married entailed, and for some long time afterwards she had felt she would not be able to endure it.

Each time she had found herself with child after Augustus's abominable demands and experienced the horror of her body swelling and distorting she had thought she'd go mad, her only comfort being that her husband did not force himself upon her again until after the confinement. She had prayed – oh, how she had prayed – that each child would be a boy after Augustus had made it clear the disgusting procedure would continue until she provided him with Greyfriar's son and heir.

And then, at long last, William had been born, and Gwendoline had found to her amazement that she felt affection for this child in a way she did not for her daughters. Perhaps part of that love stemmed from gratitude that with her son's birth her body became solely her own again, but it wasn't wholly that. She actually delighted in the boy, who from birth had shown signs of considerable beauty and definitely took after her side of the family. And now, *now* her precious son could be in dire straits, or worse . . .

Her lips thinned, and then she said, 'You judge William by your own standards, I fear. I tell you, he had formed an attachment to the girl. Look how he reacted when Francis displayed an interest in her – that should have told you how he felt. And you encouraged this attachment which had its beginnings in gratitude and would have died a natural death if you had left well alone instead of placing her with Wilhelmina. Now this same attachment, which ultimately caused William to leave us, has resulted in disaster.'

'Gwendoline, for crying out loud, see sense! I agree William felt gratitude to the chit – she'd saved his life, damn it! But it was that and only that which made him object to Francis sniffing round her. William didn't want him . . . exploiting her as he's exploited others. Neither did our son like the idea of Francis muddying the waters so close to home. Something I entirely agree with, incidentally.'

'You do not believe there was anything beyond gratitude on William's part?'

'Of course there was not, I am convinced of it.'

'Then you are more of a fool than I thought, Augustus.' Her voice sounding thin and cold, Gwendoline continued to stare at her husband who clearly couldn't believe his ears. She had never spoken to him in this way before. 'And let me tell you now, if anything has happened to my son, I hold you solely responsible.'

'You *are* mad, woman,' he growled through clenched teeth as he struggled to contain his rage. 'If you continue in this way I shall have you committed.'

Gwendoline ignored this, as she did the white faces of her daughters. Their distress did not touch her, they had too much of their father in them. 'If anything has happened to him,' she repeated slowly with great emphasis on every word, 'I shall not continue to live in this house as your wife. I shall leave, and not quietly, Augustus. There will be a public scandal. I shall demand a divorce.'

He had been staring at his wife as though he had never seen her before, and indeed felt he was looking at and listening to a stranger, but at her last words an incredulous smile touched his lips. 'Don't talk such rubbish.' He walked across to the long sideboard with ornate inlaid mother-of-pearl upon which stood a silver tray holding a brandy decanter and several small glasses. He poured himself a generous measure, lifting it to his lips and tossing it back in one gulp before he said, 'William was seen with his arms round a young woman at Calais as you very well know, even if you try to ignore the fact that the boy is a full-grown man with a man's natural appetites. The cock and bull story about visiting Rockbury's estate might well have been because he had his eye on some little filly or other, and intended to slip away with her somewhere.'

'You do not know that. And how you could have returned to England without finding out what happened . . .'

'*Gwendoline!* I have left Kirby with Marcel and the two of them are quite capable of making further enquiries.'

Gwendoline's thin upper lip curled. 'Kirby.'

'Yes, Kirby. You may have no time for the fellow but he's an excellent valet who is devoted to me. And to William too, I might add.'

Her voice cold, Gwendoline said, 'Perhaps,' because she knew such an answer would infuriate Augustus. In truth she did not doubt the valet's devotion to her husband, she had suffered from it too many years to doubt it.

A knock at the door followed by a footman announcing the arrival of Lord and Lady Routledge brought the conversation to a close, but as Gwendoline watched her husband greeting the other couple, she thought, He does not believe me about the divorce, but if anything has happened to William, he'll see.

Kirby returned to Greyfriar Hall within the week, bringing Francis Fraser with him but not the son and heir. Augustus's initial fury at his valet's actions abated somewhat as he listened to the man's explanation in the privacy of his study.

'It seems your brother has been in Paris for some months,

sir, and Mr Francis told me he's sure there is nothing to be concerned about. He said' – Kirby coughed, a polite deprecating sound which said he was well aware of the sensitivity of what he was about to reveal – 'it is common knowledge that a particular . . . amour had become a little burdensome to Mr William, and he feels your son might have taken advantage of another lady's offer to visit her abroad.'

'The woman William was seen with at Calais?' Augustus nodded. 'I knew there was one at the bottom of this somewhere. Does Francis know her name?'

'Regretfully, no, sir.'

Master and valet stared at each other, and then Augustus said, 'And how would you define my brother's mood?'

There was a pause before Josiah said, 'Conciliatory, sir. I think he is anxious to allay your fears concerning Mr William and is hoping to let bygones be bygones.'

'Hmph!' Augustus put his head down for a moment, then looking up, said, 'He's sold you a sob story, Kirby.'

'I hope not, sir. I would like to think he is genuine in his desire for a reconciliation.'

Again the two stared at each other, but when Augustus repeated his 'Hmph', his tone was not so scornful.

'I don't believe it! William wouldn't just disappear like this. He . . . he's not like that.' Gwendoline glared at her brother-in-law and husband. 'And if Francis does not know the name of this other lady, how can we be sure? No, I'm sorry, Francis, I think you are mistaken.'

'For goodness' sake, face facts, woman!' Augustus was showing his customary impatience with his wife. 'Marcel mentioned an affair which had turned sour, with a diplomat's wife no less, and where there's one there'll be others. I would have thought you'd be pleased, you've been in a constant state of nerves the last weeks.'

'I will not believe it until William himself tells me.' Gwendoline was on her feet now, refusing to be convinced. 'But I appreciate your coming to try and set our minds at rest, Francis,' she added graciously. 'I trust you will be staying for a while?'

'Augustus?' Francis turned to his brother, lowering his eyelids as he waited for the answer and trying not to let his jubilation show.

'Of course you are welcome to stay if you are able to.'

'Yes, I am able to, and thank you. I have missed the old place. Or perhaps it is my family I have missed. The years have a way of catching up suddenly.'

Augustus stared keenly at his brother and must have been reassured because he moved to stand in front of Francis, resting a hand on the other man's shoulder as he said, 'I have no wish for us to be estranged, Francis. You are my only brother after all. And I appreciate your concern over William and your wish to put his mother's mind at rest. The boy has shown himself to be irresponsible in the extreme with this latest escapade.'

'Youth has to sow its wild oats, brother,' said Francis gently, earning himself a grateful smile from Gwendoline as he added, 'William has much to commend him and this phase will pass.'

Augustus was such a fool! How long before he began to fear for William's well-being in earnest? It could be months or longer, but the beauty of it all was that the nameless corpse would carry its secret to its final resting place. Eventually Augustus would be forced to acknowledge his son was lost, and as the younger brother he was next in line, Francis thought complacently. Augustus had always taken life in small bites, he had never known how to enjoy himself. Even as a young man in his prime he had been overly concerned with upholding the pride of the Fraser name.

Francis raised his eyes as Augustus gripped his shoulder tightly. He would give it six months, a year at most, and then start pressing for a healthy increase in his allowance considering he was in line for the lot. If he knew anything about his brother, Augustus would be a broken man once he realised there was little chance his son was still alive. And he would make sure he started sowing the seeds of doubt in his brother's mind very carefully in a few months' time.

He raised his hand to Augustus's where it rested on his shoulder, pressing it tenderly before they both bowed to Gwendoline as she left the room.

Chapter Nineteen

'Lift your jaw off the floor, Mam, it'll get dusty.' Kitty spoke with a nonchalance she was far from feeling but only Daisy was really aware of this. The other girl had decided on the way home there was no time like the present to tell her parents about Alf, and once having decided had worried about the consequences until even Daisy got the jitters.

'You! You've put her up to this.' The Murrays had been sitting ensconced in front of the glowing kitchen range which had a kettle sizzling on the hob and was redolent with the smell of freshly baked bread. Wilhelmina allowed no baking on the Sabbath and therefore Gladys was always busy on a Saturday evening, something she frequently bemoaned in spite of the fact that it meant her work was light the next day.

Daisy faced the cook across the kitchen table which still held the remains of the couple's supper, and would continue to do so until Kitty cleared the dirty dishes. Part of her was thinking how warm and homely the scene could be; the shining pans, the steel and brass fender glowing rose-coloured in the light from the fire, the oak dresser full of china and fancy dishes. But then there was Gladys and Harold, and there the scene of cosy domestic bliss ended. 'If you're implying I was the means by which Kitty met Alf, I gladly accept the blame,' Daisy said evenly, 'but I can assure you they are in love with each other.'

'Love?' Gladys spat the word. 'This Alf, he's the one

who's been soft on you for years, isn't he? Got tired of him, have you, an' tossed him to her' – she indicated the white-faced Kitty with a vicious jab of her head – 'like a bone to a dog?'

'Alfred' – it was rare she gave him the dignity of his full name but Daisy felt the situation called for it – 'and Kitty love each other.'

'Oh, aye? An' pigs fly.'

'No, but it seems they enjoy a good supper.' Daisy's gaze swept contemptuously over the laden kitchen table, at which point the angry little woman in front of her seemed to swell up like a balloon.

'You hussy! You brazen hussy! You think we don't know what you're up to with your creepin' an' crawlin' round the mistress? By, we'd got your measure long afore you set foot in this place, miss. Aye, we'd been warned about you, an' rightly so.'

At this point Harold put a calming hand on his wife's arm, only to have it shaken off so violently he was forced to say, 'Gladys, Gladys lass, don't upset yerself.'

'Upset meself?' His wife was screeching now. 'When that trollop of a daughter of yours has just announced she's keepin' company with the scum of the earth? If you were any sort of man you'd have knocked her into next weekend as soon as she opened her mouth.'

'I'm not just keepin' company with Alf, we're goin' to get married.'

'I'd as soon cut your throat, aye, I would.' Gladys was leaning forward, her round body bristling with fury. 'An' I'd be doin' you a favour at that. Your life won't be worth livin', girl! Workin' day an' night for a filthy numbskull who'd make the privy smell sweet, that'll be your lot.'

'Even if that was so it'd be paradise compared to livin' with you, Mam. But Alf an' me'll be happy. I love him an' he loves me an' I want to be his wife. An' I tell you somethin' else for nothin' – I'll be more of a mam to my bairns than you ever were to me an' that won't be difficult. This house was a miserable place until Daisy come into it.'

'You satisfied now? Eh?'

As Gladys advanced on her Daisy held her ground, even as she was aware of a shrinking movement from Kitty beside her. The action brought to mind all the physical abuse her friend had suffered at the hands of this fat tyrant, and through her rising anger, Daisy said, 'That's far enough.'

Gladys remained exactly where she was but her hand came out and flapped behind her as she said, 'Harold! Are you goin' to stand there an' let her talk to me like that?'

'He is sitting, Mrs Murray, and if he wasn't man enough to stop you ill-treating his daughter, what makes you think he'd be man enough to do anything now?'

There was absolute silence in the kitchen for a moment, and then Gladys let out a long breath before she said, 'You'll come a cropper one fine day, girl, an' I pray to God I'll be there to see it. An' you' – she directed her gaze to her daughter – 'can get yerself to your room an' we'll have no more talk of you marryin' this fishing scum.'

'I am marryin' Alf, Mam, an' soon.'

That statement suggested something to Gladys that made her go white and grope blindly for a chair. Once she was sitting she said stiffly, 'How . . . how soon?'

'As soon as he can arrange it. Probably within the month.'

'You little slut!'

'Aye, well, it takes one to know one, eh, Mam? You think I'm so dim I can't work out how long it was before you had me after you got wed? But then you never expected me to find your wedding paper, I dare bet.'

Gladys stared at her daughter, and now the colour came

303

back into her face in a red flood. 'You . . . you were early. It happens.'

'Aye, an' like you said earlier, pigs might fly.'

There was no turmoil in Kitty's mind now as she looked at her mother and then her father. Her mam had made her pay all her life for what had been her own mistake, but something had happened out there on the beach tonight when Alf had taken her and she didn't mean in the physical sense. It had been afterwards, when he had held her close and whispered words she'd never thought to hear, that she'd known he loved her. Differently from how he'd loved Daisy maybe, but that was all right. With Alf loving her she could do anything.

Something of what she was feeling clearly showed in her face because Gladys ground her teeth before she said, 'You're worthless, girl, always have bin. I hope you an' your fisherman burn in hell's everlasting flames.'

'Come out of this, lass.' Daisy pushed Kitty towards the door, saying over her shoulder, 'Alf's marrying Kitty because he loves her, Gladys, and they're going to be happy. Chew on that awhile.'

Once in the hall the girls looked at each other before Daisy said, 'She took that well then, lass,' and they both began to shake with laughter born of reaction.

'By, lass.' Kitty shook her head once they'd calmed down. 'I shan't be sorry to leave here and you're the only one I'll miss.' And then she grinned. 'Well, you an' me mam's dressed crab. There's not another soul alive who does dressed crab like me mam – but then she's got a head start, bein' so crabby herself.'

'Oh, Kitty.' The two girls were holding on to each other now, trying to stifle their laughter in case it woke Miss Wilhelmina as they climbed the stairs. The landing was almost in pitch blackness but they could have found the small table holding the candles in their tin holders

304

blindfolded. Once the candles were lit Daisy and Kitty opened the green baize door and passed through to the servants' landing, and it was there that Kitty said, 'Alf said if I had any trouble from me mam when I told her about us not to stand any nonsense. He wants me to go and stay with him an' his mam till we're wed. But, well, it'll mean you being here with me mam an' da on your own.'

Daisy stared at the plump little face lit by the flickering candle. 'Alf's right, lass. Your mam'll make your life a misery for as long as you stay. When would you go?'

'Straightaway, I suppose, in the mornin'. I thought I'd nip along an' see the mistress an' explain everythin' first.'

Daisy nodded. 'You tell her word for word what your mam said, Kitty. All right? Word for word so she understands the position you're in. Your mam would do anything she could to stop you and Alf being together so don't give her the chance. Once you're with Alf and Mrs Hardy, her hands are tied.'

'Aye, that's how I feel about it.' Kitty looked at her. 'But I'll miss you, lass.'

'Not as much as I'll miss you.'

They stared at each other for a moment and it was Daisy who said, 'By, lass, the changes a day can bring!' whereupon they both started giggling again but without really knowing why.

Kitty's announcement the next day and subsequent departure barely registered on Wilhelmina. Augustus arrived at Evenley House early in the morning and he had news of William.

Daisy stayed with her mistress while Augustus told his sister about the arrival of Marcel some hours before. He had left his name and address with umpteen folk during his quest to find out what had happened to his

305

cousin, and one of these had turned up trumps. A doctor from an infirmary close to the port at Calais, who had unfortunately been away for a few weeks, had been told of the young Frenchman's search on his return to work and had contacted Marcel at Claude and Lydia's house in Paris. He remembered a man being brought in by the dockside police around the time in question, he'd told them, but doubted if it was the young Englishman they were looking for. He had been thought to be the casualty of a fight between two rival smuggling rings and had been more dead than alive. Beaten within an inch of death, but then that's what these animals were like. Anyway, the man had been taken to another infirmary almost immediately; he could give them the name of that if they liked?

'It's William, I'm afraid.' Augustus's face was white. 'Claude and Marcel went to the infirmary in Lievin. William has been there seven weeks but for the first six was in a very bad state. Even now he cannot talk much and is only just remembering who he is. He wasn't expected to pull through, apparently, but now the prognosis is good. Gwendoline, Francis and the girls are getting ready and we're leaving for France as soon as I return to the house. I wanted to see you myself before we left, though, to reassure you that he is out of immediate danger.'

Wilhelmina had cried then and Sir Augustus had sat patting her hand for some moments before he left. He had not once looked at Daisy who remained quite still and silent, numb with agony. William could have died and she would not have known. These past weeks she had been thinking . . . she could not bear to recall what she had thought, guilt piercing her heart like a sharp thorn. And all the time William had been fighting for his life in a distant town in a foreign country with only strangers to take care of him. William, William, oh, William. Who could have done such a terrible thing? How could he have made such enemies?

She tried to recall his face but his image was blurred by the mist of time. How could you love someone so much, keep loving them even though you had told yourself over and over that you hated them, and yet not be able to picture their face?

She wanted to howl out loud, give vent to the pain inside her, but she couldn't. All she seemed able to do was repeat his name endlessly in her head. William, William, my darling William.

Part 4
More Tangled Webs

Chapter Twenty

By the time of Kitty and Alf's wedding on a cold, fine day in the first week of December, the news from France was good.

William was improving daily, Augustus wrote in the latest of his weekly letters to his sister across the water. The boy was walking a little now, mainly because the physician he'd obtained to take care of William was second to none. Monsieur Richer had operated successfully on the boy's legs, and his arm and ribs were mending well. Unfortunately it was now considered doubtful if he would ever remember the hours leading up to the attack as had been hoped initially.

The last thing William recalled was leaving the coaching inn at Abbeville on the morning of the day he disappeared. After that, nothing. He had lost a considerable amount of weight but of course that was only to be expected in the circumstances, and he still slept twenty hours out of every twenty-four, but he was on the road to recovery and that was all that mattered. In fact the boy had made such progress in the last few days that he could now safely be left in the care of his mother; Gwendoline wouldn't budge from his room now he was recuperating at Claude's château.

The letter finished with best wishes for Wilhelmina's health, and the promise that Augustus would visit his sister as soon as he and his daughters returned to Greyfriar Hall, which he expected to be very soon.

This report of William's recuperation enabled Daisy to enjoy Kitty and Alf's wedding day with a lighter heart. Kitty had spent the last four weeks sewing a simple but pretty wedding dress from a dress length Wilhelmina had sent, once the reason for her maid's abrupt departure had been fully explained by Daisy.

She herself had bought her friend a beautiful stole of delicate white lace which Kitty wore over her hair in the form of a veil. As she walked down the aisle of Whitburn parish church Alf had eyes for no one but his radiant bride.

The church was full, mainly with fisherfolk but Daisy was pleased to see a number of other faces she recognised, among them Molly's sister whose husband was now back at work again.

It was a happy day, a joyous one, and Gladys and Harold were not missed, not even by Kitty. Wilhelmina's poor health had not permitted her to leave the house, but Kitty's former mistress had sent a grand wedding present to the young couple in the form of a bone china dinner service, along with her good wishes for their happiness.

And they would be happy, Daisy thought, as she sat in Mrs Hardy's cottage with the other wedding guests, cuddling a tired Tommy on her lap. The child had been ecstatic that Daisy had been at the village since early morning to help Kitty get ready, and had not left her side for a moment all day.

Alf had whisked Nellie up into his arms and carried her from her cottage to his once they had returned from the parish church, and Daisy's grandmother had sat wrapped up in blankets in one of Enid's comfy velvet-covered armchairs, thoroughly enjoying herself. Everyone had been packed into the limited space like sardines in a tin, but the feast Mrs Hardy and some of the other women had laboured over for days had been demolished with gusto, and Alf's mother's homemade wine had loosened tongues and made for much laughter.

Kitty needed this, Daisy thought to herself as she glanced round the rooms crammed with friends, almost as much as she needed Alf. Already his mam was more of a mother to Kitty than Gladys had ever been, and the two women got on like a house on fire. Everyone liked Kitty – you really couldn't do anything else – and in this close community where everyone looked out for everyone else, she would grow and blossom.

'Not too much, I hope, lass,' Kitty laughed, after Daisy told the other girl her thoughts. 'I used to eat for comfort back at the house, or that was me excuse leastways, but Alf's mam is as good a cook as me mam any day and with being so happy . . .' Kitty pulled a face and they both grinned. 'I'm going to have to watch it else I shan't get through the doors in this place, them being so narrow.'

'You're fine, Kitty,' said Daisy warmly, 'and you look beautiful today, as bonny a bride as any I've seen.'

'Aye, I'd agree with that an' all.' Alf spoke over Kitty's shoulder, his good-looking face flushed with the effects of his mother's potent brew. He put an arm round his new wife in a brief and unusual – for a fisherman – show of affection, before he said to Daisy who had Tommy asleep on her lap, 'Your granny wants to go back, lass. She's a mite tired.'

'Oh, yes, of course.' Daisy rose swiftly, Tommy still held tight to her. 'I'll just nip back quick if I can and put the bairn to bed first, and then I can look after Gran. Tilly will want to stay on a while, no doubt.' They all looked across to Tilly and Cuthbert sitting close together, Tilly's children and his all intermingled about them. Peter's widow's friendship with the big fisherman certainly didn't appear to be on the wane.

Once outside, the cold night air roused Tommy suffi-ciently for the small boy to be able to scramble up the ladder ahead of Daisy in the cottage. She sat on the edge of the bed he shared with Tilly's youngest bairns once the child was under the heaped blankets, stroking the silky soft forehead as she smiled into the enormous brown eyes fixed on her face. 'I don't want you to go.' He spoke in a whisper. 'I want you to stay here with me, *always*.'

It wasn't the first time they had had this conversation and it usually occurred when the little boy was tired and fretful. Daisy replied as she always did. 'I wish I didn't have to go too but you know I do. Where else would the pennies come from for everyone?'

'Why can't I come with you? I'd be a good boy.'

'I know you would, hinny, but bairns can't stay at Evenley House and I have to be there to look after Miss Wilhelmina. Anyway, if you came with me you'd miss playing with the other bairns, now wouldn't you? And what would Gran and Aunty do without you?'

'I don't care about playin' an' I don't care about gran an' Aunt Tilly neither.' He began to cry, not noisy child-ish sobs but silently, great teardrops slipping down his round cheeks.

Oh, Tommy, Tommy. After all the worry about William and the emotion of Kitty's big day, this was the last straw. Daisy felt like crying with him. Instead she pulled him to her, settling him on her lap with the blankets still tucked round him as she sat back against the bolster, resting against the wall. 'Don't cry, hinny,' she said very softly as he clung to her, chubby arms going round her waist as he buried his damp face with its mop of curly hair against her stomach. 'Look, I promise you, as soon as we can be together I'll tell you, all right? But in the meantime I need you to look after gran for me. You're the only one I can trust to look after her properly, you know.'

A couple of sniffs followed, then, 'Gran said she was gonna baste me backside the day.'

Oh, dear, what had he done now. 'Did she? Well, you must have upset her in some way for her to say that because you know she loves you all the world.'

'I only said Eliza was a skyet-gob.'

He had called Tilly's youngest fish-face? Daisy kept the amusement out of her voice with some effort. 'Why did you call her that? She's a nice little bairn, isn't she?'

He shrugged. 'She said you love her as much as me, but you don't, do you? You don't love her like me?'

All amusement gone, Daisy closed her eyes for a moment. She had lit the oil lamp before she had climbed the ladder and brought it up with her. Now she opened her eyes, staring into the flickering shadows as Tommy spoke again, his voice thick with tears once more. 'She said Aunt Tilly's her mam but she's only my aunty, an' that an aunty is different from a mam. She said aunties don't love as much as mams an' that you're our aunty an' you love us all the same.'

Daisy forgot all about diplomacy. She tightened her hold on his small body, her voice fierce as she said, 'This aunty loves just as much as a mam, hinny, for you anyway.'

'But not for Eliza?'

'No, not for Eliza, just you.' She'd probably get it from her grandmother and Tilly over this if Tommy repeated it, but the child needed reassurance and that came first. Eliza had her mother with her twenty-four hours a day, who did her lad have? 'To me, hinny, you *are* my bairn. All right?'

The small head with its silky curls nodded, and Daisy had to restrain herself from crushing Tommy to her. The poor little bairn. He might be a bit of a handful at times but he was so tender under all his bravado. She just thanked God that Margery's parents had never expressed any interest in their grandson. The last she'd heard of Hilda and Jacob Travis they had upped and moved Newcastle way, and nothing would convince her otherwise but that this move stemmed from the arrival of the child she held against her heart.

One day when Tommy was older and ready to understand, when he was approaching manhood, she would show him his birth certificate. But she would take care to explain fully how things had been. That his parents had loved each other, that they had made a mistake certainly but they had loved each other and fully intended to marry. She would tell him that he would have been the most precious gift of all to them, as he was to her, and he must never doubt that for a second the rest of his life. Whatever anyone else might say.

Daisy's lips compressed. People could be cruel, and the stigma of the word 'bastard' was one which broke some folk before they had even had a stab at life. But it wouldn't be like that for Tommy, not while she had breath in her body.

She didn't leave the cottage until he was fast asleep, and so it was half-an-hour later before she made her way along the path towards the Hardys' place. She had almost reached the door when a figure emerged from the shadows, making her jump.

'Sorry, lass.' Alf's voice was wry. 'I seem to have been doing that all me life, waiting for you and then frightening you half to death.'

'It's all right.' Daisy was reassured by his dry amusement but her voice expressed a hint of wariness when she said, 'Why *are* you waiting for me, Alf?'

He stared into her face, holding her eyes, his own expression changing the while from one of self-mockery to seriousness before he said, 'I need to say goodbye, lass. We never did, did we?'

'Alf—'

'It's all right, Daisy, really.' His voice dropped to a low

whisper. 'I love Kitty, more than I thought I could ever love anyone who wasn't you, an' she suits me. She suits me more than you would ever have done an' I see that now. But . . . I need to say goodbye to what might have been, if you'd felt different, an' to ask you if you'll still be me friend? If . . . if you've forgiven me for the things I said that day?'

'Oh, Alf.' She made a movement with her hand, touched by the naked emotion he was trying to conceal. 'You'll always be my friend, you and Kitty, my best friends. And you were right, in a way at least. I have to get on with my life, I can't cry for the moon or hope for what will never be.'

'He's gettin' better, the young master? So your granny said?'

She nodded.

Alf's face was solemn now as he said, 'He's got to be the biggest fool in the world, lass, for all his fine education.'

This unswerving support – something Alf had given her all her life when she thought about it – was almost too much for Daisy, tormented as she was by worry for William and sorrow at the way he had left. Her voice soft, she said, 'Thank you, Alf, and I needn't tell you to be happy with Kitty because I know you will be.'

'Aye, I do an' all. She needs me you see, lass. At heart she's like a dove with one wing down.'

Both his understanding and the simile itself amazed Daisy for the insight they displayed. She nodded at him, saying, 'Yes, that's just it, Alf. And she loves you too. She always has. Don't ever wonder about that.'

They stared at each other for a moment more before Alf rubbed his hand across his face. 'So, lass? Friends still?'

'Always, Alf.'

'That's all I wanted to hear.' He looked at her for a second longer, then turned and went towards the cottage.

'We'd better see about gettin' your granny home, an' Tilly's bairns an' all. Her an' Cuthbert can sit by the fire if he's a mind to go back with her, but I'm goin' to get George or one of the others to walk you back into Fulwell.'

'There's no need for that,' said Daisy quickly. 'It doesn't take long and I'd know my way blindfold now. There's more than enough light to see the path, it being such a clear night.'

'Stubborn to the last.' As he opened the door and a surge of voices and warmth spilled out, Alf grinned at her. 'But humour me the night, lass, eh? It's been a right grand day an' I don't want nowt to spoil it, like you turnin' your ankle in one of them potholes an' lyin' out all night without anyone knowin'. You won't have Kitty with you from now on, don't forget.'

No, she wouldn't. As Alf continued into the cottage, Daisy paused on the threshold. This was going to be yet another new chapter in her life and one she wasn't particularly looking forward to. Wilhelmina had decided that rather than replace Kitty with another live-in servant she would make do with a daily from the village, who would arrive at six every morning and leave at six in the evening. Daisy had met the young girl concerned who had seemed nice enough but who was not particularly bright, and Maud Longhurst had certainly none of bubbly Kitty's sense of fun. Maud was due to commence her new position in two days' time, and Gladys was already spitting bricks after being informed by Wilhelmina that the cook would be expected to serve and clear dinner unaided in the new way of things. Not that Gladys was talking to her, Daisy reminded herself ruefully. From the morning of Kitty's departure from Evenley House, Gladys and Harold had maintained an attitude of stony silence that was broken only when absolutely necessary.

But that didn't matter. Daisy's gaze travelled to where Kitty, bright-eyed and flushed with happiness, was laughing with some of the other fisherwomen, her brown curls bobbing and the lace stole draped about her shoulders in a cascade of white. Kitty was free of her mother now, Gladys's hold over her daughter broken, and Daisy would have endured much more than the woman's seething hostility and working with stolid Maud for that to come about.

As though her thoughts had drawn the other girl, Kitty now left the group of women and made her way over to Daisy, saying, 'Come right in then, lass, you're allowed. Most honoured guest, you are,' and she wasn't altogether joking.

'I've got to get back, Kitty. Alf's just going to bring Gran and round up Tilly and the bairns, and once they're home I'm off to Fulwell.'

'Aw, lass.' The smile sliding from her face, Kitty said softly, 'I hate to think of you there with me mam, I do straight.'

For answer, Daisy put her arms round Kitty and hugged her, whispering, 'She doesn't bother me, she never has, and that's what gets to her. You just be happy, there's no one deserves to be more than you.'

Kitty now disengaged herself enough to pull back and look into Daisy's face, and there were tears in her eyes when she said, 'There aren't words to thank you.'

'Thank me? I haven't done anything.'

Kitty shook her head, sending the high bun of curls wobbling again. 'Lass, you'll never know. You'll never know. You turned my life round when you came to Evenley House, that's the way I feel about it, and all the good things in my life now have come through you.'

'Oh, Kitty.'

'I'll miss you, lass.'

'And me you, Kitty. And me you.'

They were brought apart by Alf's voice behind Kitty saying, 'Out of me way, wife, there's folks comin' through,' and then he was stepping out of the cottage, Nellie held in his burly arms, and Tilly, Cuthbert and their menagerie of bairns behind him.

After one last quick squeeze of Kitty's hand, Daisy made her goodbyes to Alf's mother and the others and then followed the procession. She had always been aware that most of the fisherfolk had expected her to return to the cottages one day and marry Alf, but even if she hadn't been the attitude of some of them today would have told her this. Not that anyone had spoken a word out of place, it wasn't that, nor had anyone been unkind, but they had been cautious. It was as though Alf's wedding had emphasised she was now different from them, lived in a different world; by refusing him she had indicated that the old Daisy was finally gone. It made her feel sad and almost cast adrift but she couldn't do anything about it, and for the moment didn't feel up to examining herself and the whole situation any further, so she resolved to put it all on the back burner and just get on with what needed to be done.

She straightened her shoulders, set her fancy new bonnet with blue silk flowers on the brim that she'd bought specially for Kitty's wedding more firmly on her head, and went to meet the waiting George.

Chapter Twenty-one

Wilhelmina was resting on a couch pulled close to the roaring fire in her private sitting room, a thick travelling rug covering her lower torso and legs, but still she felt cold.

She glanced across to the windows beyond which more snow was swirling in a world already transformed to brilliant white. It had been snowing for the last three days. Every morning Harold cleared the path leading from the front door to the garden gate but he reported that the road beyond Evenley House was still in use so they were not cut off yet.

Would Augustus visit today, and would he bring Francis with him again? Wilhelmina frowned to herself. Why on earth Augustus had allowed their younger brother to return home with him and the girls she really didn't understand. Of course she realised Augustus was upset by Gwendoline's assertion that their marriage was over, and that she intended to stay in France indefinitely with Lydia and Claude; perhaps he found Francis's presence a comfort? For herself, she would as soon harbour an asp in her bosom than trust Francis.

Wilhelmina looked towards the door as quick light footsteps sounded in the hall outside, obviously Daisy's rather than the solid plodding of Maud.

'I've brought your luncheon tray, ma'am.' Daisy knew her mistress was finding Maud something of a trial; the girl was willing enough but painfully slow. She had to be told something at least three or four times before it penetrated her brain, and even then the pace at which she carried out the allotted task was snail-like.

'Thank you, child.' Wilhelmina glanced at the contents of the silver tray – a light meal consisting of beef consommé with a soft white roll – aware she wouldn't be able to manage more than a bite or two.

Later that afternoon Daisy had just finished massaging her mistress's feet when Maud ponderously announced that Sir Augustus and Mr Francis Fraser had called to see their sister. With Josiah Kirby ensconced in the kitchen with a venomous Gladys, and Francis Fraser staring at her in the sitting room, the afternoon proved to be a long and trying one for Daisy.

The moon was casting its cold white brilliance over the frozen vista outside the warmth of Wilhelmina's private sitting room by the time the two brothers and Josiah left. Wilhelmina had asked Daisy to see her brothers out – it being twenty-past six and Maud having left promptly at her allotted time – and out of the corner of her eye Daisy saw Francis glance meaningfully at the valet as Josiah joined him on the drive, Augustus already having seated himself in the carriage which had arrived a minute or two earlier. Josiah nodded at the unspoken prompting, at which point both men turned as one and looked at her.

Daisy bit down hard on her lip in an effort to keep her face blank and then she shut the door in their faces, her heart racing. What had all that been about? Something was afoot. As her granny would have said, you didn't need to be fiddling the same tune to know when the devil was playing.

A deep feeling of unease plagued her for the rest of the evening and by the time she left Miss Wilhelmina tucked up in bed and walked along to the kitchen – having missed dinner due to her mistress's being fretful and uncomfortable –

Daisy was tired. She pushed open the kitchen door, mentally steeling herself to meet Gladys and Harold's sour faces, but it was not the cook or her husband who met Daisy's startled gaze.

Francis Fraser rose slowly from one of the wicker armchairs in front of the range, his eyes on the young woman who had paused just inside the kitchen door. He watched Daisy glance round, her face expressing her bewilderment, and then he said, 'They've gone to bed. You were wondering where the other servants were, weren't you?'

She looked him full in the face now as she said, 'It's only just ten o'clock. Harold does not bolt the doors until half-past.'

'Is that so?' He smiled, his gaze slithering over her. 'Well, look for them, m'dear, but it will be to no avail. But please, do not let me stop you if you feel so inclined.'

Daisy said nothing to this, neither did she move, and a few moments ticked by before Francis gave a chuckle low in his throat. 'You're a cool customer, girl, I'll give you that.'

'I don't know what you mean.'

'No?'

Daisy raised her head a little, looking at the bloated individual in front of her steadily as she said, 'No.'

'Don't come your airs and graces with me, m'dear, because I am nobody's fool.' He was still speaking in the pleasant, almost jolly tone he had used since she had come into the kitchen, which made the sense of his words all the more chilling. 'You're a whore, everyone knows it, and but for the generosity of my sister in having you under her roof you would be working the Sunderland waterfront like the rest of your kind. But, don't mistake me, I don't want to get off on the wrong foot, merely to let you know I am under no illusions as to the true circumstances. And that being the case' – he reached into the pocket of his trousers and brought out a small cloth bag, throwing it on to the table where it jingled for a moment – 'I can be as generous as anyone else.'

Daisy couldn't believe her ears. For a moment she was too amazed to react and then she drew in a deep breath, forcing the tremor which had started in the pit of her stomach from sounding in her voice as she said, 'You are quite mistaken, Mr Fraser, and I think you should leave now before I raise the household.'

'What? And disturb that dimwit of a sister of mine? I doubt you'd do that, m'dear. You don't want to upset the old lady, not with her heart so dicky.' He reached out for a small glass at the side of him and swilled the contents down in one gulp, smacking his lips as he added, 'I don't know how many strings to your bow you have at the moment, but let me assure you, William Fraser has no intention of ever returning to England once he's well if that's what you're hoping. And a little bird told me the parson took fright years ago. Married to his verger's daughter now, isn't he? Even the fisherman you've tickled for years has tired of the goods, I hear? Of course I don't suppose for a minute they were the only men you've had, but I'm not one to insist on exclusive rights, never have been. No, it doesn't worry me if—'

'*Get out.*' Her voice was loud and her manner such that even Francis, befuddled with whisky as he was, couldn't doubt she meant business.

'Not till I get what I came for. Y'know, I was thinking the other day, nothing has gone right for me since you appeared. You owe me something for that, girl, and by George I intend to collect. And don't be concerned I'll let on to your mistress, I can hold my tongue when it pleases me. Got your eye on the main chance here, haven't you? Oh, yes, I know, I know.' He winked at her, moving closer. 'Think you can talk the daft old bat into leaving you a nice little nest egg as security when other . . . pastimes fail, eh? Well, nothing wrong in that. Nothing at all.'

He was mad, he had to be. It was only when he was so close Daisy could smell the whisky fumes on him that her frozen limbs sprang into action. Then she moved with a swiftness that took the drunken Francis completely by surprise. One moment the large kitchen knife was with the others, all neatly laid out for morning on their marble block, and the next it was waving in front of Francis's nose. 'You come one step nearer, just one, and I'll show you how we gut fish firsthand,' Daisy hissed through her clenched teeth.

'Wha-What?' Francis jerked back so violently from the keenly honed and razor-sharp blade that was Gladys's pride and joy he lost his balance and went sprawling on the floor, the breath leaving his body in a great gasp as he thudded against the flagstones.

'I can use this and don't think I won't.' Daisy swallowed deeply as she stared down at the grotesque figure on the floor squirming like a beached whale. 'You lay one finger on me and I'll split you in two.'

She could hear herself speaking and see the knife in her hand but still there was a sense of amazement that this was actually happening. The ladylike behaviour of the last few years had melted away like sea mist before a hot noonday sun.

'You . . . you little . . .' He began cursing, the profanities so vile that Daisy wrinkled her face against them.

'Get out.' At the back of her mind she was conscious of thinking, Gladys and Harold *know*. They must do. They had conspired with Josiah Kirby to bring this about, to have William's uncle waiting for her when she was all alone. It was almost unbelievable they could be so vicious, that they could set out to hurt her like this. She knew they had always disliked her, hated her even, but this. This was something apart.

'You think you can treat me like this? *Me?*' His flabby face was livid with anger. 'You run a brothel back where you come from, a house where no doubt the cook's brat will soon be opening her legs once your fisherman friend is done with her, and you think you can refuse me? I know all about you, including the flyblow you've tried to keep quiet about.'

Flyblow? What on earth was he talking about? For a second or two Daisy had no idea Augustus's brother was referring to little Tommy, not until he added, 'Oh, you've paid a few to fall in with the tale of your being its aunt, I don't doubt, but there's others who are on to your little game. Scum! You were born scum and scum you'll remain.'

He had staggered to his feet as he had been talking, holding on to the kitchen table for support, and when he said, 'Kirby's been on to you for years,' Daisy knew who she had to blame for all of this and found it was no great surprise.

'Josiah Kirby has a filthy mind. There is not a grain of truth in what he's said.'

'And I'm King Edward.' He stood looking at her for a moment more and it came to Daisy then that Francis Fraser was weighing up whether she really would use the weapon in her hand should he come for her again. Her body was like a ramrod now, and there was no tremor in her voice when she said, 'One step towards me and I swear I'll use this and take the consequences. I am going to tell you one last time to leave and after that I will walk into the hall and begin shouting for assistance, and then we shall see what Miss Wilhelmina makes of it all.'

Daisy couldn't find words in her mind which would

326

describe the look on his face, she only knew it was the nearest she ever wanted to come to such depravity.

It was a few more moments before his hand snatched up the cloth bag of money, stuffing it into his pocket. He straightened his back, breathing hard as he glared at her, and then turned and wrenched open the kitchen door. A layer of snow fell on to the cork mat.

Francis did not close the door behind him, and Daisy hesitated for a few seconds before walking across the kitchen, uncertain as to whether this was some kind of trick. But she had seen defeat in his eyes the moment before he had left. And then she heard a voice say, 'Mr Francis? Are you all right, sir?' and she realised Josiah Kirby must have accompanied his master's brother, the two of them concocting some tale to explain their whereabouts to Sir Augustus, no doubt.

Daisy shot the bolt on the door with trembling hands, leaning back against the cold wood as she stared down at the kitchen knife in her hand now hanging limply against her skirt. *Would* she have used this on him if he'd attempted to rape her? She didn't have to think about the answer. She could not have continued living if he had touched her. But he hadn't touched her and nor would he, he'd gone.

Daisy walked to the marble block and put the knife in its place with the others, telling herself to breathe slowly and deeply as a sensation of faintness made itself known. She had to eat something, she'd had nothing since lunch and then only a quick bite with Miss Wilhelmina being fractious.

Once in the pantry she realised her teeth were chattering with the reaction that had overtaken her now the danger was past, but she helped herself to several slices of boiled ham and put them on a plate. She placed this on a tray, along with a crusty loaf and a platter of fresh butter.

327

Once at the table a thought which occurred to her enabled her to eat the food with some measure of enjoyment.

Josiah Kirby would have been frozen half to death waiting outside on a raw winter's night like this.

Daisy lay awake for a long time deliberating on whether to inform her mistress of Francis's presence in the house, but she decided the man wasn't worth distressing Miss Wilhelmina for. The old lady was too ill to be upset over something that was done and finished with, little would be accomplished by telling her now. She had dealt with him, Daisy thought, and from that last expression on his face he would think twice about trying anything similar in the future.

As it happened, come morning Francis Fraser was the last person on Daisy's mind. A grim-faced Alf was on the doorstep of Evenley House just after dawn had broken. Nellie had had a bad turn and Tilly had sent him for the doctor in the middle of the night. Doctor Hogarth thought Daisy should come as soon as possible. 'Apoplexy' the doctor called it, Alf said. All he knew was that the night before Nellie had been the same as ever, and then Tilly had heard a crash and a bang at three in the morning and had come downstairs to find Nellie's little table with its pills and potions upturned, and Nellie herself unable to speak or move.

Daisy went in to see Miss Wilhelmina immediately and, selfish and demanding as the old lady could be at times, her mistress said Harold must drive Daisy home straightaway and she should stay with her grandmother until Nellie was better.

'I'll get a temporary nurse in for a while,' Wilhelmina said briskly, 'so don't give a moment's thought to me, Daisy. Let me know how things are when you can, dear, and rest assured your job will be waiting for you when you can return. And anything your grandmother needs, see that she gets it and charge any expenditure to me.'

'Thank you.' Daisy looked at the grand old lady whose frail little body seemed lost in the vivid pink bed, and on impulse she reached out her hands and grasped those of Wilhelmina, saying softly, 'You've been so good to me and I do appreciate it.'

'Go on with you.' The wrinkled face under the outrageous silk bonnet smiled wryly. 'I am a perverse old woman and we both know it. However, it must be said you put up with me well, child, and I like to think it is not wholly because you are paid to do so.'

'It's because I care about you.' No. That wasn't enough. 'Because I love you.'

Wilhelmina did not come back with one of the dry retorts Daisy had expected. Instead the scrawny throat worked convulsively and the grip on Daisy's hands tightened. 'Bless you, dear.' Daisy felt herself being pulled into her mistress's embrace and held close for a moment or two, and then, with a sniff, the old lady said, 'Now you get yourself home to your grandmother and I'll see you soon.'

Daisy was aware her mistress's face was wet and also that the proud old lady would hate her to mention it, so she just squeezed Wilhelmina's hands one more time before she straightened. 'I'll send word once I know how things are.'

'You do that, child.'

When Daisy entered the kitchen Gladys was about to take a tea tray through to Miss Wilhelmina. Daisy wasted no words on preliminaries. 'I haven't informed the mistress we had an intruder in the house last night but you try anything like that again and I'll make sure you're out on your ear. Is that clear? Now tell Harold to get the horse and carriage ready. He's driving Alf and me home.' She left Gladys speechless for once.

It was snowing again when Wilhelmina's carriage, driven by a silent Harold, deposited Daisy and Alf in Sea Lane, the road to the Bents being accessible only by foot due to drifts of snow some six or seven foot deep either side of the narrow path which had been cleared.

Enid was sitting with Nellie when Daisy walked into the cottage, Tilly having her work cut out to keep the little ones occupied and away from the sick woman, and for once Daisy's first glance wasn't for little Tommy.

Nellie stirred and slowly opened her eyes as Daisy bent over her, holding her granddaughter's gaze as she said, 'I'm here, Gran, and Miss Wilhelmina said I can stay until you're well again. That was nice of her, wasn't it? So you can just rest now and I'll take care of everything, all right?'

The old woman struggled to speak, her mouth opening but only an unintelligible gurgle emerging.

'Don't try and talk, Gran, not now,' said Daisy softly. 'The doctor said you need to rest and then you'll be as right as rain in a week or two.'

Nellie's mouth had closed but her desperate eyes told Daisy her grandmother knew she was lying. Now Daisy took one of her granny's gnarled hands, holding it tight as she said, 'You *will* get better, Gran, I shall make sure you do.'

She had promised herself she wouldn't cry in front of her granny, but when a tear welled up in Nellie's eye and slid down the wrinkled cheek, Daisy couldn't keep her composure. She bent closer, laying her head next to Nellie's as she said, 'Don't worry, Gran, we'll get through this together like we've got through everything else. Now you mustn't upset yourself 'cos that won't help.' In reply to the mute plea she had read in the rheumy eyes Daisy added, 'And I shall stay with you every minute, I promise. Every minute, Gran. I'll bring a mattress down, like we did for William, do you remember? And I'll sleep down here.'

Nellie's eyes closed again but Daisy didn't raise her head until she was sure the old woman was asleep. Then she stood up slowly, walking across to where Tilly stood holding Tommy who had been crying on and off for the last few minutes because he wanted her. She took the child into her arms, murmuring words of comfort to him. Over his brown curls her eyes held Tilly's.

'He said it's bad, lass, the doctor. All her left side's gone an' she's not got the strength to move, and barely to swallow. Cuthbert said I can use his cottage in the day for the bairns an' just bring 'em back here to sleep of a night if that'd help? Or do you want me here with you in case . . . well, you know,' she finished awkwardly.

'No, you take the bairns out of it.'

'I'll come of a mornin' an' stay until Tilly brings the bairns back, lass.' Enid had joined them, her voice quiet. 'Kitty can look after Alf all right, she's a good lass.'

'You don't have to, Mrs Hardy.'

'Oh, aye, I do, lass. Me an' your granny . . . Oh, aye, I do.'

It was the first time Daisy had ever seen Alf's mother cry. She put her free arm round the older woman who did the same to her, and then Tilly was holding them too, Tommy squashed between the three women who all had wet faces.

'Eeh, your gran wouldn't want this.' Enid was the first to pull away, wiping her face with her apron. 'I'll make us a nice sup tea, shall I? An' your mistress is good, lass, an' no mistake, lettin' you come like this. I've never had no time for the gentry to be truthful with you, but it seems there's good an' bad in all walks of life, eh, lass?'

'That's very true, Mrs Hardy.'

'Aye, aye, it is an' all. No one could say the Frasers haven't been fair with you after you pulled their lad out of the water, an' they seem to think a bit of you.'

Daisy could have answered this in many ways but what she did say was, 'Miss Wilhelmina is one of the kindest people I've ever come across although she doesn't strike you as such until you get to know her.'

But as for the rest of the family . . . The memory of the previous evening flashed through Daisy's head for a second before she put it out of her mind. She was here to take care of her granny and that was what she was going to do. She wouldn't let herself think about Francis Fraser for one moment. He was loathsome, filthy, and if she never saw him again in the whole of her life it would be too soon. But strangely, in spite of the disgusting things he had said and tried to do, it was the fact that he had confirmed her secret fear that William would never come back to England that had hurt the most.

'Cecilia, are you sure we are doing the right thing if we say anything? You know how Aunt Wilhelmina dotes on the girl.'

'Exactly.' Cecilia glared at her sister. 'Don't be so dim, Felicity. Uncle Francis only confirmed what I have been thinking for ages. The fishergirl is determined to get the lot when Aunt Wilhelmina goes, and you know she was going to leave everything to us. Uncle says it's common knowledge among her servants that the baggage has inveigled her way in by blackening our names. Uncle's right – Aunt Wilhelmina won't like being abandoned in favour of the girl's grandmother and it's been four days since she's been gone. Now is the time to strike. We'll just go in with the Christmas presents and make conversation, and when the time's right we'll tell her exactly what her precious companion is really like. I'm sure Aunt knows nothing about the girl having a child or carrying on with William and hundreds of others.'

Felicity looked unhappily at her sister. Cecilia was always so sure she was right, and Uncle Francis had managed to fire her up about the fishergirl so she had been beside herself the last day or two. But it was no use saying anything more.

Silence reigned until the carriage drew up on the packed snow outside the front door of Evenley House, whereupon the coachman jumped to the ground and opened the door for Sir Augustus's daughters. Although Donald Vickers hadn't been able to hear anything which had been said on the journey, his relationship with Ellen Mullen meant he knew the real reason for this visit a week before Christmas.

Once the two women had entered the house Donald settled himself down for a long wait. Normally Sir Augustus's daughters only stayed for an hour at most when they visited their aunt, but if they were about the business of ousting the fishergirl they might be a lot longer. Just his luck, Donald thought, with the wind enough to cut you in two and the air so cold it stung your throat.

He needn't have worried. The carriage was on its way home again within fifteen minutes.

Gladys and Harold sat staring at each other over the kitchen table, the wicker armchairs in front of the range empty for once. There'd be no relaxing and toasting his toes with a plate of Gladys's girdle scones on his lap this night, Harold thought despondently. Gladys was in a right tear and no mistake. Mind, it wasn't right whatever way you looked at it; if Maud hadn't been up to her eyes black-leading the kitchen range when the mistress's nieces had called,

333

him and Gladys would be none the wiser as to Miss Wilhelmina's intentions.

As though her husband had spoken out loud, Gladys now said, 'We'd know nowt about this if I hadn't taken the tea trolley along when I did an' heard what was goin' on inside afore I opened the door. You realise that, don't you? All these years of workin' me fingers to the bone an' it counts for nowt with the mistress. An' the way she went for her own flesh an' blood . . . you ought to have heard her! She told 'em straight she was goin' to change her will an' leave it all to the fishergirl. That's what was in that letter she had you take to the solicitor after they'd gone, sure as eggs are eggs. An' once he's knocked on the door an' it's done legal like, it's done for good. You know that, Harold, don't you?'

Gladys's voice had grown shriller in the face of her husband's apparent lack of response. All Harold said, as he'd done several times during the evening, was, 'Nothing you or I could say'll change matters, lass, so it's no use fretting.'

'No use!' Gladys glared at him. 'The mistress all but told me there was something in her will for us, in the days afore that baggage arrived, an' I'm not losin' what's rightfully mine. As I see it there's only one course of action left open to us.'

'Oh, aye?' It was clear Harold hadn't got Gladys's vision.

'Come mornin' Maud'll be here, an' the nurse'll be downstairs. The solicitor's comin' at ten, you say? It'll be too late to do anythin' then.' Harold's face remained blank until his wife added, 'She's only got a few weeks left in her anyway accordin' to the doctor.'

'You . . . you don't . . .' Words failed him.

'A pillow over her face for a minute an' it's done, finished. Everyone'll assume her heart's finally given out.

She'll know nowt about it if it's done while she's asleep an' it's the kindest thing to my mind, rather than let her carry on like she is.'

If Harold had spoken out what was in his mind at this point he would have said, 'You're mad – stark staring mad, woman,' but the qualities which had made Gladys choose him as a partner caused him to swallow hard before he said weakly, his head drooping to one side, 'Lass, I'm not sayin' I don't know how you feel an' you've bin treated shameful, no doubt about it, but . . . I couldn't. I'm sorry, lass, but I couldn't do it.'

Gladys's lips pursed and she brought her beefy shoulders up. 'Aye, well, that's as may be, but I could. I've had that little madam up to the eyeballs an' I'm blowed if I'll stand by and do nowt so she can thumb her nose at us when she gets everythin'.'

Harold raised his head and stared at his wife and she returned his look, her eyes having taken on a steely quality. By, she frightened him, she scared him half to death! Talking about doing away with the old lady, and all the while as cool as a cucumber.

'So? You comin' along there with me because now's as good a time as any, an' I'll do it if you're too lily-livered.'

Harold didn't know which scared him the most: the thought of being in the room while Gladys did the deed or refusing to accompany her. After a few seconds his wife took his silence to mean he was staying put and after one narrow-eyed glance didn't waste time on further words. She stood up, smoothing her apron and adjusting her mob cap, and left the room. How long Harold sat there he didn't know, but when Gladys entered the kitchen again he was surprised when she smiled at him, her voice the same as ever as she said, 'Get the teapot out, lad, an' we'll have a brew, an' I'll do you a batch of girdle cakes

335

to go with it. You're always peckish this time of night, aren't you?'

He didn't think he would ever be hungry again. As a possible reason for his wife's geniality dawned, Harold said hopefully, 'You didn't go through with it then?'

Gladys didn't answer him, at least not verbally, but as she turned from the range and her eyes met his, he read her reply from the expression on her face, and it was satisfaction.

Chapter Twenty-two

But for a visit by the clerk employed by Wilhelmina's solicitor, Daisy would not have heard about her mistress's death until after the old lady's funeral had come and gone. However, the solicitor in question was a kindly man and as astute as any in his profession. He had got to know Daisy on his monthly visits to Wilhelmina, and accurately gauged something of the atmosphere existing between his client's young companion and the older members of Wilhelmina's staff.

His December appointment had coincided with the day of Daisy's departure from the house, and after receiving Wilhelmina's letter and then the news of her death half-an-hour before he had been due to leave for Evenley House, he had been unsettled in mind enough to decide a visit by his clerk to the girl's current abode was in order. If she had already been informed about her employer's demise that was well and good; if not, then at least he had done his duty to his client who had looked on the girl more as a daughter than an employee. He had half been expecting Wilhelmina to alter her will in favour of the girl for months, but then – as he had told his clerk after explaining the reason for the visit – the old lady had not liked to reflect on her eventual demise.

Daisy had sat quietly by Nellie's bed for a long while after the clerk had gone, the tears running down her face as the old woman slept. Miss Wilhelmina had gone, and she hadn't been there to hold the old lady's hand and do whatever she could. Now it was too late. The only comfort she had was that the doctor seemed sure her mistress had gone in her sleep without knowing anything about it, and she hoped, oh, she did so hope that was true. She had to believe that, had to cling on to it.

She said as much to Kitty when her friend came to sit with her for a while, Alf's mother being indisposed with a stomach upset.

'I'm sure she didn't know a thing about it, lass,' Kitty said comfortingly, 'and if you've got to go it's not a bad way, is it, in your sleep?' They sat quietly for a few moments beside the sleeping Nellie whose breathing was barely discernible. 'What's the betting we hear nowt from me mam an' da about the mistress going. Spiteful so-an'-sos. You say the clerk said the funeral's on Wednesday?'

Daisy nodded. 'The day before Christmas Eve. Apparently it's a short laying-out because of its being Christmas and all the services arranged.'

Up until this moment in time Daisy had said nothing of what had occurred with Francis Fraser, but suddenly she felt the need to tell Kitty all of it including the part her parents had played in the proceedings. The other girl listened intently, and when Daisy finished with, 'So I think you were spot on with your prediction we'll hear nothing from your parents,' Kitty stared at her, wide-eyed.

'By, lass . . .' The words seemed to have required all the effort Kitty was capable of, because now she sat back on the hard wooden saddle, her mouth still slightly agape and her head moving from side to side in disgust. 'The old devil,' she managed eventually. 'To do something like that to another woman.'

Daisy nodded. She had no doubt that Gladys would make sure the door to Evenley House was now firmly closed to her. Suddenly what had been a temporary stay in the village was a permanent one, and it was a funny feeling. She loved her granny and her brothers and all the folk she had grown up with, but she didn't feel a part of the community in the same way as before however hard she tried. And she *had* tried over the last days.

'I'm going to go to Miss Wilhelmina's funeral, Kitty, whatever anyone might say about it not being decent. I . . . I have to. Would you sit with Gran if Alf's mam isn't better by then?'

'She will be. Constitution of a shire horse, has Mam. You sure you want to go, lass? You know they'll all whisper about it not being right for a female to attend, and an unmarried one at that. It'll be another nail in your coffin,' Kitty added with unconscious dark humour.

Daisy inclined her head slowly. She had to say goodbye properly, she'd never forgive herself if she didn't. And she hadn't taken any notice of those who said it wasn't seemly for females to attend funerals when Tom and her da died so she wasn't about to start now. 'I have to go, Kitty.'

'Then I'm coming with you.'

'Alf might not like it, lass.'

'I'm coming.' Kitty stared at her, still shaking her head. 'You know, I wouldn't have believed even Mam could sink so low as to set up something with that horrible man. By, I'm glad I'm out of it, lass. If the flow of the milk of human kindness depended on me mam it'd have dried up years ago. She's knocked me from Monday to Saturday since I was a bairn, but her fists are nothing compared to her tongue. And she'll think she's got the upper hand now, that's what gets me. Crowing like a rooster, she'll be. I don't know the Bible well enough to know if the devil had a mam, but if he did, rest assured she's alive an' well an' living in Fulwell.'

'Oh, Kitty.' In spite of everything the ghost of a smile touched Daisy's lips. Whatever else changed Kitty remained the same, and Daisy had never been so thankful for the stout, warm-hearted northern lass as she was at that moment.

The day of the funeral was one of high winds and bitter cold, but as Daisy sat shivering at the very back of Whitburn parish church next to Alf, with Kitty on the other side of the fisherman, her thoughts were on her mistress and not her own icy feet or frozen hands. Alf had insisted on escorting the two girls when he had realised Daisy was determined to go to the funeral, and Kitty was equally determined to accompany her, and in truth Daisy was glad of the big solid fisherman's presence. There was something very comforting about being under her old friend's protection when she felt so sad about Miss Wilhelmina and upset about her granny.

The congregation were waiting for the hearse to arrive, followed by the family. As a subdued stir announced its arrival Daisy closed her eyes. Oh, Miss Wilhelmina, I hope you're able to run and dance and do all those things you wanted to where you are now. Forgive me for not being with you when you needed me most, she prayed.

When she opened her eyes the cortège was filing past. As she took in the sight of a young man on crutches next to Sir Augustus her heart actually missed a beat. He hadn't seen her, all the family were looking neither to left nor right, but as her eyes followed his blond head she felt faint for a moment.

Kitty must have nudged Alf. Daisy was aware of him leaning towards his wife and Kitty whispering something, causing Alf's head to shoot up as he glanced first towards the black-clad figures and then at Daisy. This was on the perimeter of her vision and Daisy didn't turn to meet his eyes, not even when he kept them on her for some moments before looking to the front again.

William was here. Why hadn't she considered the possibility he might come to Miss Wilhelmina's funeral? And then she answered herself. The last she'd heard from her mistress before her granny took bad was that it was going to be a long old haul before William was well again, and the doctors were insisting he take it very slowly. And, after all, he hadn't bothered with the old lady in years.

Daisy could remember only parts of the service afterwards, although she was conscious of standing up and sitting down at all the right moments, and singing each of the three hymns that had been chosen, some with very poignant words. Her emotions were muddled during this twenty minutes. Part of her was aching to see William face to face, if only from a distance, and feast her eyes on the features she'd thought never to see again, but another part of her was saying, and with some bitterness, it would have meant far more to Miss Wilhelmina if her nephew had spared her just one visit in the last years, rather than making the grand gesture now when it was too late for her mistress. But over all the other thoughts one kept clamouring however much she tried to dismiss it: How could you just leave like you did, without saying goodbye?

When the service finished and the family filed out again, Daisy kept her eyes turned to the floor until the church was practically empty. Kitty and Alf said not a word as the three of them left the building, but they had stationed themselves one on either side of her, their arms through hers.

The wind was whipping round the gravestones, and by unspoken mutual consent the three of them paused some yards away from the other mourners who were standing at a respectful distance from the family gathered round the open grave. Sir Augustus was on one side of William and Francis Fraser on the other, and they were standing with their backs to the church, the parson of Whitburn church directly facing Daisy and the others. And then, as the parson began speaking, William turned, his eyes searching the crowd until they fell on Daisy whereupon they became still. And Daisy in her turn did not move a muscle. He must have seen her in the church. She acknowledged that thought as her mind said, He looks older, much older, but of course he would do with what he's been through recently. And even more handsome.

It was with some difficulty that she broke the hold of the piercingly blue gaze but she managed it, lowering her eyes again as she struggled to take in what the parson was saying and to concentrate on the last few minutes of the funeral.

Goodbye, Miss Wilhelmina. As the first thick clod of earth hit the coffin which had now been lowered into the ground, Daisy winced. She hated that sound. God bless. I love you.

'Let's go.' She turned blindly away, fighting back the tears, and Alf and Kitty moved swiftly with her, but then, as she heard her name called once, and then again, she was forced to stop, aware it was causing something of a stir.

She turned as William approached, willing herself not to betray her deep agitation and to conduct herself with dignity, and then, when he almost stumbled within feet of them, the crutches making him clumsy, her hands went out to steady him before dropping back to her sides as Alf caught him, saying, 'Steady, sir, steady.'

'Thank you.' He was speaking to Alf but looking at Daisy, and now he was so close she found she couldn't say a word. 'I'm sorry to delay you, I just wanted to say hallo.' His voice was tight, and she wasn't to know it was embarrassment at his physical inadequacy to meet the occasion that was biting at him. 'How are you?'

Daisy didn't answer this directly. What she did say was,

and stiffly, 'I'm very sorry about your aunt, Mr William. She was a wonderful woman.'

Mr William? Her emphasis on the division between them grated on him even as her presence made him light-headed. Never once in the time he had fought the doctors and his mother to come back to England for his aunt's funeral, or since he had arrived at Greyfriar the day before, had the name Daisy Appleby been mentioned, but she had been on his mind constantly. When he had seen her at the back of the church as they had followed the coffin out, he had asked his father what she was doing here and why Lyndon had allowed her to come alone. 'Lyndon?' his father had replied. 'What's he to do with the fishing wench? Your aunt fell out with him years ago as I recall and the last I heard he'd married and moved to take a parish down south.'

Now, as Alf moved back in between the two women, his hand cupping Daisy's elbow and that of Kitty, a new thought struck William. The action had been distinctly protective, even possessive. Was this rugged, good-looking individual the reason Daisy's romance with Lyndon had come to nothing?

Before he could think of a way to broach the subject, Daisy said, 'You know Kitty, Mr William, and this is Alfred Hardy.'

The two men nodded at each other, Kitty giving a little curtsey as the years of training kicked in. Now Daisy's voice expressed nothing but cool politeness when she said, 'I am pleased to see you are on the road to recovery after your accident. It must have been a trying time for you.'

'Yes.' He stared at her, his mind racing, adding as an afterthought, 'Thank you.'

After the rush of emotion Daisy was feeling slightly numb and not at all herself, but she welcomed the anaesthetising effect on her feelings. He had probably felt obliged to come across and speak to her, might even

343

have experienced a slight sense of guilt at the way he had behaved when he'd left England without warning, but the last thing she wanted was him feeling sorry for her. She could stand anything but that. He had known she . . . cared about him – at this moment she could not bring herself to acknowledge the word love – and he had led her on. Oh, yes, he had, she reiterated as though someone had challenged her. And when he had tired of his fun he had taken himself off to Paris to one of his fancy women.

She feasted her eyes on him one last time, knowing she was taking in every detail because there was little chance their paths would ever cross again, and then she turned her body slightly into Alf's in an action that deliberately hinted at intimacy as she said, 'We have to go, I'm afraid, my grandmother is not well. It was nice to see you again after all this time, Mr William. Goodbye.'

Say something. Stop me. Make everything all right somehow.

William was standing stiffly now, and his face, too, was stiff when he said, 'Goodbye, Daisy.' That was it then, she was with this fellow. Well, looking at her, in the full bloom of her beauty, he would have been a fool to expect her to stay unattached, wouldn't he? Nevertheless he felt sick as he watched the three of them walk away after Alf had nodded at him and Kitty had given another little bob. Sick to his soul.

That had shown him she didn't need any grand gestures on his part, that her life was fine without him. Daisy's head was high and her back straight as she walked away, and she was willing herself with all her strength not to turn round for one last glance at him.

'You all right, lass?' Kitty's voice was soft, and in answer to her unspoken sympathy Daisy's pride rose up again, enabling her to look round Alf at her friend and smile as she said, 'I'm fine, Kitty. It was a good turn out, wasn't it? Miss Wilhelmina would have been pleased so many people wanted to come.'

Kitty hadn't been asking how Daisy felt regarding Miss Wilhelmina's funeral and she knew Daisy realised this, but taking her cue from her friend she made a suitable reply and the three of them walked on.

It was much later that night, when Daisy was alone apart from the sleeping form of her grandmother and there was only the sound of the sea washing the shore outside the cottage, that she finally allowed the hot tears to fall.

Chapter Twenty-three

'I knew you would suffer for going, and your aunt would not have expected it. Now please, darling, let me spoil you a little. You look perfectly dreadful.'

'Thank you, Mother, that is most encouraging.' William's voice was wry but there was a quality to his smile as he glanced at his mother which would not have been there some months before. He had found, much to his surprise, that since her arrival in France he had felt altogether differently about her. But then *she* was different, he told himself. It was as though, having shaken off her marriage and more especially his father, she had taken on a warmth and lightness of spirit which made her a changed woman. All his life he had believed his mother was a social butterfly with little real substance – and he had to admit she had entered with gusto into the whirl of French society – but he had discovered over the last weeks and months when they had been together much of the time that she was more like her sister Lydia than he had previously given her credit for.

He looked at Gwendoline now, busy heaping a plate with dainty sandwiches and cake for him from a trolley one of the maids had wheeled in a few moments before. They had not really discussed the matter of the divorce, but then they had not needed to. He would have understood why she wanted to leave his father even if he had not heard her whispering about it with his Aunt Lydia one day when they had thought he was asleep. She so wished she had waited and married for love, like Lydia, his mother had murmured, rather than the prestige of a name and great wealth. It had been a mistake from the start, a grave mistake, but at least she had William to show for the years of unhappiness. That had touched him, she had sounded as though she really meant it.

'So overall you are glad you went to the funeral?' Gwendoline asked, handing him the plate before reseating herself on a couch to one side of the full-length window overlooking the grounds of Claude's château in the Loire Valley, the Garden of France. 'And your father wasn't . . . difficult about your decision to return here immediately rather than stay at Greyfriar?'

'No, he wasn't difficult.' William bit into a wafer-thin sandwich. But as to whether he was glad he had gone or not, he wasn't sure. It had been hard seeing Daisy again – seeing her with someone else was perhaps nearer the truth – harder even than he'd expected when he'd considered the matter in the past. But at least it had helped make up his mind once and for all that he would never take up residence at Greyfriar Hall again.

During the weeks he had lain in no man's land, unable to think or escape the muzziness which had penetrated his brain and kept everything – past and present – muffled in an impenetrable fog, he had expected to die. He should have done, that's what the nurses in the infirmary had told him once he began to improve, and it was a miracle he was doing so well. He agreed with them, it was a miracle, and that being the case he couldn't waste this second chance at life.

He had been speaking the truth when he had told the police and his family that he could remember nothing of the attack or the hours leading up to it, but that hadn't meant he didn't know who was responsible. He had considered mentioning von Spee's name, but after thinking about it for a while had to admit he owed the man enough to keep quiet. Make a cuckold of a man and you make an enemy; he had received rough justice but perhaps it had been no more than he deserved. Whatever, thanks to Monsieur Richer who had put his legs back together again he was going to recover, and that being the case he had resolved to put the whole episode behind him. Once he was sufficiently recovered he would follow through on the idea he had had before the attack and join the army, but until then he would keep quiet about his future, for his mother's sake. He knew she would be aghast at the thought of him becoming a soldier; time enough for her to come to terms with it when she had to. She had already been making noises about this girl or that over here, the matchmaking urge still strong, but when – or perhaps it would be if – he took a wife, it would be his choice and his alone.

'Were you aware of what was in the letter your father gave you to give to me?' his mother now asked, bringing William out of his thoughts.

'No.'

She sighed. 'Apparently he has asked Francis to come here after Christmas with papers which will then be ready for me to sign. Of course, reading between the lines, what your father is hoping is that Francis will persuade me that a divorce is not necessary. Let him try, he will not succeed.'

'I didn't think for a moment he would.'

'And in the letter your father is adamant that Francis has turned over a new leaf incidentally. Do you believe that, William?'

'No, Mother, I do not. The man is incapable of it.'

'Quite.' They smiled at each other in mutual understanding and continued with their tea.

* * *

'You saw her, didn't you, Kirby, on the day of the funeral? Butter wouldn't have melted in her mouth.'

It was a few days after Christmas and the night before Francis was due to leave for France, a trip he had been loath to agree to. However, in his new guise of Augustus's nearest and dearest, he hadn't felt he could refuse his brother. Augustus was beside himself at the thought of the ignominy of a divorce, and pinning all his hopes on 'making the damn' silly woman see reason' as he had put it to Francis when he'd asked him to go and see Gwendoline.

Not that Francis intended to do any talking round. It suited his purposes admirably to have Gwendoline out of the way and William with her; Augustus was relying on his brother more and more, and in a little while Francis intended to start planting seeds of resentment and bitterness regarding William's decision to live with his mother rather than his father. There was nothing to stop Augustus capitalising the estate's assets in his lifetime; by the time William came to inherit he could well find there was little of value left.

But for the present moment Francis's thoughts were all on Daisy. It had riled him beyond measure that she had dared to show her face at the funeral, and remain so aloof and contained at that.

'The chit's brazen! Do y'hear me, Kirby?' Francis held out his brandy glass and the valet refilled it as he had done several times since dinner. It was now nearing midnight but still Mr Francis did not seem disposed to let him go, thought Kirby, the other man's drunken breath wafting over his face.

'Does . . . doesn't know her place, that's the thing.' Francis gulped at his drink before gesturing at the valet, his tone irritable as he said, 'Have another, man. You know I don't like to drink alone.'

He waited till Josiah had dutifully poured a small measure of brandy into his own glass, then said, 'Cu . . . cunning as foxes where she comes from.'

'Indeed they are, sir.' Josiah looked at his master's brother's flushed face and red-veined eyes. Another few minutes and Mr Francis would pass out, he knew the signs. Then he would call Mallard and they could get him up to bed like they always did when the master retired early and Mr Francis took the opportunity to drink himself senseless.

'Ma . . . making up to Will . . . William. I saw 'em.'

He could barely speak now. Josiah stretched his legs in the armchair opposite, sitting quietly as Mr Francis continued to mumble on, the words incoherent in the main. He had been livid the night the fishergirl had refused him, that was what all this was about, added to the fact he must have consumed a full bottle of brandy and that after a bottle or two of wine at dinner.

'. . . arrogant young buck. Von Spee'd got the right idea . . .' There was more mumbling, and then, 'Once he'd gone to the devil it would've been easy, but they had to bu . . . bungle it, damn their eyes!'

Goodness knew what Mr Francis was on about now but he'd better get Mallard out of bed, it'd take him a few minutes to get dressed. Josiah rose to his feet, and actually had one hand on the bell rope when he froze, suddenly taking in what his master's brother was saying. '. . . only had to dump the body in the water but couldn't even get that right. Customs men be damned! Couldn't be bothered, that was the thing.'

Josiah leant against the mantelpiece for support, his head reeling as he stared at the bloated figure in the chair. This was all to do with the attack on Mr William. Mr Francis had had a hand in trying to do away with his own nephew!

Francis was still muttering away but now the indistinct

words seemed to be a string of profanities, and after a minute or two even these stopped as the brandy took hold and he slipped into unconsciousness.

Nevertheless, it was some moments before Josiah moved, and then it was only to straighten himself slowly as he covered his eyes with his hand. He remained like this for a little while. He himself had been the one to bring Mr Francis back into the fold when his master's brother had approached him in France. He had believed Mr Francis when he'd said he wanted to help, preferring to trust the old adage that blood is thicker than water. And all the time . . . He dropped his hand and turned to look at the man he had served, to a limited extent, off and on for many years. What was he going to do? It would break the master to know his own brother had played a part in the attempt to kill Mr William, especially in view of the mistress's leaving and Mr Francis growing so close to Sir Augustus again. *What was he going to do?*

At eight o'clock the next morning a carriage containing Francis Fraser and Josiah Kirby left Greyfriar Hall. It was bitterly cold, fat flakes of snow falling from a low laden sky, and Francis was in a filthy mood. He abhorred the process of travelling and was not looking forward to the journey to London and then Dover by train, or the crossing to Calais. Added to which he had the mother and father of a hangover.

He glowered at Josiah as the carriage bumped over ridges of hard-packed snow, his voice reflecting his surly disposition when he said, 'You packed my white tie, Kirby? Can't be doing with that new fashion for the dinner jacket, although it seems to be catching on in certain circles.'

'Your evening dress is at the very top of the trunk, sir, and I stood over the housemaid to make sure everything is as it should be.'

Francis grunted. 'I should think so. Damn' useless girls! There's not one of them with a grain of sense in her head.'

'Quite so, sir.'

Obsequious so-and-so. Francis belched loudly. Still, that was his job and Kirby was a damn' good valet.

When the carriage drew up outside the station the snow was coming down even more thickly. It had been arranged that Josiah would travel to Dover with his employer's brother and see him onto the boat for Calais: one of Claude's servants would meet him in France. Now Francis exited the carriage and walked into the station leaving Josiah to follow with the trunk. He turned as the valet reached him, his voice irritable as he said, 'Come on, man, come on. The train's due any moment.'

Josiah had refused the help of a porter and his face was red with exertion when he placed the trunk on the ground for a moment, only for Francis to say, as the engine puffed into the station, 'Pick it up, Kirby, I don't intend to be the last on. Look lively, man!'

'Of course, Mr Francis.'

It was talked about for months afterwards by those who had been present on the platform.

One minute the train had been chugging to a stop as usual, the next the station was echoing with the most blood-curdling screams as that poor gentleman fell on to the rails and under the wheels. Cut him in two, it did, near as damn it.

What exactly happened no one was really sure. However, the police talked to the valet who had been accompanying the dead man, and it appeared the gentleman had been standing too close to the edge of the platform and just lost his balance. Mind, it did emerge he had been drinking excessively the night before and had still been more than a little unsteady on his legs that morning. At the inquest one of the footmen from Greyfriar Hall said the gentleman had had to be carried to bed after midnight; incapable of even undressing himself, he'd been. You can't get into a state like that and it not have consequences, can you?

The valet was as upset as the family, poor devil. 'Course, he'd seen it happen, hadn't he, and it'd live with you for ever something like that. What a way to go, eh?

Chapter Twenty-four

Nellie died on New Year's Eve and her end was peaceful, with those she loved gathered about her and Daisy holding her hand. It was a gentle, slow slipping away and Daisy knew her grandmother wouldn't have wanted to continue living with many of her faculties gone. Nevertheless, as the old woman breathed her last she found herself inwardly crying, Granny, don't go. Please don't go. Not yet, I can't bear it. You can't go. But she had. And in death the lines and wrinkles of years of pain and suffering were smoothed away and she looked young again as she went to meet her Abe.

Daisy sat for a long time stroking the gnarled old hand, her eyes streaming and her heart sore, and then she asked Enid to help her lay her granny out. Cuthbert had had all the bairns at his house since it had been obvious the end was nigh, and while Daisy and Enid did what needed to be done, Kitty, Alf and Tilly joined him, Daisy's brothers and their wives returning to their own homes.

Daisy and Enid had just finished and Daisy was filling the poss-tub to soak the soiled linen when a grim-faced Harold knocked on the door of the cottage. He had brought her clothes and belongings, he said quietly. Miss Cecilia and Miss Felicity were in the process of clearing the house before they sold it, and the solicitor had advised them they had to return what was hers.

'Thank you.' Even in the midst of her grief over Nellie

Daisy thought how ill he looked, and something made her say, 'Are you all right, Harold? I would ask you in for a hot drink before you go back but my grandmother died today.'

He stared at her long enough for her to become sure there was something terribly wrong with him, actually wringing his hands before he said, still in the same quiet flat voice, 'I'm sorry, lass, about your granny. Give . . . give Kitty me best when you see her, will you? Tell her me an' her mam'll be movin' on in the next few days.'

'Where to?'

'Don't know, lass. Gladys was hopin' they'd fit us in at Greyfriar Hall but they've given her short shrift.'

'But you'll be all right? I mean, with what the mistress must have left you?'

'For a while, aye.' He chewed on his lip for a moment. 'But it weren't as much as Gladys had hoped an' it won't last long if we don't get work. Gladys is gettin' on an' I'm not as young as I used to be, an' there's not many places'd be lookin' for a cook an' gardener both.'

Daisy didn't know what to say. There was silence for a moment beyond the sound of Enid pummelling at the washing in the scullery, and then Harold said, 'I'd best be gettin' back, Gladys is in a state. Miss Cecilia has made a list of everythin' in the place down to the last teaspoon, an' Gladys has got it into her head the young mistress thinks she might pinch somethin'.'

Well, Daisy for one wouldn't put it past her old enemy.

Her face must have reflected her thoughts because Harold dropped his eyes, switching his gaze to one side as he said, 'You . . . you won't forget to remember me to Kitty?'

'No, I won't forget, Harold.'

'I wish . . . I wish things could have been . . . been different, lass, when we was all up at the house together.'

'So do I, Harold, but I think the person you really need to say that to is your daughter.'

His neck stretched, craning out of his coat. 'Aye, mebbe, but it's too late.'

'It's never too late, not if you mean what you say.'

'Oh, aye, it is, lass. You don't know . . .' He swallowed hard, his Adam's apple jerking. 'Just give the lass me best.'

He turned on his heel, leaving indentations in the freshly fallen snow as he made his way back to the horse and trap. His bowed head and drooping shoulders gave the impression of someone who was in utter despair. Daisy stared after him for a moment before she picked up the package Harold had placed on the mat and shut the door slowly, turning to face the room in front of her. She glanced across at the bed on which lay Nellie's still figure, and all thoughts of Kitty's father fled her mind.

Her granny had gone, her lovely granny had gone, and right at this moment she would have given the world to be able to step back in time and become a child again, feeling her granny holding her tight and telling her that she was her own precious bairn.

When Tilly brought Tommy and the other children back to the cottage, Cuthbert accompanied her.

'We need to talk to you, lass, an' I'm sorry it's like this but it might affect what you decide to do and so . . .' Tilly stopped abruptly, aware she was gabbling.

'I've asked Tilly to marry me, Daisy, and she's said yes.' Cuthbert's voice was low in acknowledgement of her grief but he couldn't quite keep a thread of elation from it. 'It will mean she'll move in with me, her and the bairns, and . . .' He paused, not knowing quite how to put it.

'That's wonderful, Tilly.' Daisy reached out and grasped her sister-in-law's hands, keeping her voice steady. She

357

had known immediately what Cuthbert was trying to say. There would be no room for Tommy at his cottage. Almost from the first the two of them had not hit it off. Cuthbert's children were placid, like Tilly's, but Tommy had all of his father's assertive, enquiring nature and then some. 'Tommy and I will be fine.'

'Lass, things can stay as they are for as long as they need to—'

'But it would be nice to have the wedding as soon as we can,' Cuthbert interrupted hastily.

Daisy looked at him, a straight look. Cuthbert was a good man and would make Tilly a sound husband, but, like Tommy, she had never liked him. She said quietly, 'I have a little money saved, enough to bury Gran properly and rent somewhere in Sunderland while I look for a job and someone to look after Tommy in the day, so you must get married as soon as you like. I shall rent somewhere unfurnished and take all the stuff from here, of course.'

'Oh, of course, lass, of course. You've bought it all.' Tilly nodded violently. 'But won't you carry on in service somewhere, now you're so far up the ladder? As a companion or governess, I mean?'

'No, I won't go into service again.' It was said very definitely. Suddenly there was only Tommy and herself to support and the change in her circumstances over the last two weeks had knocked Daisy for six. Or perhaps it was the loss of two dear old ladies, born at opposite ends of the social scale but still alike for all that. Suddenly she couldn't discuss the future anymore, and was grateful for Tommy's voice calling for her in the room above.

By the end of January Daisy and Tommy were established on the upper floor of a two-up, two-down terraced house in Mainsforth Terrace West off Hendon Valley Road, opposite the Villette Brick Works.

The location of the house was not ideal being close to the brick works, but a short walk down Villette Road and the better part of Hendon was at hand. Although Sunderland had absorbed the small villages of Hendon and Grangetown in latter years the main bulk of the heavily built up area lay eastward towards Hendon Dock and the Wear Fuel and Chemical Works; but westward, just past Barley Mow Cottage was Hendon Hill with trees and flowers, a fountain and well, and Hendon Burn.

Daisy was determined that Tommy – born to the sound of the sea and used to playing on the sands and running wild most of the time with the other fishermen's bairns – would not be confined to the grim terraced streets more than could be helped.

The district had been electrified three years before so now the journey into the heart of Bishopwearmouth was not reliant on the old horse trams and was much quicker. But Daisy would have walked there and back every day if it had been necessary, rather than take accommodation in Sunderland's stinking East End or the main part of the town where thick black industrial smoke hung in the air like a stifling blanket.

An added advantage with the house in Mainsforth Terrace West was that the landlady – a retired schoolteacher who was nevertheless a very active and agile sixty year old occupying the downstairs of the dwelling – had been very pleased to alleviate the boredom of her days by taking charge of little Tommy while Daisy looked for work. Furthermore, Miss Casey had assured her new lodger that the arrangement could continue when Daisy had employment, right up to the time Tommy started school. Tommy, a child of definite and immediate opinions, had cast the plump, merry-eyed little spinster in the role of grandmother from the first moment he had seen her, and their relationship was proving to be a happy one.

This, along with the fact that he had not once asked for Tilly or his old playmates but still seemed as ecstatic about being with Daisy as when she had first broached the news to the little boy, was a great encouragement but Daisy was anxious to find suitable employment quickly. By the time she had paid for her grandmother's funeral – and she had been determined Nellie wouldn't have a pauper's send off like her father and brothers had had but a decent service and a nice plot in the churchyard – and other expenses, her carefully saved little nest egg was severely depleted.

But their two rooms were a real home. Daisy glanced about the sitting room, having just left the bedroom after settling Tommy down in one of the two single iron beds the room held. She had bought these along with new mattresses after selling Nellie's bed and the two double beds at the fishing cottage.

In the sitting room the hard wooden saddle was standing by the wall under the window, but now its seat was festooned with flock cushions. Daisy had bought these from the second-hand stall in the old market in Bishopswearmouth and covered them in bright red material, some of which she had used to make matching curtains. The square wooden table was also from the cottage but Daisy had only brought two of the chairs, selling the other four. With a thick new tablecloth covering the old oilcloth and a pot holding a flowering azalea in the middle of the table, it was barely recognisable.

When Miss Casey had decided to rent the two upper rooms as a small flat she had had the fireplace in the room she had designated the sitting room replaced with a kitchen grate with cast-iron hobs. Although small, this now enabled pots and kettles to simmer in front of the fire. Daisy had bought a large guard for this with Tommy's exploring hands in mind, but the child had made no effort to get too near, merely lying on the thick clippy mat in front of the range when he was tired, dreamily watching the flames flickering in the fire.

A small dresser and kitchen cupboard in the sitting room, and a wardrobe in the bedroom – again courtesy of a second-hand shop – completed Daisy's small home. She felt it was clean, cosy and comfortable, and moreover that she and Tommy could be happy in it. There was just enough room for the privy and a washline in the back yard which was accessed by means of a door at the end of the hall, but no washhouse. This meant water from the tap in the yard had to be carried upstairs for washing as well as cooking, but Daisy didn't mind this. All she wanted now was a job which would pay enough for her to support Tommy and herself.

She had considered asking Sir Augustus for a character reference but decided against it. William's family had made their feelings about her clear on numerous occasions, and she wasn't about to give them the satisfaction of refusing her. If it became necessary she would approach Miss Wilhelmina's solicitor to vouch for her. Mr Crawford's premises were situated in Fawcett Street in between the cabinet maker's and the ironmonger's and she could easily call and see him.

Daisy walked across to the table, pulling one of the chairs out from under it and sitting down. He was nice, Mr Crawford. He had written to her after the funeral saying that he was sure Miss Wilhelmina had been about to change her will in Daisy's favour just before she died, that he had been due to visit the house regarding that very thing the morning they had found the old lady. It had been kind of him to let her know, and she was glad Miss Wilhelmina had felt that way, but in a sense she was relieved that this severance from the Frasers was final. It was her and Tommy now, and no one else – *no one* – mattered.

*   *   *

The next week's search for a job proved fruitless and by the end of it Daisy was seriously considering forgetting all thoughts of office work or something similar, and approaching one of the factories or the curing houses at the docks. It seemed a shame because she had come on well with her shorthand and was sure she'd pick up typing, given a chance, but she had little money left. She'd paid Miss Casey a month's rent initially, but three weeks had passed already. She'd done the rounds and answered some advertisements and got interviews for two positions – one in a tea agent's office and the other in Heatherdene Convalescent Home office – but as soon as she had admitted she had a child to support she had sensed a withdrawal on the part of the interviewer. She had explained the circumstances in both instances – that Tommy was her late brother's child and she had assumed responsibility for the boy on the death of his mother – but it was obvious neither man had believed her. They had clearly both labelled her a 'fallen' woman and the interviews had been brief from that point.

She had thought then about concealing Tommy's existence, but apart from the fact that these things inevitably came out into the open sooner or later and then it would definitely look as though she'd had something to hide, everything within her rebelled against denying her nephew. So, it looked as though it would be a manual job in one of the curing houses or rope works where the only criteria were how strong you were and how hard you could work. Filthy, back-breaking work often among coarse and foul-mouthed companions. But needs must.

That was on the Friday evening. On Saturday morning Daisy took Tommy with her to post a letter to Kitty. The post office was on Villette Road, and afterwards she intended to walk down to Hendon Burn. Tommy liked the little footbridge there and would spend an hour or more throwing leaves into the water and watching his 'boats' float downstream.

Daisy bought the stamp for her letter along with some more writing materials while Tommy held on to her skirt, large-eyed as he took in the shining counter and brass scales beyond which a latticework of pigeonholes stretched from floor to ceiling full of letters, parcels, official-looking forms and a hundred and one other things besides.

Daisy had moved away from the counter and was putting her change in her purse when she heard the postmaster – who had served her – say to one of the postmen who was standing leaning on the counter, 'Anyway, like I was saying, I told her to hop it.'

'She was lucky you didn't call in the law.'

'Aye, that's what I told her. And do you know what the cheeky baggage said? Where's me pay for the week? Her pay! She's probably thieved the equivalent over the last months. I told her her pay would be a boot up her backside if she wasn't out of the door in sixty seconds.'

'Left you in a bit of a mess though, eh, Cecil?'

'Aye, but better that than having someone around with light fingers.'

Daisy raised her head and looked at the postmaster. He was a middle-aged man of medium height with a full head of grizzled grey hair and strikingly blue eyes which reminded her of William's. She didn't think about her next action, stepping forward with a suddenness which surprised Tommy who was still hanging on to her skirt with one hand. 'Are you looking to employ someone?' she asked with no preamble whatsoever.

'What?' He stared at her, the postman too.

'I couldn't help overhearing your conversation and I am at present seeking employment.'

'Are you indeed?' The blue eyes flashed from her to Tommy and then back again. Cecilia had been chary in exactly what she had returned to Daisy via Harold. One or two little gifts Miss Wilhelmina had given her had been missing, along with Pastor Lyndon's book and the three evening dresses she had possessed. However, the rest of her clothes had been in the package, and Daisy had never been so glad of her mistress's generosity as when the postmaster's sharp blue eyes took in her coat and hat, both of good quality. 'And in what capacity, Mrs . . . ?'

'Miss.' She knew her face had turned scarlet but her voice was clear and steady. 'Miss Daisy Appleby. And this is my nephew, Tommy Appleby.'

The postmaster said nothing for several screamingly long seconds and he didn't glance at Tommy again. Then he said, 'Like I said, in what capacity, Miss Appleby?'

'The capacity of the job you've just had to sack the other girl from.' He knew and she knew she didn't have a clue what that was.

'Mm, you're so sharp you'll cut yourself, girl.' It could have been meant nastily but it wasn't. 'Septimus' – he turned to the postman who was still watching with considerable interest – 'you keep this little chappie happy for a minute or two while I talk to his aunt in the back, all right?' Now the man did look down at Tommy, smiling as he said, 'I bet you don't like sweets, eh? You do?' He reached behind the counter and brought out a bag of boiled sweets. 'Well, you chew on these bullets and be good for this nice gentleman. Here' – he came round and lifted Tommy on to the polished wood of the counter – 'you can help Mr Riley serve any customers that come in.'

Daisy left Mr Riley looking none too happy about the arrangement and followed the postmaster past the counter and into the back of the shop which was clearly a small office. Her heart was beating fit to burst and she could feel her hands beginning to tremble, so after the postmaster had indicated for her to be seated on a hardbacked chair to one side of one of the two desks the room contained, she clasped them together tightly in her lap.

'So, lass.' He sat down behind the bigger desk in a chair which although old looked comfy. 'I'm Mr Shelton and as you've already picked up I sacked my office girl this morning.' He settled himself comfortably, relaxing back in the chair as he said, 'And if I'm not mistaken there's more to you than meets the eye at first. You say you want a job?'

Daisy nodded, her eyes wide and fixed on his face.

'Then why don't you tell me all about yourself, lass, and start at the beginning, all right? I can't abide half a story.'

'The beginning?'

'Aye. Who your mam and da are, where you live, what you've been doing with yourself for the last . . . How old are you, lass?'

'I'm nineteen.'

'For the last nineteen years.'

This wasn't at all like the other two interviews. Daisy stared at him, thinking as she did so, Do I tell him I haven't got a proper reference because William's family didn't like me, that I've never had an office job before, that I have Tommy to take care of?

Bushy eyebrows rose over his vivid blue eyes. 'Well? I haven't got all day.'

She drew in a long breath. He had asked for it all and that was what he'd get, but if he thought she could tell it in sixty seconds he'd got another think coming.

It took ten minutes, and by the time Daisy had finished speaking Cecil Shelton had forgotten all about how busy he was. He had edged forward attentively in his chair once Daisy had begun speaking but now he leant back once more, his attitude relaxed again. It was some moments before he spoke, and then he said quietly, 'So I take it you can't type, lass?'

Daisy didn't know what she had been expecting but it wasn't that. 'No, I can't. My shorthand isn't too bad, but no, I can't type. Not yet.'

'Then you'd better learn smartish. One finger'll do for a week or two but I'm not a patient man as you'll discover. And you'll have to help out behind the counter oft times.'

She stared at him enquiringly. He couldn't be saying he was giving her the job?

'I paid Muriel seven and six a week, but of course she could type as well as being pretty good on the shorthand.'

Daisy nodded, she didn't know what to say.

''Course she'd had it on a plate, her da had paid for lessons for her, not like you getting a book and teaching yourself. I like that, lass. Shows gumption. Now, hours here are from eight in the morning until eight-thirty at night but you get every other Saturday off. My wife comes in on those days. And it's early closing Thursday, we finish at three then. As for your wage . . .' He stared at her and Daisy stared back. 'How much rent you paying for yourself and the bairn?'

'One and nine a week. I'm lodging with Miss Casey in Mainsforth Terrace West off—'

'Aye, aye, I know where Mainsforth Terrace is and I know Miss Casey an' all. You won't go far wrong with her, and one and nine is fair. I know a few round here who would try it on at two bob and more given half a chance, and their places wouldn't be as clean as Grace Casey's, not by a long chalk. Well, with your rent and fuel and food you'll have to be canny with your money. Are you canny, lass?'

'I think so.'

'Aye, I think so an' all, and that being the case I wouldn't want to lose you to someone else, eh?' For the first time Daisy noticed the kindness in the bright blue eyes. 'So we'd better keep the wage at seven and six assuming you're going to pick everything up in double quick time.'

'I will, Mr Shelton.' Seven and six a week! It would have been good pay for a girl living in the family home and paying board, but she was on her own, renting and with Tommy to take care of. Could she manage? She already knew the answer. This was the first rung up the ladder, and moreover she was independent. She had everything she needed for their two rooms and wouldn't need to buy any clothes for herself for a long time, thanks to Miss Wilhelmina. Tommy was a different matter but she'd cross that bridge when she came to it. For the moment the little boy was well kitted out with boots on his feet and a warm winter coat.

'You say you worked for the sister of Sir Augustus Fraser of Greyfriar Hall? Bad business with her brother, weren't it?'

'I'm sorry?'

'Her brother, the one that went under a train. Don't you know about it?' Daisy shook her head. 'In all the papers at the time. Just after Christmas it was, in Central Station.'

Daisy had to clear her throat before she could say, 'Which . . . which brother?'

'Oh, not him, the lord of the manor,' Cecil said dryly. 'No, this was another one.'

Francis. It had to be Francis Fraser. 'Is he . . . dead?'

'Oh, aye, he's dead all right. Chopped his legs clean off. All the money in the world don't make no difference in an argument with iron and steel.'

Daisy shivered. She had loathed Francis and couldn't say hand on heart she was sorry he was dead, but the manner of his death was too awful to contemplate. 'How horrible.'

Cecil nodded. He wasn't really interested in the likes of Sir Augustus Fraser and his brother. Didn't know they were born, that lot. And reading between the lines of what

367

this lass had told him only bore out his theory that the less you had to do with the gentry, the better. 'So, you'll start Monday then? On the dot of eight, mind. I can't abide unpunctuality.'

'I'll be here, Mr Shelton, and thank you. Thank you very much indeed.'

The postmaster seemed to echo her previous thoughts when he said quietly, 'Got to start somewhere, haven't you, lass? And rest assured, if you play fair by me I'll play fair by you. I come from mining stock meself but I couldn't hold with being under the ground. It was old Mr Howard who ran the post office on Nelson Square in Monkwearmouth who took me on as a lad. "I'll give you a chance, lad, and it's up to you what you make of it," that's what he said. And I reckon that still holds good today, don't you?'

Daisy nodded.

'And now we'd better go and rescue the bairn from Septimus. Twelve bairns, him and his wife have got, but he can't stand any of them, or his wife for that matter.' He grinned widely now and Daisy smiled back. She had done it! She'd got a job, and close to home too which was a bonus. And as for the typing – she'd noticed a book with exercises explaining the right way to learn when she'd got the shorthand one but it had been no use without a machine to practise on. She could get that and practise in her lunch hours, perhaps even take the typewriter home on a Sunday if Mr Shelton didn't mind. She would go into town now – Tommy loved the aviary and the pond with the goldfish at the Winter Garden, and the library was at the front of the building. A flood of relief that things were finally working out made her lightheaded for a second.

She hadn't visited Kitty and Alf or her brothers since she had moved to Hendon, although she had written to Kitty twice to let her friend know she and Tommy were fine.

There were several reasons for this. She had told herself she wanted to give Tommy some time to settle fully into his new environment and avoid confusing the little boy, also there had been lots to do with making the two rooms a home and not least looking for work each day. But it was only now, this very second, that she realised the main reason had been a matter of pride. She wanted to go back only when she had a job and it was clear she was able to support herself and Tommy.

She didn't know when she had first become aware of it but for some time now, especially in the last months, she had come to understand that there were those in the fishing community who were resentful of her. They thought she had done too well and had let her know it in various ways, especially over the time of Kitty and Alf's engagement and swift wedding. She had been labelled an upstart, and at the wedding there had been several instances – put to the back of her mind on the day but which had sunk deep into her subconscious – when conversation had died when she had joined this person or that, along with snide glances and whispers, some of which she knew were meant to register on her. She had ignored it all and would continue to do so, but knowing there was more than one person who would like her to fall flat on her face had given her a funny feeling in the pit of her stomach. These people used to be her friends, they would have done anything for her once and she for them, and the loss of them hurt. Perhaps she was silly to care but she couldn't help it.

However, given the choice she would do the same thing over again. And she wouldn't apologise for setting her own course either, or Tommy's. He would have an education, a good one which would enable him to hold his own with anyone. She wasn't denying her da or Tommy's for that matter, and she would make sure he fully appreciated the unique breed he'd come from, a people who were strong and sound with the ability to survive the most appalling adversities, but she wanted more for him. A fisherman's life was one long harsh battle for survival and the North Sea a cruel master. She hated it. The sea had taken her da and Tom and Peter, it wasn't going to have Tommy too.

The child was still sitting on the counter when she walked through with Mr Shelton and it appeared he had won over the dour Septimus. The postman was showing the little boy how the scales worked and smiling at Tommy's fascination. As though he had been caught at something shameful, Septimus wiped the smile off his face and straightened immediately he saw them. 'Time I was getting on,' he said gruffly. 'Haven't got time to waste.'

'Aye, you go then, and thanks, man.' Cecil Shelton's voice was brisk but Daisy had noticed the twinkle in his eye and guessed his thoughts had been similar to hers.

'Thank you again.' As the postman left, Daisy lifted Tommy down and took the child's hand. 'I'll be here at eight on Monday then.'

'Righto, lass.'

As Daisy left the post office, Tommy still clutching the bag of bullets which Mr Shelton had said he could keep, her mind was spinning with elation. She felt bright and eager, like she'd got the top job in Sunderland, and she didn't care if that was daft, she told herself happily. She suddenly whisked Tommy up into her arms and spun round a few times, making the child squeal with excitement and causing passers-by to tut-tut at such a spectacle or smile indulgently, depending on their disposition.

'I love you, Tommy Appleby. Do you know that?' Daisy said softly as she stopped her spinning and held the little boy close to her heart, his arms tight around her neck.

'Me love you, Dadi.' It was his pet name for her, first spoken when he couldn't pronounce her name properly.

'We're going to show them, you and me. We'll show them all, Tommy.'

He grinned at her, his rosy red cheeks plumping out still more as he strained back in her arms to touch her face, one of his most endearing habits and something which never failed to touch Daisy's heart.

Yes, she would show them. She was going to make something of her life and she would succeed. It was time to say goodbye to the old life and embrace the new.

Tommy was now wriggling in her arms, anxious to be off to the burn, and she set him down, saying, 'Instead of going to the burn, would you like to see the goldfish and the birds again in town?' and then laughing at his rapturous response.

Mowbray Park was about half a mile from the post office but the Museum and Library stood at the far end which put another quarter of a mile on the walk for Tommy's little legs. Daisy knew to the farthing how much she had in her purse, and the tram fare would pay for enough scrag ends to make a good broth for the two of them which would last for two dinners, eked out with stottie cake. She decided to walk, even though it would mean slipping and sliding on the frozen snow for most of the way, probably with Tommy in her arms. But it wouldn't always be like this.

She caught him by the hand, her head high, and together they set off for Mowbray Park.

Chapter Twenty-five

'So she's come out into the open and has got the child with her now, has she? Well, well.'

'It might not be hers, Mr Kirby.'

'Don't tell me you've been taken in by that cock and bull story about it being her brother's bairn? The servants who worked with her at Evenley House weren't, and they should know. I'd say with the grandmother gone who ran the house for her she's decided to set up somewhere else and taken her flyblow with her.'

'She's not running a – well, one of them places, Mr Kirby. I told you.'

Josiah shook his head at Ellen Mullen. 'Girl, you're too trusting by half. Her type don't soil their hands, they get others to do it for them. She had the grandmother as the madam in the other place. Likely she's got the same set-up with someone else in Hendon and the post office is just a cover.'

Ellen Mullen's teeth dragged at her lower lip for a moment. Why hadn't she kept her big mouth shut about seeing the fishergirl yesterday? she asked herself miserably. It was only because she had saved her last two half-days so she could visit her sister in Hendon who had just had her first baby that she'd seen the Appleby lass in the first place. She'd been right surprised to notice her walk out of the post office just as she and Delia had passed, and perhaps because she'd been pushing little Millicent in her perambulator, the fishergirl hadn't spotted her. Then once she'd let on to Delia that it was the lass she'd told her so much about in the past, nothing would content her sister but that they should go in the post office and find out what the girl had been doing so far from Whitburn. Delia was like that, nosy as they come. And it being her local post office and the postmaster knowing her, she had soon found out the lass was the postmaster's new office girl starting Monday, and that her and the little lad had lodgings in Hendon.

Ellen now glanced across the huge kitchen table where the servants were sitting at breakfast. As Donald caught her eye he shook his head ever so slightly. She knew what that meant – don't argue with Mr Kirby. Ellen's lips pressed together. Next step down from God Himself was Mr Kirby, or that's the impression he liked to create anyway.

'She's a wrong 'un, Mr Kirby, that much is for sure.' Cook was determined to put her two pennyworth in. She hadn't forgotten how the fishergirl had talked to her, and in her own kitchen! 'Looks like butter wouldn't melt in her mouth but she's got a tongue on her like Sheffield steel. Hard as nails, that one.'

Josiah nodded slowly. 'You're right, Mrs Preston.'

'Worst thing the master's sister ever did, taking that one on,' said Mrs Preston, warming to her theme.

'Well, Mr William wouldn't be here now if it wasn't for the fishergirl.'

As though connected by a single wire, all eyes turned to Ellen.

'Well, he wouldn't,' she said again, noticing that Donald had shut his eyes for an infinitesimal moment and wishing she was near enough to kick him.

'That is neither here nor there.' Josiah's voice was cold. 'Although personally I feel the incident in question was grossly exaggerated.'

'I disagree.' Stuart Middleton the butler didn't care about the fishergirl one way or the other but he couldn't miss this opportunity to bring Josiah down a peg or two. 'I was present when the doctor examined Mr William and he was in no doubt the girl had saved his life at, I might add, the risk of her own. It might stick in your craw, Josiah, but those are the facts. What do you say, Miss Finlay?'

The housekeeper seated opposite the butler at the prestigious end of the table inclined her head in agreement as everyone knew she would. Stuart Middleton had been visiting her room in the middle of the night for years although they were under the illusion they were the only ones who knew of the arrangement.

'You could have twenty doctors swearing on oath but I know what I know.' Josiah glared at his old enemy before rising abruptly to his feet. 'Have you got the master's breakfast tray ready, Cook?'

'Nancy?' Mrs Preston turned and spoke to the youngest kitchen maid who had been scurrying about like a mouse while the others ate, having been forced to bolt her own meal as she did every morning. 'Let's look at it.'

'I've done it right, Cook.' It was said anxiously and there was a tense moment as the cook surveyed the silver tray and its contents.

'It'll do.'

It was the highest praise Nancy was likely to hear but she beamed as though she had been awarded the most gracious accolade.

Once Josiah was in the hall his thoughts returned to the matter of the fishergirl. He had seen the way Mr William's eyes had followed her on the day of the funeral when the chit had left with her fisherman friend and the former maid, and the look on his face when he had returned to his father. Of course the master's son was in France and out of harm's way at the moment, but it stood to reason he would be visiting his father now and again. There must be no searching her out. Young men could be foolish where women were concerned, he'd had proof of that himself. He hadn't wanted to believe the signs that his own sweetheart was carrying on, but when May had run off with someone else on the eve of their wedding he'd been forced to. Josiah made a sound of irritation deep in his throat. Why on earth was he thinking of May now? Possibly because the fishergirl reminded him of her, a separate part of his brain answered. They had the same indefinable power to attract, something more than mere beauty. Something dangerous. He had sensed there was something between the young master and the fishergirl from the first moment he had set eyes on her. And that being the case . . .

The valet had reached the master suite now, but paused for a moment outside Sir Augustus's rooms. There was bound to be an opportunity to let the young master know the fishergirl had a child the next time he saw him but if not he would make one, Josiah decided. Of course it wouldn't do to intimate the girl's precise circumstances, not with Mr William. Young men sometimes made the mistake of thinking they could reform a fallen woman, and in view of the fact that Mr William insisted the girl had saved his life . . . He would suggest she was happily married, hint at it, that would do the trick. If Mr William thought she was settled and playing happy families, he wouldn't interfere. He knew the young master well enough to know that, as he'd known how that fool of a parson would react to that letter too. The parson! By, she'd have eaten him alive and not bothered to spit out the pips.

Josiah nodded grimly to himself, opened the door and walked briskly into the room beyond.

Part 5
And Then There Was War
1916

Chapter Twenty-six

The last thirteen years had seen Daisy's life and that of the people of Britain in general change irrevocably. The country was at war, and with thousands of men volunteering to fight each month, women were taking over their jobs.

They were working in the dangerous munitions factories, becoming tram drivers, porters, window cleaners. Still others worked on the land, in shipyards, drove ambulances, lorries and motor bikes.

There were some in government circles who worried less about the war than about what sort of country their brave soldiers would be coming back to. Before you knew it women would be granted the right to vote, and then they would go on to demand political equality with men. Unthinkable? Don't you believe it! Give the suffragettes an inch and they would take a mile. And as Lord Curzon had said, what sane man, in the face of great issues like war and peace, would like his destiny at such a moment to be decided by a *woman*?

Daisy had busily carved out a career for herself some time before the war began, but the widespread change in women's work brought fresh unexpected benefits. Women all over the country ceased seeing themselves as tied irrevocably to hearth and home, worthy only of being paid a mere pittance compared to their male counterparts, or yet again – for the upper classes – as fragile social ornaments.

They no longer felt they needed male company if they wished to eat or drink out. Suddenly it was acceptable for even 'nice' girls to dine alone or with each other, to smoke cigarettes in public, and to wear make-up.

Clothes became more practical, hemlines rising dramatically until the glimpse of a lady's ankle ceased to thrill. Women had reached out and seized a measure of liberation, but not even the fiercest suffragette would have wished this freedom to have come into being at the cost of thousands of England's finest young men.

Word of the terrible reality of this war, which had begun with working-class men enlisting in a flood of swashbuckling patriotism, was seeping back from the front. Men were dying in unbelievable numbers in France, and the awful results of the German Army's use of mustard gas at Yypres had quenched the public ardour for such songs as 'Keep the Homes Fires Burning' and 'Belgium Put the Kibosh on the Kaiser' for some loved ones at home, of which Daisy was one.

Already George's two eldest boys had been reported missing and Art's youngest killed in the first few weeks of the war. George had two more sons in France and Ron's twin boys hadn't long since left for the front.

Daisy raised her head from where she was busy slicing a freshly baked loaf into thick slices and glanced round the kitchen table. Tommy and three of his pals were busy devouring great wedges of ham and egg pie, meat roll, shives of cheese and pickles, and hot potatoes in their jackets. They had already drained three pots of tea. He caught her eye and grinned. 'Been thinking of this all day.'

'Go on with you.' She flapped her hand at him, laughing, but the thought that her lad and his three pals could have been at the front if they had been just three or so years older was frightening. The four of them had been beside themselves when German cruisers had shelled the towns of Hartlepool, Scarborough and Whitby just down the coast, killing a hundred and thirty-seven people and wounding hundreds more in an attack just before Christmas last year, and the incident had sent a stream of northern lads to the recruitment offices. Thought he'd frighten us, the Kaiser, did he? had been the general opinion among Tommy's age group and the older lads. Barking up the wrong tree then, wasn't he? Didn't know the British bulldog very well, did he, but he'd soon learn.

When Daisy had first heard Tommy and his friends talking this way she had taken him aside when the others had gone home. War was a terrible thing, she'd told him soberly, and it *was* frightening. Only a fool wouldn't be scared. Men and lads were being killed and maimed and leaving their womenfolk half-demented with grief.

'Aye, I know, Mam.' He had taken to calling her this just after they had moved to Hendon from the fishing village. 'But someone's got to stop the Kaiser.'

She had just nodded while offering a silent prayer of thanks it wasn't *her* boy engaged against the forces of that madman. And then she had prayed for the ones who were.

'And where are the four of you off to tonight?' she said now, as the last of the loaf was finished and she put a baked jam roll and a plate of gingerbread on the now virtually empty table.

'The Palace. Jimmy's got free tickets again,' Tommy said, his mouth full of gingerbread. On leaving school he had secured an apprenticeship in the machine shop of the North Eastern Marine Engineering Company on the South Docks in Sunderland, along with his pal Joe. Phil had been taken on at the Castle Street brewery, while Jimmy had pulled off the by no means easy feat of inveigling himself into the Palace Theatre as general dogsbody and jack-of-all-trades. Consequently the four of them enjoyed many evenings of free entertainment, usually after a meal at Daisy's. The other boys all came from large poor families, and having started feeding them after school when the four of them had chummed up while still knee-high to a grasshopper, Daisy had never really stopped. But she loved doing it, she loved them, and there was rarely an evening went by when the house didn't resound with their laughter and chatter.

And Tommy appreciated it, like now. As the others all said their thank yous and left the house by the back door, he hung back until he and Daisy were alone. 'Thanks, Mam.' At fifteen years old he was an inch taller than her and still growing strong, but he never left without kissing her. 'That meal was grand, an' the lads love it round here, especially poor old Joe.'

Daisy nodded. Joe's father was the type who thought nothing of using his fists on his family, and as a little lad Joe had often been black and blue. Many were the nights he had slept on a shakedown by the side of Tommy's bed; in fact, Daisy thought Joe had lived more with them than he ever had with his own family. She just thanked her lucky stars she had been able to offer all Tommy's pals a free meal and hospitality when it was needed.

Twenty months after starting work for Mr Shelton at the post office, equipped with new certificates for excellent speeds in shorthand and typing, she had left the kindly postmaster – with his blessing and good wishes – and taken a job with Woods & Company, bankers, for twice the salary. Swift promotion had followed, and by the time Miss Casey had decided to move to Newcastle to live with her recently bereaved sister, Daisy was in a position to take out a mortgage and buy a property of her own. The house had been modest, a two-up, two-down terrace in Maritime Terrace opposite the Almshouses, but when Tommy had just turned eleven another change of job and increase in salary had meant the two of them being able to move to a bay-fronted end of terrace with a tiny railed front garden and a patch of lawn at the back in Grangetown, in view of the old windmill which had ceased operating some time before.

Tommy first and then work was Daisy's life. Although in latter years she had had several men friends they had always remained just that – friends. There had been two she had thought she might grow fonder of, but in the event the more serious they had become the more she had withdrawn. Tommy often teased her, saying she was too particular, and he might be right at that, but she couldn't force feelings that weren't there and that was that as far as Daisy was concerned. And it wasn't as though her life wasn't busy, what with him and his pals, work, friends including Alf and Kitty and their four children and the rest of her family at the fishing village, and now the fund-raising and such she was involved in for the war effort. Tank Week, Gun Week, Cruiser Week – they all demanded time and attention, and as a member of the Grangetown Women's Support Group Daisy was heavily involved in delivering food and clothing to needy families whose menfolk were missing or killed, helping to man the twice-weekly soup kitchen, opening up her home for committee meetings and organising ongoing aid for the old folk.

It was the thought of the last venture that now made her say, 'The others'll be waiting, Tommy,' as she gave her lad a hug and sent him out the door. She had three visits to make and the old folk didn't like being disturbed too late at night, even if she did come bearing gifts!

The February night was raw, and Daisy was glad to get home again once she had done the rounds. By the time Tommy came in at half-past ten she had the kettle on and some scones singing on the girdle, which she and Tommy ate hot and dripping with butter while he told her about his evening.

'Bought you a few sweets, Mam.' His voice was casual but his eyes were bright as he sent a box of chocolates skidding across the table into her hands as he left the kitchen.

'Thanks, hinny.' Daisy's voice was soft. It was rare a week went by that he didn't buy her something: a bunch of flowers, a women's magazine, sweets or chocolate, in spite of an apprentice's wage being next to nothing.

He thought of her as his mam, she knew that, and it was precious, although she had been careful to talk often about Margery and Tom to the boy, trying to draw a mental picture for him of how they had looked, what sort of people they had been and so on. She had waited until she'd felt he was old enough before she had told him the full story about his parents not being married – she hadn't wanted him to find his birth certificate some day and see the bald details in black and white, or for some kind soul to acquaint him with the facts before she had had a chance to do it properly. She had stressed that Margery and Tom were planning to marry, that they had loved each other with a love known to few people, and that Margery had been comforted after he had died to learn that she was bearing his child and in that way Tom would live on.

Tommy had taken it well but had been quiet for a few days. After that he had come to her one day when she was in the kitchen preparing a meal and said very softly that he wished he had a picture of his da. 'We never had the money for things like photographs or pictures,' Daisy had said gently, 'but if you look in the mirror, hinny, you'll be seeing your da. You are the spitting image of him, anyone would tell you that. Your hair might be a bit curlier but that's all.' And after that Tommy had been his old self again, although she had noticed from that point he spent some time each morning trying to straighten his hair with brilliantine.

Daisy sat on for some time in the quiet kitchen when Tommy had gone to bed. There was talk of conscription for married men now, where was it all going to end? Two of the three old couples she had visited that evening had lost sons and grandsons in this war; as one of the old gentlemen had said, 'It's not just them as die out there that stop livin', lass. Me wife used to be a big girl, but since we lost our two lads she's nowt but skin an' bone. Don't want to go on, see?'

She had seen, and her heart had bled for the old woman who had looked at her with vacant lost eyes.

After a while she cleaned the girdle and put the kitchen to rights, preparing Tommy's bait-can for morning before she went quietly upstairs. She paused at his open bedroom door, looking across at the boy who was fast asleep under his eiderdown, one arm flung out across his pillow as always. The temperature could be minus ten and thick ice coating the inside of the window, but still that arm would be out.

She walked across, as she did most nights in the winter, to tuck it under the covers again, but this time she stared down at the sleeping form. His hands had been so plump and dimpled as a baby, so soft and small, but now it was a man's hand she was looking at. She reached out and took his fingers in hers, looking down at the rough oil-stained skin that spoke of his work in the machine shop. She stroked the callused flesh gently. Pray God this war would be finished before he was eighteen and called up. Pray God . . .

When Daisy got home from work the next evening she knew immediately something was wrong. Tommy was always back before her, usually with one or all of his pals in tow, and invariably the house was filled with chatter and activity. Tonight it was cold and empty.

She called his name as she walked through to the kitchen, and then she saw it. A note propped against a vase of flowers. And the breakfast things had all been cleared away, the crockery washed and the table scrubbed. Something was terribly wrong.

She picked up the note and sat down hard on a kitchen chair, her heart pounding in her throat as she slit the envelope open. She read the single sheet of paper it contained right through to the end, but in fact she had known the minute she'd seen it what he had done. Oh, Tommy. *Tommy*. She screamed his name in her head.

A frantic knocking at the front door brought her to her feet, and when Phil's mother all but fell into her arms on the doorstep Daisy had to help her through to the living room.

They had lied to the recruiting sergeant, all four of them, and even now were on their way to France. They had all been well over the minimum height of five foot three inches admittedly, but the sergeant must have known they were still just bairns, Phil's mother moaned. But the army didn't care whether they were old enough or not, that was the thing. By, if she could get her hands on that man for just one minute . . .

Daisy listened to the woman going on and on, feeling frozen with fear. Tommy hadn't gone to work that morning. He had joined up the day before and now he was gone, they all were. And not one of them a day over fifteen.

She had gone into the kitchen to make them both a cup of tea at some point, and there she had read his letter through again.

Don't be mad, Mam, but I have to go. I've wanted to for months and months and I can't wait any more.

I'll be all right, I promise, but you never know when it's going to end and I don't want to miss it.

He didn't want to miss it. Oh, God, God, help her.

I'll write as soon as I can and please don't worry. I'm doing what I want to do. I'll see you again soon.
Love, Tommy

Daisy spooned tea into the pot, adding the hot water and then placing the kettle back on the hob. She put the teapot, along with the milk and sugar and two teacups, on to a tray, and then she saw the bait-can on the side of the cupboard. It was standing all alone, the top half open and hanging forlornly to one side . . .

Chapter Twenty-seven

It was May, and a brilliantly sunny Sunday the day before had marked the start of a new scheme to put the clocks throughout Britain forward an hour at two o'clock to launch 'daylight saving time' as it was officially known.

This scheme would produce hundreds of thousands of tons of extra coal for the war effort by lengthening working hours, and, apart from vehement objections by farmers, the prospect of lighter evenings had been welcomed generally. Daisy had left for work that morning knowing that in spite of the late meeting which took place every Monday, she would be returning home in daylight.

In the three months since Tommy had been gone, she had often thought she would have gone mad with worry but for the exacting nature of her job. Tommy's letters home said little to worry her, but she would have expected that. However, she knew full well the true character of the war. The newspapers had long since finished their first love affair with it and were now full of reports of men being slaughtered in fruitless offensives. Women were receiving letters from loved ones who spoke of being driven out of their wits by living with the unrelenting bombardment and daily likelihood of a violent death.

All over the country people lived in dread of receiving a black-edged telegram, and it had shocked everyone in the north east when just three days ago Ann Gilmore from Blackburn had committed suicide by cutting her throat. She had had four sons at the front, the newspapers had reported, and when her fifth and only remaining boy had been called up, the poor woman's mind had snapped.

There were few mothers who would have been unable to identify with Mrs Gilmore's desperation, and when Daisy had read the item she had again thanked God, as she had done so many times over the last weeks, that the hours she spent at work were so full and hectic they left her little time for brooding and worrying. Her job carried a great deal of responsibility which could be daunting at times, but now was just what she needed.

Daisy was one of the thousands of women who had just entered government service for the first time. The traditional male clerk with his quill pen and copperplate handwriting was now holding a gun in his hands, and the female shorthand-typist had taken his place.

In the first year of the war it had become clear that the hand-to-mouth growth of welfare associations in the country had resulted in chaos in local authorities up and down the land. Daisy's last job before her present one had been as private secretary to the manager of a bank, and when she had started work for the local government board three months into the war, she had needed all the efficiency and diplomacy she had acquired. But she had soon settled in and found she loved the work.

Once in the pleasant office she shared with her boss, Mr Newton, chief coordinator between Sunderland's branch of local government and the military as well as the local community, Daisy set about the pile of correspondence she knew would be waiting for her.

Mr Newton was an unmarried man of fifty years of age to whom work was an obsession. But for the fact that first thing every Monday morning he met the mayor he would already have been at his desk when Daisy arrived, and would work long after she left, even though she often stayed late now Tommy was gone. But he was a nice man, his sense of humour reminding her of Mr Shelton's, and the two of them got on very well. He had been wonderfully understanding when Tommy had up and enlisted and thrown her all at sea.

Mr Newton arrived at the office mid-morning and as usual dictated steadily until just before lunchtime, Daisy's pencil flying over the pages of her notebook. At twelve she left the office in the town hall and walked along to Binns the cake shop and restaurant which was situated next to Binns the store, with two of the other girls. Since Tommy had been away she had taken to eating her main meal of the day at lunchtime in the restaurant, rather than cook for herself at night.

She listened to the two other girls who were considerably younger than herself discussing their respective sweethearts and what they had got up to at the weekend, but did not join in the conversation. Not that they expected her to. When she had first worked for Mr Newton one of the girls had said to her, 'We've all been trying to work out why you aren't married or courting, looking like you do and with a head on your shoulders an' all. You could have anyone you liked.'

She had smiled and replied she was happy as she was, thank you very much, and it hadn't been too far from the truth then with Tommy still at home.

Now, as she continued to sit there, she wondered – as she had done more than once in the last weeks – what she would do with herself in the future. When Tommy came home – and she always thought when, never if – she would be lucky if he lived with her for more than a few years before he found himself a wife and got his own place. And that was good and natural and as it should be.

But she was only thirty-one years old. Daisy shifted restlessly in her seat, moving a piece of potato round and round on her plate. She wanted to meet someone one day, get married, have a family with her husband. She wanted – oh, she didn't know what she wanted. The moon she supposed. But the last weeks had shown her that the house was just a building without Tommy and the others to turn it into a home, and she didn't want to live in a building for ever. Neither did she want to turn into a grumpy old woman, or the sort of mother-in-law who had no life of her own and was always calling in on their children whether they were welcome or not. She could work her way up even higher within local government, of course, now jobs were opening up for women who were dedicated and determined in a way which wouldn't have been dreamt of before the war. But would that be enough? She thought of the cold, empty house she went home to every night, and shivered.

Once back in the office Daisy worked quietly and competently. It was just before ten to six when she finished the last letter, placing the thick pile of correspondence in front of Mr Newton as she said, 'I'll set the chairs out, shall I? They'll be here soon.'

'Aye.' He nodded without looking up. 'Didn't realise that was the time. Thanks, lass.'

Within five minutes several of the leading lights of the town had filed into the room. The original intention of the Monday meeting had been to iron out problems due to the war which might be occurring in the factories and shipyards day by day, to 'keep on top of the damn' nit pickers' as Mr Newton himself put it.

Daisy had just seated herself at her desk, notebook at the ready to take the minutes once the meeting began, when she heard Lionel Bainsby, an advocate of industrial welfare who frequently irritated Mr Newton, say, 'I've brought a friend along who's home on leave, Edwin. All right if he sits in a corner?'

Daisy lifted her head, and there, standing in front of her, was the moon.

'Hallo, Daisy.'

Hallo, Daisy. A stillness took possession of her body, a stillness which mercifully enabled her to swallow and say quite normally, 'Hallo.' One word, and not as she had imagined it sounding when she had pictured this meeting in her mind over and over and over again. It was flatly said. Not cool and collected. Just flat.

She stared at William and he stared back. He was more handsome than ever but different, very different. He had been little more than a youth when she had seen him last, but the person in front of her, looking at her with eyes that were still as beautiful as ever but now with a crystal hardness, was a full-grown man. He looked bigger, broader and taller, with a mature air that spoke of a wealth of experience. There wasn't an inch of spare flesh on him and she noticed, with a curious little jerk in her heart, that the fair hair was liberally sprinkled with grey. His face had taken on some lines, a couple of crevices radiating from his mouth as deep as sabre cuts. He must be, what, approaching forty? And still more attractive than any man had the right to be.

Daisy knew she ought to say something more and was aware of Lionel Bainsby staring at them with interest, but she couldn't speak. It was William who broke the silence and still he did not smile when he said, 'You have not changed at all.'

'Thank you but you flatter me. It has been thirteen years.'

'Not quite. Not until December.'

Her eyes widened ever so slightly and she prayed the pounding of her heart was not apparent as it began to drum against her breastbone. William was in uniform. Why that suddenly registered she didn't know, but it enabled her to say more formally than she had thought herself capable of, 'You are in the army?'

He nodded. 'For the last twelve years. I am home briefly to see my father. He is not well.'

'I'm sorry.'

'And your . . . husband? Is he in the forces?'

'My . . .' It was a full ten seconds before she could say, 'I am not married.'

'Not married?' His brow wrinkled but then Lionel Bainsby took his arm, drawing him across the room as he said, 'Edwin, meet Captain Fraser, Captain William Fraser. William, Edwin Newton.'

When William walked back a moment or two later and quietly took a seat by the door, Daisy felt the colour sweeping over her face. He was now on the perimeter of her vision and by moving very slightly she managed to cut him out completely. Nevertheless, every nerve in her body was vitally aware of the big figure across the room and her hands were trembling so much she could barely hold her pencil, let alone transport the squiggles and dots in her head on to the lined pages of her notebook.

An hour later she had pages full of double Dutch she had no hope of translating and tension had produced an ache in her neck which was radiating pain in all directions. Mr Newton wound the meeting up, and at this informal stage of the proceedings Daisy normally put her notebook away in her desk and made her goodbyes, the men invariably leaving as a group and spending an hour or two in a public house before they went their separate ways.

She tidied her desk quickly, put the cover on her typewriter and walked across to the coatstand in a corner of the room for her coat and hat. As she did so she was aware of William speaking softly to Lionel Bainsby, and of the other man – his voice louder – replying, 'Of course not, old man. Quite understand. I'll talk to you tomorrow.'

Her head was buzzing, and as she was about to slip into her coat she felt it being taken out of her hands.

'May I?' William's voice was still soft and low.

It was either let him help her on with the coat or cause a scene. 'Thank you.' Her voice was clipped, and Daisy did not look at him as she began to do up the buttons, neither did she glance at him when he said, 'Might I be permitted to escort you home?'

'I don't think so.'

'Please, Daisy.'

And he needn't talk like that, in such a soft, smoky tone, either. What did he expect her to do, for goodness' sake? Smile and thank him for deigning to remember her after all these years? Fall at his feet in humble adoration? She knew she was being irrational but she had never wanted to hit someone so much in all her life. He had broken her heart, didn't he realise that? And just to assume he could walk her home as though they were old friends who hadn't seen each other for a while. It was . . . it was a typically *Fraser* action. Arrogant and high-handed.

'I'm sorry, I have things to do.' She raised her eyes at this point, steeling herself to meet the piercing blue.

'Tomorrow then?'

'I have things to do tomorrow too.' She bent forward and picked up her handbag, turning away, but then he brought her round to face him with a restraining hand on her arm and again they were staring at each other. 'Daisy . . .' He hesitated. 'What's wrong? Can't we talk?'

What was wrong? She was burning with anger and hurt and a hundred and one feelings she could never have put into words, but she managed to keep her voice cool and clipped as she said, 'No, William, we cannot talk.'

'Well, at least that's an improvement on *Mr* William,' he said, unforgivably.

He was mocking her? How dare he! How *dare* he treat this as though it was a game, something amusing.

Over the last years Daisy had learnt a lot about freezing out annoying and persistent callers who were pestering her boss; now she brought all that experience to the fore. Her voice icy, she said, 'I mustn't keep you from your friend any longer. Goodnight.'

This time he did not stop her, and she managed to call out a fairly normal 'Goodnight' to the rest of the company as she left. She was aware that Mr Newton was staring at her, and that although the other men were being more tactful they must all be wondering what the little tête-à-tête between Newton's secretary and Lionel Bainsby's military friend was all about, but she didn't hurry as she walked across the room and out of the door. She was not going to scurry away from his presence like a confused little mouse, she told herself grimly, aware her cheeks were hot and her hands were shaking now she was outside the room. She was a grown woman of thirty-one, not a young lass bedazzled by the lord of the manor.

All the way out of the building she kept her back straight and her chin high, but once outside in the busy street where she soon blended into the anonymous crowd, reaction set in. She wanted to cry and that horrified her. She couldn't do that, not in the street, she told herself. It was just the shock of it all that had upset her, that was all.

She continued to tell herself that for the rest of the evening, forcing herself to make a sandwich she didn't want and read a book in which she had no interest. But later, in bed, she found she couldn't escape the truth so easily. She still loved him. Hot tears slipped down her cheeks and dampened her pillow. Which made her the most stupid person in the world after all that had happened. But seeing him like that today, so unexpectedly, had made her face the fact that the reason all her other men friends had never measured up was because they weren't William.

By morning she was telling herself that it was good she had seen him again. It had laid a lot of ghosts, she told herself firmly over breakfast. And Tommy, bless him, was right. She had been too particular in the past, too quick to end a relationship which might have blossomed if she had stuck with it. Part of it had been because with Tommy filling so much of her life she hadn't needed anyone else, but things were changing now with her lad becoming a man. She had to look to the future and put common sense before ridiculous feelings which should have died years ago. But she knew what was what now so that was good.

She was overwhelmingly grateful when Mr Newton didn't refer to the previous evening later at the office, and after a few minutes of feeling a little embarrassed she settled into work and got on with what she had to do. As always the day flew by, and before she knew it she was putting on her coat and saying goodnight.

She exited the building into bright sunlight, the warmth pleasant on her skin, and then she turned and William was in front of her. 'Don't walk away.' His voice was urgent. 'Listen to me for just a minute. I realise I did it all wrong yesterday and I'm sorry. I must have embarrassed you in front of Mr Newton and that was the last thing I wanted. I did, didn't I?'

If embarrassment had been her only concern she would

have considered herself well blessed. Daisy forced herself to look into the blue eyes without shivering. Although her whole body was tingling in the most peculiar way, her face did not give her away when she answered quietly, 'No, not really.'

'I didn't think how it might look—' He stopped abruptly. 'No, that isn't quite true. Seeing you again was the most wonderful thing that has happened to me in a long time and . . .' He paused again, thinking as he did so, You've had women in every port in your time and here you are stuttering and stammering like a lad still wet behind the ears. But Daisy had always had this effect on him.

'Perhaps it would be better to have this conversation elsewhere?'

Her voice, the northern inflection warm and soft on his ears, was pointing out that people were having to step round them as they stood in the middle of the pavement.

He flushed, aware he felt younger than he had in years but in all the wrong ways. The last time he had felt as gauche and awkward as this had been standing outside his aunt's cottage watching her with Lyndon. 'Why didn't you marry the parson?' He hadn't meant to say it but with the words came the realisation he had wanted an answer to this question for years.

'What?'

Her surprise made him feel even more stupid.

'Parson Lyndon. My aunt made it very clear marriage was on the cards when I told her how I felt about you.'

They had begun walking, a full two feet between them, and as her head turned towards him he rubbed his hand across his mouth. *He was nervous.* As the knowledge registered with Daisy she stumbled. His hand came shooting out to steady her, stopping before he touched her.

She took a deep breath, willing some sort of composure back. 'I did not marry Parson Lyndon because he did not ask me,' she said truthfully, 'but if I had done so it would have been for all the wrong reasons. I did not care for him, not in that way.'

'No?'

'No, and I cannot imagine how your aunt could have thought so.' She hesitated. She wanted to ask him what he had meant when he'd said he had told Miss Wilhelmina how he felt about her but it would have been too forward.

'Last night you said you were not married. You are a widow?'

'A widow?' Now it was Daisy who stopped, oblivious of the late-night shoppers. 'Why would I be a widow? I am not married, I have never been married.'

'But they told me—'

'What did they tell you?'

'That you were married, that you had a little boy, a son. It was some time after my aunt's funeral, when I knew I had missed my chance again . . .'

'Again?'

'I was going to ask you to marry me on your sixteenth birthday but my aunt persuaded me your affections lay elsewhere. I was stupid.' His voice was clearer now. 'If I had known then what I know now I wouldn't have listened to anyone else.'

At some point in the conversation he had reached out and gripped her hands. Now he pulled her closer towards him, becoming aware for the first time that her whole body was trembling. 'I was told you had a son.'

'I do have a son.' He didn't blink or withdraw in any way, his blue eyes steady on her face, and in that moment Daisy knew just how much she loved him and why she always would. 'But I did not give birth to him. Tommy is my brother's child. His father died before he was born and his mother gave her life for his when she brought him into the world. He is a wonderful boy . . .'

William's arms went around her and he lifted her right off the pavement and against his chest as he kissed her, the hunger of years in his embrace. Fawcett Street had never seen such a blatant display of carnal desire and it caused several passers-by to gasp in horror as they hastily scurried by whilst averting their eyes.

'Oh, Daisy, Daisy.' When they surfaced his face was still close to hers and they breathed each other's breath as he said, 'I can't tell you how much I love you, how I've always loved you. I've been such a fool.' He gradually let her feet slip down to the ground, only to whisk her up again as though he couldn't bear to let her go. Their eyes on a level, he laughed, the sound so triumphant the war could have been over. 'I should have listened to my heart. Damn it! I should have listened to my heart.' And then he said quickly, 'Forgive my language, sweetheart.'

Sweetheart. Her head spinning and all the strength drained from her, she leant heavily against him, the smell and feel of the man she loved intoxicating. She couldn't believe it was happening, not so suddenly, so quickly, and yet in the same instant she was looking back down the years to the source of this consuming love and wondering why it had taken so long.

'Would you ever! 'Tisn't right. I blame this war. Never had such goings-on when we were young, Fanny.'

'No . . .'

This last utterance came so wistfully from one of the two old women clothed in black with shawls covering their heads who were passing by that again William was laughing, Daisy joining in as she leant against him for a moment or two more before drawing away.

'Can we go somewhere?' His voice was soft and urgent, and as Daisy nodded, he said, 'I want to be able to hold you in my arms while we talk and unravel the tangle of it all. And it has been a tangle, sweetheart, has it not?' Bringing her hands to his breast he pressed them tightly there, his eyes holding hers. 'I want to hear you say you love me. You do love me, Daisy?'

'So much.'

'Oh, my love, my love. We'll never be separated again, I swear it. We've so much time to make up for, so many wasted years.'

Daisy's gaze dropped momentarily to his uniform and as she looked at him again something in her eyes made him say brokenly, 'Oh, darling. It will be all right. I promise it will be all right.'

'I know.' It had to be, it just had to be. Fate couldn't be so cruel as to take him now. But the things you heard in the newspapers . . . 'Come back to my house.'

William stayed the night. They sat wrapped in each other's arms on Daisy's sofa, clearing the dross of sixteen years in between long drugged kisses. But, contrary to the desire which emanated from him, William asked no more of her than that. This was Daisy, his Daisy. When they became one it would be as man and wife and she would have the protection of his name. If nothing else in his life he would get this right.

In the cold silver light of a May dawn they stood in Daisy's hall, lips clinging and their bodies moulded as one before William left for Greyfriar Hall. Daisy's heart was full as she waved him goodbye. He had promised to return for lunch and for the first time in her working life Daisy played the malingerer.

William did return just after noon, but as she opened the door to him, her face alight, she knew immediately something had happened in the few hours they had been apart.

He had some news, he said softly, drawing her into him and holding her very tight. His father had passed away at ten o'clock that morning. He was now Sir William Fraser and had inherited the vast bulk of his father's estate. And there was something else. All leave had been cancelled. He was leaving for France that evening.

Chapter Twenty-eight

William stayed for as long as he could that afternoon before returning to Greyfriar Hall. He had asked Daisy to come back with him so that his sisters and the rest of the household could be told the news that she had consented to become his wife, but Daisy wouldn't hear of it. 'Think, darling,' she said softly. 'Your father has just died and the house is in mourning. It wouldn't be proper.'

Proper. He had stared at her before inclining his head, knowing he couldn't speak what was in his mind. The war had shown him horrors he had never imagined in his worst nightmares, unspeakable abominations amid chaos and mayhem with men dying in their hundreds and the generals moving divisions around with little thought for strategy as though it was all some grotesque game. 'Proper' would never feature in his vocabulary again. He had found his love despite all the odds, and wanted to shout it to the rooftops and damn the rest of the world. He could hardly believe that after all the hurt and bitterness and pain a few hours could turn everything round, but it had. In truth it hadn't even taken that long. From the moment she had told him she had never married he had felt reborn. The wonder of it, the absolute wonder of it, was that Daisy felt the same.

'Then you'll come to the station to see me off?' he had asked once he'd realised she was adamant about not returning with him to the Hall.

'Oh, of course. Of course I will.'

'Come early, at five-thirty, so we can have a few minutes before the train leaves.'

Daisy was standing on the platform from five o'clock. The evening was a mellow one, devoid of the sharp north-east wind for once, and as she had walked to the station through terraced streets her thoughts had been similar to William's. Sixteen years. Sixteen years of longing and heartache that need never have been, but they had been wiped away with that one sentence: 'I was going to ask you to marry me on your sixteenth birthday'. Her hand went to the small diamond and pearl pin William had given her earlier that afternoon and she recalled the look on his face when he had said, 'I couldn't bear to get rid of it even though I knew you would never wear it.'

But she was wearing it now. Her heart thudded, and for the hundredth time that day she prayed, 'Keep him safe, God. William and my precious boy, keep them both safe. Let them both come home to me.'

She saw him immediately he came on to the platform, a tall, lean, handsome figure who stood head and shoulders above anyone else, and because she had eyes only for him she did not notice the small man behind him. His hands stretched out and gripped hers as he reached her, drawing her to him and holding her close for a moment as he kissed her hard and swiftly.

'Are you sure they won't let you stay a little longer if you tell them about your father?' she asked as his mouth left hers. 'Compassionate leave or something?'

'I've tried.' His lips moved over her brow again as though reluctant to stop kissing her. 'There's an offensive and they need experienced officers. There are so many officers and men who have only been in five minutes and don't know one end of a gun from the other.' Which added to the carnage a thousandfold. Mind, even the oldest hands made mistakes when lack of sleep due to the ear-deafening continuous bombardment from the enemy took its toll.

'An offensive?'

'Oh, darling, don't look like that. I'll be all right. Look, for the first time I have my own batman. What about that? You remember Kirby, don't you?'

As William put his arm round her waist and pulled her to his side, Daisy found herself staring into the face of the man who had worked against her in one way or another from the first moment they had met. William had told her it had been Kirby who had related she was married with a son, and when she had said the valet had done it on purpose because he didn't like her, William hadn't taken her seriously. 'Nonsense, my sweet, how could he not like you?' And because there had been so much else to talk about Daisy had not pursued the matter of Sir Augustus's valet. But now William was Sir William and it appeared Kirby was equally determined to serve him as he had been to serve Augustus. She should have told William, she thought frantically. Told him about the incident with Francis Fraser in the kitchen which the valet had played a part in, about all the insults the man had heaped upon her head over the years, all the trouble he had caused. She should have made him *see* and then he would have dismissed Kirby.

Above her head she heard William say, 'I told him he should stay at home and look after Greyfriar but he insisted on coming with me.'

'Your father would have expected me to serve you as I did him, Sir William.' Kirby was speaking in his normal obsequious tone but his eyes were fixed on Daisy. She stared at the valet and he stared back, and it came to her then in a flash of intuition that the man was expecting her to give him away. Something in his eyes told her

405

so. Their expression reminded her of a dog one of the travelling tinkers who used to call at the fishing village selling trinkets had had. Skin and bone that dog had been, and when she had taken pity on it and tried to give it a ham shank she had got bitten for her trouble.

The tinker had appeared as the dog had gone for her, saying, 'You leave 'im alone, you. Bin taught to refuse food from strangers, 'e 'as, so's 'e don't get 'imself poisoned like me last dog. Taught 'im, I 'ave.' Daisy hadn't asked how, but it couldn't have been pleasant because the animal was clearly starving but unable to trust any show of kindness. She had cried herself to sleep over the look in the dog's eyes, and when Tom had risked getting bitten later that night and untied the scrawny creature from the tinker's caravan, taking it to old Ma Stratton who lived in the woods Boldon way and had the reputation of being a witch but wonderful with animals, she'd been nice to her brother for a whole week.

Before she could reconsider, Daisy said, 'I was sorry to hear about Sir Augustus, Mr Kirby. I know you had been with him for a very long time and you must be upset.'

The man continued staring at her without speaking for a second or two, and there was both amazement and embarrassment in his eyes now. Then it was almost as if he deflated before her eyes. He swallowed twice before saying, 'Thank you, Miss Appleby. Yes, I served the master for a long time.' He turned to William, saying, 'I will see to the bags and tickets, sir.'

'Thank you, Kirby.'

Once the valet was walking away, his back stiff and straight once more, William turned his head to the side, saying in an undertone, 'The damnedest thing, Kirby insisting on coming with me like this. Frankly the last thing I want is a batman, but the fellow got quite distressed when I tried to put him off.'

'He needs you.'

'What?' And then before she could reply, William said, 'Oh, what are we wasting time on him for? Come and sit with me, my darling. You will write, won't you? Every day? Ten times a day?'

'A hundred.' She smiled back at him as he drew her over to one of the station benches.

'We haven't discussed anything of importance. Do you want children? But of course you do, you're that sort of woman.'

'What sort?'

'Soft, warm, beautiful, good . . .'

'Do *you* want children?' she interrupted him, laughing softly.

'Lots. I want to fill Greyfriar with them so they get into all the cobwebbed corners and bring new life with none of the formality I was brought up in.'

Greyfriar. Daisy felt a chill strike her before she brushed it away. Of course he would expect her to live at the Hall, it was his home. But that house and its army of servants . . . And then it came to her, in a blinding flash, and Daisy being Daisy she had to speak out straightaway. 'Do you really want to fill Greyfriar?' she said. 'Because there are going to be children of all ages who will need a home after the war, even if it is just for a few weeks at a time for some of them, to give a break to mothers who have lost husbands. We . . . we could do something for them.'

'What a marvellous idea.' He touched her mouth with one finger. 'Think about it until we are together again.'

'Oh, William.' Something in his voice made a shiver flicker down her spine. Both the men she loved, Tommy and William, out there in all the mayhem . . .

For the rest of the time until the train chugged into the station they sat very close together, talking softly and kissing now and again.

407

Kirby magically reappeared as the train drew to a halt although they hadn't been aware of his presence before then, and Daisy found she couldn't let go of William. He was very gentle as he dried her face with a crisp white handkerchief, tucking it in her pocket as he said, 'I'll collect it when I return, all right, darling? When I return.'

'Oh, William, William.'

He had to put her from him and get into the carriage, the door closing behind Kirby and the bags just as the train began to move. For a crazy moment Daisy wanted to run after it. William was going and she didn't know if she would ever see him again. It wasn't fair. Sixteen years, and then they had barely had twenty-four hours together. It wasn't *fair*. None of it was fair. How could God let it happen like this?

She stood there long after the sound of the train had faded away, one hand pressed tightly over her mouth and the other resting on William's brooch. She might have remained there longer such was her state of mind, but a voice saying, 'You all right, lass?' brought her out of the whirling panic. She glanced quickly at the young man who had spoken to her, intending to nod and walk away, but then her eyes returned to the empty sleeve tucked into the pocket of his jacket and stayed there.

She had to drag her gaze away to look him in the eye and say, 'Yes, thank you. I . . . I'm all right. I was just . . . seeing someone off.'

'Aye.' He nodded. 'I saw. A captain no less. Rum 'un, this war, ain't it, lass? Don't matter if you're in the ranks or an officer, there's still family at the back of you. Mind, I'm out of it now after copping this little lot.' He nodded to the empty sleeve. 'I was a miner afore I joined up so it's put paid to that. Funny thing, when I come round in the hospital the main worry on me mind was how me an'' the wife'd manage, but do you know what she said? She'd rather have me alive an' home with one arm than out there with two. She meant it an' all. Canny lass, me wife.'

Daisy smiled a little shakily. 'I'm sure she is and I know exactly how she felt.' She said goodbye and began walking. One arm, and he couldn't have been more than twenty-one or two. And there would be so many who would come home minus limbs, perhaps blinded or driven out of their minds. Even more who wouldn't come home at all. But William would. *He would.* She had to believe that, like she did with Tommy, or else she'd go stark staring mad. And William had Kirby with him now. If nothing else the valet would try to make his master's life as comfortable as he could.

Her hand went to her mouth again as she thought, Will Kirby try to poison William's mind against me? Would it have been better to say something, to have it all out once and for all? But how could she have done, with William about to leave for France and Kirby with him? But it wasn't really that. She had felt sorry for the man, just like the tinker's dog. Kirby would be thrilled to bits if he knew of the comparison! A dart of humour pierced the blackness for a moment. Ma Stratton had got the dog round fine, it had been a good-natured animal at heart. As for Josiah Kirby – she just hoped it wasn't a case of extending the hand of friendship only to have it bitten off. But it was too late now. She couldn't change what had occurred on the platform although in hindsight she had to admit she had followed her heart rather than her head. Still, she had enough to worry about with both William and Tommy over the water. She didn't need to anticipate trouble.

The last remnants of sunshine were dappling High Street West when Daisy emerged from the station. She stood for a moment looking about her. Everything seemed the same.

The same shops, the same busy crowds, the same barefoot urchins darting here and there.

She breathed deeply, willing herself to start walking as though this was just another fine summer evening. She supposed she ought to count her blessings that her three brothers were too old to be caught in the latest net of conscription which had been extended to cover all men between the ages of eighteen and forty-one, regardless of their marital status. She knew Kitty was worried out of her wits that Alf might be called up soon. They had said the war would be over by Christmas when it had started, so what had gone wrong?

But the war couldn't go on for ever. She walked faster now, her chin lifting as it always did when she was telling herself to buck up. One day Tommy and William would come home, and if things worked out Tommy might never have to go back to that noisy, dirty machine shop. Unless he wanted to, of course. He could join them at Greyfriar Hall; they would need all the help they could get to make the place into a working children's home.

It was that night that Daisy first lit the two candles. She placed them in the window, whispering, 'One for each of them, God. Guide them safely home. And let them know how much I love them.'

On 31 May seven thousand British sailors were lost when Dreadnought fleets clashed at Jutland, causing the sea to be awash with bodies. But it was the sinking of the *Hampshire* on 5 June with Kitchener on board which caused a pall of grief and dismay to descend on the British people. He had been the ordinary man's hero, and England went into mourning.

Towards the end of June William was called to operational headquarters. On his return, Josiah took one look at his young master's face and feared the worst. 'Sir?' He paused in his task of pressing William's trousers. They might be in the thick of it but Sir William's uniform would always be immaculate while Josiah had breath in his body.

'We're in the hands of lunatics, Kirby.' William brushed a weary hand across his face. 'It's the Somme. Damn it, the least intelligent strategist can see there's nothing to be gained on the Somme. Victory will merely free the Germans from an awkward salient, or, if we're too successful, saddle us with one of our own.'

Josiah nodded. He didn't understand the ins and outs of it all like the master, but he trusted Sir William's judgement more than the old generals in their bath chairs. Always a man of few words, he said, 'When, sir?'

'We start now. You're coming with me in the staff car. See to things, would you?'

Within an hour they were on their way, the car passing soldiers making for the front, heavily laden with their packs but marching at a smart, swinging pace, some singing music-hall tunes accompanied here and there by a mouth organ. They were heading towards the points of flame stabbing the darkness where British shells were falling.

Josiah sat very still in the vehicle which bumped and jolted along, the motor cycles of despatch riders passing it now and again. It was hard to believe he had only been out here with the young master for a matter of weeks. It seemed like months, years, an eternity. Once there had been another life but it seemed unreal now, the blood and guts of the last weeks wiping it away.

Now, he was surprised he had ever been concerned about Mr William having a fancy for the fishergirl. Mind, the last time he had seen her she hadn't looked the same as the fierce little upstart he remembered. He had looked at Daisy Appleby on that platform and she had seemed a woman of presence with a self-possessed air about her, aloof and cool. Until she had seen Mr William that was. Then her face had lit up. It still pained him to remember how her face had lit up. Certainly May had never looked at him like that in all the time he'd known her. Perhaps that should have told him something? But he had let go of May now, in his head. What was the point of holding on when he would be dead soon? And he was going to die, they all were. No one could survive this butchery. So it didn't matter about May or the fishergirl, the only thing which was important was staying alive as long as Sir William and serving the young master right to the end.

It was probably better it was going to end out here in France because he couldn't have stood by and done nothing if Mr William had persisted with this notion of marrying a girl from the common people. There had been enough disgrace to the family name with his mother insisting on the divorce and then up and marrying a French count before the paper was even dry. But at least she had made a new life for herself in France and was out of the way, unlike the fishergirl. No, he would have had to step in and, strangely, it would have given him no pleasure, not since the incident on the railway platform. The fishergirl had shown herself to be kind there and kindness was a rare commodity in a woman, or so he had found.

The car catapulted into the air a few inches, courtesy of a large pothole, and Josiah heard Sir William swear profusely.

The last of the Frasers he would be, which was a shame. A great shame. A grand old name which Josiah had been proud to serve would die with him. This damn' awful war . . .

At 7.30 the next morning the artillery barrage was lifted and the British went over the top in regular waves. In the first five minutes of the battle thousands of British men and lads were cut down by relentless German fire. The enemy's machine guns mowed men and officers down in rows, and the German defences were formidable and deep.

Later that night William walked amongst what was left of his division. The day had cost the British Army nineteen thousand dead and fifty-seven thousand casualties – all William knew was that they were going to have to do it all again tomorrow.

They did do it again, and again, and again. They did it all through July and August, and by September William and Josiah, like thousands of other men, had become numb and accepting.

But now it was the first week of September, and the morning was dry after days of heavy rain which had turned the trenches to mud. William's lieutenant was counting down before they went over the top, and as he listened one of his hands was on his gun and the other on a letter in his pocket which he had received from Daisy a few days before. It was a little bit of sanity amid all the madness.

'Three, two, one. Over, lads! Over!'

William knew Kirby would be following behind him as he climbed out of the trench. He had given up telling the valet to stay put and keep his head down because the man always appeared at his shoulder a few seconds later. By rights Kirby should be serving some doddery old master he had grown old with while enjoying the mellow fruits of his years of service, not existing minute to minute in this hell-hole. But as far as Kirby was concerned a valet's rightful place was beside his master at all times, be it in the land of plenty or the land of want.

A shell exploded to the left of William, blowing him right off his feet, but he knew when he got up again he still had two arms and two legs, which was more than could be said for some of the poor blighters who had been nearer to the deafening blast.

The screams and cries and pounding noise of the artillery always produced a kind of whirling vacuum in his head; he could usually remember very little of the action afterwards. Anything specific, that was.

The nights were different. The men composed songs once darkness fell, their tunes usually adapted from music-hall hits to relieve the tedium of life in the trenches. The words were usually self-deprecatory and often obscene, but William thought no other army had ever gone to war proclaiming its own incompetence and reluctance to fight like this one, and no army had ever fought better.

There were rolls of barbed wire in front of him. It caught at his clothes with cruel barbs, tearing at his skin. There were men to either side of him and behind, Germans in front, and the barrage indiscriminately blasted away with no respect for friend or foe. Once free from the wire he continued to move, and when another shell burst just behind him, the force of the explosion blasting William and several other men into a trench, he didn't realise for a moment or two that he was injured. It was only when he tried to get up that he realised one of his legs was shattered, bone sticking out at all angles, and that his arm on the same side was hanging useless. He lay panting for a second before turning to the other men, intending to tell them to carry on, but they had done all the fighting they were ever going to do.

How long he sat there surrounded by dead bodies he didn't know. He made no effort to staunch the blood from his wounds but remembered wondering why he felt no pain, and then, at the same moment it hit with white-hot savagery, Kirby flung himself down into the trench beside him.

'You're hurt, sir.'

It wasn't like Kirby to make unnecessary remarks, William thought dazedly, managing to grind out, 'So it would seem,' through teeth clenched in agony.

'If you will allow me, sir.' Josiah had unceremoniously stripped the shirt off one of the dead men which he now tore into several strips before getting to work on William's leg. The rough bandaging did the trick and stopped the worst of the flow of blood, but William's clothes were already soaked a deep red and there was a pool beneath his injured leg.

'We have to get you back to the medics, sir.'

William watched as Josiah cautiously raised his head above the parapet only to duck down swiftly as machine-gun fire whizzed by. 'L . . . later.' Every little bit of William was concentrated on holding on to consciousness. 'Let our men advance first. We . . . we're too close to the . . . enemy line. They'll pick . . . pick us off like rabbits.'

'You haven't got time for later, sir.'

'Be that as it may, there . . . is no point in both of us . . . dying.' The pain was unbearable now, excruciating. It brought back memories of von Spee's thugs and he found himself thinking, as he glanced through pain-dazed eyes at his leg, All that work the surgeons did and this is how I reward them. Monsieur Richer would have my guts for garters if he could see how I'd treated his artistry. He turned his head to look at his arm which was now hurting every bit as much as his leg.

'Dislocated, I think, sir, badly.' Josiah had noticed the direction of his master's gaze. 'Or it could be broken. It isn't bleeding too much anyway.' He didn't mention the wound towards the back of the younger man's head where it looked as though he had been all but scalped in part.

'And I'm sorry, sir, but I really am going to have to get you back to base.'

The valet's tone was such that he could have been an adult addressing a recalcitrant child who was insisting on remaining at a party too long. William would have smiled if he had been able. Daisy would have appreciated the humour. He glanced at his shattered leg. Or maybe she wouldn't.

'We can get back to where there's assistance if we crawl, sir. All you have to do is to get over the top and I can pull you.'

'Not . . . not with the snipers. You'll be a sitting duck.'

'Snipers or no snipers we have to try, Master William.'

This was the Kirby of his childhood, the stern but caring disciplinarian who in many ways had been more of a father to him than his own. It came to William with a real shock of surprise that Kirby had been an anchor to the small confused boy he had been, and furthermore that he felt some affection for the dour individual. William knew he wouldn't make it if they waited but it seemed crazy two lives being lost in what he saw as a suicide mission. 'We'll wait, Kirby. I'll tell you when—'

And then Kirby took the decision out of his hands, grabbing him by the collar as he said, 'Forgive me for the liberty, sir,' and hoisting him upwards with a strength William would not have believed him capable of.

He must have passed out with the pain because the next thing he was aware of was being dragged through mud on his back, and then an English voice yelling through the din, 'Get down, you fool! What do you think you're doing – providing target practice for Jerry?'

'I've a badly injured officer here, I need help.'

'We all need help, mate. Another dozen or so divisions'd be nice.'

Again William fainted but help must have been forthcoming because when he next surfaced he was on a canvas stretcher which two soldiers were dragging as they crawled along, and Kirby's voice was behind him, saying, 'Not long now, Master William.' There was something very comforting about becoming Master William again. It spoke of toasted muffins thick with raspberry jam in the nursery, of walks with his nurse and one of the footmen when the worst that could happen was that he fell over and got his clothes dirty, of playing war with his lead soldiers in front of the nursery fire . . . Oh, Daisy, Daisy. This was no game.

He felt a weight on his chest as the shell hit but no surprise. He had been expecting it.

It had been a strange sort of day. Daisy had awoken early in the morning after a nightmare which had left her sweating and shaking, and long before dawn had broken she had been downstairs in the kitchen, drinking tea and telling herself the feeling of foreboding she couldn't shake off was nothing more than the residue of the dream.

She had got to work very early, and when by nine o'clock Mr Newton still hadn't arrived she was beginning to get worried. Then she'd received a message to say his widowed sister had collapsed the night before and he had had to go to Hartlepool. He expected to return the next day and could she hold the fort until then? Due to his absence the day had been even more hectic than usual, and by the time she got home that evening all she wanted was a hot bath, a couple of aspirin for the headache which had been with her since the nightmare had woken her, and an early night.

Daisy stoked up the kitchen range and put the kettle on, flopping down on one of the hard-backed chairs while she waited for it to boil. She normally scurried about doing this and that in the evenings, having found it was the best defence against brooding about how quiet the house was with Tommy gone, but tonight she felt too tired. And then there was a knock at the front door. She opened it to find Kitty on the doorstep, beside herself with worry. Alf had had his call-up papers and had already left for the front.

'His mam's going up the wall an' all.' Once Daisy had got Kitty established at the kitchen table, a strong cup of tea at her elbow and a plate of biscuits in front of her, the other girl calmed down a little. 'But she can always take her mind off things with the bairns, that's why I left them with her.'

Daisy nodded. Kitty was a good mother and loved her children, but not the way she loved Alf. He was her reason for living.

'He'll be all right, lass.' Worthless words of comfort and they both knew it, but there was nothing else to say. You had to believe and pray for the best, it was the only way to cope. 'And this war can't go on for ever.'

Kitty inclined her head, settling back in her chair as she said, 'I don't mind the shortages of this and that, and the petrol rationing and meatless days don't affect us being as we don't go nowhere and never ate much meat anyway, but the men and the lads that've been called up . . . I don't know a family that hasn't lost someone, Daisy, and with this bright idea of the powers-that-be of keeping brothers and whole groups from one place in the same regiments, some folk are losing all their family in one go. You can't wonder some women are going doo-lally.'

Kitty munched a biscuit and they both sipped their tea, Daisy reflecting that Tommy and the rest of the lads were in that very position. Of course it was good for soldiers' morale to have friends and family with them, but it did prove devastating when the worst happened. She felt she'd played a part in bringing Phil, Jimmy and Joe up, she'd seen so much of them – especially poor little Joe – and she had to admit Tommy's three pals meant more to her than George, Art, Ron and Peter's bairns, although she'd never have said so to her family.

Kitty must have realised her words were less than tactful because now she said, 'I'm sorry, lass, I do go on, don't I? Take no notice of me. You didn't mind me coming, did you?'

'Mind? Don't be daft. Our shoulders have always been available for each other to cry on, haven't they?' It was true too. Although they didn't meet often these days, when they did they were as firm friends as ever. Daisy had been the first person Kitty had come to when she'd heard her mam and da had passed away in the Newcastle workhouse a few years ago. Kitty hadn't known Gladys and Harold had ended up there, but nevertheless had been consumed with guilt at the manner of her parents' passing, insisting she should have prevented it somehow, even if it had meant their coming to live with her.

Daisy had privately thought it was just as well her friend had not known in that case, because ten to one Gladys would have found some way to put a spoke in Kitty's marriage. But she had kept that reflection to herself, instead spending hours talking Kitty through her guilt and remorse until the other woman had finally come to see her sense of guilt was completely unfounded.

Kitty spent another half-an-hour with Daisy before rising, drawing her coat from the back of the chair as she said, 'I'd better be making tracks, lass. The bairns'll be running

Alf's mam ragged. She can't say no to any of them and the little monkeys know it.'

'I'll walk with you to the tram stop.'

Daisy actually had her hand on the door when the knock came from outside, making both women jump. She raised her eyebrows at Kitty as she opened it, and then she was staring at the young lad holding out the black-rimmed telegram. 'Miss Appleby?'

She couldn't answer him. It was Kitty who said, 'Yes, she's Miss Appleby,' and reached out and took the telegram.

Fear assailed Daisy then such as she had never felt before. It caused her to open her mouth and pull in a great draught of air to combat the feeling she was drowning, but she turned and walked with Kitty back to the kitchen, sitting down at the table and then holding out her hand for the telegram. Kitty, her face drained of colour, handed it to her without a word.

'Lass?' Kitty's voice was tentative as she watched Daisy's eyes scan the paper.

Daisy had been sitting rigid, but now, as if she had suddenly turned into a rag doll, she crumpled, her mouth emitting a wail which frightened Kitty to death.

Her heart thudding, Kitty sank down beside her friend and without a word took Daisy in her arms, rocking her as she would a little bairn. After a few moments Daisy clung to her, sobs shaking her body and the tears rolling down her cheeks. While she held her Kitty caught sight of the words on the telegram which had fallen on to the kitchen table. It was several lines long, but the only words which registered on her were '. . . regret to inform you that soldier Thomas Appleby serving with the Durham Light Infantry has been killed in action . . .'

Outside, there were all the normal street sounds, children playing, voices calling, the barking of a dog somewhere in the distance, but inside there was only the sound of Daisy's agony. And the telegram on the kitchen table.

Chapter Twenty-nine

In the first week of October the Allies broke the Somme front along ten miles, but Daisy, along with tens of thousands of other women whose loved ones would not be coming home due to this disaster of strategical misjudgement, felt no pleasure in the hollow 'victory'. Kitchener's army had found its graveyard on the Somme, but not only men perished with it. There perished also the zest and idealism with which nearly three million Englishmen had marched forth to war.

Daisy returned to work just a couple of days after hearing the news of Tommy's death, feeling she would go mad if she had to stay in the house another minute. Every nook and cranny held memories of her boy; she kept seeing him sitting at the kitchen table agonising over his homework or racing down the hall to answer the door. At times she thought she even heard him call to her. Phil, Joe and Jimmy's families had received similar telegrams on the same day as Daisy – the four had enlisted together, fought together and died together – and at times Daisy thought her heart would crack wide open with the pain of it all. It didn't help her torment that she had heard nothing from William for the last little while either, and such was her state of mind that she had lost nearly half a stone in the last weeks, causing a worried Kitty to remark that she looked as though a breath of wind could blow her away.

Her anguish drove her to arrive at work very early in

the morning and leave hours after everyone else had gone; everyone except Mr Newton, that was. He had been marvellous, supportive and understanding but not over-fussy. And then, in the second week of October, Daisy received a telephone call. It sent her dashing to the train station, bound for London, without even bothering to go home to change.

A few hours later she was standing in the private rooms of Mr Mark Baxter, an eminent medical consultant, her nerves stretched to breaking point but a light in her eyes for the first time in weeks.

'Miss Appleby? I'm pleased to meet you.' Mr Baxter was small and rotund with the same sort of gentle voice his secretary had had when she'd spoken to Daisy earlier in the day on the telephone. They had already shaken hands, and now he said, 'Do sit down, I won't keep you long, but I wanted a word with you before you see Captain Fraser.'

He was alive, he was safe! Injured, but safe. Oh, William, William. His name had been a refrain in her heart sung in time with the wheels of the train all the way down to the capital.

'Now I ought to make it clear Captain Fraser only arrived here from France yesterday, before that he could not be moved. To put it bluntly he would not have stood the journey. I understand from my nursing staff that Captain Fraser was under the impression his family had carried out his wishes and let you know what had happened, but this is apparently not so?'

Daisy shook her head.

'Dear, dear.' The surgeon shook his head but said no more on that matter, beyond, 'My secretary had a word with him and put him in the picture about that when she went along to say you were coming. Now, as for his condition . . . You will find him somewhat changed, my dear. There is an element of shell shock which can be distressing for the uninitiated, although Captain Fraser's is manifesting itself more in nightmares than anything else. Badly fractured arm, broken ribs, wound to the head – all of which will heal in time.'

Daisy waited. There was more to come, she could tell.

'The worst injury occurred to his right leg. I'm afraid it had to be amputated below the knee.'

Daisy swallowed. 'How has he taken that?'

'Remarkably well. Of course he has seen others a great deal worse off than him.' Mr Baxter paused. 'Yes, a great deal worse off, but that does not always count for anything in these circumstances. He's been made aware that science is progressing in leaps and bounds in the realm of prosthetic limbs, and with the positive attitude he seems to have I'm sure to all intents and purposes he will be the same as ever he was. Certainly his mobility will not be affected too severely.'

'So he will be all right, in time?'

'Yes, Miss Appleby, he will be all right in time.' The consultant smiled. 'And I am sure with you beside him his recovery will be all the more swift. Your first reaction was concern for how the patient is coping, and from where I am sitting that is always a good sign.'

'But surely everyone who has a loved one in these circumstances reacts the same?'

Mr Baxter didn't say anything for a moment and then his voice was flat when he said, 'You would be surprised, Miss Appleby. You would be surprised.' It became considerably brisker as he continued, 'One last thing. I presume you are unaware of the part Captain Fraser's batman played in all of this?'

'Josiah Kirby?'

'I don't know the fellow's name, only that he was reported to have acted with great bravery. Sacrificial bravery. At the last moment, when he must have realised death was imminent, he apparently shielded the Captain's body with his own. Undoubtedly saved his life.'

'He was . . . ?'

'Oh, yes. More or less a direct hit according to eye witnesses. Threw himself on top of Captain Fraser and took the full force of the blast. We aren't sure how much the Captain understands of this, but we feel it is best for details to be divulged gradually. Patients in Captain Fraser's condition do not always understand that their mind, as well as their body, has been affected.'

She had to see him. She had to see him now.

Mr Baxter seemed to read Daisy's mind because he rose to his feet, saying, 'I will get Sister Clark to take you along. He is in a ward with other surgical cases; we find this best rather than separate rooms although I am aware the Captain could afford it. It's all a matter of morale, you see. They help each other to come to terms with the mental conflict.'

'Thank you.' Daisy, too, rose to her feet, her face pale and her eyes enormous. She wanted to hold him, to tell him it would be all right now he was home and the war didn't have a hold on him anymore. But it did, it did have a hold from what Mr Baxter had said, in his head. But they would work it out together. Whatever it took, she would make him well; mind, soul and body.

She hadn't been aware of Mr Baxter pressing a bell but he must have done because when the door opened and a fresh-faced, middle-aged nurse said, 'You rang, sir?' he nodded, saying, 'This is the Captain's young lady, Sister. Perhaps you would be so kind as to take her along to the ward?' And to Daisy, 'The Captain is under Sister Clark's care and there is none better in the whole of the hospital.'

Sister Clark smiled primly before saying, 'Would you come this way please?' but once outside in the corridor she seemed to unbend a little. 'Mr Baxter's secretary didn't let on that you were actually coming today, we thought it would be a nice surprise for the Captain that way.'

Daisy nodded, saying, as though she hadn't just spoken to William's doctor, 'How is he?'

'Eating and sleeping most of the time. I consider those two of the best medicines. Physically he is very weak, of course, but that it is to be expected. In himself . . .' The sister paused, turning to look at Daisy. 'In himself he is experiencing something which I think he finds harder to come to terms with than the loss of his leg. Most of the men are like that. They seem to think shell shock is some kind of weakness rather than a psychological disturbance of the brain resulting from exposure to what they have seen and heard and had to do. They speak sometimes in their nightmares . . .' The sister shook her head. 'What a world we live in, Miss Appleby, that it could send good, honest, decent men to such depths.'

Daisy said nothing. They had just reached the ward doors and although her whole body was sweating her mouth was dry.

'But he has something to aim for, unlike some of the poor souls in here,' the sister continued softly as she pushed open the doors. 'Hasn't he, Miss Appleby?'

It was a question not a statement; the expression on the woman's face declared this although her tone had been even.

Daisy's answer came promptly and with her whole heart. 'Yes, he has.'

'That is what I thought.' The sister smiled, and for a moment Daisy glimpsed the real woman beneath the uniform and thought William was indeed lucky to be under her care. 'Third bed on the right. We draw the curtains round them at this time of the afternoon to encourage a sleep after lunch. It works . . . mostly.' Sister Clark pointed down the row of cubicles before giving Daisy's arm a gentle pat. 'And good luck with the children's home,' she added quietly. 'He told me all about it last night when he awoke with one of the nightmares. I think it is only the thought of what he can do in that realm that is helping to make sense of all the madness he has been through.'

A reply was clearly not expected. Daisy smiled, leaving the sister at the door to her small glass-walled office just within the entrance to the ward and walking quickly to the set of curtains the woman had indicated.

He was lying with his eyes closed when she stepped inside. That William was aware of someone's presence became apparent when he said, his tone irritable, 'If Sister has sent you to check my temperature or blood pressure, Nurse Pearson, you can forget it. And before you ask, I do not want anything.'

'Well, shame on you then, Captain Fraser, with me having come all the way from Sunderland.' Daisy hoped her voice hid the shock she'd felt when she had seen him lying so still and grey-looking, the cage over his right leg telling its own story.

'Daisy?' He sat up in bed with enough force to make himself wince and bite down hard on his lip, but then she reached his side. He pulled her down on to the stiff linen coverlet with his good arm, his strength belying his infirmity. 'Daisy . . . oh, Daisy! My love, my love. I didn't know you were coming today.'

'William, darling.' She couldn't say more, he was kissing her until her head swam.

It was a good few moments before he drew back a little, his eyes roaming over her face as he murmured her name again and again. He touched her mouth with a hand that was shaking. 'I didn't think I'd ever see you again. Out there, on the battlefield, I was sure my time was up.'

For a moment she thought of Tommy, her mother's heart

crying, Oh, my boy, my boy, but she couldn't tell William about that now.

Daisy's lips trembled as she said, 'Oh, darling,' and now it was she who held him close, seeing the large patch of red skin where shrapnel had sliced his scalp raw with a feeling of painful love and tenderness.

'I've been such a fool, Daisy. I don't think I fully realised how much time I had wasted until I thought it was the final parting.'

'Both of us, darling. We've both been fools.'

'No, not you, never you.' He kissed her again before he said, a smile touching his pale lips, 'Call me darling again. I like it.'

'Darling, darling, my precious darling . . .'

When they next surfaced, William's lips reluctantly leaving hers, he said, 'I wouldn't have made it but for Kirby, you know. He came for me, wouldn't take no for an answer, and it cost him his life. And at the end—' He stopped abruptly, shaking his head before he said, 'Do you know . . . what he did when the shell hit?'

'Yes, darling. Mr Baxter told me.'

'They think I can't remember. I *couldn't* remember but I heard two of the nurses talking when they thought I was out of it. Why do you think he did that, Daisy? He must have known he was going to die.'

'Perhaps he thought losing one life instead of two made sense. And he cared about you and your father very deeply.'

William nodded, drawing her against his chest, and again the fact that only one arm held her caused a rush of emotion that caused her to blink furiously as she thought, Thank you, Kirby. Whatever you thought of me, thank you.

'My . . . my injuries. I would understand if they made a difference—'

She answered him by raising her face and covering his

lips with hers. When one of the nurses bustled in a few moments later with a cup of tea for the patient and one for his visitor, Daisy was flushed and dishevelled but William looked a lot brighter.

It was as the nurse left that he said, 'And Tommy? How is Tommy?' And then as he looked into her face, he whispered, 'Oh, no, my love. Not that.'

She had promised herself on the train all the way down to London that she wouldn't cry when she told him, in the event she couldn't help it. But William held her close and that in itself was a comfort. They sat quietly after that, William holding Daisy's hand tightly in his, and she realised just how ill he still was when he started to speak but went to sleep between words.

The nurse popped in for the tea tray at one point, whispering to Daisy, 'Best he's looked since they brought him in. I thought he might be getting over-tired but you stay on if you want, dear. Seems you're the medicine he needs.'

It must have been over an hour later when William's eyelids suddenly opened wide from what had been a deep sleep. His eyes searched immediately for hers and then they were staring at each other, his gaze as blue as the sea on a perfect summer's day, and the sounds of the hospital ward melted away.

For a moment they were two young people on a storm-tossed beach again and life was stretching out before them, full of wonder, joy and promise.

William didn't move when he said softly, 'I love you, Daisy Appleby. Marry me soon?'

Daisy's was just as soft when she whispered, 'I love you, William Fraser. As soon as you like.'

'We'll never be separated again. Say it, Daisy. We'll always be together. Working together, living together, loving. We'll make up for the lost years.'

430

There was a plea in his voice, and now she brought his hand to her lips, kissing it before she said, 'Together for eternity, darling.'

She would light no more candles. There might still be storms in the new life she was about to embrace, but William would be right beside her and they would face them together. She asked for nothing more.

Epilogue

Daisy and William founded their children's home.

They took the little ones no one else wanted; children who carried all the tragedy of poverty and disease and abuse in their small faces. They needed warmth and food and care, but most of all love. This they received in abundance at Greyfriar Hall.

William's two sisters took themselves off the minute they heard of the impending marriage, the legacy from Wilhelmina providing them with an allowance which covered the rent of a small town house where they could gossip with others of a like mind to their hearts' content. Gwendoline and her new husband attended Daisy and William's wedding; Gwendoline's gracious attitude did not quite hide the fact that, mortified at her son's decision, she was prepared to accept Daisy under sufferance rather than lose William. But she was civil, and as there would normally be an ocean between them that was all Daisy asked of William's mother.

The staff who chose to stay on at the announcement of William's nuptials to the fishergirl and their plans for the old house became co-workers with Daisy and William.

Ellen Mullen said it was the best sound she had ever heard when the grand building began ringing with children's laughter. What did it matter that the woodwork got chipped and the imposing staircase became a clandestine slide for many a small backside? The Hall had come alive, turned into a place of sanctuary and hope. Swings and slides stood on the once pristine croquet lawn; treehouses, sandpits and a football pitch replaced the immaculately landscaped grounds at the back of the house. Daisy and William thought Greyfriar had never looked more beautiful.

In the second year of the Home's life, the same year that saw Alf safely returned to Kitty and their bairns, a school was built where the stables had once stood and experienced teachers were hired.

At the end of this year Daisy gave birth to the first of their five children, a boy whom they named George. Two more boys and then two daughters followed in quick succession, and it caused tongues to wag in a certain town house when it became common knowledge that it was impossible to distinguish the little Frasers from all the other children at the hall. But then, what else could you expect? William had married beneath himself, and letting his children fraternise with those of common blood without any distinction being drawn between them only proved how far he had fallen.

Of course it was all *her* fault, the fishergirl's. It was upstarts like her who had forced through the vote for women, encouraged working-class girls to shun domestic work and demand employment in offices and working places hitherto barred to them, and – worst of all – encouraged married ladies to take up careers and meddle in all kinds of things.

She had never known her place, the fishergirl, that was the thing.

The Urchin's Song

Rita Bradshaw

Growing up in the 1890s amid crushing poverty in Sunderland's East End, Josie Burns is no stranger to dirt, cold and hunger. Every day Josie and her younger sister are sent out to beg by their brutal father, but Josie has a special gift – a beautiful voice. By singing in the rough dockside pubs, Josie earns enough for her father to leave them alone.

When Josie is twelve years old, she learns that her father has sold her older sisters to his evil friend, Patrick Duffy, to work the streets. Josie flees to Newcastle, obtaining refuge with a kindly mining family, but for Josie even this sanctuary is not free from pain or the long arm of Patrick Duffy.

Josie is drawn to the music halls, but the road to success is not an easy one. Josie must fight for what she believes in before she can find true happiness.

Acclaim for Rita Bradshaw's novels:

'If you like gritty, rags-to-riches Northern sagas, you'll enjoy this' *Family Circle*

'Catherine Cookson fans will enjoy discovering a new author who writes in a similar vein' *Home and Family*

'What an emotional rollercoaster ride of a book! It grabs your attention from page one and does not let go until the end' *Sunderland Echo*

0 7472 6708 1

<u>headline</u>

The Stony Path

Rita Bradshaw

Growing up on a small, struggling farm on the outskirts of Sunderland in the early 1900s, Polly Farrow has a tough life, but she has gifts money can't buy – a joyful disposition and a loving heart that is reflected in her beautiful face. And her heart has been given to her beloved cousin, Michael, since childhood. They share a special bond, and Polly knows that one day they'll be man and wife.

But a terrible family secret is to shatter her dreams for ever. The lovers are rent apart and Polly is left to bear the responsibility of the farm and her family single-handed. Life is now a battle for survival, and Polly wonders if she will ever find true happiness, unaware that the answer to her prayers is closer than she thinks . . .

'If you like gritty, rags-to-riches Northern sagas, you'll enjoy this' *Family Circle*

'Catherine Cookson fans will enjoy discovering a new author who writes in a similar vein' *Home and Family*

'A warm-hearted tale of tough family life in the North' *Teeside Evening Gazette*

'What an emotional rollercoaster ride of a book! It grabs your attention from page one and does not let go until the end' *Sunderland Echo*

0 7472 6322 1

headline

Now you can buy any of these other bestselling
Headline books from your bookshop or
direct from the publisher.

FREE P&P AND UK DELIVERY
(Overseas and Ireland £3.50 per book)

TO ORDER SIMPLY CALL THIS NUMBER

01235 400 414

or visit our website: www.madaboutbooks.com

Prices and availability subject to change without notice.